THE PENTAMERONE

(THE TALE OF TALES)

By GIAMBATTISTA BASILE

Translated by RICHARD F. BURTON

The Pentamerone (The Tale of Tales)
By Giambattista Basile
Translated by Richard F. Burton

Print ISBN 13: 978-1-4209-7111-8

Cover Image: a detail of "Vastolla and Peruonto approaching the Ship, from Peruonto", an illustration by Warwick Goble, from "Stories from the Pentamerone", Macmillan & Co, London, c. 1911.

Please visit *www.digireads.com*

TO THE VIRTUOUS NEAPOLITAN READERS!

MASILLO REPPONE

Most illustrious gentlemen, and my most reverend patrons. The what-do-you-call-it is so full of pulp and solid, that it hath thrust the pen into my hand, and maketh me write without shame this scrawl in form of a petition, so that in your mercy ye may defend a poor man, who, being a foreigner, hath gone from door to door seeking for alms of some Neapolitan words.

Therefore be ye informed that a certain printer, who hath become a foe to Naples, although he was born ten hundred miles distant therefrom, would once more print the Tale of Tales for the Diversion of Little Ones by Cav. John the Baptist Basile, who would call himself Gian Alessio Abbatutis: and, knowing not whom he should chance to meet, laid hold of me, so that I should correct it, because the ink in the last print had daubed it in such a manner that not even the father (and may Heaven receive him in glory), if he were alive, would have recognised it for his own son. Now I, who am possessed of an heart like the lungs, and a door to my will, which, if any one knocks at it, at once is opened wide, promised with every charity at a simple opening of the mouth to do him this service: and so much the more in that it concerned a poor pupil, son of such a very learned father, awakened about an hundred miles behind by the evil practice of the players. I have done my best and all, that I might to force into its body what was missing, so that it should be mended, and be known again even as when it was born.

And what have I not done? I have put myself in torments all the night and the day, to rid him of so much filthiness. But after having done this, and many more charitable fatigues, certain young masters, who wear glasses upon their noses, and believe they can carry all the world behind them, have gone about with a twist of the muzzle, and a casting up of the eyes, saying, 'And how can one who hath been born in the ice have dared to come and be the corrector in this city, and set a price upon a cabbage stump? The presumptuous man would deserve a most cruel stripping. A Pugliese flat-cap wanting to make fine love in a Naples where are to be found folk who weigh a ton each, and perhaps more. Look ye if he knoweth how to write, and if he wanteth to pass for learned in the Partenopean language? Here two m's are lacking, again two s's are missing, and here two other e's, and so on!'

Now these folk believe that they have found me alone, broken down, and mournful, with no friends on my side. And therefore I will scorn and affront them, and let them know they speak at random, and they know naught of tum and bus,* and of this quarrel I appeal myself straightly to the just tribunal of your genius: and so that ye may give me reason if I am wrong, I present to you these writings as proof of these facts. And first and foremost know ye, O most illustrious gentlemen, that I, although I am not a Neapolitan, neglected naught to learn well this language, for when I came to this country (that with another eight will be nineteen years), I fell in love with these pretty words, and they seemed to me as so many coins with which I could enrich my brain, and the much more so in that I bethought me of having read in Cicerone's Epistles to Atticus that Pompeius, the great Roman emperor, left off speaking the Latin language and would speak the Neapolitan, as that great man Sommonte found out, and noted down in the History of Naples, Chap. VI., Book I., because the Neapolitan language being half Greek and half Latin, it seemed to him a more tasteful mixture. Now I, who have always followed after the Greek to fill myself to bursting with it—I have not left quarters, squares, warehouses, streets, little streets and even those without

---

*In the old a. b. c. books the alphabet ended in cyphers 'et, con, rum, bus,' like those that very often are used in the ancient Latin books. And from that the last of these cyphers was thought of great importance, like a full stop at the end.

an issue: and although the washerman speaketh one way, and washeth worse, he hath changed in all the way of speaking, and he of the little pier in another way: but, thanks be to Heaven! I have eaten cabbage-stumps and broccoli, that is to say, I have read good authors, and I understand them a little. And I will now say that I know also how wrote those men of ancient date, and how the moderns write. But because the Neapolitan speech carrieth not dictionaries with it as do the other languages—viz., the Latin hath Colapino, the Tuscan hath la Crusca, the Greek studieth the Lexicon, and thus do also all the other nations—it seemed to me most convenient to let this poor pupil rest with that orthography which his father had left him, that is to say, as I found it in the first book, and as it was printed by several printers, day by day, when it came forth. And his good father liked not the superfluous, which breaketh the lid, nor the two m's, and two n's, and other such things, which were sought by the sages. Those words, therefore, that it has not by nature I have signed with a sign, which a Greek would call spirit, so that they could gently hit them, in the same way that these folk do hit us with so many m's and n's. And without that only one who is a Neapolitan can well read it, and who is a foreigner let him add as many letters as he liketh, for never will he read it well, if he doth not hear it read by a Neapolitan, or by some other who is an expert in this language. And besides, the other languages would spoil it, because they pronounce an hundred miles distant of what they write. But this is a ball which if I would unwind there would be enough for to-morrow, and after to-morrow, and the day after, and the day thereafter. Enough: another day, if time carrieth away certain sickness from mine head and certain scab from my neck, I will prove this to you with an hundred rules of orthography, and perhaps I will let you read the phenomena and the phrases of the Neapolitan speech that I have gathered until now, with an hundred thousand observations, and I will make you say, 'Oh 'tis good indeed: this man deserveth great praise, because he hath done things that our countrymen cared not to do.'

Now, my most reverend, these are my writings in the style of Rome, brief and to the point, and if ye will judge it spurious and

TO THE VIRTUOUS NEAPOLITAN READERS

will call me to good purpose, be sure that I shall not prove myself contumacious. And with this I expect the sentence in my favour, and if for naught else, only because I have been charitable so readily that from a maimed book I have made it cast away its crutches: and with this I take my leave. May your lordships well maintain yourselves, whilst I pray Heaven, to pour upon you a deluge of happy days. I give myself peace.

YE ARE INVITED TO READ

THE TALE OF TALES

CORRECTED BY MASTER MASILLO REPPONE

ALL AGES ARE FOUND IN THIS SONNET

BY M.R.S.D.

Rest ye for a little, and a-pleasuring we'll go:
Come my merry little ones and hasten with all speed;
Gossiping Masillo hath a fairy book to show,
Written and re-written so that all the world may read.

Know, both youths and maidens, an ye yield ye to my wiles—
Whether ye be churlish or light laughter is your cheer—
Not e'en Master Grillo with his smirking and his smiles
At your new-found knowledge can himself afford to sneer.

But no bush for my wine's needed. Here's enjoyment with good
      fruit:
In the vineyard of my narratives no weed hath taken root;
Tuneful, always tuneful, is the music of my lute.

Last of all, ye elders, with your growing weight of years,
Smile the smile of comfort through the tempest of your tears,
And listen as in childhood with your childhood's hopes and fears!

CONTENTS

CONTENTS

CONTENTS OF VOLUME THE FIRST

IL PENTAMERONE

INTRODUCTION TO
THE DIVERSION OF THE LITTLE ONES

I

IT was a proverb established after those of an antique usage that whoso seeketh what he should not findeth what he would not; and clear thing it is that the ape, for drawing on boots, was trapped by the foot. This also befell a beggarly handmaid, who, never having worn shoes to her feet, must needs wear a crown on her head; but, as all wrongs meet their requital, and anon comes one that compensates for each and every, at last, having by wicked ways usurped what belonged to others, she was caught at the wheel, even as says the by-word, 'The higher the height, the lower the lapse': and this shall be shown after the fashion that follows.

It is said that once upon a time there was a king of the Bushy Valley that had a daughter named Zoza, and she, like another Zoroaster or Anacretus,* was never seen to smile. The afflicted father, having none other life and spirit than this his only daughter, left nothing undone to lighten her melancholy. The better to provoke from her a laugh, he summoned now drolls who walk upon maceheads, and then fellows who jump through circles, and anon boxers, and rivals of Master Roger the juggler, and workers of legerdemain, and anon fellows strong as Hercules, and now the dancing dog and the leaping old man, and then the ass that drinks from a tumbler and the bitch Lucia Conazza †: briefly, now one thing, and then another. But 'twas all lost time, for neither the remedy of Master Grillo,‡ nor the herb sardonion, nor a dig in the diaphragm would make her smile in the least.

At length the unfortunate father, wishing to make a last at-

* Heraclitus.　　† A Neapolitan dame.　　‡ A noted medico of the day.

1

tempt and not knowing what else to do, gave orders to build a great fountain of oil fronting the palace gate, with design by so doing that the folk who crowded like ants passing to and fro that way should be obliged, so as not to soil their clothes, to skip like crickets, and buck-jump like goats, and scurry like hares, pushing and knocking one against another; thus hoping that somewhat might occur which would make his daughter laugh.

So this fountain being built, as Zoza was standing at her lattice window, looking sour as vinegar, she saw an ancient woman coming to the fountain, and soaking up the oil with a sponge, filling therewith an earthen ewer she had brought with her; and whilst so doing, a certain court page threw a stone so true to an hair that he hit the ewer and broke it to bits. Hereat the old woman, who was by no means hairy of tongue, nor held herself from speaking her mind, turned to the page, and thus began to say: 'Ah, kindchen, scatter-brains, piss-a-bed, goat-dancer, petticoat-catcher, hangman's rope, mongrel mule, spindle-shanks, whereat if ever the fleas cough, go where a palsy catch thee; and may thy mammy hear the ill news! Never mayest thou see the first of May! May a Catalan lance thrust thee through! Mayest thou be touched with the rope and never lose a drop of blood! A thousand miseries reach thee, with the rest to boot; and, in short, may the wind blow away thy sail, so that the seed may be lost, thou knave, pimp, son of a whore!'

The lad, who had little beard and less discretion, hearing this flow of abuse, repaid her with the same coin, saying, 'Wilt thou not hold thy tongue, devil's grandam, bull's-vomit, children-smotherer, turd-clout, farting crone?' The old woman, hearing all the news of her household thus cried aloud, waxed so wroth that, losing all patience, she raised the curtain of her clothes, and showed a truly rural scene, whereof Silvio * might have said, 'Go, wake the eyes with the horn.' When this spectacle was beheld by Zoza, she fell backwards, laughing so much that she had well-nigh fainted. Hereupon the old woman became even more furious, and turning a fierce look upon Zoza, cried, 'Go! and mayest thou never see the

---

* *Dialectic,* Sirvio: a personage in some pastoral, perhaps the pastor.

bed of an husband, unless thou take the Prince of Campo Rotundo!'
Zoza, who heard these words, summoned the crone and perforce
would learn if she had meant to lay a curse upon her, or only to
abuse her; and the other answered, 'Now thou must know that the
prince I have named is a wonderful creature, Thaddeus hight, who,
having been cursed by a fairy, came to the last picture of life, and
was laid in a tomb outside the city walls, and upon his tombstone
an inscription is graven: "Whosoever of womankind will in three
days fill with tears an earthen vessel which hangs upon an hook, she
will bring him to life and strength, and will take him to husband."
But as it is impossible for two human eyes to run so much with
weeping as to fill an earthen vessel which holds half a flagon, save,
as I have heard recounted, it were a certain Jinniyah who became
at Rome a fountain of tears, I, because I saw myself derided, have
given you this curse, which I pray Heaven may fall upon you in
revenge for the injury done me.' And thus saying, the old woman
ran down the steps and went her way, being afeard that something
might happen to her.

Meanwhile the princess pondered over the words of the old
woman, and meditated, and doubted, and feared, and at length drew
from them that passion which blindeth our judgment and darkeneth
the mind; and she determined to fly from her father's house, and
taking with her many thousand crowns and jewels, left the palace,
and fared along until she reached the castle of a fairy, to whom
she told her story. The fairy, taking compassion of such a beautiful young maiden, and desiring to help her on account of her
youth and her great love to an unknown being, gave her a letter of
recommendation to her own sister, who was also a fairy; and taking
kindly leave of her, presented her with a walnut, saying, 'Take this,
O my daughter, and keep it by thee, but open it not save in time of
great stress.' The princess took the gift and the letter, and proceeding on her journey, ceased not wayfaring until she arrived at
the castle of the second fairy, who also received her graciously, and
well entreated her. And on the next morning, before taking leave,
the fairy gave her a letter for another sister of hers, and presented

to her a chestnut, with the same advice which had been given to her before. She fared on until she reached the castle of the third fairy, who also welcomed her, and entreated her kindly. The following morning, before her departure, the fairy presented her with an hazel-nut and the same injunctions as the other sisters.

Having received these things, Zoza fared on through cities and villages, wilds and wolds, passing seas and rivers, until after seven years she arrived, tired and worn by so much wayfaring, at Campo Rotundo, where, before entering the city, she perceived a mausoleum of marble at the foot of a fountain where a porphyry criminal wept tears of crystal: and hung thereon was the earthenware flagon. Taking the vessel down, and putting it before her, she shed two rivulets of tears rivalling the fountain, never lifting her head from its mouth, so that at the end of two days the tears had filled it to the neck, and there remained only two inches more. But, wearied by so much stress and trouble, she was taken by a deep sleep, so that she lay perforce under a tent close by for well-nigh two hours. In the meantime a certain slave, Cricket-legs hight, who came often to that fountain to fill an hogshead, and who knew well the matter of the inscription, which was spoken of everywhere, hid herself when she beheld Zoza weeping, awaiting that the earthen flagon should be nearly full, hoping by some wile to win the remainder to herself, and thus leave the princess with a handful of flies. And as she beheld her asleep, she thought the time had come for her advantage, and dexterously taking the earthen juglet, and putting her eye upon its mouth, filled it to the brim in a short time. Hardly was it full when the prince, awaking as from heavy sleep, arose from the marble sarcophagus, and threw his arms around that mass of black flesh, and leading her to his palace, with feasts, and joyance, and revelry took her to wife. But no sooner did Zoza awake to find the grave open, and the juglet gone, and with it all her hopes and joys, than she came near to unpacking the bales of her soul at the custom-house of death. At last, seeing that for this evil there was no remedy, and that she could blame nought but her own eyes which had watched so ill that which held her desire, she arose, and fared on, and entered the city. And when she heard of the bridal feasts of the prince and of the fine wife he had taken to himself, she imagined how the misfortune had come to pass, and said to herself, sighing, 'Alas! two black things have crushed me to the earth; black sleep and a black slave.' Then, desiring to struggle against death, from which every kind of animal trieth to defend itself, Zoza took a fine house fronting the prince's palace, from within which she could not behold the idol of her heart, but could at least look upon the walls of the temple which held him for whom she longed with excessive longing.

Herewhile Zoza was seen one day of the days by Thaddeus, who had been flying until then like a moth around that black, hideous slave. When he beheld her, he became as an eagle, and held ever present in mind the beauty and comeliness of Zoza, even as it is one of the privileges of nature to be taken by a beauteous form and face. The slave failed not to perceive of what had taken place in the prince's mind, and she was wroth with exceeding wrath, and being with child by Thaddeus, threatened him, saying thus: 'If thou wilt not close the window, I will punish my belly and murder little George.' The prince, who loved his race, trembled like a leaf, and liked not to anger his wife, and therefore shut himself in, although it seemed to him he had taken the life out of his body in depriving himself of the sight of Zoza's beauty. The princess, perceiving herself deprived of the only means of beholding Thaddeus, and having lost every hope, not knowing what to do in this her time of need, bethought herself of the three gifts of the fairies, and cracking the walnut, out flew a handsome bird, the handsomest that had ever been seen in the world. The bird began to sing, and trill, and quaver at the window as no other bird had done before, and having been seen and heard by the slave, she could not rest without it, and so, calling the prince, said to him, 'If thou wilt not get for me that bird that sings so well, I will punish my belly and murder little George.' Thaddeus, who had let himself be ridden by her, sent at once to the princess to ask if she would sell it. Zoza made answer that she was not a seller of birds, but if he would accept it as a gift, she would present it to him. The prince, desiring to please his wife on account of the child she would bring to light, accepted the offer; but about four days after Zoza opened the chestnut, and out of it stalked a fowl with twelve chicks of gold, which were seen by the slave upon the same window-sill, who at once longed to have them, and sending for the prince, pointed to them, saying, 'If thou bring me not that fowl and chicks, I will punish my belly and murder little George'; and Thaddeus, who allowed this bitch to pull him by the nose, sent again to the princess, offering her whatever she chose for such a priceless fowl, and he received the same answer as before: that he might have it as a gift, but to ask of buying it would be but lost time. And as he could not, and dared not, refuse, necessity had the best of his discretion; and he was humbled by the generosity of a woman, their liberality being very scarce, as they are never spoiled, not even by owning all the ores of India. But having passed another four days, Zoza opened the hazel-nut, from which came forth a doll, who was spinning gold, a most marvellous thing. No sooner was she put at the same window than the slave saw her, and sending for the prince, said to him, 'If thou bring me not that doll, I will punish my belly and murder little George'; and Thaddeus, who let his wife swing him about as yarn-blades, by whom he was ridden at her pleasure and crushed by her pride, not having courage to send for the third time to the king's daughter for the doll, thought it best to go himself, remembering the old saws, 'There is no better messenger than thyself,' and 'Who wanteth goeth, and who wanteth not sendeth,' and 'Who will eat fish must take it by the tail,' and beseeching her to forgive his boldness for begging these things because of the whims of a woman great with child, asked for the doll. Zoza, who was nigh a-fainting because of the cause of all her travail, hardened her heart, and allowed him to pray and beseech of her the gift of the doll, so as to have her lord near her and hear his voice, and to enjoy the light of his presence a little longer—he who had been stolen from her by an hideous slave. At last she gave him the doll, as she had done all the other things; but before she handed it to him, she begged the doll to make the slave long to hear tales and stories. Thaddeus, who beheld the doll in his hand without spending a single crown, felt crushed by so much kindness, and he offered Zoza his kingdom and his life in exchange for so much pleasure; then returning to his palace, he gave the doll to his wife.

No sooner did she place it in her bosom to play with it than it appeared as Cupid in the form of Ascanius before Dido, and lit a fire in her heart, and great desire to hear stories and tales, so that at last, fearing to lose her life on account of her great longing, and to give birth to a man-child who would corrupt a shipful of beggars, she sent for her husband, and said to him, 'If thou wilt not call folk to tell me stories, I will punish my belly and murder little George.' Thaddeus, desiring to get rid of this March nuisance, gave orders to the crier to publish that all the women of the city should come to the palace on such a day, and on the appointed day, at the shooting forth of the star Diana, which forerunneth the dawn to prepare the way by which the sun must pass, they should meet all at the same place. But the prince, unaccustomed to see such a crowd, and having no particular taste for the whims of his wife now that she longed to see so many folk around her, chose only ten of the noblest in the city, who seemed to him the more provoking and full of talk. And there were limping Zoza, crooked Cecca, wen-necked Meneca, long-nosed Tolla, hunchbacked Popa, flabbering Antonella, musty Ciulla, cheekless Paola, hairless Ciommetella, and rough-hewn Giacova; and, having written their names on a paper, he discharged the others.

Then they arose with the slave from under the dais, and all fared slowly to the palace garden, where the trees and boughs were so well interlaced one with another that the sun's rays could not penetrate underneath their leafy screen, and they seated themselves under a pavilion covered with a creeping vine, amiddlemost of which played a fountain. Grand Master of the School of Courtiers Prince Thaddeus thus began to say: 'There is nothing more pleasing and glorious in the world, O my noble women, than to hearken to the deeds of others; and not without reason did Aristoteles, that great philosopher, place man's greatest happiness in listening to pretty stories, since in hearkening to them care and gloom vanish, and life is lengthened. And with this desire doth the artisan leave his workshop, the merchant his traffic, the doctor his patient, the druggist his business; and they all go abroad in search of those clever storytellers, whose tales can rival the best gazette ever written. By which reason I must excuse my wife, who, having become of a melancholic mood, desireth so much to listen to some pleasant tale: and therefore, if ye are willing to fulfil her wants and to catch mid-air also my desire, ye will be pleased in these four or five days that ye will remain to empty your stomachs and recount every day a story, such as those old women tell for the entertainment of the children, meeting always in this same site, where, after having eaten, ye will begin by recounting, and will end the day by reciting an eclogue, and thus we will spend joyously our life, and all the worse for him who dieth.' Hearing these words, all bowed their heads downwards in humble assent to Thaddeus's command.

In the meanwhile the tables were spread, and food was laid upon them, and they all began to eat; and having ended, the prince made a sign to Zoza the limping that she should open the fire. Rising and bowing low to the prince and his wife, Zoza thus began her say:

STORY OF THE GHUL

First Diversion

Of the First Day

ANTONY OF MAREGLIANO, BEING A CLOWNISH PRATTLER, IS EXPELLED BY
HIS MOTHER. HE TAKETH SERVICE WITH A GHUL, AND AS HE DESIRETH
TO VISIT HIS HOUSE, IS REGALED WITH A SOUND BASTINADO. QUARRELLING
WITH A TAVERN-KEEPER, AT LAST HE IS PRESENTED WITH A CLUB,
WHICH PUNISHETH HIS IGNORANCE, AND MAKETH THE TAVERN-KEEPER
PAY THE PENANCE FOR HIS TRICKERY: AND THUS HE ENRICHETH HIMSELF
AND FAMILY.

THOSE who said that fortune is blind spake sooth (and knew
more than Master Lanza, who truly passed some of these matters), for she raiseth some folk to greatest height who should be
kicked out of a field of beans, and throweth to the ground folk
who are the best and noblest of men, as I will now relate.

It is said that once upon a time there lived in the country of
Maregliano a good woman, Masella hight, who had, besides six
virgin daughters, a son so clownish and idle that he was not worth
even a snow game, and no day passed but that she said to him, 'Why
do you stay at home, accursed bread-eater? Disappear, lump of
laziness, dirty Maccabeus, depriver of sleep, carrier of evil news,
chestnut-boiler, thou who must have been exchanged for me in the
cradle, where instead of a pretty, dearling child was put a pig
lasagne-eater.' And whilst Masella thus apostrophised him, he kept
whistling, showing that there was no hope that Antony (thus was
the son hight) would turn his mind to any good. And one day of
the days it happened that his mother washed his head without soap,
and hending a stick in hand, took measure of his doublet. Antony,
who when least expecting it found himself well warmed, as soon
as he could escape from her hands, took to his heels, and walked
till the twenty-four hours had elapsed and the stars began to peep

9

out, at which time he reached the foot of a mountain so high that its head touched the clouds, where, in an avenue of poplar-trees, at the entrance of a grotto built of pumice-stone, was sitting a ghul. O mother mine, how hideous was he! His head was larger than an Indian vegetable-marrow, his forehead full of bumps, his eyebrows united, his eyes crooked, his nose flat, with nostrils like a forge, his mouth like an oven, from which protruded two tusks like unto a boar's; a hairy breast had he, and arms like reels; and bandy-legged was he, and flat-footed like a goose; briefly he was an hideous monster, frightful to behold, who would have made a Roland smile, and would have frightened a Scannarebecco; but Antony, who cared not for ugliness or aught else, nodding his head slightly to him, said, 'Good-day, master; what mayest thou be doing? How dost thou do? Dost thou want anything? How far is it from here to the place whereto I am bound?' The ghul, hearing such foolish queries addressed to him, burst out a-laughing, and because he was pleased with that humourous beast, said to him, 'Wilt thou be my servant?' and Antony rejoined, 'And how much wilt thou give me a month?' and the ghul answered, 'Mind and serve me honourably, and we will not dispute about the wage.' Thus, having concluded this accord, Antony remained to serve the ghul.

With him was abundance of food, and of work very little, so much so that in four days Antony found himself in such good condition that he became as a Turk for stoutness, an ox for roundness, courageous as a game-cock, red like a lobster, green as garlick, and flat like a whale. But nearly two years had gone by when his pleasant life began to weary him, and he became sad and sore at heart, thinking of his home, and for stress of longing had nearly come to his first state. The ghul, who could see into his innermost thoughts by a look at his nose and a move of his back parts, called him to his presence, and said to him, 'Antony mine, I know that thou art sickening with a great longing and desire to behold once more thine own flesh; and because I love thee as mine own entrails, I will permit thee to fare forth and take thy pleasure; and I will give thee this ass, which will spare thee from the fatigue of the journey: but be very careful never to say to it, "Ass dump!" or thou shalt repent it, by my ancestor's soul.'

Antony took the ass, without even saying good-evening, and vaulting into the saddle, put it to the trot; and he had not gone yet a hundred paces when, dismounting, he began to cry to the ass, 'Ass dump!' and hardly had he opened his mouth to say so, when the beast began to ease itself, and pearls came out of it, and rubies, and emeralds, and sapphires, and diamonds, each of the size of a walnut. Antony watched all this with mouth wide open, and a feeling of great joy at the rich evacuation of the ass; and he took down the saddle-bags, and filled them with the jewels, and mounting again, continued faring on till he arrived at a tavern, and there dismounting, the first thing he said to the innkeeper was, 'Make fast this ass to the manger, and give it good food; but be thou careful not to say to it, "Ass dump!" as thou shalt repent so doing; and also put these things in a safe place for me.' The innkeeper, who was not wanting in cunning, hearing these words, and beholding the jewels which glimmered and glittered in the saddle-bags, was overcome by curiosity, and longed to know the meaning of the words forbidden him by Antony: therefore giving to Antony a plentiful supper and wines to drink, awaited until he saw him overtaken by sleep and snoring loudly, when he made his way to the stable, and said to the ass, 'Ass dump!' At the sound of those words the ass eased itself again of gold and jewels. The innkeeper, beholding this evacuation, bethought himself of exchanging the ass and of befooling Antony, thinking that he could easily blind and deceive him, and make him take a glow-worm for a lanthorn, believing him a simpleton who had come to his hand.

Therefore as soon as Antony arose, when morning dawned, and Dame Aurora appeared at the east window, all rose-hued, to empty the night-vase of her old man, stretching himself and talking the while, Antony at last called the innkeeper, and said to him, 'Come here, comrade, short accounts and long friendship! friends are we, and our purse let us combat: give me my bill, and let me pay.' And this was done, so much for bread, so much for wine, so much for soup, and so much for meat, for stabling five, and ten for the bed, and fifteen for thanks: he paid his account, and taking the ass with a load of pumice-stone in the saddle-bags instead of jewels, fared on towards his village, and before entering his house he began crying, 'Run, mother, run; we are rich: display towels and spread bed-linen, and thou wilt behold treasures.' The mother, with great joy, opening a large coffer where she held all her daughters' linen, brought out all the bed-linen, and covered the floor with it. Antony drew the ass upon it, and began to cry out, 'Ass dump!' but he could say, 'Ass dump!' as much as he liked: the ass took no notice of the words, no more than if they had been sounds of music; moreover he returned three or four times to repeat the words, but all was thrown to the winds. Thinking the beast obstinate, he took a strong stick, and began belabouring it therewith, until the poor animal let go a run of yellowish matter upon the white bed-linen. The unhappy Masella, beholding this evacuation of the ass, and scenting enough stink to infect all the house when she expected to enrich her poverty, was wroth with exceeding wrath, and hending a staff, let Antony feel its weight on his shoulders, without awaiting to look at the pumice-stone, for which warm reception he again took to his heels, and the ghul beheld him returning to him faster than he had seen him depart. But the ghul already knew what had happened to him, because he was a sorcerer, and gave him a good scolding because he had let himself be tricked by the innkeeper, calling him Ascadeo, foolish, simpleton, deformed, silly, brainless, that for an ass full of treasures he had taken a vulgar beast full of dung. Antony was obliged to swallow in silence all these pills, and swore to himself that nevermore, no never, would he allow any man living to laugh at him.

A year passed by, and the same longing came in his heart as heretofore, and he became once more desirous to behold his kith and kin. The ghul, who was hideous of favour but handsome of heart, gave him permission to go, and presented him with a fine napkin, saying, 'Take this to thy mother, and take care not to be a simpleton, as thou wert with the ass; and till thou comest to thy house, mind and

do not say, "Open and shut, thou napkin," because maybe some
great mishap will befall thee, and all the loss will be thine; now go,
and good speed, and come back soon': and thus Antony took his
leave. But having fared not very far from the cave, he at once put
the napkin on the ground, and said, 'Open and shut, thou napkin,'
whereupon in opening the napkin displayed many precious things
which were marvellous to behold. As Antony saw them, he said
at once, 'Shut, napkin,' and everything being shut inside it, he fared
on to the same tavern, where on entering he said to the innkeeper,
'Put away for me in a safe place this napkin, and be careful not to
say, "Open and shut, thou napkin."' The astute host, who knew
a thing or two, answered, 'Let me do it for thee'; and having given
him a plenteous repast and copious draughts of wine, watched till
he slept soundly, and then, taking the napkin, said, 'Open thou, O
napkin,' and the napkin opened, and showed to sight all kinds of
precious things which were marvellous to behold. And having
found another napkin similar to that one, he put it in its place.

When Antony awoke in the morning, he rose, and thanked the
host, and went his way, and after a time arrived at his mother's
house, and as soon as he saw her exclaimed, 'Now, indeed, O my
mother, will we bid adieu to our beggarly lot; now in very sooth
shall we have the wherewithal to remedy all our wants'; and thus
saying, he laid the napkin upon the ground, and cried, 'Open thou,
O napkin:' but he could cry out as much as he liked, all was time
lost. At last, perceiving that it was useless, turning to his mother,
he said, 'Well, I wot that again have I been befooled by that innkeeper: but never mind. I and he, we are two; better for him not
to have done it: far better if he had gone under a cart-wheel. May
I lose the best house-furniture if, when I pass that way, I do not
smash to atoms all his belongings in payment for the jewels from
the ass and the napkin he hath stolen.' The mother, hearing this
new silliness, became greatly enraged, and said to him, 'Decamp,
accursed son! break thy neck, take thyself off. I cannot bear the
sight of thee. Begone at once, and think of this house just as if it

were fire. I shake the dust off my clothing of thee, and I will think as if I never had given birth to thee.'

The ill-treated Antony, seeing the lightning-flash, would not await the thunder, and, like a thief, lowering his head and lifting his heels, he wended his way towards the abode of the ghul, who, on seeing him coming quite quietly, gave him another good dressing, saying, 'I know not what holds me that I do not kill thee, ass, beast, blister, farting mouth, rotten throat, gaol's trumpet, that of all things thou publishest the banns, and vomitest all that is in thy body, and canst not hold a bean in thy mouth. If thou hadst held thy tongue at the tavern, it would not have happened; but having a tongue like the sail of a windmill, thou hast been grinding the happiness which came to thee by my hands.' The ill-fated Antony, putting his tail between his legs, swallowed all this music, and lived quietly on another three years in the ghul's service, thinking about his house as much as he thought of being an earl; but after all this time came to him again the fever of longing and desire to wend home, and he asked leave to go from his master, who, desiring to rid himself of this lack-wit, gave his consent, and presented him with a finely chiselled mace, and said to him, 'Take this mace and keep it in remembrance of me, but be careful not to say, "Lift thyself, mace," or "Lie down, mace," for I want no part with thee.' Antony, taking the gift, answered, 'Thou mayest rest in peace. I have grown the wisdom-tooth, and I know full well how many pair make three oxen; I am no longer a child: who desireth to cheat Antony must kiss his elbow.' To this the ghul rejoined, 'The work praiseth the worker; words are females, and deeds are males; we will wait and see; thou hast heard me more than a deaf man, and man forewarned is man forearmed.' And whilst his master continued thus to speak, Antony sneaked off towards his dwelling-place; but he had not gone half a mile, when he said, 'Lift thyself, mace.' But far better had he not spoken these words. At once the mace uplifted, and belaboured Antony's shoulders with a good will, so much so that the blows rained faster than hailstones in the open sky. The unlucky man, seeing himself so much ill-treated, said,

'Lie thee down, O mace,' and the mace ceased to punish him: and therefore, having learnt a lesson at his own expense, he said to himself, 'And lame may he be who tries to escape!   I will not leave this mace a single moment: yet he is not abed who is to have a bad evening': and so saying, he arrived at the usual tavern where he met with the greatest of welcomes, because they knew what sap could be drawn from the root.

As soon as he entered, Antony said to the host, 'Put away in a safe place this mace; and be thou careful not to say to it, "Lift thyself, mace," lest thou suffer a mishap; understand well what I tell thee, and afterwards do not blame Antony for what may befall thee, as I protest and advise thee beforehand.'   The innkeeper, delighted at this third venture, sent him a goodly supper and the best of vintage; and as soon as he beheld him asleep he took up the mace, and calling his wife to this new treat, said, 'Lift thyself, O mace,' and the mace did at once devoir on the man and his wife's shoulders, down here and down there, piff-paff with lightning speed; and finding themselves in a direful plight, they ran, and the mace after them thumping right and left, crying out with loud cries for Antony, who on awakening beheld that the macaroni had tumbled into the cheese, and the cabbages into the lard: therefore he said to them, 'There is no help for it but that ye both die under its blows unless ye return to me what ye stole.'   The innkeeper, who had had enough, cried, 'Take all I have, but deliver me from this evil'; and moreover, to assure Antony of his good will, he sent for all that which he had stolen from him.   As soon as Antony had it between his hands, he said, 'Lie thee down, O mace,' and the mace lay still: and he, taking his ass, the napkin, and the treasure, wended his way homewards to his mother, where, after showing real proof of the ass's behind, and sure sight of the napkin, he hired good cooks for himself and lived right royally, and giving all his sisters in marriage, and enriching his mother, made the old saw come true that

‘ God helpeth madmen and children.’

THE MYRTLE-TREE

Second Diversion

Of the First Day

A COUNTRYWOMAN OF MIANO GIVETH BIRTH TO A MYRTLE-TREE. A PRINCE FALLETH IN LOVE WITH IT, AND OUT OF IT ISSUETH A BEAUTIFUL FAIRY. THE PRINCE GOETH OUT AND LEAVETH HER INSIDE THE MYRTLE-TREE, WITH A LITTLE BELL ATTACHED TO IT. SOME LIGHT WOMEN ENTER THE PRINCE'S CHAMBER IN HIS ABSENCE, AND BEING JEALOUS, THEY TOUCH THE MYRTLE-TREE, AND THE FAIRY COMETH FORTH, AND THEY KILL HER. THE PRINCE RETURNETH, AND FINDETH THIS MIS-FORTUNE, AND COMETH NEAR UNTO DEATH FOR GRIEF; BUT, BY A STRANGE ADVENTURE RECOVERING HIS FAIRY, HE COMMANDETH THE COURTESANS TO BE SLAIN, AND TAKETH THE FAIRY TO WIFE.

DEEPEST silence reigned whilst Zoza recounted her story; but no sooner had she ceased speaking than all began to talk, and no mouth would keep silent because of the evacuation of the ass and the charmed - mace: they kept saying that it would be very useful to own such maces, that at least servants and cheaters would be rightly treated, since one commonly met with more asses than ground flour. And after discussing all these things, the prince ordered Cecca to continue the story-telling, at which command she began, saying thus:

If man could think what evils, and what ruin, and what loss of honour and home happen through the accursed women of the world, he would be more prudent, and would fly instead of following the footsteps of a dishonest woman, as when sighting a scorpion, and would not lose his reputation for the dregs of a brothel, and his life for a lazaretto, and all his rent-rolls for a public whore, who for the smallest coin maketh him swallow disgusting pills and fits of anger: as you will hear from what happened to a prince who had had some traffic with this evil race.

In the village of Miano there lived a husband and wife who had no children, and they longed, and pined, and prayed God to

16

grant them an heir; and the wife above all things kept saying, 'O God, could I bring to light something in the world, I would not care even though it were a myrtle-bough': and for so long did she sing this song that at last she tired ·Heaven with her prayers, and her belly began to swell, and became round, so that at the end of nine months she gave birth, in the arms of the midwife, instead of a pretty man-child, to a myrtle-bough which, with great affection, she had laid in a fine flower-pot, and carefully tended it morning and evening.   But one day the son of the king, who had gone out a-hunting, passed that way; and he took a fancy for the pretty myrtle-bough, and sent a message to the owner, asking her to sell it to him, stating that he would pay her whatever she demanded. After much denial and opposition, at last, caught by great offers, and taken by good promises, and frightened by threats, and won by prayers, she gave to him the tree, beseeching him to hold it with care, as she loved it more than a child, and held it as dear as if it had come out of her entrails.   The prince, with the greatest joy, had the tree brought into his chamber and put in the balcony: and with his own hands he tended, and watered, and dug around it.

Now it so happened that one night the prince went to bed, and put out the candle, but could not sleep.   All the folk around were slumbering, and all the world was quiet, when the prince heard a soft footstep pattering about the room.   And it came towards the bed, and the prince bethought him that mayhap it was some servant who wanted to lighten his purse; but like the courageous youth that he was, whom Satan himself would not have frightened, he feigned sleep, and waited for what would follow.   And he felt some one come near and touch him very lightly, and very gently he put forth his hands, and felt something soft and tender, with skin like velvet, and more tender and delicate than bullfinch's feathers, and softer than Barbary wool, and more flexible than a marten's tail; and believing that it must be a fairy (as it really was), he caught her in his arms, and began to play with her at dumb-sparrow.   But before sunrise she arose and disappeared, leaving the prince full of all sweetness, and curiosity, and surprise.   And this joyance continued for seven days; and he burned with great desire to know what good was this which rained on him from the stars, and what vessel loaded with sweetness and love had anchored at his bed. And one night, whilst the beauty slept, he tied a lock of her hair to his arm so that she could not escape, and calling one of his servants, bade him light the candles. He then beheld the princess and flower of beauties, the marvel of womankind, another Venus, goddess of love; perceived a doll, a dove, the Fairy Morgana, a golden bough, a huntress falcon-eyed, a full moon in her fourteenth night, a face of pigeon, a mouthful fit for kings, a jewel; he beheld, in fact, a being that made him lose his senses: and looking at her, he said, 'Now mayest thou hide thyself, O goddess of love: and thou, Helen, mayest return to Ilium and put a rope round thy neck, as thy beauties, so much descanted, are as nought compared with this beauty by my side, beauty accomplished like a sun, worthy a throne, solid, graceful, and full of pride, wherein I cannot find a single blemish. O sleep, O sweet sleep, weighten down with poppy-juice the eyelids of this beautiful joy: deprive me not of the enjoyance of beholding this the end of all my desires, this triumph of beauty. O beautiful lock that closely binds me! O beautiful eyes that burn me! O sweet lips that give me such joy! O beautiful breasts that console me! O beautiful hand that holds me close! In which shop of the marvels of nature was made this perfect form? What part of India gave the threads of gold to that hair? What part of Ethiopia gave the ivory for that brow? which place the carbuncles for those eyes? what part of Tyre the purple for that face? and what part of the East the pearls to make those teeth? And from which mountain came the snow to cover that neck and breast: snow against nature, that maintaineth the flowers and warmeth the heart?' Thus saying, he put his arms around her as a creeping vine, to enjoy his life; and whilst he clung to her neck, she awoke from sleep, and answered with a trembling and soft sigh the enamoured prince, who, on see-ing her awake, said to her, 'O my beloved, if, holding thee without candles, this temple of love was nearly burnt to ashes, what will there be now of my life, that I can behold those two lights? O

dear eyes, that with a lightning glance rival the stars, ye, and ye
alone, have burnt a hole in my heart, and ye alone may salve it,
as new-laid eggs; and thou, O beauteous doctoress mine, be moved
to pity for this my stress, and be careful of one sickening for thy
love, so that, for having changed the night to day and beheld the
light of thy beauty, a direful fever burneth his entrails. Put
thine hand upon my breast; feel my pulse; order a prescription.
But what do I say? what prescription do I seek? O my soul, kiss me
on the lips with thy sweet mouth; I do not want other cure for my
life than a handling of thy dear hand; and with the cordial of thy
sweet grace, and the root of this thy tongue, I shall be well and
free.' Hearing these words, she became red as a flame of fire, and
answered, 'Do not praise me so much, O dear my lord. I am thy
slave, and to serve thy kingly person I would throw myself into the
privy; and I hold it great fortune that this myrtle-tree, planted in
that earthen pot, hath become a branch of laurel, and hath found
a resting-place in a heart of flesh, a heart where dwelleth so much
greatness and virtue.' The prince, hearing these words, melted like
a tallow candle, and again embracing her, sealed that letter with a
kiss, and held out his hand to her, saying, 'Here I plight thee my
troth: thou shalt be my wife, thou shalt hend the sceptre, and thou
shalt have the key of my heart as thou holdest the wheel of my life.'
And after this they continued their joyance, and then arose, and took
food and drink, and continued so doing for about five days. But
fate and fortune upset all play, and divide matrimony, and are
always contrary to love, and are as a black dog which eateth itself
amidst the pleasures of those who love: so it happened that the prince
was called to go to the chase of a big wild boar that infested the
country, for which cause he was obliged to quit his wife, and to
leave behind two-thirds of his heart.

And because he loved her better than his life, and saw her beauteous above all beauty and love, he burned and melted: for it was
as a tempest in the sea of amorous joyance, a copious rain of the joy
of love, a cobweb dropping into a saucepan full of the butter of
the pleasures of lovers: it was as a serpent that bites, a moth that

nibbles, the gall which embitters, the coldness which freezes, that
for which life wearies, and the mind becomes unstable, and the heart
suspicious: therefore, calling the fairy, he said to her, 'O my heart,
I am obliged to remain two or three nights away from home. God
knoweth with what grief I fare forth from thee, who art my
soul; Heaven knoweth if before I go to this chase I will be able to
endure it; but I cannot avoid it, as I must go to satisfy my father:
and therefore I must leave thee: and I beseech thee, for that love
which thou bearest me, to enter inside the earthenware pot, and not
come out of it until my return, which will be before long.' 'I will
do so,' answered the fairy, 'because I know not, and I will not, and
I cannot disobey what pleaseth thee: therefore go in peace, and God-
speed, as I will serve thee as thou wilt: but do me a kindness, leave
attached at the end of the myrtle-bough a silken thread tied to a
small bell, and when thou shalt arrive, pull the thread and ring, and
I will come forth and welcome thee.' And thus did the prince,
and calling one of his valets, said to him, 'Come here, come here
thou, open thine ears, and hearken to me well. Make this bed every
evening, just as if in it had to take rest my own person; water
always this myrtle-tree, and be careful that nothing should happen
to it, as I have counted its leaves: and if I find only one missing, I
will kick thee out.' And having thus spoken, he mounted his steed
and departed, sad at heart, more like a sheep going to the slaughter-
house than a hunter going to chase a boar.

In the meantime seven women of pleasure whom the prince had
kept, seeing that he had cooled towards them, and had no more love
for them, and worked no more in their territory, began to suspect
that he had in hand some new intrigue, which had made him forget
the old friendship. And being desirous to discover country, they
sent for a builder, and giving him a good sum of money, bade him
build a passage under their house which reached to the chamber of
the prince, where, as soon as it was ready, they quickly entered to
see what new thing they could find, and if another wanton had taken
their place and stopped accounts. But finding no one, and looking
all round, they perceived only the beautiful myrtle-tree. Each one

took a leaf from it, and the youngest took all the end to which was tied the tiny bell, which was no sooner touched than it rang; and the fairy, thinking it was the prince, came out at once, but the dirty bitches, as soon as they beheld the beauteous fairy, laid their claws upon her, saying, 'Thou are the one who drawest to thy mill all the waters of our hopes; thou art the one who hast won in thy hand a fine balance of the prince's good grace; thou art the splendid creature who hast put thyself in possession of our flesh. Mayest thou be welcome! Thou mayest go now, as thou hast reached to the last dregs; better, far better, had not thy mother filthed thee! Go, for thou art ready: thou hast taken the bean, but thou art caught this time. May we not have been born at nine months if thou shalt escape!' And thus saying, they hit her a blow of the mace on her head, smashing her into five pieces, and each took a piece: but the youngest would have no part in this cruelty, and invited by her sisters to do as they had done, she would accept nothing else than a lock of the golden hair. And having done thus, they took their departure by the same way they had come.

In the meanwhile came the valet to make the bed, and to water the plant according to his master's orders; and finding what had happened, nearly died with affright, and picking up the hands and teeth, lifted up what was left of the flesh and the bones, and wiping up the blood from the ground, he buried it inside the pot, and having watered the tree, made the bed, shut the door, and putting the key under it, took to his heels out of the country.

Now the prince, having returned from the chase, pulled the silken string and rang the bell: but ring and catch quails, and ring that the bishop passeth, he could ring as much as he like, for the fairy was deaf, by which reason as he went to the door of the chamber, and being unable to keep cool and call the valet with the key, he kicked the lock and pushed the door open. And he entered and ran to the balcony, where he beheld the myrtle-tree despoiled as its leaves, at which sight he began to cry out with loud cries, and weep with bitter weeping and wailing. 'O unlucky, O unfortunate, O miserable that I am, who hath made me this tow-beard? who hath ruined

and crushed a prince? O my leafless myrtle-tree! O my lost
fairy! O my darkened life! O my joys ended in smoke! O my
pleasures turned to vinegar! What wilt thou do, O unfortunate
Cola Marcione? What will become of thee, O unhappy one?
Jump over this pit! arise from this dunghill: thou art fallen from
every good thing, and thou dost not kill thyself? thou hast lost every
treasure, and thou canst live? thou hast lost all pleasure in life: why
dost thou not end it? Where art thou, where art thou, O myrtle
mine? And what hellish arm hath ruined thy beautiful head? O
accursed chase, that hast been the cause of my great loss! Alas!
I am forlorn, my days are ruined: it is impossible that I can live
without my life, and there is no help for it but that I stretch my
feet, as without my love, sleep will not restore me; the food will be
poison, and life and pleasure desert.' And thus weeping and lamenting enough to move to compassion even the very stones in the
road, the prince, unable to take food or take rest, sickened, and his
colour yellowed, and the carmine of his lips became white.

Now the fairy, being charmed, had begun to form herself again
from the flesh and bones buried in the pot by the valet, and after a
short time became the same as before, and seeing the sorrowful
plight of her lover, who had become of the colour of a sick Spaniard, and like unto a lizard, and juice of leaven, and wolf's fart,
had compassion upon him, and coming out of the pot, like the
glimmer of candle out of a dark lantern, came in sight of Cola
Marcione, and clasping him in her arms, said, 'Cheer up, cheer up,
O my prince, leave off this lamenting, put an end to thy weeping,
wipe thy tears, abate thine anger, show a happy visage. Here am
I, alive and beautiful, in spite of those strumpets who brake my
head, and did with my flesh that which Tesone did with the monk's.'

The prince, on beholding her when least he expected her, returned from death to life: the colour came back to his face, the
warmth to his blood, the spirit of to his breast, and after a thousand
caresses, and sporting, and playing, he bade her tell him how all
had happened, and hearing that the valet was not to blame, sent for
him; and having ordered a banquet, with the consent of his father,

he wedded the fairy: and having invited all the grandees of the realm, he ordered that the seven serpents who had so ill-treated that lamb should be present. And when they had eaten their fill, said the prince to each one of his guests, 'What would the persons deserve who would do a damage to this beauteous girl?' pointing to the fairy, whose radiant loveliness shone, and glittered, and took all hearts by storm. Now all those that were sitting at table, beginning with the king, said, one that they deserved to be hanged, another that they should be put to the wheel, one decreeing one thing and the other another: and at last it came to the turn of the seven vipers. Although this discussion was not pleasing to them, still they dreamt not of the bad night which awaited them: and as all truth lies where wine playeth, they answered that he who could have the heart even to touch that jewel embodiment of all the joys of love would deserve to be thrown into the privy. The bitches having given this sentence with their own mouth, the prince said, 'Yourselves have discussed the cause, and yourselves have decreed the sentence: it only remaineth that your orders should be executed, as ye are the ones that, with a heart like Nero's and cruelty similar to Medea's, wanted to make a fricassee of that graceful form and beauteous shape: therefore quick, we must lose no time: let them be thrown into a large public privy, where they will end their life.' And the prince's order was at once executed, sparing only the youngest, whom he married to his valet, giving her a good dowry; and then he sent for the father and mother of Myrtle, and presented them with the wherewithal to live in ease and plenty to the end of their days; and the prince and the fairy lived happily together; and those daughters of Satan, escaping with great difficulty with life, certified the truth of the old proverb,

> 'Passeth e'en a lame goat,
> If she findeth none to stop.'

PERUONTO

Of the First Day

PERUONTO GOETH TO THE FOREST TO GATHER A FAGOT OF WOOD, AND
BEHAVETH KINDLY TOWARDS THREE GIRLS WHOM HE FINDETH SLEEPING
IN THE SUN, AND RECEIVETH FROM THEM A CHARM. THE KING'S
DAUGHTER MOCKETH HIM, AND HE CALLETH DOWN A CURSE UPON HER
THAT SHE SHOULD BE WITH CHILD OF HIM, WHICH COMETH TO PASS.
KNOWING THAT HE IS THE FATHER, THE KING COMMANDETH THAT HE
SHOULD BE PUT INSIDE A CASK WITH HIS WIFE AND LITTLE ONES, AND
THROWN INTO THE SEA; BUT IN VIRTUE OF THE CHARM HE HAS RECEIVED,
HE FREETH HIMSELF OF THE DANGER, AND BECOMING A HANDSOME
YOUTH, IS MADE KING.

ALL were pleased with the recital, and heard with great satisfaction of the happiness of the prince, and of the punishment of the evil women. And now it was Meneca's turn to speak, and the chattering of the others was silenced, and she began recounting the story which followeth:

A good deed is never lost: whoso soweth the seed of kindness meeteth with due reward, and whoso soweth the seed of love gathereth love in return. The favour which is shown to a grateful heart is never barren, and gratitude giveth birth to gifts. Instances of these sayings occur continually in the deeds of mankind: and ye will meet with an example of it in the tale that I am about to relate to you.

A countrywoman of Casoria, Ceccarella hight, had a son named Peruonto, who was the silliest body and the ugliest lump of flesh that nature had ever created; so that the unhappy mother always felt sad at heart, and cursed the day and the hour upon which she had given birth to this good-for-nothing, who was not worth a dog's hide. The unfortunate woman could cry out as much as she liked, but the ass never stirred to do her the lightest service. At last, after screaming herself hoarse, and assailing him with all the epithets she

24

could think of, she induced him to go to the forest and gather a
fagot of wood, saying, 'It is nearly time that we should have something to eat. Run for this wood, that I may get ready somewhat:
and forget not yourself on the way, but come back at once, that I
may cook the needful so as to keep the life in us.'

Peruonto departed, and fared on like a monk among his brethren
in a procession. Away he went, stepping as one treading down eggs,
with the gait of a jackdaw, counting his paces as he went. At last
he reached a certain part of the forest through which ran a stream-
let, and near by he espied three young girls lying on the grass, with
a stone for a pillow, fast asleep, with the sun pouring his rays
straight upon them. When Peruonto saw them like a fountain amid
a roaring fire, he took compassion upon them; and with the axe
which he carried to cut the wood he severed some branches from the
trees, and built a kind of arbour over them. Whilst he was busy
so doing the young girls awoke (they were the daughters of a fairy),
and perceiving the kindness and goodness of heart of Peruonto, in
gratitude they gave him a charm, by which he might possess whatever he knew how to ask for.

Peruonto, having performed this action, continued faring
towards the forest, where he cut down a fagot of wood so large that
it would require a cart to carry it. Seeing that it would be impossible for him to lift it, he sat upon it, saying, 'Would it not be a fine
thing if only this fagot would carry me home?' and behold, the
fagot began to trot like a Besignano horse, and arriving before the
king's palace, it began to wheel round, and prance, and curvet, so
that Peruonto cried out aloud, enough to deafen all hearers. The
young ladies who attended the king's daughter, Vastolla hight, happening to look out of the window and behold this marvel, hastened
to call the princess, who, glancing out and observing the freaks
played by the fagot, laughed until she fell backwards, which thing
was unusual, and the young ladies were astonished at the sight, as
the Lady Vastolla was by nature so melancholy that they never remembered to have seen her smile. Peruonto lifted his head, and
perceiving that they made a mock at him, said, 'O Vastolla, mayest

thou be with child by me!' and thus saying, tightened his heels on the fagot, which at once moved away, and in an instant arrived home with a train of screaming children behind: and if his mother had not quickly shut the door, they would have slain him with stones.

In the meantime Vastolla, after a feeling of uneasiness, and unrest, and the hindering of the monthly ordinary, perceived that she was with child, and hid as long as possible her plight, until she was round as a cask. The king, discovering her condition, was wroth with exceeding wrath, and fumed, and swore terrible oaths, and convened a meeting of the council, and thus spake to them: 'Ye all know that the moon of mine honour is wearing horns, and ye all know that my daughter hath furnished matter of which to write chronicles, or, even better, to chronicle my shame. Ye all know that to adorn my brow she hath filled her belly: therefore tell me, advise me what I had better do. Methinks I had rather have her slain than have her give birth to a bastard race. I have a mind to let her feel rather the agonies of death than the labour of child-bed: I have a mind to let her depart this world ere she bring bad seed into it.' The ministers and advisers, who had made use of more oil than vinegar, answered him, saying, 'Truly deserveth she a great punishment, and of the horns which she forceth on thy brow should the handle be made of the knife that shall slay her: but if we slay her now that she is with child, the villain who hath been the principal cause of thy disgust, and who hath dressed thee horns right and left will escape unhurt: he who, teaching thee the policy of Tiberius, hath put before him a Cornelius Tacitus, and to represent to thee true sleep, hath made thee issue forth from the horn-gate. Let us await, therefore, until it comes to port, and then we are likely to know the root of this dishonour: and afterwards we will think and resolve, with a grain of salt, which course we had best follow.'

The king was pleased with this rede, perceiving in it sound sense, and therefore held his hand, and said, 'Let us await the issue of events.' But as Heaven willed, the time came: and with little labour, at the first sound of the midwife's voice, and the first squeeze of the body, out sprang two men-children like two golden apples. The king, who was full of wrath, sent for his ministers and counsellors, and said to them, 'My daughter hath been brought to bed, and the time hath come for her to die.' Answered the old sages (and all to gain time upon time), 'No; we will tarry until the children get older, so as to be able by their favour to recognise their father.' The king, not desiring his counsellors to think him unjust, shrugged his shoulders and took it quietly, and patiently tarried till the children were seven years of age, at which time he again sent for his counsellors, and asked them their rede: and one of them said, 'As thou hast not been able to know from thy daughter who was the false coiner that altered the crown from thy image, it is time that we seek to obliterate the stain. Command thou that a great banquet should be got ready, and ask all the grandees and noblemen of the city, and let us be watchful, and seek with our own eyes him to whom the children incline most by the inclination of nature: for that one without fail will be the father, and we will at once get hold of him like goat's excrement.' The king was pleased with this rede. He gave orders for the banquet, invited all folk of any consequence, and after they had eaten their fill he bade them stand in line and pass before the children: but they took as much notice of them as did Alexander's courser of the rabbits, so that the king became enraged and bit his lips with anger: and although he was not wanting in shoes, because of the tightness of those he was compelled to wear he stamped the ground with the excess of pain; but his advisers said to him, 'Softly, Your Majesty! Hearten your heart. We will give another banquet in a short while, no more inviting the noblest of the land, but instead folk of the lower class, as women are ever wont to attach themselves to the worst: and perchance we will meet with the seed of your wrath amid cutlers, comb-sellers, and other merchants of small wares, as we have not met with him among the noble and well-born.' The king was pleased with this rede, and commanded the second banquet to be got ready, whereto came, by ban invited, all folk from Chiaja, all the rogues, all adventurers and fortune-hunters, all quick-witted, all ruffians, and villains, and apron-wights that were to be found in the city, who, taking seat like unto noblemen at a long table spread with rich abundance, began straightway to load themselves.

Now it so happened that Ceccarella, having heard the ban which invited folk to this banquet, began to urge Peruonto to go to it also, and so much did she say and do that at last she prevailed upon him to depart, and he went: and he had hardly entered the place of feasting, when the two pretty children ran to him, and embraced him, and received him with great joy, and sported and played with him. The king, beholding this sight, wrenched off all his beard, seeing that the good name of this lottery and this lump of copeta * belonged to a sorcerer, scirpio,† hideous, and badly made, who sickened the sight so that one could not even gaze upon him without flinching. He was, besides, velvet-headed, owl-eyed, and had a nose like a parrot-beak, a mouth like that of a Lucerna fish, and was all in rags, so that, without reading, thou couldst have an insight into all the secrets; and sighing heavily, the king said, 'Hath ever any one seen anything like this, that that light-o'-brains daughter mine should have it in her head to fall in love with this sea-monster? hath ever any one seen one that could take to the heel of such an hairy foot? Ah, infamous woman, what blind and false metamorphoses are these: to become a strumpet for a pig, so that I should become a ram? But why do I tarry? what am I thinking of? Let them feel the weight of my just chastisement, let them be punished as they deserve, and let them bear the penalty that ye will adjudge: and take them out of my sight, for I cannot endure them.'

The ministers all took counsel together, and resolved that the princess and the malefactor, with the two children, should be put into a cask and thrown into the sea, so that they should thus end their days without the king soiling his hands with his own blood. No sooner was the sentence pronounced than the cask was brought,

---

* *Giuggiolena,* paste condensed with honey, hazel-nuts, and almonds, made in different shapes and figures, and seasoned with comfits.

† *Scirpio,* fem. *scirpia,* sour-looking, Lat. *scirpus;* a woman thin, lurid-looking, bronzed with shaggy hair, a witch.

and all four were put therein; but before they were thrown in, some of the handmaidens of Princess Vastolla, who were weeping with bitter weeping, put inside the hogshead raisins and dried figs, so that they could live for a little time. Then the cask was closed, and taken away, and flung into the sea, and it kept sailing on whither the wind blew it. Meanwhile Vastolla, weeping with sore weeping, her eyes running two streamlets of tears, said to Peruonto, 'What great misfortune is ours that our grave should be Bacchus' cradle! Oh, could I but have known who it was that worked in this body to have me thrown into this prison! Alas! I am come to a sad end, without knowing the why or wherefore. O thou cruel one, tell me, tell me, what magic art didst thou use, what wand didst thou hend, to bring me to this pass, to be shut herein by this hogshead's hoops? tell me, tell me, what devil tempted thee to put into me the invisible pipe, and gain nothing by it but the spectacle of a blackened factor?' Peruonto, who had for a time listened and pretended not to hear (making merchant's ear), answered at last, 'If thou wilt know how it came to pass, give me some raisins and figs.' The princess, desiring to draw from him something, gave him a handful of each; and as soon as his desire was satisfied, he began to recount all that had happened to him with the three young girls and the fagot of wood, and how at last he came under her window, and how, when she laughed at him, he wished her to be with child by him: which when the lady Vastolla heard, she heartened her heart, and said to him, 'Brother mine, why should we make exit of life inside this hogshead? Why not wish for this vessel to become a splendid ship, so that we may escape from this peril and arrive in good port?' And Peruonto rejoined, 'Give me figs and raisins, if it be thy desire to know.' And Vastolla at once satisfied his gluttony, so that he should be willing to speak: and like a carnival fisherwoman, with the raisins and figs she fished for the words fresh out of his body. And Peruonto said the words desired by the princess: and at once the cask became a ship, with all the sails ready for sailing, and with all the sailors that were needed for the ship's service; and there were to be seen some lowering the sheets, some hauling the shrouds, some holding the rudder, some setting the studding-sails, some mounting to the upper-main-topsail, one crying, 'Put the ship about!' and another, 'Put the helm up!' and one blowing the trumpet, and others firing the guns, and some doing one thing, and some another, so long as Vastolla remained on board the ship, swimming in a sea of sweetness.

It being now the hour when the moon played with the sun at going and coming, Vastolla said to Peruonto, 'Handsome youth mine, wish that this ship may become a palace, so that we may be more secure. Thou knowest what is usually said: "Praise the sea, but dwell on shore"'; and Peruonto answered, 'If it be thy desire that I should say so, give me some figs and raisins'; and she at once gave him what he asked, and Peruonto, having eaten, wished his wish, and the ship became a beautiful palace, adorned in all points, and furnished with such splendour that nothing was wanting. So that the princess, who would have parted with life easily but a short time before, now would not have exchanged her place with the highest lady in the world, seeing that she was served and entreated as a queen. Then, to put a seal upon her good-fortune, she begged Peruonto to obtain the grace of becoming handsome and polished, so that they could joy together: remarking that, although saith the proverb, 'Better a pig for an husband than an emperor for a friend,' if he could change his looks she would take it as the greatest good-fortune: and Peruonto in the same way answered, 'Give me figs and raisins, if it be thy will that I should thus desire.' And Vastolla at once remedied the costiveness of his words with the raisins and the figs, so that as soon as the wish was spoken he became from a sparrow a bullfinch, from a ghul a narcissus, and from an hideous mask a handsome youth. Vastolla, seeing such a transformation, was beside herself with excess of joy, and throwing her arms around him, tasted of the sweet juice of happiness.

Now it so happened that at this same time the king, who from the day on which he had pronounced the cruel sentence had not lifted his eyes from the ground, was entreated to the chase by his courtiers, who bethought themselves thus to cheer him. And he

went; and night surprising him, sighting from afar a light from a
lanthorn at one of the windows of the palace, he sent one of his
followers to see if they would receive him there: and he was answered that he might not only break a glass, but he could also shatter
a night vase. So the king accepted the invitation, and mounting the
steps, entered: and going from room to room, he could see no person living except the two children, who kept at his side, saying,
'Grandsire! grandsire! grandsire!' The king wondered with greatest wonder, and marvelled with greatest marvel: and being wearied,
seated himself by a table, when he beheld spread on it by invisible hands a white cloth and divers dishes of food, of which he
partook, and wines of good vintage, of which he drank truly as a
king, served by the two pretty children, never ceasing: and whilst
he was at meat, a band of calascioni * and tambourines discoursed
delicious music, touching even the marrow of his bones. When
he had done eating, a bed suddenly appeared made of cloth of gold;
and having had his boots pulled off, he took his rest, and all his
courtiers did the same, after having well supped at an hundred tables,
which were ready laid in other rooms.

As soon as morning came, the king got ready to depart, and was
going to take with him also the little ones, when Vastolla and her
husband appeared, and falling at his feet, asked his pardon, and recounted to him all their fortune. The king, seeing that he had won
two nephews that were like two grains of gold and two priceless
gems galore, and a son-in-law like a jinn, embraced first one and
then the other, and took them with him to the city, and commanded
great festivals and rejoicings to be made for this great gain, which
lasted many days: solemnly confessing to himself that

'Man proposeth, but God disposeth.'

* *Calascione* (Gr. χήλυς), an ancient and famous instrument with gut-strings.

VARDIELLO

Of the First Day

VARDIELLO BEING OF A BRUTISH DISPOSITION, AFTER AN HUNDRED BAD
TRICKS PLAYED UPON HIS MOTHER, LOSETH FOR HER A PIECE OF CLOTH,
AND STUPIDLY DESIRETH TO RECOVER IT FROM A STATUE, AND IN SO
DOING BECOMETH RICH.

As soon as Meneca had ended her story, which was praised and
esteemed by all for the number of curious adventures, which held
the hearer in suspense unto the end, Tolla, at the command of the
prince, without any loss of time thus began her say:

If nature had made it necessary for the brute creation to think
of dressing and of buying their food, by this time the race of quad-
rupeds would have been destroyed. But finding food readily, they
have no need of gardener to gather it, buyer to buy it, cook to dress
it, and carver to cut it up; their hide defends them from the rain
and the snow, they need no merchant to sell them cloth, no tailor
to make it, and no apprentice to ask for a gift. But man is ingenious, and Mother Nature cared not to give him the same indul-
gences, because she kenneth well that he can procure whatso he
needeth. This is the reason why the wise are often needy, and the
brainless rich: as ye will learn from the story that I will relate.

Grannonia of Aprano was a woman of sound judgment, but had
a son, Vardiello hight, the greatest simpleton of the village: but as
the eyes of the mother were charmed and saw not aright, she perceived no blemish in him, and loved him with a passionate love, and
was for ever caressing him and fondling him, as if he were the
handsomest creature in the world.

Now Grannonia kept a fowl, which was sitting upon a nest of
eggs upon which she set all her hopes, expecting to have a good
brood and thereby to derive some profit. And having one day to

32

go on some needful errand, she called her son, and said to him, 'O beloved son of thy mother, listen to me: keep watch upon this hen, and if she cometh down from her nest, be careful and drive her back again, otherwise the eggs will grow cold, and we shall have neither eggs nor chicks.'

'Leave it to me,' said Vardiello; 'thou hast not spoken to a deaf ear.' And another thing his mother begged of him, saying, 'O blessed son, in that cupboard there are several things in a jar which are poisonous: do not be tempted to touch them, for they would make you stretch your feet.'

Answered Vardiello, 'Far be it from me: poison will not catch me, and thou hast done well to forewarn me of it, for I might have been caught in it, and there would have been left neither thorn nor bone.' Thereupon his mother departed, and Vardiello remained; and not knowing what to do to spend his time, he descended to the garden, and began to dig small pits, which he covered with straw and soil, so that the children might tumble into them. And as he was in the midst of this pleasant work, he perceived the fowl strutting outside the house, whereupon he began to say, 'Hish! hish! away from here! march there!' but the fowl moved not, and Vardiello, seeing that she was as headstrong as an ass, after screeching, 'Hish! hish!' began to stamp with his feet, and to throw his cap at her, and picking up a stick, threw it also, and catching her in the middle, made the hen reel forward and stretch her feet.

When Vardiello saw what had happened, he bethought himself of what would be the best to do not to let the eggs get cold, and making a virtue of necessity, thought of remedying the evil by taking off his trousers and seating himself on the nest: but in doing so, his body being heavy, he quickly made an omelet of the eggs. Beholding this sight, he was ready to beat his head against the walls. At last, as all grief turns to the mouth, feeling an emptiness in his stomach, he resolved to feast upon the fowl. Therefore, plucking off the feathers and putting her on a spit, he lit a large fire, and began to roast her; and when she was cooked, to do all things in due order, he laid a fine-coloured cloth on an old chest, and taking an earthenware juglet, went down to the cellar, and filled it with wine. But whilst so doing, he heard a great noise, and a great crash, and a rushing about the house like the clattering of horses' hoofs. Whereat starting up in alarm and turning his eyes, he saw a large tom-cat running off with the fowl, spit and all, and another cat chasing after the first, swearing and miauwing for a share.

Vardiello, wishing to remedy the mishap, threw himself like an unchained lion upon the cat, and in his haste left the tap open and the wine running. And after racing after the cat all over the house, he recovered the fowl, but meanwhile all the wine was spilt; and when Vardiello returned and saw what had happened, he took the tap away from the cask; and because his sense helped him to remedy all this damage, so that his mother would not perceive it, he dragged forward a sack full of flour, and began to scatter its contents about the floor. Nevertheless, keeping account with his fingers of the mishaps which had happened that day, and thinking that he had committed stupidities that would lose for him all play with the love of his mother, he resolved in his heart not to let her find him again alive. Therefore he went to the cupboard, and taking out the jar full of preserved walnuts, which his mother had told him contained poison, he began to eat its contents, and never ceased until he came to the last; and when he had filled his stomach, he went to sleep inside the oven. Meanwhile his mother came, and knocked for some time, and seeing that no one heard her, gave a kick to the door and entered: and calling her son in a loud voice, and finding that no one answered, bethought her that a bad day had come, and shouted louder, 'O Vardiello, Vardiello, art thou deaf, that thou hearest not? Hast thou weights on thy feet, that thou comest not? Hast thou a pip on thy tongue, that thou answerest not? Where art thou, O rogue? Where art thou, son of a bad race? Would that I had strangled thee in thy birth!' Vardiello, listening to all this noise, at last with a pitiful voice said, 'Here am I! I am inside the oven, and you will never see me more, mother mine.' 'Why?' answered the distressed mother. 'Because I am poisoned,' answered the son. 'Alas and well-a-day! How didst thou do it? What cause hadst thou to commit this slaughter, and who gave to thee the poison?' And Vardiello related one after another all the fine deeds that he had done, and for which cause he desired to die, and not remain in this world as an example of folly.

The poor woman, hearing thus all that had happened, was wroth, and embittered, and aggrieved also, and had something to do to take out of Vardiello's head all his melancholy humour: and because she loved him dearly, she gave him other sweetmeats, so as to cheer him and undeceive him from his belief that the walnuts were poison, saying that they were good to restore the stomach but not to poison him. Having appeased him with many kind words, she drew him out of the oven, and giving him a piece of cloth, told him to go and sell it, advising him not to treat of this business with anybody that spake too much. 'Bravo,' said Vardiello; 'doubt not but that I shall serve thee well'; and taking the piece of cloth, Vardiello fared to Naples city, where he brought his ware, and began crying, 'Cloth! cloth!' But to all those who said to him, 'What cloth is this?' he answered, 'Thou art no good for my house, because thou speakest too much.' And to another who said to him, 'How dost thou sell it?' he answered that he had deafened him with his shouting.

At last, beholding in the courtyard of an untenanted house a statue of stucco, and being very tired and sore-footed, he seated himself upon a heap of stones; and seeing no one entering that house, that seemed as if it had been plundered, he marvelled with exceeding marvel, and turning to the statue, said, 'Tell me, comrade, doth anybody live in this house?' And as the other answered not, he thought that this must be a man of few words, and said, 'Wilt thou buy this piece of cloth? I will let thee have it cheaply': and seeing that the statue answereth not, said, 'By Jupiter, this is the very man I have been seeking: take it, let some one price it, and give me for it whatsoever thou wilt, and shortly I will return for the moneys.' Thus saying, he put the piece of cloth where he had been sitting; and the first one who entered therein for some want of nature, finding it there, took it away. Meanwhile Vardiello returned to his mother without the cloth; and relating the facts to her, she felt heart-sore, and said, 'Whenever wilt thou put thy brains in order? See how much mischief thou hast done to me: remember it well. But I am to blame for being too tender-hearted: I have not at first put thy legs to rights, and now I feel assured that a pitiful doctor maketh a wound sorer: and so much mischief dost thou do that at last I will pay thee back, and we will square all accounts.' Vardiello kept saying, whilst she thus spake, 'Hush, mother mine, it is not what thou sayest. Thou wantest nought but the coins. Thinkest thou that I am such a dunce, and do not know how to keep counts? It will come by-and-by: thou wilt see in a short time if I do not have an handle put to the shovel.'

As morning dawned, when the shadows of night flee, persecuted by the sun's troops of light, Vardiello made his way to the courtyard where was the statue, and said, 'Good-morrow, master. Will it be convenient to give me that small amount of money? Now dost thou hear? Pay me for the cloth.' But the statue answered not, he took hold of a stone, and throwing it with all his strength, caught the statue in the middle of its breast, and broke a vein which was the health and benefit of his house, for, having knocked down a few pieces of stone, he discovered a vessel full of gold pieces, and hending with both hands, he ran to his house, crying, 'Mother! mother! look what a number of red lupins: oh, how many; how many!' The mother, seeing the gold, and knowing that her son would soon publish the fact, told him to stand at the door and wait for the curdled milk seller, because she would buy him some. Vardiello, who was a glutton, at once seated himself before the door: and the mother, going upstairs, sent down for more than half an hour a rain of raisins and figs from the window, which Vardiello beholding, he began to cry, 'Mother! mother! put out basins and tubs, and if this rain lasteth, we shall be rich': and as soon as he was well filled, he went upstairs to sleep.

Now it happened that one day of the days two working men were quarrelling because of a golden coin they had found on the ground; and whilst thus engaged, Vardiello passed that way, and seeing the cause of their dispute, said, 'What asses ye are to quarrel about a red lupin, which I hold of no account, since I found of them a potful!' The men, hearing this, took him before a court of justice, where the judge asked him, 'How, when, and with whom didst thou find these lupins?' to which answered Vardiello, 'I found them in a palace, inside a dumb man: and it rained raisins and dried figs.' The judge, hearing this jumping of emptiness, decreed that he should be taken to the madhouse as a competent judge of it. Thus the son's ignorance made the mother rich, and the judgment of the mother balanced the stupidity of the son: and by this it is clearly seen that

' 'Tis great misfortune if ship, governed by good pilot, wrecks on rock.'

THE FLEA

Of the First Day

A THOUGHTLESS KING GROWETH A FLEA TO THE SIZE OF A SHEEP, AND
ORDERING IT TO BE SLAIN AND SKINNED, OFFERETH HIS DAUGHTER IN
MARRIAGE TO WHOSO SHALL, ON SEEING THE HIDE, RECOGNISE TO WHAT
MANNER OF ANIMAL IT BELONGED.   A GHUL RECOGNISETH IT BY THE
SCENT, AND TAKETH THE PRINCESS TO WIFE: BUT SHE IS FREED FROM
HER THRALDOM BY SEVEN SONS OF AN OLD WOMAN, EACH ONE GIVING
PROOF OF HIS WIT TO DELIVER HER.

THE prince and the slave laughed aloud at Vardiello's tricks, and
praised the sound sense of the mother, who had the wit to fore-
see and remedy her son's folly; and it being now Popa's turn to
relate her story, all the company became silent, and she began thus:

A resolve taken without wise judgment bringeth always ruin
without remedy.   Whoso guideth himself as a madman suffereth
cark and care as a wise one: as happened to the King of Automonte,
who, through a measureless folly, did a mad deed, imperilling greatly
both his daughter and his honour.

The King of Automonte, being once bitten by a flea, caught it
with dexterity, and seeing it nicely rounded, deemed it a cruelty to
sentence it to be crushed on the nail.   Therefore, putting it into a
bottle, he nourished it with the blood from his own arm, and it
was so well fed that in seven months' time it had to change lodging,
for it had become of the size of a sheep, whereat the king at once
ordered it to be slain and skinned, and the hide tanned, and bade
the public crier proclaim, 'Whoso will recognise to what animal belongeth this hide, the king will give him his daughter to wife.'
When the folk heard this, they crowded from all parts of the world
to tempt their fortune: and some said it belonged to a wild cat, and
some to a wolf, and some to a crocodile, and some gave it to one
animal, and some to another; but all were a thousand miles from

38

the truth, and not one hit the nail on the head. At last came a ghul to this experiment, who was the most hideous being ever seen, since to look upon him was enough to make one tremble, and the most courageous youth in the world would have felt faint at the sight. Now no sooner had this ghul arrived than, putting his nose to the hide, he said, 'This skin belongeth to the largest of fleas.'

The king, hearing that he had known it straightway, and desiring not to fail in his promise, sent for his daughter Porziella, a beauteous lady, with a face like milk and roses that would charm all beholders; and the king said to her, 'O my daughter, thou knowest the edict that I had cried about the city, and thou knowest who I am. I cannot gainsay my promise: I must be a king or the bark of a poplar-tree: my word once given must be maintained, even though in so doing I break my heart. Who could suppose that this lottery would be won by a ghul? But as not a leaf falleth without the will of Heaven, we must believe that this marriage is made first above and afterwards here below. Be patient, therefore, and if thou art a blessed daughter, do not rebel against thy sire's will, for my heart whispers to me that thou wilt be happy, because often hidden behind a rude stone is treasure found.' Porziella hearing this behest, all things became dark before her sight, and her colour changed and paled, and her mouth drooped, and her limbs trembled, and she came nigh unto death for her stress of sorrow.

At last she wept with sore weeping, and spake in a tremulous voice, and said to her sire, 'What evil deed have I done to our house, that I am doomed to so cruel a fate? what evil words have I uttered to thee, that I should be given in hand to this monster? O wretched Porziella, as a weasel I must be eaten by a toad, and as a trembling sheep I must be dragged to the den of a wolf! Is this the love thou bearest to thy race? Is this the affection thou showest to me, whom heretofore thou calledst the doll of thy soul? Is it thus thou hast expelled from thy heart her who is a part and parcel of thy flesh and blood? Is it thus thou sendest from thy sight her who was the apple of thine eye? O father, O cruel sire, thou art not born of human flesh: the sea-ghuls gave thee birth, the wild cats suckled thee.

But what am I saying? Every brute, be it of the sea or of the land, loveth its own breed. Only thou goest against thy own seed: thou hatest thy child. Oh, far better had it been if my mother had strangled me at my birth, if my cradle had been my death-bed, the breast which suckled me a bladder of poison, and the necklace they put round my neck a rope to strangle me: better all these things than to see the evil day in which an harpy's hand should caress me, and to be embraced by two bear's paws and kissed by a bear's mouth.'

She would have added more, but the king interrupted her, saying, 'Be not angry, as the sugar costeth dear; softly, as the forks are made of wood; hold, for out of it come the dregs: be silent; say no more; thou speakest too much; thy tongue goeth too fast; what I do is well done; a father knoweth what to make with his children; put thy tongue behind thee, and raise not mine anger, for if I put my hands upon thee I will not leave thee a whole bone, and I will see thee bite the dust, thou breath of my arse, wanting to play the man and lay down the law to thy sire. Whence comes it that one whose mouth yet stinketh of milk can contradict my will? At once take his hand and wend thy footsteps to his home, for I will behold thy brazen face no longer.'

The unhappy princess, having reached this pass, with a face like a corpse, and eyes glaring, and mouth foaming, and a heart crushed with cark and care took the ghul by the hand, and he dragged her to the forest, where the trees were her palace, and the sun's rays never shone; the rivers met, and being in a darksome place, touched each other; and the wild beasts joyed to their hearts' content in the security of the bush, where man never entered, unless he had strayed and lost his road. And in a dark place, fearful to behold, like a very hell, was built the ghul's palace, adorned and bedecked with the bones of all those wretches whom he had slain and devoured. Bethink, ye that are Christians, the affright, the straitened breast, the trembling of limbs, the anguished heart, of the wretched princess: she had no blood left in her! But this was as nought to what followed, since the ghul had gone a-hunting, and shortly returned laden with slaughtered men, saying, 'Now thou canst not say, O my wife, that I do not feed thee well: see what a fine meal I have brought thee; take and eat, and love me: for the heavens may fall, but I will never leave thee meatless.' The unhappy Porziella, spitting like a woman with child, turned her head the other side.

The ghul, seeing her disgust, said, 'It is like giving sweetmeats to pigs: but never mind, be patient till to-morrow morning, for I have been bidden to the chase, and will hunt wild boars, and I will bring thee a pair, and we will have a feast, and all our kith and kin shall partake thereof in honour of our wedding.' Thus saying, he fared onwards into the forest; and Porziella was left to think and repine at the window.

Now it chanced that an old woman passed that way, and feeling faint with hunger, begged of Porziella some refreshment, to which the unhappy princess answered, 'O my good old woman, God knoweth the heart, but I am in the power of a Satan, who bringeth me home nought but quarters of slaughtered men, and I know not how I have any appetite left in sighting such horrors, and I am spending the most miserable and wretched day that was ever left in store for a baptized being, and I am a king's daughter to boot, and was brought up with delicacy, and all my wishes were gratified': and thus saying, she wept with bitter weeping.

The old woman felt her heart softening for her, and turning to her, said, 'Weep not, O beauteous lady: do not wear out thy loveliness, for thou hast met with thy chance: here am I to help thee and watch over thee. Now hearken to me: I am the mother of seven sons, like seven giants, Mase, Nardo, Cola, Micco, Petrullo, Ascadeo, and Ceccone, and they have more power in them than the rosemary, and especially Mase, since every time he leans his ear to the ground he can hear what is done for thirty miles' distance; Nardo, every time he spits, makes a great sea of soapy water; Cola, every time he throws on the ground a hairpin, it becomes a field of sharpened razors; Micco, every time he sets a bough, it becomes an intricate forest; Petrullo, every time he drops a drop of water, it becomes a large river; Ascadeo, every time he throws a stone, it becomes a strong fortress; and Ceccone pulls the bowstring with such dexterity that he can hit a fowl in the eye at a mile's distance. Now, with the help of these my sons, who are all good and loving, and will take compassion of this thy estate, I will try to wrench thee out of the ghul's claws, because this sweet morsel is not for his mouth.'

'There never will be a better opportunity than now,' answered Porziella, 'for that hideous shadow hath gone to the chase, not to return till this evening, and we would have time to take our departure and escape.'

'It cannot be this evening,' answered the old woman, 'because I live at a distance from here; but to-morrow morning early I and my sons will ease thee of thy travail.' Thus saying, she went her way: and Porziella's heart was heartened, and she rested cheerfully that night. And when the maids of dawn cried, 'Hail to the sun!' behold, the old woman came with her seven sons, and bidding the princess to walk in the midst of them, they all fared cityward: but they had not journeyed half the way, when Mase, putting his ear to the earth, cried, 'Be on guard: let us be careful! The ghul hath returned home, and finding not this child, is coming after us with all speed.' Hearing these words, Nardo turned, and spat on the ground, when a roaring sea of soapy water rose up. The ghul, sighting this hindrance in his way, returned to his home, and took up a sack of bran, which he tied about his limbs; and thus accoutred, he passed this first difficulty. But Mase, again putting his ear to the ground, said, 'Look out, brother mine; 'tis thy turn, for he is coming,' whereupon Cola threw the hair-pin on the ground, and it became at once a field of sharpened razors. The ghul, sighting this new obstacle, ran home, and donned steel raiment from head to foot, and returning, passed on. But Mase, putting ear on ground again, cried, 'Up, up, to arms! The ghul is coming in all haste'; and Micco, ready with the bough, set it on the ground: and a forest of great intricacy sprang up.

But as soon as the ghul reached this impediment, he drew a knife from his waistband, and began to cut down trees, one here and one there, so that in a short time he had nearly cut down all the forest, and had come out of this difficulty easily. Mase, who held his ear close to the ground, lifted his voice and cried, 'Let us not be idle, for the ghul is coming, and will be at our backs in a trice.' Petrullo, hearing these words, took from a small fountain, which ran near the roadside, a shell full of water: and throwing it on the ground, behold, a great river sprang up.

The ghul, perceiving this new obstacle, took off his raiment and remained quite naked, and putting his robes on his head, plunged into the stream, and swimming powerfully, soon reached the other side. Mase, who kept his ear in every hole, cried, 'This matter is becoming stale, and already the ghul beateth his heels on the ground behind us, and may Heaven guard us: therefore let us be wise, and let us repair this evil: let not the storm overtake us.' Then said Ascadeo, 'Doubt not; I will clear thee of this hideous ragamuffin'; and thus speaking, he took up a stone and threw it at a distance, when a strong fortress appeared, and all entered therein, shutting the door.

Now the ghul, perceiving that they were in a safe place, returned home, and took up a ladder, and came back with it. Mase, who was always on guard, heard from afar that the ghul had returned, and said, 'Now we have reached the last candle of our hopes; Ceccone is the final refuge for our lives; the ghul is returning in a great fury. Alas! my heart is beating against my breast, and I dream already of a bad day.'

'Art thou so faint-hearted?' said Ceccone. 'Dost thou dump thyself in thy small-clothes with fear? Let me deal with this villain, and thou wilt see if I hit the nail on the head.' Thus saying, they beheld the ghul coming with the ladder, which he leant against the wall, and began mounting: but Ceccone took aim, and drew the string, and caught him on the eye, and he fell headlong on the ground, when Ceccone, issuing from the tower, took the ghul's knife from his belt, and cut off his head, just as if it had been a new cheese, which they brought to the king, who rejoiced with exceeding joy in having recovered his daughter, having repented sorely of the rash deed which had obliged him to wed her to the ghul. After a short time he gave her in marriage to a handsome prince, and enriched the seven sons and their mother, who had saved his daughter from unhappiness and death, never ceasing to reproach himself for having exposed his daughter to so much peril for a worthless caprice, and thinking of what a grave error is committed by those who seek

'A wolf's eggs and comb of fifteen.' *

* *Ova di lupo*, a thing impossible or without price, for a worthless thing, viz., *pettine de quìnneci*, a comb of fifteen soldi. *Ova di lupo* is also used for several kinds of pastry fried together.

THE CAT CINDERELLA

Of the First Day

ZEZOLLA IS TAUGHT BY HER GOVERNESS TO SLAY HER STEPMOTHER, AND
BELIEVING THAT IN PERSUADING HER FATHER TO MARRY HER TEACHER
SHE WOULD BE WELL TREATED AND HELD DEAR, INSTEAD IS SENT INTO
THE KITCHEN: BUT, BY VIRTUE OF THE FAIRIES, AFTER PASSING VARIOUS
ADVENTURES, GAINETH A KING FOR A SPOUSE.

THE hearers were silent as statues, listening to the story of the
flea, and as soon as it was ended, all declared that the king had
behaved like an ass in placing in jeopardy his own flesh and blood
and the succession of his realm: and all having said their say, Antonella began to relate as follows:

Envy is ever a sea of malignity, and giveth in exchange for bladders a rupture, and when it desireth to see folk drowned in the sea,
findeth itself under water or impelled against a rock, as I am now
going to relate.

Once upon a time there lived a prince who was a widower, and
he possessed an only daughter, so dear to him that he saw nought
but by her eyes: and the princess had a governess, who taught her all
kinds of fancy work, and educated her in many other feminine en-
dowments.

Now this woman made a great show of affection for her pupil,
more in sooth than can be expressed. The prince took to himself a
wife after a little while, and she chanced to be an evilly-disposed
woman, who looked with disfavour on her charming stepdaughter,
treating her with contempt, and coldness, and spite, so much so that
the unhappy child used to complain of the ill-treatment she received
to her teacher, saying to her, 'O God, would that thou hadst been
my darling mother, thou who lovest me and art always caressing
me!' And so long did she continue this song that the governess at

45

last lent a pleased ear to it, and blinded by Satan, spake to the child thus: 'If thou wilt do as I bid thee, I will become thy mother, and thou shalt be dear unto me as my very eyes.' She was going to end her say, when Zezolla (thus was the princess hight) interrupted her, and said, 'Pardon me if I thus stop the words upon thy lips: I ken quite well that thou lovest me: therefore say no more, but teach me only by what art we can come to the end of our desires. Write thou, and I will sign the deed.' The teacher rejoined, 'Open thine ears, and hearken well, and thou shalt have bread as white as snow. When thy sire fareth to the chase, say to thy stepmother that thou wouldest like to wear one of the old raiments which are to be found in the large chest stored away, as it is thy desire to save for high occasions the one thou wearest now. Thy stepmother, who loveth above all things to see thee in rags, will at once consent, and will go and open the chest, and will say to thee, "Hold up the lid," and thou wilt hold it: and when she searcheth therein, thou wilt let it fall, and thus her neck will be broken. And after this thou knowest thy sire will do anything, even to false coinage, to please thee: therefore, when he caresseth thee, beseech thou him to take me to wife: and then wilt thou be blessed and happy, since thou wilt be the mistress of my life.'

Having listened to the bidding of her governess, every hour seemed a thousand years to her until she could execute her teacher's rede. And after a time she did so: and when the mourning for her stepmother's untimely end had passed, she began to speak to her sire, telling him that she would be very happy if he would wed her teacher.

The prince at first heard not; but the daughter kept ever speaking and persuading him, till at last he lent a willing ear to her desires, and took Carmosina (thus was the teacher hight) to wife, and ordered great joyance and feasting in all his realm. Now it so happened that whilst the bride and bridegroom were toying and playing, and spending their time in joyance, Zezolla was looking out of one of the windows in the palace, and beheld a pigeon flying about, which at last settled upon a low wall in front of her, and addressing her in human voice, spake thus: 'When thou desirest to have something, send to the pigeon of the fairies in the island of Sardinia, and thou shalt have thy wish.'

The new stepmother for five or six days caressed and petted the young princess, seating her in the best place at table, giving her the choicest morsels, arraying her in the finest raiment: but having passed a short time, forgetting the deed Zezolla had done to serve her (and sad the soul who hath a bad master), she brought forward six daughters of her own, whom she had kept hidden secretly: and so much art did she use that, having ingratiated her daughters in the stepfather's favour, he lost all love and affection for his own child, so that (argue to-day and speak to-morrow) Zezolla was sent from the chamber to the kitchen, from the dais to the fireplace, from the silken and golden raiment to the coarse cloth, and from the sceptre to the spit. And not only did she change her estate, but her name was changed also, and she was hight the Cat Cinderella. So it chanced one day of the days that the prince her sire had to journey to the island of Sardinia on matters concerning his realm; and before departing he asked each one of his stepdaughters—Mperia, Calamita, Sciorella, Diamante, Colommina, and Pascarella—what they would that he should bring to them on his return. One asked for fine raiment, another jewels for her hair, another cosmetics and pomade for the skin, another divers playthings to pass the time, another fruits, another flowers: and at the last, in contempt for his own daughter, he turned and said to her, 'And thou, what wilt thou?' and she answered, 'I want nought, but I desire that thou recommend me to the pigeon of the fairies, bidding her tell them that they would send me somewhat: and an thou shouldest forget to do my bidding, mayest thou not be able to stir forward or backward from thy place. Remember well my saying: thine is the weapon, and thine is the sleeve.' The prince fared to Sardinia, ended all his affairs, bought all the things desired by his stepdaughters, and forgot quite Zezolla's bidding. He took ship for his return: but do as they would, the ship would not move from its place, neither backward nor forward, and it seemed glued to its mooring.

The vessel's master was in despair, and in the evening, being very tired, he lay down and slept: and he beheld a fairy in his sleep, who said to him, 'Knowest thou wherefore thy ship cannot sail? 'Tis because the prince thou hast on board hath failed to keep his promise to his daughter, remembering all his stepdaughters, and forgetting his own flesh and blood.' The master awoke from sleep, and related his dream to the prince, who, confessing the fault he had committed, fared at once to the fairies' grotto, and recommending his daughter to them, begged that they would send her somewhat: and at his words out of the cave came a beauteous young lady, who said to him that she thanked his daughter for her kind remembrance, and that she bade her take for love of her these her gifts: and thus saying, she gave him a date-tree, a mattock, a golden bucket, and a silken napkin, the one to transplant, and the others to cultivate the tree. The prince marvelled at the present, took leave of the fairy, and journeyed with the ship towards his country. On his arrival he gave his stepdaughters that which they had bidden him bring, and lastly to his daughter the gifts of the fairy. Zezolla accepted the gift with great joy, and transplanted the date-tree in a larger and finer vase, and watered it, and dug round it morning and evening, and dried it with the silken napkin, and in four days it grew to a woman's stature: and the fairy came out of it one morning, saying, 'What wilt thou?' and the princess answered, 'I would like to fare from this house, but should desire that my stepsisters should not know of it': and the fairy rejoined, 'Each time that thou wouldest fare out and enjoy thyself, come to the date-tree, and say,

> "My date-tree tall and golden,
> With a golden mattock I dug thee around,
> With a golden bucket I watered thee,
> With a silken napkin I wiped thee dry:
> Undress thyself, and robe thou me."

And when thou wouldst undress, change the last verse, and say, "Undress thou me, and robe thyself." ' '

Now it so chanced that a great festival was held by the king: and the daughters of the teacher went to it in fine raiment, and jewellery, and ribbons, and fine shoes, and flowers, and perfumed, with roses and posies. As soon as they departed, Zezolla ran to the date-tree, and repeated the verse taught her by the fairy: and at once she was arrayed as a queen, and put on a steed, and twelve pages followed her, all dressed with luxury and taste: and she went where her stepsisters had gone before her, who knew her not, and were ready to die with envy. But as fate decreed, came to that same place the king, who on beholding Zezolla fell enamoured of her, and desired one of his most trusty followers to learn who was this beauty and where she dwelt. The king's servant at once followed the princess: but Zezolla, perceiving the snare, threw an handful of golden coins to the ground, at the sight of which the man forgot to follow the courser as he stooped to gather the gold, which Zezolla had begged the date-tree to give her for this same purpose. Thus she had time to run ino the house, and undress herself as the fairy had taught her. And when those witches, her stepsisters, arrived home, they said many things in praise of the festival, of what they had done and what they had seen, to cause her vexation, as they supposed. In the meanwhile the follower returned to the king, and related to him about the handful of coins and how he had lost sight of her, at which the king waxed wroth, and said to him that for a few dirty pieces of gold he had deprived him of his delight, but that he would forgive him this time, but he must be sure to follow her on the next feast-day, and to discover for him who this beautiful bird was.

The next feast-day the stepsisters went their way all bedecked in finery, and left the despised Zezolla at the fireplace. As soon as they were gone, she ran to the date-tree and said the usual charm: and some young girls came forward, some with the mirror, some with the perfumes, some with the curling tongs, some with the comb, some with the hair-pins, and others with the raiment, some with the necklace, and others with flowers: and decking her like a bride, she looked like the sun, and setting her in a carriage, with six horses, with footmen, and servants, and pages in livery, she arrived at the same place where had been held the festival heretofore:

and she lit more marvel and envy in her stepsister's breasts, and
greater love and fiercer fire in the king's heart. But having departed, the same servant followed her: but she threw at him a handful of jewels, and pearls, and precious stones, and he could not
withstand the temptation to gather them, as they were too precious
to lose. And the princess had time to reach her home, and to undress
as usual. The man returned to the king, who said, 'By the bones
of my ancestors, if thou findest not this lovely being for me, I will
give thee as many kicks on thy backside as thou hast hairs in thy
beard.'

The third festival came: and the stepsisters having departed,
Zezolla went to the date-tree, and saying the charmed verse, she
was at once apparelled most splendidly, and seated in a golden carriage, followed by many servants, pages, and retainers. And thus
she caused more envy in the sisters' breasts: and the king's follower
stuck to the carriage. And the princess, sighting him always beside
her, said to the coachman, 'Hasten on,' and the horses raced with
such speed that nothing could be discerned clearly, and in the fury
of the race a slipper of the princess flew out of the carriage. The
servant, unable to follow the carriage, which seemed to fly, picked
up the slipper and brought it to the king, and related all that had
happened; and the king, taking it, said, 'If the foundation is so
beautiful, what must be the house? O beauteous candlestick, which
holdest the candle that consumeth me! O trivet of the beauteous
kettle where boileth my life! O fine cloth, to which is tied the net
of love wherewith thou hast caught this soul! I embrace thee and
hold thee to my bosom; and if I cannot have the tree, I worship the
root; and if I cannot hend the chapiter, I kiss the foundation.
Thou wert the covering for a white foot, and now art thou the
pulley of this blackened heart; by thee stood thy fellow, an inch
tall and more, who is the tyrant of this life of mine; and by thee
groweth so much sweetness in my soul, whilst I gaze upon thee and
possess thee!' And thus saying, he called his secretary, and commanded him to send the public crier to publish a ban that all the
women in the land should be invited to a banquet by the king.

And the day came. O goodness me, what a banquet was that, and what joyance and amusements were there, and what food: pastry, and pies, and roast, and balls of mincemeat, and macaroni, and ravioli, enough to feed an army! All the women came: noble and commoner, rich and poor, old and young, wives and maidens, beautiful and ugly; and the king, arrayed in costly raiment, tried the slipper on each one's foot to see if it would fit one of them, hoping thus to find the one he was seeking: but he found not what he sought, and he came nigh unto despair. At last, commanding perfect silence, he said to them, 'Return to-morrow to do penance with me: but an ye love me, leave not a single female in the house, be she who she may.' Said the prince, 'I have a daughter who sitteth always in the kitchen by the fireplace, because she is not worthy any one's notice, and she deserveth not to sit at thy table.' Said the king, 'Let this be the very one at the head of all: such is my desire.' Therefore all departed, and on the morrow all came again, and with the daughters of Carmosina came also Zezolla, and when the king beheld her he knew her for the one he sought: but he dissembled.

The banquet was more sumptuous that the last, and when all had eaten their fill the king began to try on the slipper: but no sooner came he to Zezolla than the foot was caught by love like steel to the magnet; and the king surprised her by putting his arms around her, and seating her under the dais, and putting the crown on her head, commanded that all should do her obeisance as to their queen. The stepsisters, beholding this sight, full of wrath and envy, and being unable to support this blow without showing their chagrin, departed quite quietly towards their mother's home: confessing, in spite of themselves, that

''Tis a madman's deed to dispute the stars' decree.'

THE MERCHANT

Of the First Day

CIENZO BREAKETH THE KING'S SON'S HEAD, AND IS OBLIGED TO FLEE FROM
HIS COUNTRY. HE DELIVERETH FROM A DRAGON THE DAUGHTER OF KING
PIERDISINNO, AND AFTER VARIOUS ADVENTURES SHE BECOMETH HIS WIFE.
ENSORCELLED BY A WOMAN, HE IS FREED FROM THE CHARM BY HIS
BROTHER, MEO HIGHT, WHOM FOR JEALOUSY HE SLAYETH: BUT BEING
APPRISED OF MEO'S INNOCENCE, WITH AN HERB HE RESTORETH HIM
TO LIFE.

WORDS fail to express how the good fortune of Zezolla touched
all hearers, even to the marrow of their bones, and how they praised
Heaven for its liberality towards her; but they deemed the punishment small for the stepmother and her daughters, since there is no
chastisement great enough for pride, nor ruin strong enough to crush
envy. But listening awhile to the whispering about that which had
been related, Prince Thaddeus at last put the forefinger of his right
hand upon his lips, and signed to them to be silent: and they ceased
instantaneously, just as if they had seen a wolf, or like a pupil who,
in the midst of his game beholding the teacher approach, loseth all
power of speech. The prince signed to Ciulla to proceed with her
story, and she began thus:

Oft-times man hath sorrows and travail which, like flames and
shovels, straighten the road to that good fortune which he never
dreamt he could achieve. And such a man curseth the rain because
it wetteth his head, and knoweth not that it bringeth him plentiful-
ness, so that he may expel dark hunger from his side: as will be seen
in the story of a youth which I will relate.

There lived in Naples city a rich merchant, Antoniello hight,
who had two sons named Cienzo and Meo; and they so much resembled one another that one could hardly tell which was one and
which the other. Now Cienzo, who was the eldest, was playing

with the son of the king at throwing stones, when it chanced that he struck and broke the prince's head; and Cienzo's sire, hearing of the mishap, said, 'Bravo! thou hast done a good deed. Write now to thy country, boast of thy doings, bag of emptiness, and I will unpick thee. Mount on thy high horse, for thou hast gained that which is worth six soldi: thou hast broken the head of the prince. Hadst thou not the measure, son of a goatherd? Now what will become of thee? I would not give three farthings for thy skin, for thou hast cooked thy soup badly; even shouldst thou enter the womb whence thou camest forth, I would not answer that thou wouldst escape the king's wrath: thou knowest that king's arms are long and reach far, and he is certain to do something that will stink.'

Cienzo listened patiently to his father's saying, and when he had ended, thus rejoined: 'O my father, I have always heard it said that it is better to go to a court of justice than to have the doctor in the house. Would it not have been worse if he had broken my head? I was provoked: we are but children, and we quarrelled; it is a first crime, and the king is a just man; at worst what will it matter in an hundred years? Who will not give me the mother may give me the daughter, and who will not send me cooked food may send it uncooked; all the world is a country, and he that is afraid may become a constable.' Antoniello answered, 'What can he do to thee? He can send thee out of the world; he can send thee for a change of air; he can make thee a schoolmaster in a twenty-four feet galley,* to be a horse for the fishes, so that thou mayest teach them to speak; he can send thee a three-feet collar well starched,† so that thou mayest enjoy thyself with the widow: and instead of touching the hand of the bride, thou shalt touch the feet of the groomsman. Therefore stand not with thy skin between the cloth and the cloth-shearer; but march at this same step, that we may never hear tidings, neither old nor new, of thee and thy doings, so that thou mayest not be caught by the foot. For it is better to be a bird in the wilderness than a bird in a cage. Here,

---

* Galley-slave.
† To be hanged.

take this gold, and go to the stable, and mount one of the two charmed steeds I have therein; and take a bitch which is also ensorcelled, and wait for nothing more. It is better to lift thine heel than to be caught by the heel; it is better to carry thy legs than to put thy neck under thy legs; it is better to walk a thousand feet than to remain with a rope three feet long. If thou takest not thy saddlebags, neither Baldo nor Bartolo will help thee.'

Cienzo begged his father to give him his blessing, and mounting horse and taking the bitch on his arm, journeyed away from the city; but as soon as he fared forth from the Capuan gate, turning his head backwards, he began saying, 'I am going to leave thee, O my beautiful Naples; who knoweth if I evermore will see thee, O thou whose bricks are sugar, and whose walls are made of sweet soft pastry, where the stones are manna, and the beams are of sugarcane, and the doors and the windows are of sweet cakes? Alas! separating myself from thee, O beautiful Apennine, it seems to me as if I fared away with the standard; withdrawing myself from thee, O thou Great Place, my soul is straitened; removing myself from thee, Ermo's Place, my spirit is ready to depart from this body; dividing myself from you, Lancers, I feel the stroke of a Catalan lance in my side. Where shall I ever find another harbour like thine, the sweetest harbour in all the world? Where shall I find another hole, receptacle of all virtuous men, where another lodge where dwelleth all that pleaseth and enticeth the taste? Alas! and woe is me, I cannot leave thee, O dear bay mine, if I do not let mine eyes run a sea of tears; I cannot leave thee, O market, without deep grief burning in my breast; in leaving thee, O beautiful Chiaja, I must bear in my heart a thousand wounds. Farewell, sweet carrots, and cabbages, and cauliflowers! adieu, dear tripe and lovely trots! adieu, tarantella and elegant ladies! adieu, flower of the city and Talia's luxury, Cupid of Europe and Ass of the World! farewell, Naples, where ends all virtue, and all grace abideth! I go, and shall be for ever a widower of married pottage; I fare away from this beauteous country, where I leave all my strength and peace.'

And thus saying, he made a winter of tears and a summer of
sighs, and journeyed onwards, and never ceased faring till the evening, when he came to a forest, where he sighted an old house at
the foot of a strong tower. He knocked at the door, but the master,
fearing brigands, it being a dark night, would not open to him;
and Cienzo was obliged to take refuge in a dilapidated part of the
old house: and tethering the horse in the adjacent field, he lay with
the bitch by his side on some straw he found there. But hardly
had he closed his eyes, when he started up at the barking of the
bitch; and listening, he heard footsteps creeping around. Now
Cienzo was brave and courageous, and he drew his sword and began
to lunge and plunge in the dark; but finding that he caught no one,
and that he fought with the wind, he lay down once more. But
after a little while he felt some one pulling him gently by the foot;
and again rising and drawing his sword, he cried, 'Ho, there, whoever thou art, thou annoyest me now; it is no good playing hide-
and-seek: if thou art valiant, let me see thee, and if thou wilt fight,
let us fight, for thou hast found the shape for thy shoe.' In answer
to this he heard a light laugh, and a muffled voice said, 'Come down
here, and I will tell thee who I am.' Cienzo fearlessly replied,
'Wait a minute, and I will be with thee'; and he crept in the dark,
feeling about till he found a staircase descending to the cellar; and
he went down, and perceived, by the light of a small lantern, three
gnomes who were weeping bitterly and crying, 'O beautiful treasure, how can we lose thee?' Cienzo at the sight began also to weep
and lament, to keep them company; and after bemoaning for some
time, and the moon being high amidst the heavens, the three gnomes
said to him, 'Go and take this treasure: it was decreed by the Decreer that it should be thine; take it, and know how to use it.'
And having spoken thus, they disappeared.

Now as soon as Cienzo beheld a ray of the sun from a little fis-
sure, he tried to find the stairs to mount; but he could see no mode
of exit, at which case he began to cry out so very loud that the master of the tower, who had entered those ruins to make water, heard
him, and asking him what he was doing there, and hearing how it

fortuned, went to fetch a ladder, and in descending thereon found the hoard, which he wished to share with Cienzo. But Cienzo would accept none of it; and taking the bitch on his arm, he mounted his steed, and fared on. After a while he came to another forest, very dark and gloomy; and there at the sea-shore he found a fairy, who, being enamoured of the shade and its coolness, liked to spend her time in the wood in the shape of a serpent: and she was persecuted by several others who desired to slay her, which Cienzo seeing, he laid hand on sword and sliced right and left, thus saving the fairy's life and honour. Then she appeared to him as a beauteous lady, and thanked him, and complimented him on his valour, and invited him to her palace, which was not very distant, for that she desired to show him proof of her gratitude. But Cienzo said to her, 'There is no need; a thousand thanks! Another time I will accept thy favour; now I cannot, for I am pressed for time'; and taking leave of her, he fared on for some time, and he came to a king's palace, all tapestried in mourning, so that it made the very heart be darkened to look upon it.

Cienzo went forward and inquired the cause of this mourning; and they answered him that into that country had come a dragon with seven heads, the most terrible that could be seen in the world. On each head he had a cock's comb and a cat's face, eyes of fire, a dog's mouth, a bat's jaws, and he had a bear's paws and a serpent's tail. And this dragon ate a human being each day, and so it had been for some time; and now, by decree of the Decreer, it had come to the turn of Menechiella, the king's daughter, to serve as food for the monster. 'And this is the reason why the king's palace is in mourning,' continued they, 'because the loveliest and most graceful creature in this country must serve as food for this horrible monster.' As Cienzo heard this he stood aside, and beheld Menechiella coming dressed all in mourning, and followed by the young ladies of the court and by all the women of the land, who buffeted their faces, and struck at their breasts, and tore their hair, and wept and wailed, bemoaning the lot of the unhappy princess, saying, 'Who could have dreamt that this poor child should give up all the joys and pleasures of life in the body of this hideous beast? If any one had told us that this pretty bird should serve as food for this dragon, we could not have believed it; we could not dream that this bright young angel would lose her life in this monster's belly'; and as they spake thus, behold, out of a hidden place came the dragon. O mother mine, how hideous! The sun would hide its face behind the clouds for fear, and the sky would darken. And the hearts of all beholders shrivelled up, and the fear was such that a pig's head could not have entered amid the crowd.

Cienzo, beholding this sight, hent sword in hand and came forward and sliced at the dragon; and tiff and taff, down went one of the dragon's heads. But the dragon, rubbing the fallen head on some grass which grew hard by, stuck it on again, like a lizard gluing on its tail. But Cienzo seeing this, said, 'Who followeth not up his work will fail,' and tightening his lips, lifted his sword and gave such a powerful blow that all the seven heads fell at a single stroke; and they jumped to a distance like beans from a wooden spoon. Taking hold of them, and wrenching their tongues, and putting them aside, he carried them about a mile's distance, for fear that they should cleave together again; and taking a handful of the grass with which the dragon had glued on his head, he put it carefully by; then he sent Menechiella back to her father's house, and he went to take some rest at a tavern.

When the king beheld his daughter his joy and gladness knew no bounds, and hearing how she had been delivered, he sent the public crier round the city to publish an edict 'that whosoever had killed the dragon, by the king's command should come and wed the princess.' A cunning rustic, hearing the crier, went and picked up the dragon's seven heads and fared to the presence, and after paying due homage to the king presented him the heads and said, 'My prowess saved Menechiella, and these hands saved our land from direst ruin. Here are the heads as witnesses of the deed; and every promise is a debt.' The king hearing this, took off the crown from his head, and put it on the clown's; and it looked like an exile's head on the top of a pillar. The news went round like wildfire in all the land, till it reached the ears of Cienzo, who said to himself, 'I am in very sooth an ass; I held Fortune by the hair, and I let her slip from my grasp; the master of the tower offered me a moiety of the treasure, and I refused, holding it of such account as a German does water; the fairy invited me to her palace, desiring to do some deed of kindness, and I took so much heed of it as the ass doth of the fly; and now I am sent for to wear a crown, and I behave as a drunkard doth with the spindle, allowing that a clodhopper should set his hairy foot before me and bear away from me this beautiful being by a dishonest gambling to his advantage.' And thus saying, he searched for pen, ink, and paper, and began to write:—

'To the most beauteous jewel, above all women, Menechiella, Infanta of King Pierdisinno.

'Having, by the sun's grace, saved thy life, I find that another is enjoying the fruit of my labour; another beareth the honours for the service which I rendered thee; therefore I ask of thee, that wert present and a witness of my doings, to undeceive the king thy sire, and let him know the truth, and do not thou consent that another should win thee, when I imperilled my life to gain thy safety. And this is written so that thou shouldst bestow upon me with thy queenly grace the guerdon due to my valour; and I end this kissing thy lily-white hands.

'From the Pot Tavern to-day, Sunday.'

Having written and sealed this letter, he put it in the bitch's mouth, saying to her, 'Haste thee, and tarry not till thou hast taken this missive to the king's daughter; and let no one have it but herself, and let her hand take it, my princess, with her face like a silvern moon.' The bitch went to the palace nearly flying, and ascending the stairs, entered the saloon, where she beheld the king paying great homage to the bridegroom. And when they sighted the bitch with a letter in her mouth, they ordered that it should be taken from her; but the bitch would not let any one touch her till she reached the princess, and laid it in her hands. And Menechiella arose and read it, and bowing low to the king, laid it in his hands, so that he might see it. And the king having read it, ordered some of his officers to follow the bitch wherever she went and bring back with them her master.

The officers and courtiers followed the bitch to the tavern, where they fould Cienzo; and delivering their message from the king, they returned, and Cienzo with them, to the royal presence. The king asked him, 'How canst thou boast of having killed the dragon, if this man, who is crowned here by my side, brought the seven heads?' and Cienzo rejoined, 'This clodhopper deserveth rather a paper hat than a crown, and he hath been so impudent as to make thee believe that bladders are lanthorns; and to prove to thee that it was I that delivered thy daughter, and not this tow-bearded villain, let the dragon's heads be brought here, and thou wilt see that not one of them can bear witness against me, as they are tongue-less, and I have brought the tongues to the judgment.' Saying thus, he drew forth the seven tongues and showed them to the king; and the rustic stood still as if carved in stone, hardly knowing what had happened to him. And Menechiella came forward and said, 'O my sire, this is the one that saved me,' and turning to the boor, said, 'Ah, accursed dog and villain, I had nearly believed thee.'

The king, hearing and seeing all this, took off the crown from the head of that hardened hind, and put it on Cienzo's head; and would have sent the clown to the galleys, but Cienzo besought the king to be gracious and forgive him, desiring to heap coals of fire upon his head, punishing his indiscretion with generosity and kind-ness. And the king married his daughter to Cienzo, and tables were spread, and abundance of victuals was brought, and all ate and were satisfied; and when all was ended, the bride and bride-groom retired to a perfumed bed, where Cienzo, lifting the trophy of his victory over the dragon, entered in triumph into love's capitol. But as morning dawned, when the sun, having drawn his sword of light chaseth away the stars, crying, 'Stand back, canaille,' Cienzo donned his raiment, and looked out of the window; and in a house opposite he beheld a beautiful lady at the window, and turning to Menechiella, said to her, 'What a pretty thing that is opposite our

palace!' 'And what dost thou want with it?' answered his wife;
and pursued she, 'Hast thou opened thine eyes already? Art thou
in a bad humour? Hath thy good surfeited thee? Doth it not
suffice thee what thou hast at home?' Cienzo bowed his head like
a cat which hath done some damage, and said nothing; but pretending to go out on some business, fared forth from the palace, and
entered the house of that young lady, who was in sooth a choice
morsel, a curdled milk, a sugarcane, a sweet paste. She never
turned her eyes without ensnaring a thousand hearts, and she never
opened her lips without setting fire to all breasts, and never moved
a foot without crushing down the hopes of her adorers. But, besides such grace and comeliness, she had the power through sorcery
to charm, chain, and tie all men with her hair, as she did with
Cienzo, that no sooner did he put foot where she abode than he was
tethered like unto a pony. Such was his case.

Now his younger brother Meo, receiving no news from Cienzo,
begged leave of his father to go and search for him, and he let him
go willingly, giving him another steed and a bitch, as he had done
to his elder son. And Meo, bidding farewell to his sire, departed,
and fared on the same road whither his brother had forwent him,
till he reached the tower. The master, believing him to be Cienzo,
received him and welcomed him with joy and affection; and offered
him some money, which Meo refused; but seeing himself so well
entreated, he bethought him that his brother must have been there
before him, and he waxed more hopeful of finding him. But as
soon as Luna, with her enmity to poets, turned her shoulders to the
sun, he fared on once more, and never ceased faring till he arrived
at the fairy's palace; and when she saw him, believing him to be
Cienzo, she welcomed him with joy and gladness, saying to him,
'Be thou welcome and well come, O youth mine, thou who hast
saved my life.' Meo thanked her for her kindness, and said, 'Forgive me, if I do not stay longer, as I have some pressing matters
to attend to; I will come and visit thee on my return'; and joying in
himself at having thus perceived traces of his brother, he pursued

the same road, and never ceased wayfaring till he came to the king's palace.

On the evening of the day on which Cienzo had been ensorcelled, Meo entered the palace, and was received with great honour by the officers, and guards, and pages, and servants, and was embraced by the bride with great affection; and she said to him, 'Welcome, my darling, to thy wife! This morning thou wentest, and this evening thou returnest; when every bird seeketh for food the owl sleepeth. Where hast thou been so long, O Cienzo mine? How canst thou stay so long away from Menechiella? Thou hast saved me from the dragon's mouth, and cast me deep into suspicion's chasm; and thou holdest me not as the light of thine eyes.' Meo, who was sharp-witted, understood at once that the one who thus addressed him was no other than his brother's wife, turning towards her, said, 'Pray, excuse me for being away so long'; and he embraced her, and went with her to take food. But when the moon, like a breeding fowl, calleth the stars to enjoy the dews, they rose to go to their rest, and Meo, who respected his brother's honour, divided the bed-linen, so that there should be no chance of his touching his sister-in-law; and she, beholding this new system, with a darkened face and wrathful mien said to him, 'O my love, since when? What game are we playing at? Are we two disputants, that thou hast put a division? Are we two belligerent armies, that thou hast dug a trench? Are we two strange horses, that thou dividest the manger?' Meo, who knew well how to count till thirteen, rejoined, 'Do not be angry with me, O my dear love, but I do so by the doctor's orders; it is he that hath advised me this diet, fearing that chasing too much would make me powerless.'

Menechiella knew nought of troubled waters, and swallowed this pear, and peacefully went to sleep. But when Night, exiled by the sun, took her flight, Meo arose, and began dressing near the same window where heretofore his brother had looked out, and beheld the same sorceress in whose bonds was Cienzo; and she pleased him, and turning to Menechiella, he said, 'Who may that girl be?' and the princess answered in wrath, 'Ah! this is it. And if it be so, the thing is ours. Yesterday thou didst sing the same song to me about that dog-fish, and I fear me that the tongue goeth where the tooth acheth; thou oughest to show respect unto me, for, after all, I am a king's daughter. Was it not enough that last night thou playedst at eagle imperial shoulder to shoulder, deeming not sufficient thy withdrawal of expense? I hear thee; the diet of our bed is convincing proof to me of a banquet in the house of others; but if I find this to be true, I will do some mad deed, and will not heed what evil may come.'

Meo, who was a youth who had eaten bread from several bakers, soothed her with kind words, and sware an oath, and said that for the handsomest leman in the world he would not exchange what was his at home, and that she alone was engrafted in his heart and entrails. Menechiella, comforted by these words, retired to her chamber, and sent for her tirewomen to dress her hair, and to paint her eyebrows, and to anoint her face, and have recourse to all arts so as to look bewitching to her lord; whilst Meo, suspecting by her words that Cienzo might be at the house of that sorceress, fared forth, taking the bitch with him, and entering the house of the sorceress, came to the saloon, where no sooner did she behold him than she said, 'O my hair, bind him fast'; and Meo rejoined readily, 'O my bitch, eat this witch'; and the bitch, obedient to her master's words, swallowed the sorceress just as if she had been the yolk of an egg. Then he fared from room to room till he came to the chamber where lay his brother, ensorcelled by the witch. And Meo took a few hairs from the bitch's tail and burnt them over him, when Cienzo awakened as from a deep sleep; and when he beheld his brother, he joyed with exceeding joy, and asked how he came there: and Meo related to him how he had decided to come in search of him, and how he had fared on his journey, and, lastly, how he came to the palace, and how Menechiella had mistaken him for her husband, and how he had slept with her; and he was about to continue his narrative, and explain to his brother how he had divided the bed-linen, when Cienzo harshly interrupted him, and tempted by the demon of jealousy, he took up an old sword which lay near at hand, and cut off his brother's head. At the noise and cries the king came with his daughter, and looked out of the window; and they beheld Cienzo, who had cut off the head of some one very like him, at which sight they inquired of him the cause; and Cienzo made answer, 'Inquire it of thyself, thou who hast slept with my brother, believing that thou didst sleep with me, and for this reason have I slain him.'

'Alas! how many are slain and punished wrongfully,' exclaimed Menechiella. 'A fine deed hast thou done! Thou wast not worthy to have such a brother; he did find himself in the same bed with me, and so great was his respect for thee that he divided the bed-linen, so as not to come in contact with me.' Cienzo hearing these words, repented with deep repentance of having committed such a direful error, born of a rash judgment, and fathered by crass stupidity, and buffeted his face, and tore his hair and plucked his beard. But after a little while remembering the herb used by the dragon, he rubbed his brother's neck with it, and stuck his head on again. And he at once became whole, hale, and hearty, as he was before, and embracing him with exceeding joy and pleasure, and begging him to forgive him his hastiness in thus sending him out of the world without listening to the end of his say, they entered the palace, and the king sent a messenger to bring hither Antoniello, and all his family and belongings. And when he arrived he became very dear unto the king, who made him his companion, and he beheld verified in the person of his son the old saw,—

'A ship sailing crossways reacheth harbour straightway.'

GOAT-FACE

Eighth Diversion

Of the First Day

A PEASANT'S DAUGHTER BY THE GOODNESS OF A FAIRY BECOMETH A KING'S WIFE; BUT BEING UNGRATEFUL TO HER WHO HAD DONE HER SO MUCH GOOD, IN PUNISHMENT THE FAIRY CHANGETH HER FACE INTO A GOAT'S FACE. AND THUS SHE IS DESPISED BY HER HUSBAND, AND SUFFERETH A THOUSAND ILLS: BUT AT LAST HUMBLING HERSELF TO A GOOD OLD MAN, IS CHANGED TO HER FORMER FAVOUR, AND REINSTATED IN HER HUSBAND'S LOVE.

CIULLA having ended her say, which was duly praised by all, and deemed sweet as sugar, Paola, whose turn it was to enter the ball, began thus:

All the evil deeds committed by man have some cause which urgeth him on, as wrath that provoketh him; or necessity, that compelleth him; or love, that blindeth him; or fury, that enrageth him. Ingratitude is the only vice that hath no reason, either true or false, whereunto to attach itself; and therefore it is the worst, to which the fountain of mercy is dry. It extinguisheth the fire of love, it closeth the roads to all benefits, and bringeth punishment to the ingrate, and tardy repentance: as ye will hear of in this story that I am going to relate.

There once lived a peasant who had twelve daughters, each but little older than the other, as every year his goodwife Ceccuzza gave birth to one; and the poor man desiring to maintain honourably his home, arose in the morning and went early to work, and with the sweat of his brow could scarce contend with the hunger of so many mouths. Now it so chanced that one day of the days he was digging at the foot of a mountain whose summit reached the clouds, and at the further side thereof was a grotto so darksome and fearsome that no sunrays ever entered there. And from this cave came a large green lizard as big as a crocodile, and the poor peasant was sore frightened, and stood open-mouthed, expecting the end of his days from that hideous animal. But the lizard came near him and said, 'Be not afraid, my good man, I came not here to do thee hurt, I came only to do thee service.' Masaniello, so was the peasant hight, hearing the lizard speak thus, knelt before her, and said, 'My lady, what is thy name? I am thy slave; be thou kind-hearted, and take compassion of this poor body, as I have twelve children to feed.' Answered the lizard, 'I came to help thee; therefore bring me to-morrow morning the youngest of thy daughters, and I will bring her up as my own child, and will hold her dear as my own life.'

The father, hearing this, remained confused as a thief found with whatso he had been stealing in hand; his breast straitened to think that his youngest and tenderest child should be desired of a lizard, perchance to assuage its hunger, and he said to himself, 'If I give it my child, I give my soul; if I refuse it will take my body; if I bring my daughter, I lose my entrails; if I deny the beast, it will suck my blood; an I please it, I give it part of myself; an I refuse, it will take all. What must I do? What will be best? What is most expedient? Alas, and woe is me, what a bad day is this for me! What a misfortune hath rained from Heaven upon me!'

The lizard perceiving his indecision, said, 'Let me know thy say, at once, and do thou as I bid thee, otherwise thou wilt lose thy cloth: this is my will, and thus must it be done.' Masaniello, hearing what the lizard decreed, and knowing not how to refuse, fared home-wards, sad at heart and yellow-faced, and Ceccuzza seeing him in such a case, said to him, 'What hath happened to thee, O my husband? didst thou quarrel with some one? Has some one served thee with a writ? or is the ass dead?'

'Nought of all this hath occurred,' answered Masaniello, 'but a lizard hath threatened me with all kinds of evils, if I take not to her cave my youngest daughter; and my head is swimming like a top; I know not what fish to catch; in one way am I constrained by love, and in the other am I constrained by fear. I love very dearly Ren-zolla mine, but I love also my own life; if I give not to the lizard this part of myself, the beast will take me: therefore advise me,

Ceccuzza mine; if not, I shall die.' Hearing this, the wife said, 'Who knoweth, O dear my husband, but that this lizard will be double-tailed for our house? Perhaps this lizard will put an end to all our miseries and woes. Remember that oft-times we ourselves toss the axe upon our feet, and when we should have an eagle's sight to understand the weal which cometh to us, we are blind as a bat: therefore obey thou the lizard's behest, and take the child to its cave, as my heart whispers to me that it will be the fortune of our daughter.' Masaniello followed his wife's rede, and in the morning, as soon as the sun brightened the heavens with his rays, he took his child by the hand, and fared towards the grotto.

The lizard was waiting for his coming, and as soon as she saw him, came out of her hiding place, and taking the child, give to the father a bag full of gold pieces, saying, 'Go home, take this coin, and give thy daughters in marriage, and hearten thine heart, for Renzolla hath found a mother and father; thrice happy is she, to be blessed with such good fortune.' Masaniello, with heart full of gladness, thanked the lizard, and taking leave of her and his daughter, fared back home to this wife, relating to her what had taken place and showing her the ducats. She joyed with exceeding gladness, and after a time, with the help of the money, they gave all their daughters in marriage; and they were left alone to engage with pleasure in the daily labour of life. Such was their case. But no sooner was Renzolla left alone with the lizard than a splendid palace arose in sight, and they both entered therein; and there Renzolla dwelt in great ease and luxury, like unto a queen never wanting for anything. Ye may suppose that even if she had desire to drink ant's milk she would have had her wish. She ate, and dressed as a princess, had an hundred handmaids to do her bidding, and being so well entreated, she became tall and strong, beauteous and healthy.

One day of the days the king fared out a-hunting, and night surprised him in that forest; and not knowing where he might seek a resting-place, he looked round about till at last he beheld a light shining afar, and going nearer he found it came out of the window of a splendid palace. He called one of his suite and sent him to this mansion, to beg permission from the house-master to rest therein for the night. The officer did the king's behest and knocked at the palace-gate, when the lizard came forth in the shape of a beauteous lady, to whom the man delivered his message, and she answered, 'The king is welcome, and a thousand times well come; neither bread nor knives will be wanting here.'

The messenger returned to the king and reported the answer, and he at once fared forward with his suite, and was met and received as a true knight, an hundred pages coming to meet him, with torches alight, like as if they were going to the funeral of some rich man. An hundred pages more brought food and drink, and spread the tables, looking like so many hospital valets bringing food to the sick; and an hundred more played on instruments of music deafening all hearers. And Renzolla stood as cupbearer to the king, and filled his cup so often and well that he drank as much love from her eyes as wine from her cup. But having eaten their sufficiency, they all retired to rest, and the king with them, and Renzolla attended him and pulled his socks from his feet, and his heart from his breast with such good will, that feeling the pressure of that lovely hand the poison of love burned in his soul; and to remedy this evil, for his love-longing and desire were such that he felt he would die if he had not his desire, he sent for the fairy, and there and then begged her to give him Renzolla to wife. And the fairy, desiring naught but the girl's good, gave her consent freely, and also bestowed upon her a dowry of seven millions of gold.

The king joyed with exceeding gladness, and prepared to take his departure with Renzolla, and she with base ingratitude, forgetting all the goodness of the fairy towards her, was ready to follow her husband without uttering a single word of thanks, or bestowing a kindly glance upon one who had done so much for her welfare. The fairy, perceiving her ingratitude, laid a curse upon her, saying, 'O thou ingrate, may thy face become like unto a goat's': and hardly had she spoken the words, when her mouth lengthened, and a beard a foot long hung down her chin, and her cheeks tightened, and hair grew on her face, and the curls and tresses on her head became pointed horns. The king, seeing this transformation, nearly lost his wits, and knew not what had happened, beholding an incomparable beauty thus changed, and sighing, and weeping, and bemoaning his lot, he wailed, 'Where is the golden hair which bound mine heart? Where the sweet eyes which darted fiery darts? Where the mouth which burnt my soul, mastered my spirits, and enchained my heart? But, what? Must I be the husband of a goat, and thus acquire the title of Caprone*? Have I come to this pass? No, no, I will not let my heart be crushed by a goat-faced creature, a goat that will cause me war and dissension wherever I go, with her crapping of olives.'

And thus saying, as soon as he reached his own palace he sent Renzolla with a maid to the kitchen, and gave to each some flax to spin; bidding them end their work in a week's time. The maid obeyed the king's command, and began by combing the flax, and filling the distaff, and twisting the spindle, and forming the skein; and she worked on so well that on the Saturday evening she had ended her share of the work. But Renzolla believing herself the same as when she was in the fairy's palace, as she had not seen her own figure in the mirror, threw the flax out of window, saying, 'The king wants something to do, to give me such hindrances; if he needeth shirts, let him buy some, he must not think that he found me in the street. He must remember that I brought him seven millions of gold pieces, and that I am his wife, and not his leman, and I think him an ass to treat me thus.' But although she spake thus, when Saturday morning came, seeing that the maid had ended her work, and fearing some mishap because of her disobedience, she fared to the fairy's palace, and related to her her disgrace and fear. The fairy embraced her with great love and affection, and brought her a bag full of thread; and bade her give it to the king, showing to him thus that she had been an industrious woman and a good mistress. But Renzolla, taking the bag, without saying thank you for

* A nasty large he-goat.

the service, returned to the king's palace; leaving the fairy wroth with exceeding wrath at the ingratitude of the girl.

Meanwhile the king, having taken away the thread, brought two dogs, and gave one to his wife and one to the maid, telling them to bring them up well. The maid fed her dog with crumbs and treated it like a son. But Rensolla, saying, 'Yes, this thought was left me by my sire; there are the Turks; must I comb a dog's tail, and take him to crap?' and thus grumbling threw a dog out of the window, which was not so pleasant for the brute as jumping over a stick. But after some months had passed the king came seeking the dogs, and Renzolla being sorely afraid, ran once more to the fairy's palace and found at the door an old man who was the door-keeper who inquired of her, 'Who art thou, and whom seekest thou?' and Renzolla hearing his question answered, 'Dost thou not know me, thou goats-beard?' Replied the old man, 'Goats-beard to me? The thief runneth after the constable! Stand aside, for thou soilest me, said the boiler-maker; throw thyself forward for fear to tumble backward. I am a goats-beard: and thou? thou are a goats-beard and a half; because of thy great presumption thou deservedst this and worse; and await a little while, impudent hussy, and I will clear thee, and thou will perceive where thy fine airs, and thy smoke, and thy forwardness have brought thee.'

Thus saying, he went to a little chamber and brought out of it a mirror, and putting it before Renzolla, told her to look at herself, and she, beholding her own ugly hairy face, came nigh unto death with sorrow; neither such grief did Rinaldo suffer when looking at his own image in the charmed shield, than felt she in viewing her metamorphosis, and she knew not herself, and the old man continued, 'Thou must remember, O Renzolla, that thou art the daughter of a peasant, and the fairy had thus entreated thee and cared for thee and loved thee, that thou becamest as a very queen; but thou, disobedient and discourteous, hadst no gratitude nor thankfulness for so many favours thou hadst received. Thou hast ever been un-kind, showing not the least sign of love or affection. Therefore thou hast thy desert; take this and return for the rest; see to what brought thee thy bad conduct; look, what face hast thou; see to what plight thy ingratitude hath brought thee: the fairy having cursed thee, thou hast changed not only face but also position. But an thou wilt do as I bid thee, go to the fairy, and throw thyself at her feet, buffet thy face and beat thy breast, and weep and lament, and beseech her forgiveness: she hath a tender heart, and will be moved to compassion at thy stress of pain.' Renzolla, thinking the old man's rede right, did as he bade her; and the fairy, seeing her plight, kissed and embraced her, and returned her to her pristine shape, and arraying her in costly raiment, sent for a carriage and put her therein, and accompanied by a train of followers, pages, and servants, took her to the king. And when he beheld her looking so beautiful and queenly, he loved her with a deep love, and held her dear as his life, and beating his breast, begged her forgiveness for that which he had made her suffer; excusing himself by saying that that accursed goat's-face had caused all this disunion. And thus Renzolla became humble and patient and grateful, and joy and gladness returned to her, and she loved her lord dearly, and honoured the fairy, and was ever thankful to the old man, having found out at her own expense that

'It is ever best to be courteous.'

THE CHARMED HIND

Of the First Day

FONZO AND CANNELORO ARE BROUGHT INTO THE WORLD BY ENCHANT-
MENT; THE QUEEN, MOTHER OF FONZO, ENVIETH CANNELORO, AND
BREAKETH HIS HEAD. CANNELORO FARETH FORTH FROM HIS COUNTRY
AND BECOMING KING, IS IN GREAT DANGER. FONZO, BY MEANS OF A
FOUNTAIN AND MYRTLE-TREE, COMETH TO THE KNOWLEDGE OF HIS
BROTHER'S PERIL, AND DEPARTETH TO DELIVER HIM.

ALL the company remained open-mouthed, listening to the story
related by Paola, and they one and all came to the conclusion that
humility is like a ball, the more one throws it to the ground the
more it rebounds; it is like the he-goat, the more ye pull him backwards the harder he will hit you. But Prince Thaddeus having
signed to Ciommetella to continue the rubric, she put her tongue
in motion, and thus began:

There is no doubt that the strength of a true and loyal friendship
is such that all fatigue is thought as naught, and to serve a friend
the dangers we incur are but as child's play, our wealth but a straw,
our honour but smoke, our life as nothing: and to do service to him,
we lose freely: as is often related in romances and histories, of
which to-day I will give you an example, such as my grandam (may
her soul be at rest) used to relate, if ye will hearken to me, shutting
your mouths and lengthening your ears.

Once upon a time there lived a certain king, Jannone hight, and
he being childless had great desire to have offspring, and he commanded that public prayers to the gods should be said, so that his
wife might soon be with child. And he largessed the people, and
gave alms, and well entreated pilgrims, and was charitable and kind
to all. But after a time, seeing that there was no sign of his wife

being with child, he shut his doors, and sent away all that came to seek hospitality.

Now one day of the days a great sage passed that way, and knowing not the change in the king's habits, or perhaps knowing it but desiring to remedy this evil, he made his way to Jannone's presence, and begged him to let him rest in his house. And the king with severe mien replied brusquely, 'If thou hast no other candle than this one, thou mayest go and sleep in darkness; the time is past when Bertha spinned; and the cats have opened their eyes; and the mother is here no longer.' And the old sage enquired the cause of this change, and rejoined the king, 'I longed to have a son; and I have spent and thrown away in every side to all those that came, and have thus wasted my substance; and finding at last that it was all time lost I ceased so doing.'

'If this be all,' replied the sage, 'I will cause her to be pregnant, and if I do not, thou mayst cut off mine ears.'

'If thou wilt do this,' said the king, 'I will give thee half of my kingdom.' And the sage replied, 'Now pay attention to my say, let a heart of a sea-dragon be brought, and a virgin maid cook it, and she will be with child with the smell issuing from the pot, and when it is ready, give it to the queen to eat and thou wilt see at once, that she will be with child, just as if the nine months were passed.'

Rejoined the king, 'How can this be? It seems to me, thou biddest me swallow a hard morsel.'

Said the old man, 'Do not marvel: if thou hast ever read fables thou wilt have found that Juno passing one day through a field, leant down to inhale the scent of a flower, and that was enough to fill her belly.'

'If it be so, let us at once get this dragon's heart. At the worst I lose nothing,' said the king; and he sent an hundred fishermen out a-fishing with spears, and nets, and bow-nets, and they tried, and turned so long, that at last they caught a dragon, and taking out its heart, they brought it to the king. And he sent for a beauteous damsel, who shut herself in a chamber, and as soon as the heart began

cooking, and the smoke and smell filled the room, not only the beautiful cook became pregnant, but the furniture of the house became
full and at the end of a few days gave birth, the bedstead to a small
bed, the chest to a small chest, the coffer to a small coffer, the chairs
to smaller chairs, the table to a smaller table, and the night-chamber
to a smaller vase, graceful, and comely, and captivating to the eye.

Now when it was ready they brought the heart to the queen, and
no sooner did she eat of it than she felt her stomach fill, and within
four days the queen and the damsel each gave birth to a man-child,
like the full moon, and so like one another, that one could not be
known from the other when apart; and they grew up together and
loved each other with such deep affection, that they could not live
apart one from the other.   And the queen beholding the great tenderness each bestowed to the other, waxed envious, and she could not
endure the thought that her son should bear more affection to the
son of one of her handmaidens than to herself, and she knew not by
what device she might rid herself of this eye-sore.

Now it so chanced that one day the prince was desirous to go to
the chase with his brother, and he bade his followers light a fire in
his chamber, and began melting the lead to make some small shot,
and wanting somewhat, left his brother in care of the lead, and went
to fetch that which he desired himself.   Meanwhile the queen came
to her son's retreat and finding Canneloro alone (thus was the damsel's son hight) though it was a good opportunity to send him out
of the world, and taking an heated iron from the fire struck with
it a blow on Canneloro's head, so that he perceiving the blow coming
lowered his head, and it struck him on the eyebrow, and wounded
him seriously.   And she was on the point of repeating her blow
when Fonzo, her son, returned, and feigning that she had come
to enquire after his health, after a few insipid caresses, she went her
ways.

Now Canneloro, putting on his hat, hid thus from Fonzo the
wound on his head, and firmly and stoutly bore in silence the suffering and pain and burning of the cut; and when the prince had ended
the casting of the shot, he begged his leave to depart.   Fonzo mar-

velled with exceeding marvel at the request and enquired of him
the cause of this sudden resolve: and he answered 'Seek not to know,
O Fonzo mine, enough is it for thee to know that I must depart
hence; Heaven knoweth, that when I part from thee, who are mine
heart, I part with my soul, my spirit goeth, and life leaveth the body,
and the blood leaveth my veins; but I cannot do otherwise, it must
be so, do not forget me.' And weeping and lamenting he embraced
the prince and went to his chamber where he donned an armour, and
buckled his sword (a sword that had come to the world when the
heart was cooking), and arming himself cap-a-pie, went to the
stables and saddled his horse, and he was putting his foot on the
stirrup when Fonzo came to him weeping and wailing, and saying,
that if in very sooth he desired to forsake him, at least he should
leave him some thing by which to remember him while he was
gone, and with this token of his love he might crush down the anguish caused by his absence. Canneloro hearing these words drew a
poinard from his side, and struck it on the ground and a beautiful
fountain sprung up, and turning to the prince said, 'This is the best
remembrance that I can leave thee, as in this fountain thou canst
apprise thyself what happeneth in my life: if thou seest its waters
clear and tranquil, then thou wilt know that my life passeth in ease
and peace; if thou perceivest the water to be troubled, then thou mayest suppose that some travail and sorrow is upon me; and if thou beholdest it dry (but Heaven forbid), thou mayest believe that there is
no more oil in my lamp, and that I shall have reached that bourn
from whence no wayfarer returneth, and paid my debt to nature.'
And as he ended speaking, he drew his sword and struck the earth
with it, when a myrtle-tree sprung up, and turning to the prince, he
added, 'Until thou seest this myrtle-tree green, know that I am hale
and well, and green as garlic; if thou beholdest it withered, think
that some trouble vexeth me; and if thou findest it perfectly dry,
thou mayest say a requiem for Canneloro, leathern shoes and wooden
shoes.' And saying thus, he embraced his brother and fared on,
and in wayfaring he met with many adventures, as quarrelling with
the postillions, disgusts with the tavern-keepers, fights with robbers,

and many others, but at last he reached Longa-pergola when a grand tourney was taking place, and the king's daughter was the prize awarded to the winner.

Canneloro presented himself to the lists, and fought boldly, unhorsing the bravest knights who had come there to win a renown. And thus he obtained the hand of the Lady Fenizia, the king's daughter, and was married, and great festivals and banquets were held in honour of the bridal, and for a month all was peace and joy and gladness.

After this time had passed, Canneloro became sad at heart, and desiring a distraction, asked leave of his father-in-law to go a-hunting, and the king rejoined, 'Mind thy limbs, O my son-in-law, do not be blinded by Satan, keep thy brain clear, open thine eyes, my master, for about these wilds and wolds whereto thou wilt go a-hunting dwelleth a ghul, who changeth shape every day; now he appeareth as a wolf, to-morrow as a lion, now as a deer, and to-morrow as an ass, and every day changeth form and colour. And he enticeth all wayfarers, with a thousand devices, into the cave wherein he dwelleth, and he maketh his meal of them. Therefore, O my son, do not endanger thy safety, and beware that thou lose not thy cloth and skin together.'

Canneloro, who had left all fear in the body of his mother when he came into the world, heeding not his father-in-law's rede, as soon as the sun came forth, and with his bristle-broom of light swept off all the cobwebs from the darksome night, fared forth to the chase, and coming to a forest, where under the thick boughs the shadows met to monopolize and conspire against the sun's rays, he beheld a hind (the ghul seeing him coming had taken that shape), and as soon as he sighted her, he began to chase her, and she leapt from place to place, till she enticed him to the darkest part of the forest. Then the ghul by magic made a great fall of snow to come down, so that it seemed as if the heavens were falling, and Canneloro finding himself before the ghul's cavern, he entered therein to save himself from the downpour. And being very cold, he took a handful of wood that he found therein, and putting aside his gun, he lit a fire and stood before it to warm himself and to dry his clothes; and as he stood thus, the hind came to the cavern's mouth, and thus addressed him, 'O sir knight, give me leave, I beseech thee, to come in and warm myself for a little while, as I am frozen with the cold.'

Canneloro, who was gentle and kind-hearted, answered, 'Come in, and be thou welcome.'

Replied the hind, 'I would enter, but I fear me, that thou wilt slay me after.'

Said Canneloro, 'Fear naught, and doubt not my promise.'

Continued the hind, 'If thou wilt let me come in, do chain these dogs, that they may not worry me, and tether this horse, that he may not kick me.'

And Canneloro did so; and said the hind, 'I feel more sure now, but if thou do not put aside thy sword and fire-arms, by my father's soul I will not enter therein;' and the youth, willing to be friendly with the hind, put aside his sword, but the ghul, beholding him unarmed and defenceless, came forth in his own shape, and lifting him up, threw him into a pit at the further end of the cave, and rolling a large stone over the top, left him there until he should require him for his meal. Such was his case.

Meanwhile Prince Fonzo every morning and evening visited the fountain and the myrtle-tree, so as to be aware of how it passed with his brother, but on that very morning when the ghul had imprisoned Canneloro, Fonzo, going to the fountain and myrtle-tree as was his wont, found the waters of the one troubled, and the leaves of the other withered, and he knew at once by these signs that Canneloro was in stress of danger; and desiring to go to his aid, without speaking to any one, or taking leave of his sire or his mother, he saddled his own steed and donned his armour, and taking with him two charmed dogs, he mounted, and fared forth, and never ceased wayfaring first in one place and then the other, seeking tidings of his brother, till he came to Longa-pergola, and in entering the city he beheld all the houses and palaces decked in mourning, and the folk in mourning raiment, for the supposed death of Canleroro. But no sooner had the prince entered the city, than the folk, supposing him to be Canneloro, because of his great likeness to him, all hastened to bring the good news to Princess Fenizia, and when she heard it, she ran down the palace-stair, and threw her arms round Fonzo's neck, saying, 'O my husband, O my love, O my heart! where hast thou been all these days?' Fonzo understood easily by this that Canneloro had been there, and had gone, and he thought that he must dexterously examine the princess, and draw out from her where he had gone; and she spake to him of that accursed chase, and of the danger he had incurred, especially if he had been met by the ghul who was cruel with mankind. By this the prince inferred that Canneloro must have fallen into the ghul's power; and when night darkened they went to their rest. But Fonzo, telling the princess that he had made a vow to the goddess Diana not to touch his wife that night, placed his naked sword between Fenizia and himself, and laid himself down, anxiously waiting the first ray of dawn when the sun giveth the golden pills to the heavens to ease them of the darksome shadows of the night.

Then he hastily left his bed and equipped himself for the chase, and neither Fenizia's prayers, nor the king's command could change him from his purpose. And mounting horse, and taking the two charmed dogs with him, he fared to the wilds and wolds, and entered the same darksome forest, and it chanced to him, as it had fortuned with Canneloro; and entering the cave he beheld his brother's dogs, and the steed, and his sword and fire-arms; at the sight of which he was now assured that Canneloro was in the ghul's power either dead or alive. And he determined to avenge his death, if he came too late to save him; therefore when the hind bade him lay aside his arms, and chain the dogs, and tether the horse, Fonzo in answer to her bidding threw himself upon her and slew her, and after heaping upon the slain ghul stones and whatsoever he could find, he looked about in search of tidings. And he heard a sound of moaning at the further end of the cavern, and going there he saw the pit, and rolling off the stone out came Canneloro and several others, whom the ghul kept there to fatten them; and they all embraced him and thanked him for their deliverance, and then they fared to the king's palace, where the princess beholding two princes so much alike knew not which was her husband. But Canneloro lifting his hat shewed her the cicatrix on his brow, which when she beheld she embraced him, and there was feasting and joyance and gladness; and Prince Fonzo tarried with them one month, enjoying all the sights and pleasaunces of the country; but at last he longed to return to his own nest, and Canneloro writing a letter to his mother bidding her to come and share his grandeur and happiness, gave it to him, and taking leave from each other, promising to visit one another often, he departed. And Canneloro's mother came to him, and from that hour he would not hear any more, neither of dogs, nor of chase, keeping in mind that true sentence,

'Unhappy is he who learneth and is corrected at his own expense.'

THE OLD WOMAN DISCOVERED

Tenth Diversion

Of the First Day

THE KING OF ROCCAFORTE IS ENAMOURED BY THE VOICE OF AN OLD
WOMAN; IS DECEIVED BY A FINGER, AND GOETH TO BED WITH HER; BUT
DISCOVERING THE DECEIT, COMMANDETH HIS SERVANTS TO THROW HER
OUT OF THE WINDOW, AND IN FALLING SHE REMAINETH HANGING ON A
TREE. SEVEN FAIRIES SIGHTING HER, THEY GIVE HER A CHARM, AND
SHE BECOMETH A BEAUTIFUL GIRL, AND THE KING TAKETH HER TO WIFE;
THE OTHER SISTER BEING ENVIOUS OF HER GOOD FORTUNE, AND WISH-
ING TO BE MADE HANDSOME ALSO, DESIRETH TO BE FLAYED ALIVE, AND
IN SO DOING DIES.

ALL hearers were pleased with Ciommetella's story, and were
delighted to hear of Canneloro's safety, and the ghul's punishment
for such deeds of cruelty. Then Prince Thaddeus signed for all to
be silent, and commanded Ghiacova to seal with her recital this letter of entertainment, when thus she began:

The accursed vanity born with us women is our besetting vice,
and through the great longing to seem beautiful and adorn the brow
we spoil our faces; to whiten our skin we mar the whiteness of our
teeth; and to give light to the limbs we darken our sight; and thus
we pay the tribute to Time before the hour, enfeebling the eyesight, lining the face, and withering the skin. If a young girl deserveth blame for such emptiness, how much more so an old woman,
who, eager to seem young, becometh the laughing stock of all beholders and the ruin of herself: as I will relate to you if ye lend me
an ear.

In a garden, opposite the king's palace in Roccaforte city, were
sitting two old women, who were the most hideous creatures that
could be seen. They had dishevelled hair, and wrinkled brow, and
crooked, stiff eyebrows, eyes red and watery, yellow skins full of
wrinkles, large and crooked mouths, and hairy breasts. They were

hunchbacked, with shrivelled arms, and were lame, and cloven footed; and so that the sun should not light upon that ugly looking sight, they were hidden under the trees near one of the windows of the king. And it had come to this, that he could not even belch but that these two would talk and observe his doings; sometimes saying, that a jasmine had fallen upon their heads, and had given them an head-ache; another time, that a letter had fallen upon their shoulders and disturbed them; and at another, that the dust had suffocated them.

Now the king, listening to this talk, supposed that under him must be the quintessence of beauty, and the first cut of flowers, and the sweetest of all sweetness: and thus thinking, he longed with excessive longing to behold these hidden beauties, and to be enlightened upon their charms: therefore he began to sigh with deep sighs, and cough without a cold, and lastly to speak softly, saying, 'Where, where art thou hidden, thou most precious jewel? Come forth, O thou, the most beauteous in the world! Arise, thou sun! Come forth, thou gem worthy an emperor! Make manifest thy graces, let me behold the beaming lights which kindle fire in love's domain! Chase from thee, O thou accursed bench, this flower of beauty: be not so ware of thy excellencies: open the gate to a poor falcon, and cage me if thou wilt! Let me behold the mouth from whose lips these sounds come forth: let me behold the bell whose sound I hear: let me behold this bird whose sweet song I listen to: do not leave me as a sheep from Ponto to be fed with cresses, do not deny me the joy to behold and contemplate thy beauteous form.' These and other words did the king say, but he could ring gloria, the old women's ears were deaf to his prayers, and it was like adding fuel to the fire.

And the king burned with the heat of desire, and his thoughts were held ensnared by a form created in his own mind, and his heart was enslaved by amorous longing, and he fain would have found the key that could open the casket where this priceless gem was hidden, that caused him to die in despair; but nothing daunted at the silence which followed his sighs and petitions, he continued to beseech and pray, never ceasing until one day of the days the old women, having become proud, gave themselves airs, through the flattering speeches of the king, and took counsel each with the other, so as not to let this opportunity escape them to catch this fine bird, who of his own accord came to throw himself into the snare. Therefore one day when the king, according to his wont, made sweet speeches from the window, they spake to him through the trees with a sweet whispering voice, that the greatest favour that they could confer upon him was to show him in eight days' time one finger of one hand.

The king being an expert soldier, knew that fortresses are taken inch by inch, and therefore refused not the offer, hoping thus to win step by step his will of this strong place which he besieged unceasingly; knowing the old adage, 'Take first and ask afterwards.' He accepted the peremptory terms and awaited the eight days, desiring to behold this eighth marvel of the world.

Meanwhile the old women all this time did naught else but trim and anoint their fingers, so that when the appointed time should arrive she whose finger was smoothest and finest, should hold it for inspection to the king; and he, impatiently waiting, counted the days, dragged on the nights, weighed the hours, measured the moments, noted the points, and examined carefully the atoms that should elapse till the longed for good should be vouchsafed to him, beseeching the sun to shorten his ways through the heavenly fields, so that he should sooner reach the end of his daily route and water his fiery steeds, tired of their long journey. And he adjured the night to chase away all darkness, and let him gaze on the light that, yet not seen, made him burn in a furnace of love; and he apostrophised Time, saying that he walked on crutches, and had put on leaden boots to spite him, so that the hour should not arrive so quickly in which their obligation should be fulfilled. But the time came at last, and the king descended to the garden, and knocked at the gate, and said, 'Come, come!' And one of the old women, the oldest and ugliest, seeing that her finger was the finest and smoothest, put it through the key-hole, and showed it to the king. For

him, this was not a finger but a pointed dart, which struck his heart
with deadly aim: 'twas not a dart, but a mace that struck his head
with fiercest blow: but what do I say?   Dart and mace?   It was a
lighted match to his desires, which took fire and burned with fiercest
flames: but what am I saying?   Dart and mace, and match?   It was
a thorn unto his thoughts, which cost him a thousand sighs; and
holding the hand, and kissing that finger, that from a woodcutter's
scraper had become a gilder's burnisher, he began saying, 'O sweet
bow of love, O receptacle of all joys, O register of all love's privileges, for which I have become a warehouse of sorrow, and a magazine of anguish, and a custom-house of torments: is it possible, that
thou wilt remain so hardened, and cruel, and feel no compassion of
my complaints?   O my sweetheart, if thou hast shown me the tail
by the key-hole, put there thy lips, and we will have a jelly of
happiness; if thou hast shown part of thy sweetmeats, O thou river
of beauty, let me behold all thy body, let me behold those eyes of
hawk peregrine, and let them wither and scorch mine heart with
their leven glances.   Who holdeth prisoner the treasure of thy
beauteous face; who keepeth this beauteous ship in quarantine; by
whose power is held prisoner this charming and graceful gazelle in
a pig-stye?   Come out of that pit; issue forth from those stables,
come out of that hole; leap, sweet May, and give thine hand to
Cola, and pay me what I am worth; thou knowest that I am the
king, I am not a cucumber, I can bid and forbid: but that false
and blind son of the lame Vulcan and the strumpet Venus, who hath
full authority over all sceptres, hath made me thy subject, so that I
beg of thee that of which I could command the gift; and I do as
the old saw saith, for "with caresses and not with talk is Venus
won." '

The old woman, who well knew where the devil kept his tail,
an old fox, a decrepit cat, an old crow, a superannuated owl, thinking that, when your superior begs of you something, it is a command, and that the disobedience of a liege rouseth the wrath of the
master, which may bring ruin, in a voice like a flayed cat's said, 'O
my lord, as thou art willing to submit thyself to one that is beneath

thee, an thou hast designed descend from the sceptre to the spinning-wheel, from the royal hall to the stable, from pomp and luxury to the petticoats, from grandeur to misery, from the belvedere to the cellar, from the steed to the ass, I cannot, and I must not, and I will not contradict the will of so great a king; therefore as it is your desire to tie this knot between prince and liege, this binding of ivory with wood of a poplar-tree, this setting of diamonds with glass, I am ready to do thy will, but I must beseech thee to grant me, as a sign of thine affection, what I will beg of thee, and that is, that I may be received in thy bed at night without a candle, because I could not bear to be seen naked.'

The king, joying with exceeding gladness, sware an oath, laying hand upon hand, that he would grant her request willingly. And giving a kiss sweet as sugar to a mouth stinking like assafœtida, he went his ways, and the time seemed longsome to him till the sun, tired of ploughing heaven's fields, before sowing the stars went to repose, and he thought of naught but the field he would plough and the seed he would sow, the joyance by hundredweights and the happiness by tons. But when the night darkened, and all marauders issued forth to empty the pockets of the wayfarers, and ease them of their cloaks, the old woman, conducted by one of the king's valets, came in the gloom, covered from head to foot with a thick veil looped up behind. And reaching the king's bedchamber, she unrobed at once, and went into bed.

The king, who had waited like match near a powder-cask, when he heard them coming, and heard her get into bed, perfuming his person with sweet scented musk and civet, and anointing his beard with perfumed ointment, jumped into bed. And it was well for the old woman that he was thus anointed and perfumed, so that he could not smell the stink of her mouth, and the vinegar of her arm-pits, and the mustiness of that ugly thing. But as soon as he felt her limbs, he perceived the deception; he felt her bottom and found it fleshless, the limbs thin and withered, and the breasts as empty bladders; and he marvelled with exceeding marvel, but kept silence, so as to be better assured of the case; and forced himself to do that for which he had no more desire, and entered this pig-stye whilst he believed he would enter the coast of Posillaco; and sailed with a fishing-smack, when he believed himself on board a galley.

But when sleep overtook the old woman, the king drew out from an ebony casket inlaid with silver a leathern bag, and out of it a small lanthorn which he lit, and made a perquisition under the bed-linen, and beheld an harpy instead of a nymph, a fury instead of a grace, Medusa instead of Venus. And at the sight he was wroth with exceeding wrath, and he had a mind to cut the rope which held this ship. And foaming at the mouth with rage, he cried aloud and called all his household, and when the servants heard the king's outcries they hardly stopped to don their shirts, but ran to his help, and said he to them, 'Behold, what trick hath this witch of Satan played me! Thinking I had a suckling-lamb, I find an old buffalo; believing I held in hand a dove, I find an owl; supposing I was enjoying a mouthful worth a king, I find between mine hands this filthy morsel, sickening to taste; but this, and worse, deserveth he who buyeth the cat inside the bag. But she hath vexed me beyond measure, and she will do just penance, therefore take her up as she is, and throw her out of the window;' which command hearing, the old woman began to defend herself, kicking, and plunging, and biting, and saying, 'I appeal against this sentence: thou wouldest that I came to thy bed, and I will bring an hundred doctors to my defence,' and she spake the proverbs, 'An old fowl maketh good soup;' and 'Whoso leaveth the old way for the new findeth worse will ensue;' but with all this talk she was lifted up by the servants and thrown out of the window, and that was her fortune. She fell, and being hung by the hair of her head on the bough of a fig-tree, remained hanging there without breaking her neck.

Now at early dawn some fairies passed through that garden, and being sad-hearted, having had some great sorrow to bear, for some time had neither spoken nor smiled; but perceiving that hideous shadow hanging on the tree, they all laughed till they fell backwards, and putting their tongue in motion, they never ended talking about this spectacle they beheld. And to repay the old woman for the enjoyment she had caused them, they each and all gave her a charm. The first said, 'Mayest thou become young;' another, 'Mayest thou become beautiful;' another, 'Mayest thou be rich;' the next, 'Mayest thou be noble;' and another, 'Mayest thou be virtuous;' and the next, 'May all folk love thee;' and the last, 'Be thine all good fortune.' And when they ended their saying they departed, and the old woman found herself seated on a velvet chair with fringe of golden threads under that same tree, which had become a green velvet canopy purflewed with gold. Her face was as the face of a young girl, just fifteen, so beauteous that all other beauties would seem like old slippers near satin shoes: compared to this grace sitting on that velvet chair, the three Graces would seem as old iron; and if she would but smile and talk and glance, all others would play a losing game beside her. And she was decked and arrayed in costly raiments all purflewed with gems and gold, and the flowers that adorned her, scented the air with their perfume, and pages and servants and handmaidens surrounded her, and she looked every inch a queen.

In the meanwhile the king, wrapping himself up in a blanket, and putting on a pair of light shoes, looked out of window to see what had happened to the old woman, and beholding a sight so marvellous and unexpected, he remained with mouth wide open, and gazed upon this beauty as one charmed, admiring first the golden hair falling lightly upon the white shoulders, and the curls tied with a golden cord, whose sheen would put to shame the sun's rays; then the pencilled brows, like bows whose darts pierced the heart; and those eyes whose leven glance caused him a thousand sighs; and the sweet mouth, full of love's witchery, where all graces sat enthroned; and he gazed at the jewels and the robes, and he was beside himself, and murmured to himself, 'Am I sleeping, or awaking? am I in my right senses, or am I mad? do I know or do I not know whence came this ball to strike me in such manner which maddens me? I must be a senseless spindle if I do not find out all about this marvel. How hath this sun appeared? how did this flower open? whence did this bird come hither, to draw by magnet all my desires? what ship hath brought her to this country? which cloud rained her down? This fountain of beauty hath brought me a sea of trouble!'

And speaking thus he ran down the steps into the garden, and went where the made-young old woman sat, and throwing himself at her feet, said to her, 'O dove-faced mine, O thou graceful doll, O thou pigeon from Venus' car, triumph of love, thou hast put this heart in soak in the river Sarno. If thine eyes are not blinded by the cane-seed, and thine ears deafened by the excrement of Rennena, thou wilt hear and perceive the love-longing and pain, the anguish and sore distress that I endure for thy beauty's sake; an if thou dost not believe, at the yellowing of my face, the heat which boileth in this breast; if thou believest not the flames of sighs, and the scorching fire which burneth in my veins; thou who art of good understanding, and judgment, thou canst comprehend how thy golden hair bindeth me like a chain, from thy dark eyes what coal burneth me, and from thy red lips like Cupid's bow, what darts strike me: therefore shut not the gate of pity, and draw not up the bridge of mercy, and dry not up the rill of compassion: and if thou do not believe me worthy to possess thy beauteous form, at least give me a safeguard of good words, a guide in a promise, and a deed of expecting hope, an if thou dost not, I will die and thou wilt lose the form.' These and other words did the king utter from the depth of his heart, which touched the made-young old woman, and at last she accepted him for her husband. And then she arose and he took her by the hand, and they went together in the royal palace, and he commanded them to get ready a banquet, and invited all the nobles of the country.

Now the old bride would have her sister there, but the messengers had great difficulty in finding her, and she was sadly afraid and would not go. She had been hiding carefully, but at last they prevailed upon her to go, and she went, and now was seated by her sister's side, and it was long ere she knew her, and when at last she did know her, they joyed together with exceeding gladness. But the old woman could not eat, because other hunger consumed her entrails. Her heart was bursting with envy in sighting the youth and beauty of her sister, and every now and then she pulled her by the sleeve, saying, 'How hast thou done it, how hast thou done it, O my sister? Blessed art thou within those bonds.' And her sister answered, 'Eat now thy sufficiency, we will converse afterwards.' And the king enquired what she wanted, and the bride answered that her sister desired some green sauce, and the king sent at once for garlic sauce, peppered mustard, and a thousand other appetizing sauces to tickle the appetite. But to the old woman all kings of sauces seemed bitter as gall, and again she pulled her sister's sleeve, saying, 'How didst thou do it, O sister mine, how didst thou do it? as I wish to do the like under the mantle;' and the sister answered, 'Be silent, we will have more time than money, eat now, and I will help thee, and we will speak afterwards.' And the king, being curious, asked what she wanted, and the bride was perplexed, and felt like a chick among the straw, and would have liked to be let alone from that nuisance, and answered that her sister wanted some sweetmeats, and the king sent for some pastry, and blanc-mange, and other sweetmeats raining from the heavens in great quantities. But the old woman could not rest, and again sang to the same tune, and the bride unable to bear her persistency any longer answered, 'I made them flay me, O my sister.' And the envious sister hearing these words said to herself, 'Go thy ways, thou hast not spoken to deaf ears; I will also tempt Fortune, and a courageous spirit perchance winneth, and if I succeed, thou wilt not be alone in thy enjoyment, as I also will require my share.' And thus saying, feigning to leave the table on some necessary requirement, she went to a barber's shop, where finding the master, she took him apart, and said to him, 'Here thou hast fifty ducats, if thou wilt flay me from head to foot.'

The barber, believing her to be mad, answered, 'Go thy ways, O my sister, thou speakest oddly, and surely thou wilt find some company very shortly.'

And the old woman, with a brazen face, replied, 'Mad thou art, as thou knowest not thy luck when it cometh to thee; because besides the fifty ducats, if my attempt be successful, I will make thee barber to Fortune herself; therefore do as I bid thee, tarry not, as this will be thy fortune.' The barber contradicted, quarrelled, snapped, and protested for a long while, and at last feeling himself pulled by the nose, did as the proverb saith, 'Tether the master where the ass willeth,' and making her take a seat upon a bench, began to flay her, and the blood rained down, but she, firm as a damant, now and again said, 'Ugh, who beauteous wisheth to be, with anguish and pain must troubled be!' and the barber continued his work and she continued her say, till at last the barber reached the naval, when her strength failed her, and giving vent to a strong wind in sign of departure, she proved at her own risk Sannazaro's verse:

' Envy, O my son, her flesh doth rend.'

This story ended, and it wanting an hour yet to sunset, Prince Thaddeus sent for Fabiello and Jacovuccio, the one Master of the Robes, and the other House Steward, and desired them to give a dessert to this furnished table of entertainments; and they were ready as serjeants, the one dressed in tights, and surtout bell-fashion with large brass buttons, and a flat cap drawn over the ears; the other with a long cap, surtout with breastplate, and trousers as a spider's legs. And they came forth from behind a myrtle-bush, just as if they were on the stage acting a scene, and spake thus:

ECLOGUE

The Crucible

Fabiello and Jacovuccio

Fab. Where away in such haste?
    Where are thou going, O Jacovuccio?
Jac. I am taking this parcel home.

Fab. Is it something very good?

Jac. Most excellent, it is Mescescia.*

Fab. And what else?

Jac. And a tub.

Fab. And what is that for?

Jac. Ho! there, come not nigh me,
And keep thy brains clear.

Fab. What for?

Jac. Who knoweth, but that
Satan would blind thee;
Thou understandest my meaning.

Fab. I understand thee;
But thou comest not near it by an hundred miles.

Jac. How do I know?

Fab. Who knoweth not, keepeth silence, and a dry mouth.
I know thou art not a jeweller,
Nor art thou a distiller:
Now draw thou out the consequences.

Jac. Let us retire apart, O Fabiello,
And thou shalt hear marvellous matters and wondrous.

Fab. Let us go whither it pleaseth thee.

Jac. We will stand near this gutter,
And thou shalt listen to most surprising things.

Fab. O my brother, tell me quickly,
Do not keep me in suspense.

Jac. Softly, O my brother.
Do not be so hasty.
Did thy mother give birth to thee in a hurry?
Seest thou this utensil?

Fab. I see it, 'tis a crucible
Wherein silver is refined.

Jac. Thou hast hit the mark;
Thou hast divined it at first sight.

---

* 'Mescescia' (Gr. μεσοτομος) beef cut in pieces, and dried in the wind and smoke: 'dried beef.'

Fab. Hide it from sight, lest some peasant see it,
    And we be taken to the filthy den.
Jac. Do not crap thy breeches:
    Tremble not, 'tis not of those
    Where pastry is worked ingeniously
    And out of fifteen thou gettest three.
Fab. Tell me, what dost thou with it?
Jac. I keep it to refine this world's goods,
    Clearly to know a garlic from a fig.
Fab. Thou hast taken too much flax to spin:
    Thou wilt grow old before thy time,
    Too soon thou'lt have a hoary head.
Jac. There dwelleth not a man upon earth's face
    Who would not give his teeth and eyes
    To be quick-witted as I am,
    What at first glance can clear away the blot
    Of all the bad that man in mind contains,
    And value truly each art, and fortune's ways.
    Because herein is seen
    If 't be an empty marrow, or meat with salt,
    If this be profitless, or a thing of worth.
Fab. What dost thou mean?
Jac. Listen with care,
    Till I explain to thee;
    When at first sight a countenance
    Seemeth a thing of worth,
    Know thou, that 'tis deceit,
    The folk are blind to all,
    See naught, but what may seem:
    But thou, look not from smoke to smoke,
    Nor fare from bark to bark,
    But pierce that bark, and enter thou within,
    For those that angle not in waters deep
    Are nothing but clodhoppers in this world;
    Then use this crucible and thus thou'lt prove

If all be substance or appearance only,
If it be shooting onion, or sweet pasty.
Fab. 'Tis truly wondrous
By the life of Lanfusa!
Jac. Hearken to me, and marvel,
Let us go on, and fear not,
Thou shalt hear things most wondrous,
Listen to me, *verbi gratia:*
Thou art bursting with envy
And jealousy and wrath
If thou beholdest earl or knight,
In rolling chariot, with jewels dight:
Thou seest them followed by their servants' train.
All bend to them with humble flattery.
One cringeth like a cur,
One boweth to the ground,
One lifteth cap from head,
One saith, 'I am thy slave,'
(All these be done to silken raiment and gems and gold).
When they feel warm, they have ready fans,
Even their night-commode is silver and gold.
Be not deceived by this parade and pomp,
Sight not, and envy not this ostentation:
Put them into this crucible,
And thou shalt see the canker-worm
Under the velvet vest;
Thou shalt see how many serpents
Lurk hidden amid the flowers and in the grass;
And if thou but unlid the night-commode,
And lift its silken cover purfled with gold,
Thou'lt smell what cometh forth, if stink or scent.
Thou shalt perceive, they basons have of gold:
Look in and thou wilt see they spit their blood.
Dainty in their food,
It chokes them in their throat;

An if thou ponder well and measure right,
That which thou thinkest Fortune's proudest gift,
It is but Heaven's punishment.
They feed with delicacies many crows,
Which at the last pluck out their eyes from head;
They keep a pack of hounds,
Which bark continuously around;
Wages they give to their greatest foes,
Who stand about them;
And they are flayed alive;
And on all sides are robbed,
And flattered by their panders
With false humility and affectation.
One urgeth them to things due and undue;
Another to give help and alms pretendeth,
The wolf concealing under the sheep's hide,
With kindly manner, and a brutal heart,
Compelleth them to unright and injustice;
One plotteth against their peace;
Another spieth their doings,
And bringeth sorrow and anguish
To their hearts.
One betrayeth them,
And thus they lose their rest,
And eat not with desire,
And joy to them is not known;
The music played at dinner deafeneth them,
Sleep, when they rest, hath frightful visions,
And dire suspicion driveth away all peace.
Like Tizio's bird, water and fruit surround them,
They stand amongst them, and they die with hunger.
Reason fights against reason,
And Ixion's wheel,
Never lets it rest,
And the chimerical designs

Upon the stones rolled
By Sisyphus up the mountain,
Only to fall to lower depth.
And they sit on their golden throne
Encrusted with ivory and gems;
Under their feet
Brocaded cushions, and carpets soft
Of Turkish texture: but the plumage
On the top of their heads
Is always ruffled;
And whilst they sit, fear standeth by their side;
Suspended by an hair's breadth is their life;
Their days are spent in doubts and fears;
Their lips are wreathèd in false smiles,
Whilst dreads of unknown dangers sap their vitals.
And at the last, bethink thyself,
This sumptuous grandeur and this luxury
Are in vain shadows, worldly emptiness:
A handful of earth and a narrow grave
Holdeth the king and the vilest slave.

Fab.   Thou art right, by my godsire's soul,
By Jove, 'tis very true, this, and more thou **sayest**,
That the noblest and the highest in degree
Feel keenly misadventures more than we;
And in very deed spake sooth
The man of Terrapiena,
Who went about with walnuts, saying,
' 'Tis not all gold, oh no, all that which glitters.'

Jac.   And now hearken to this, and gape with wonder;
Some folk praise war,
And lift it to a high pinnacle,
And when the time cometh
That from afar they sight the standard flying,
And listen to the tramping and neighing of steeds,
They sign their names to the roll,

Feeling themselves drawn to the fight
By sighting a few medals laid on a bench:
They take a few new coppers,
And dress in Jewish garb,*
And don a rusty sword,
And look as mules of burden,
With drooping plume, and foot in stirrup.
If a friend asketh, 'Where do we go?'
They answer cheerfully,
With foot aloft,
'To war, to war,'
And go from tavern to tavern,
Bespeaking triumphs in advance,
Run to their lodgings
Bid farewell to all,
Kick up a shindy, overthrow all things,
And would not stand aside even for a Gradasso.
But if thou put them in this crucible,
Thou wilt perceive that all this merriment,
And all their boast, and all their proud disdain,
Are but a mask to cover for their sore anguish.
They freeze with cold,
They burn with heat,
Their entrails are gnawed by hunger,
Their tongue is swollen with thirst,
They are fainting with fatigue,
And danger standeth ever by their sides;
The guerdon is afar,
And wounds and death are near;
The wage on credit;
Long the disasters, and all joyance short;
Life is uncertain, most are sure of death.
At last, worn out

---

* An expression used in Naples, which means buying second-hand clothes
in the ghetto at the old Jew vendors'.

By a thousand mishaps, they fly from the plain,
Or instantly are struck by cannon-ball,
Or bound like asses with a rope,
Or killed in fight,
Or lose their limbs;
And naught to them remaineth
Else to do, but walk with crutches,
Or troubled be with a perennial itch,
And when the evil is least
Fill empty places in the hospital.

Fab. Thou speakest sooth, and cuttest out the rotten—
Naught can be said:
'Tis truth, and more than truth,
As a poor soldier's fate
Is to return a beggar, and crushed down.

Jac. But what wilt thou say of a genial man
Who treadeth on the air,
Whose self-conceit is great,
Who boasteth of himself
And of his ancient race,
Referring to Achilles or Alexander,
And all the day draweth trees of genealogy,
And from a chestnut-bough
Bringeth forth an holm:
Writing all the day,
Stories and biographies
Of fathers who never had children:
Insisting that a vendor of oil by quart
Is noble in his quarters:
With privileges, upon parchment writ,
Hung in a smoky place, so as to seem old,
To feed his self-esteem, and overbearing pride.
He buyeth a mausoleum,
And hath engraved thereon a lengthened epitaph,
With praise of virtues which have birth in the clouds;

And prayeth well for stock
To amend his worn old coat;
Willingly giveth to put new bells
Into a church-steeple;
And to lay a new foundation
In a tumbling old house
Wasteth on stones his gold.
But put him in the crucible,
And thou wilt see, that he who delayeth longer,
And he who pretendeth more,
And weareth sumptuous robes,
And exacteth more encomium,
His hands have yet the corns of when he worked the fields.

Fab. Thou touchest the wound to the quick,
Naught can be said more; thou hast hit the nail on the head;
I remember on this subject
(And the words I keep in mind)
That once a sage did say,
'There is naught worse than a boor set in high place.'

Jac. And now for the proud vain man,
The coxcomb full of vainglory and pretensions,
Expecting cheeses to drop from the air,
Who maketh a point of great prosopopœa,
Who swelleth out balloons,
Who filleth thine ears with falsehoods,
Spitting a round of words, all boasts of self,
Twisting his mouth in shapes of affectation,
And when he speaketh sucking his lips:
He measureth every step:
Canst thou divine in what rank the man may be?
And he crieth and swelleth forth:
'Olá, send for some pastry;
Call twenty of my followers;
Go some of you to the palace
Of the earl, my nephew;

Bid him come to me,
That we may go to enjoy an airing
When our coachman bringeth the chariot round;
Go to the tailor, and bid him bring before night
My coat and vest purfled with gold;
Write and say to that lady,
Who is dying for my sake,
That perhaps, and may be, some day I will love her.'
But put him in this crucible,
And thou wilt find not one mite of truth:
'All is a fire of straw;'
The higher he mounteth, the lower he falleth;
He speaketh of ducats, and hath not a soldo;
Dainties are on his lips, and emptiness within;
A full kerchief hath he to hide his withered neck;
Lightly he trippeth along, with empty purse and pockets;
And in conclusion
Every beard he passeth for a fin,
Every pump becometh a hammer,
Every hunchback is perfectly straight,
And every gun resolveth into a cannon.

Fab. Blessed by thy tongue:
How prettily hast thou explained it;
And in very sooth it is an ancient say
That, 'A coxcomb is a bladder, full of wind, for children's
    play.'

Jac. Who followeth the court,
Charmed by that hideous witch,
And filleth himself with wind,
And feedeth on smoke, leaving the roast for others;
With bladders full of hope,
Who expecteth bells
When blowing soapy waters
Which reach but half the way,
And there dissolve;

Who sumptuously arrayed
Standeth with open mouth
Gazing on pomp and grandeur:
And for this old vain rag,
And to sip broth from a tub,
And eat a dry old loaf,
He selleth his liberty, man's greatest prize.
If thou purify this gold from all its dross,
Thou'lt spy a labyrinth
Of fraud and treachery;
Thou'lt find, O brother, an abyss
Of deceit and falsity;
Thou a country shalt discover
Of wicked tongues, with poison as an asp's;
Now he is held aloft, but shortly downcast;
Now to his master dear, but soon an outcast;
Now rich, and briefly a beggar;
Now stout and well fed, and shortly thin and hungry:
He worketh hard to get forward in the chase,
Perspireth like a dog,
Runneth rather than walketh,
And carrieth even water with his ears.
But it is loss of time,
He loseth the work and the seed,
All is thrown to the winds,
All falleth into the sea.
Do what he will, they are gone;
Let him make drawings and models
Of hopes, of merits, and travails:
A little contrary wind
Casteth them down to the ground:
And he beholdeth before him
A jester, a spy, a Ganymede,
A hardened hide,
One who buildeth

A house with two entrances, a two-faced man.

Fab. O my brother, thou givest me new life.
Believe me, I have learned
More in this short time,
And from this thy say,
Than in all the years I spent at school:
And 'twas a sage who said,
'Who serveth courts, upon a straw-rick dieth.'

Jac. Thou hast heard what is a courtier:
Hearken now what is a servant of lower degree.
Take a man-servant,
Handsome, polite, and clean
He must be of good parentage,
He boweth an hundred times,
He keepeth the house in order, draweth water,
Cooketh thy food,
Brusheth thy vestments,
Currieth thy mule, washeth thy dishes;
If thou send him to market,
He is back before thy spittle drieth on ground.
He is never idle,
His hands are never still,
He cleanseth the glass, emptieth the night vase.
But put thou him to the test,
In this true crucible:
Thou shalt find that all new things are fine,
And the race of an ass endureth not,
And before three days are past
Thou shalt discover him to be a flatterer,
Deceiver, and idle for dear life;
A first class pander,
A meddling fellow, a glutton, and a gamster.
If he goeth to market, he defraudeth;
If he giveth corn to the mule,
'Tis given from grapes to rice;

He corrupteth the maid-servant,
He emptieth thy pockets,
And when he is so inclined,
To put the last stroke to his deeds,
He taketh thy best things, and lifts his heels;
And thou may'st tether thy pigs to the cucumber.

Fab. These are substantial words
With wit and juice:
O unfortunate, O thrice unhappy is he
Whose trust hath met with servants' treachery.

Jac. And now for the man of valour,
The first of Spartan braves,
The chief of all swashbucklers,
The prompter of all disputes,
Fourth in the art of neck-breaking,
Bravest of the brave,
Commander-in-chief of the valiant:
He pointedly presumeth
To frighten all the folk,
To make thee tremble
With a side-glance of his eyes;
He walketh with a swagger,
He weareth a slashed coat,
His hat drawn over his eyes,
His hair disorderly,
His mustachios twisted on end,
His eyes fiercely rolling,
One hand on side,
Swearing, and stamping with his feet;
Even a straw causeth him to be wroth,
And he squabbleth with the flies;
He companieth with soldiers and brigands;
If thou hearken to his speech,
He speaketh of naught, but of cutting,
Of slashing, and piercing, and hanging,

Of killing, and running through the body;
Of one he draweth out the heart,
Of another the liver,
Of one he draweth out the entrails,
Of another the kidneys,
He trampleth on one,
Another he heweth in quarters.
If thou listen to his boasting,
The earth is too small to hold them
This one, he writeth his name in the book,
That other, he sendeth out of the world,
This one, he sendeth unto his friends,
That other, he emptieth his pockets of gold,
This one, he salteth,
That other, he striketh to earth,
Of this one, he maketh mince-meat:
An hundred he turneth, and an hundred he gathereth,
And always passing truth, and with havoc,
Splitting heads, and breaking limbs.
But the sword hung by his side,
No matter how strong and sharp its edge,
Is virgin of blood, and widowed of honour:
And this crucible will to thee make clear,
That the big words carried so high
Hide the heart's trembling;
The rolling of the eyes,
Retreat of feet;
The eastern thunderclaps,
Looseness of ice;
The visionary boastings
Indicate the wakeful hours of night;
And the swearing and stamping
Is but an excuse to keep sword in sheath,
Which, like an honoured woman,
Feeleth ashamed to show itself naked.

Seemeth he bitter as gall,
He hath but a chicken's heart;
Seemeth he an eater of lions,
He is but a catcher of rabbits;
Challengeth he, he gaineth a thrashing;
Threateneth he, he receiveth annoyance double weight;
Gambleth he with his boasting dice,
He always meeteth his equal;
In words he is brave,
But in actions brief;
Layeth hand on hilt,
But draweth not sword;
Seeketh quarrel, and withdraweth from it;
And he lifteth heel easier than show valour,
If he lighteth upon one who bendeth him down,
Or one who sets his coat to rights,
And dealeth him a rain of blows with change,
Who settleth his accounts,
Who cardeth out his wool,
Who beateth well his sides,
Who whistleth in his ears,
Who knocketh down his teeth,
Who pusheth him down a pit,
Who bravely throttleth him,
Who passeth his blood through a sieve,
Who breaketh his lantern to pieces,
Who giveth him a good dressing,
Who prepareth him for a feast,
Or casteth him with the box,
Or boxeth well his ears,
Or giveth him back-handed cuffs,
Kicks, pushes, knocks, and cuts,
Or thrusteth a knife in his side.
Enough for him to cut and thrust,
And speak in manly voice:

He steppeth deal faster than a deer;
He soweth spittle, and gathereth marrows;
And when thou thinkest
That he is about to lay waste an army,
Then it is that the scene changeth;
Goodby, farewell, and good-day,
He disappeareth, weigheth anchor, is gone,
And shooting the parting shaft,
Lifteth his heels, and runneth away;
Taketh with him his saddle-bags well-filled,
'And help me, O my feet, because I cover ye,'
His heel toucheth shoulder,
And rivalleth hare in speed;
And well he playeth with his two-legged sword,
And like a great poltroon
In haste he flieth, is caught, and taken in gaol!

Fab. It is the true portrait
Of these fire-eaters:
It is in sooth quite natural.
And hereabout thou findest more than one
That answereth well to this description,
That with their tongue do giants slay,
And are not worth a cur nor yet a quail.

Jac. And now for the flatterer, who ever praiseth thy doings,
He lifteth thee aloft above the moon's circle,
He agreeth always to all thou choose to do,
He feedeth thy pride, and filleth himself,
He giveth fair wind to thy sails,
And never contradicteth what thou sayest.
If thou art a ghul or an Æsop,
He will tell thee thou art a Narcissus;
If thou hast a mark upon thy face,
He'll swear 'tis but a patch, a mole;
If thou art a poltroon,
He will assert thou art Hercules or Samson;

If thou art of vile descent,
He will attest thou springest from a count;
He is always flattering thee and caressing thee:
But be not caught by the sweet words
Of these sycophants;
And do not trust them,
Nor hold them in esteem;
Do not let the false glitter dazzle thee,
But try them in this crucible,
And thou shalt feel with both hands
That these folk are double-faced,
One visage frontward, and another backward,
And what is on their tongues is not in heart;
They are all face-washers, and false dealers,
And tricksters, and deceivers;
They knit thee, and perplex thee,
And blind thee, and deceive thee.
When he agreeth with thee in every matter,
Be watchful, for 'tis then thou'lt have a storm.
With a sweet smile he biteth thee,
He soileth thee with his flattery;
He swelleth thy balloon,
And emptieth thy money-bags.
The end he hath in view
Is thee to cheat and upon thee spunge.
And with his praises and eulogium,
And his long stories and enormous boasting,
He draweth from thy heart thy secrets' core,
And all this doth this sharper
To get from thee gold or silver;
That he may spend to his leman, and in taverns,
He selleth to thee bladders for a lanthorn.

Fab. May the seed be lost of such vile race,
Men wearing masks!
They ought to be thrown within a sack;

Out, fair Narcissus, and with Satan back!

Jac. And listen now about a woman, who kisseth
Those which come, and those that go:
Thou shalt behold a pretty doll,
All grace and gallantry, a dove,
A fair white ass, a jewel,
A parrot, a Fairy Morgana,
A moon on her fourteenth night,
A form worthy a painter's brush
Thou couldst drink her in a glass of water
A delicate morsel fit for kings,
A charmer and heart stealer.
With her golden locks she bindeth thee,
With her glances she consumeth thee,
With her voice of honey seduceth thee.
But no sooner is she put within this crucible,
Thou shalt behold great flames,
And traps, and snares,
And skains, and clews;
A thousand sly snakish deeds she'll do,
A thousand malices invent,
A thousand snares, and ambushes,
And stratagems will lay,
And lead thee first one way and then another,
And from the one perplexity to the other.
She will draw thee, like an hook,
Bleed thee, like a barber,
Cheat thee, like a gipsy;
And a thousand times thou wilt believe
She'll bring thee a cup of good strong wine,
And instead thou'lt find
She mixeth mince-meat.
If she speak, she enticeth,
And if she walk, stiffeneth:
Her smile is a guile,

And her touch will soil thee,
And if thou wilt escape from all harm
And not be thrown in an hospital,
Thou shalt be treated as a bird, or beast,
With her accursed manner,
And she will pluck thee of thy feathers
And will leave thee hideless.

Fab. If thou shouldst write on paper all these words,
It would be sold six times over,
As in publishing this history,
Some one will take example,
And thus every man will be on his guard,
And not easily give himself in hand
To these blood-suckers:
Because they are false coin,
Which ruineth the meat and all the sauce.

Jac. If thou by chance beholdeth at a window
A girl who seems to thee a beauteous fairy,
With golden hair,
In glancing at whose sheen
Thou wouldst suppose it
Threads of gold or chains of golden cheese;
The brow like mirror, or a colt of ass;
A speaking eye; and, juiceful fruit,
Two lips, red as two cherries, like
Two slices of ham:
For a time thou standest afar
Sighing at this rising star,
She standeth on high as a standard flying,
And thou hast hardly gazed on her,
And with desire and longing art dying,
Thy vitals gnawed with despair.
O thou clodhopper, O thou lack-wits,
Put her in the crucible,
And thou wilt see that what seemeth to thee

A beauty without compeer
Is but an enamelled doll,
A wall newly plastered,
A Ferrarese mask,
And the bride is all made up.
The lovely golden hair is not her own,
The pencilled brows are painted,
The rosy cheeks are covered by a cup-full
Of chalk and varnish, and of cochineal.
She smootheth her wrinkles, and raileth at thee,
All cosmetics and pomade.
Arrayed in silks, and laces, and flowers,
Powder, scent-bottles, and perfumes,
She seemeth ready, with kerchief in hand,
To bandage all the wounds of some sick man.
How many faults are hid by all this train
Of petticoats, and jewels, and costly garments,
Her feet misshapen, covered full with corns,
Are hid by slippers red purflewed with gold.

Fab. Thou fillest me with wonder:
'Tis truly marvellous, I am become a mummy,
And with surprise I am beside myself.
Every sentence, O my brother, uttered by thee,
Is worth full seventy golden pieces to me;
Thou canst engrave thy sayings with the engraver
Upon a stone, for thou agreest in thy thoughts
With that old saw:
'That a woman is like a chestnut:
Handsome outside, and with a worm inside.'

Jac. Now we come to the merchant,
Who changeth, and exchangeth,
Ensureth vessels, and findeth accounts;
He trafficketh, intrigueth, and deceiveth,
Shareth with the custom-house,
Loadeth, and unloadeth,

Taketh share in all, and gaineth ducats;
Buildeth ships and buildeth houses,
And thus filleth well his sink;
Furnisheth his house with sumptuousness,
 With pomp and luxury equal to an earl's,
And wasteth silks and trimmings,
And keepeth serving-men, and servant-maids,
And free born women,
And is envied by all folk.
Unhappy is he, if put into this crucible,
For his riches are but of air,
And his fortune hath birth in smoke.
Fortune inconstant,
Subject to changeful winds,
In power of the waves,
Is beautiful to gaze at.
But it cheateth the eyesight,
And when thou seest it
More prosperous to view,
The game is lost by a very slight mistake.

Fab. Thou speakest sooth: of these I count by thousands,
Whose houses have failed down,
And all their riches
Disappeared quickly: as, thou seest me
And seest me not; and joyed in this world
To the beard of the third, and fourth, who had lack of wits,
And filled their pots, and made bad testament.

Jac. Now for the lover:
Happy thinketh he the hours,
Spent in the service of love:
Sweet holdeth the flame, and dear the chain,
Loveth the dart,
Which wounded him for a beauty.
He confesseth that he dieth
When afar from his love;

'Tis not life far from her side;
He calleth joy, the pains,
The turns of the head, and reproaches;
Delight, the doubts and the jealousy.
He cannot enjoy his food,
His sleep is broken and restless,
He suffereth without sickness,
He maketh without wage the round
Of the doors of his beloved;
No architect, he draweth designs
Of castles in the air;
And although he is not the executioner,
He is always tyrannising over his life.
But nathless all this woe,
He groweth red and stout;
And the harder he is hit by the dart
The better he cometh in form.
And always feasteth, and playeth,
Until the fire lasteth;
And thinketh himself lucky, and happy is he,
To feel himself in bondage and not free.
But if thou put him in this crucible,
Thou shalt perceive that 'tis a lunacy,
A species of consumption,
Living in uncertainty,
Always between hope, and fear,
'Tis like being half way hung
Between doubts and suspicions:
'Tis living ever badly,
Like the cat of Messer Basil
Which weepeth this moment and laugheth the next:
'Tis a stepping badly on uneven road,
A speaking brokenly and interrupted,
At all hours sending
The brains out feeding;

'Tis like ever having
The heart for a napkin,
The face discoloured,
Warm the breast, and the soul sickening.
And if at last
The ice is broken, and the stone is moved
Of the being he loves,
That the further he is from her, the nearer he feeleth
He proveth the sweet at last, and soon repenteth.

Fab. O unhappy he unto whom happen
These unjust weights;
And sad his heart whose foot is caught,
For the blind god sendeth
Joys short-lived, and troubles by the ton.

Jac. And now we'll speak of the sad poet,
Pouring down stanzas, and bowling out sonnets,
Spoiling much paper, and torturing the brain,
And tearing his coat's elbows,
And his time,
Only that the folk
Should hold him as an oracle in the world.
He goes about as if possessed,
By legions of evil spirits,
With empty stomach and foolish aspect,
Thinking of the conceptions
He kneadeth in his mind;
And whilst he is walking in the roads,
He talketh to himself,
Finding new voices by the thousand;
And rolling his eyes about,
Saith, 'Liquid surmounting of leaves and flowers,
Funereal croaking of the waves!
O life-giving pear-tree!
O lubric hope!'
O unmeasured presumption!'

But put him in this crucible,
And all evaporates in smoke:
'O what fine composition,' and there
Endeth the madrigal, and spendeth.
And having scanned the verse,
The more he writeth the less they agree:
He praiseth whoso despiseth him,
Exalteth whoso troubleth him,
Keepeth ever in remembrance
Whoso hath clean forgotten him,
Expendeth all his strength
For those who never give him aught:
Thus is his life broken;
For glory singeth he, and weepeth for want.

Fab. And in fact they are past,
Those days of Saint Martin, when
On high hand every poet stood;
But in this darksome age
The patronisers are ground upon the wheel;
And besides, in Naples, I must say,
Even though I died of grief and great distress,
The laurel leaf is not thought of like other leaves.

Jac. The astrologer standeth well:
From every side he hath put to him
An hundred questions and more:
One wants to know if she'll bring forth a son-child;
Another, if this is a suitable time,
And most propitious, to win a law-suit;
And one, if his unluckiness will change;
One, if his lady-love is true to him;
And one, if he will have a thunderstorm
With her he loves, or great enjoyance reap.
And the seer answereth well to all,
And he deserveth a good thrashing;
For half the questions put he wisely guesseth,

And the other half are cunningly invented.
But in this crucible
Thou mayest discern, if dust or flour it is;
That if he formeth aught in a square form,
Thou wilt behold it oblong, and deal larger;
And if he buildeth houses,
Thou wilt perceive he hath no fireside;
He showeth figures, and discovereth stories;
Ascendeth to the stars,
And droppeth arse on ground;
And at the last, having lost all vogue,
He is seen in tatters, reduced to beggary,
And rags and lice his only company.
His trowsers fall from his hips,
And there mayest thou behold a truer astrology
Than shown in the astrolabe with all the spheres.

Fab. Thou hast cheered me, O my brother,
And I must laugh at this description,
Although I had no desire, and I must smile
At the most foolish credulity of those
Who put their trust in such mendacity;
And they pretend to foretell unto others,
Who cannot divine what evil will befall them,
And whilst star-gazing, fall into a pit.

Jac. And another pretendeth to be a sage,
And stretcheth his legs,
And measureth his words, spitting them round,
And holdeth himself the best in all the world.
Dost thou discuss upon poetry?
He knoweth more than Petrarca.
Speakest thou of philosophers?
He will mention fifteen more than Aristoteles.
In arithmetic he surpasseth Cantone;
In the art of war toppeth Cornazgaro;

In architecture goeth back to Euclid;
In music he rivalleth Venosa;
In law he knoweth more than Farcinaccio;
For language taketh precedence of Boccaccio;
He speaketh in sentences, offereth advice;
And the play is not worth a leaf of Indian corn.
But if he is tried,
And put into this crucible,
In a library full of books he playeth the ass.

Fab. How foolish it is to be overmuch presumptuous;
And a clever sage used once to say:
'He who believeth himself most clever
Is the most ignorant.'

Jac. And now for alchemy, and the alchemist:
He holdeth himself to be a happy man,
And is always cheerful,
And in twenty or thirty years hence
Promiseth thee great doings,
And relateth marvellous things:
Of a new drug he hath distilled;
Of his great hope of having riches.
But put him into this crucible,
And thou wilt see, that after squandering all
He perceiveth how sophistical is that art;
He findeth how blind, and filthy,
And full of smoke he hath been,
To lay all his best hopes
On a scaffold of brittle glass,
And to put all thoughts and designs
Amongst the smoke.
And whilst he fanneth lustily
The flames with words, meanwhile
Replenisheth the longing and desire
Of him who waiteth for what never comes.
He seeketh after secrets,

And all the folk believe him mad;
And trying to find the first matter
Loseth his own form.
He believeth he is going to multiply his gold,
And he diminisheth whatsoever he possesseth;
He thinketh the sick metals he will heal,
And he instead is sent to the hospital;
And instead of hardening
Quick-silver, so that he may coin and spend it,
His own life thus fatigued he melteth down;
And whilst believing he'll transmute
Into fine gold all baser metal,
He but transmuteth himself from a man to an ass.

Fab. Doubtless 'tis madness
To enter on such enterprise: I have seen
An hundred houses in this way thrown down,
And none ever built.
But having great hopes, he evermore despaireth,
Is sad at heart, and hungry stomach beareth.

Jac. And now tell me, dost thou want more for a penny?

Fab. I stand here open-mouthed to hear thy say.

Jac. And I could still continue even to roses.

Fab. Then do so, whilst the mood is on thee still.

Jac. Yes, so I would, if my soul was not departing
For want of food, as my meal-time is past:
Therefore let us be going,
And come thou to my shop
If so it please thee,
And thus we'll something find for our teeth to‧grind,
For food's ne'er wanting in a beggar's home.

The words of this eclogue were companied by such graceful gestures, and with such ludicrous grimaces, that all hearers perforce must needs show their teeth: and because the crickets called the folk to take their rest, therefore Prince Thaddeus took leave of all the women, and bade them depart and return on the following morning to continue the enterprise: and then he and the slave retired to their own chambers.

END OF THE FIRST DAY

SECOND DAY OF THE

DIVERSION FOR THE LITTLE ONES

THE dawn arose and came forth to anoint the wheels of the sun's chariot; and the fatigue endured by her in turning the grease with her mace in the stock of the wheel had reddened her cheeks like unto a sweet apple. And Prince Thaddeus, leaving his bed, after stretching himself and gaping called the slave, and dressing in the twindling of an eye, both descended to the garden, where they found the ten women assembled. And bidding them each gather a few fresh figs, which looked so inviting, and with their ragged coats and their long necks, and their glistening tears (like unto a prostitute's) made the spittle gather into the mouth, they played a thousand games to pass the time till the dinner hour, and they left none of the games untouched: they played 'Here is Nicholas;' 'The Wheel of Kicks;' 'Look to thy Wife;' 'The Knight;' 'O my Companion, I am Wounded;' 'By Edict and Commandment;' and 'Welcome, O my Master;' and 'Rentinola, my Rentinola;' 'Jump over this Cask;' 'Jump a Foot;' 'Stone on Lap;' 'O thou Fish of the Sea;' 'O thou Angel, and Anola;' 'The King Thrasher;' 'The Blind Cat;' and 'Lamp to Lamp;' and 'Stretch the Curtain;' and 'Drum and Fife;' 'I find no Room;' 'A Long Beam;' 'The Little Chicks;' 'The Old Man is Come;' 'Unload the Barrel;' and 'Mammara and Hazelnut;' and 'The Exile;' and 'Take out this Dart;' and 'Come come;' 'Hold the Needle and Thread;' 'Sweet Bird, Sweet Bird;' and 'Iron Handle;' 'The Greek and Vinegar;' and 'Open the Door to a Poor Hawk.'

But when the meal time came, they took their seats round the table, and after they had eaten their sufficiency, the prince told Zeza, that she should bear herself as a clever woman should and begin her story; and Zeza, who has so many tales in her head that they overflowed, asking them to listen to her story, chose the one which I am going to relate.

PETROSINELLA

Of the Second Day

A WOMAN WITH CHILD EATETH SOME PARSLEY OUT OF THE GARDEN OF
A GHULA, AND BEING CAUGHT WHILST SO DOING, PROMISETH THE GHULA
THE CHILD TO WHOM SHE SHOULD GIVE BIRTH. SHE GIVETH BIRTH TO
PETROSINELLA; THE GHULA TAKETH THE CHILD AND SHUTTETH HER UP
IN A TOWER. A PRINCE STEALETH HER AWAY, AND BY THE VIRTUE OF
THREE ACORNS BOTH ESCAPE THE PERILS SET THEM BY THE GHULA, AND
BEING TAKEN HOME BY HER LOVER, SHE BECOMETH A PRINCESS.

My desire to please the princess and to maintain her in good
humour hath kept me awake all the night. When all other folk
were fast asleep and no footstep was heard, I did naught else but
turn in the old pockets of my brain, and search in all the corners
of my memory, choosing those things, that that good soul of Ma-
dame Chiarella Usciolo, grandmother of my uncle may (God have
her in His glory), used to relate: an ye be all in health, I will tell
to you, of these tales, one each day, whichever seems to me more
à propos; and of these ye will remain well satisfied. If I have
not turned mine eyes the wrong way, I imagine that ye will be all
pleased with them; or if they will not be pleasing enough to chase
the annoyance and gloom out of your minds, at least they will be
as trumpets to excite these my companions to come into the field
with more power than my poor strength doth allow, and to supple-
ment with the abundance of their wit the deficiency of these my
words:

Once upon a time there lived a woman who was with child, Pascaddozia hight. Looking out of a window into a garden belonging
to a ghula, she sighted a pretty bed of parsley, and she longed for
some, and her longing increased so much that she felt faint, and
could not withstand the temptation to go and gather some, and

watching till the ghula went out, she descended to the garden and gathered a handful.

The ghula, returning home, and wanting some parsley for some sauce, discovered that some had been stolen and cried, 'Whosoever hath taken it, I hope to break his neck. If I once catch him and put these hooks upon him, I will make him repent of the deed, for an example to others, so that they shall know how to eat at their own fireside, and not put their spoons in other folk's pots.'

Pascaddozia, continuing her despoiling, was at last caught in the act by the ghula, who in sighting her became wroth with exceeding wrath, and cried 'I have caught thee, thou thief, thou robber. Thou must pay me for the theft thou hast committed in my garden, as thou hast come to steal my sweet herbs and hast used so little discretion in taking them. Doubt not, but that I will take thee to Rome to do penance.'

Pascaddozia, frightened and ashamed, began to excuse herself, saying that it had not been taken to satisfy her greed. Satan had blinded her, and she had stolen it because she was with child, and feared that the child's face would come covered all over with parsley if she did not satisfy her longing; and she begged the ghula to forgive her, and trusted that she would not punish her by sending her something evil. Answered the ghula, 'Words are fit for brides, thou shalt not fish me up with all this prattling: thou hast put an end to thy life's thread, if thou promise not to give me the child that thou wilt bring forth, either male or female.' The unhappy Pascaddozia, to escape the peril in which she was, sware, laying hand upon hand, to do the ghula's bidding, and the latter let her go unhurt.

When the time came of child-bed, she brought forth a beauteous woman-child, like unto a gem, with a face like the moon in her fourteenth night. But on her breast was wrought a bunch of parsley, whereupon her mother had her named Petrosinella. Day by day she grew, and when she was seven years old, Pascaddozia sent her to school, and every time she went her ways, she was met by the ghula, who kept saying to her, 'Tell thy mother to remember her promise'; and so often did she recite these words to the child, that the wretched mother, being tired of hearing this music repeated, and having lost her wits with fear, said to the child, 'If thou shouldst meet the old woman, and she again ask of thee that accursed promise, answer thou, 'Take it.' '

Petrosinella, who was not possessed of too much wit, soon met the ghula, who asked her the same question, and she answered innocently in the words her mother had bade her say. Then the ghula, seizing her by the hair of her head, carried her into the forest, where Phœbus' horses never entered, desiring not to graze in that dreary darkness. And the ghula put her in a tower, which arose by means of magic. And the tower was without doors or stairs, and possessed only a small window, by which the ghula came and went, using Petrosinella's hair, which was very long, as a ladder; and she mounted and descended as a sailor-boy mounts and descends from the masts to the sails.

Now it so chanced one day of the days that the ghula having gone out of the tower, Petrosinella put her head out of that small window, and let her tresses hang out in the sun. Whilst she was in this plight, passed that way a prince's son, and beholding those two golden standards, calling to arms to enroll himself under the banner of love, and sighting between those precious waves the face of a mermaid, which charmed all hearts and took his own by storm with her grace and beauty, he sent her a petition of a thousand sighs, and it was thus decreed that the fortress should be taken and be at his mercy. And the merchandise had good success, and the prince had in return bowing of head, hand-kissing, languishing glances, thanks and offers, hopes and promises, good words and salutes: which continued for some days and they became so used to each other, that they made appointments together, but only when the moon plays with the stars. And Petrosinella would give the ghula somewhat to make her sleep, and then would hang her tresses out of window for her lover to climb up; and thus they combined together, and then came the hour when the prince stood beneath the tower window, and Petrosinella lowered her tresses, and he caught hold of them with both hands, saying, 'Lift up.' Jumping in from the window into the room, he sated his desire, and ate of that sweet parsley sauce of love, and before the sun brought forth his horses to jump over the zodiac, he descended by the same golden ladder to his affairs.

So this continued for some time, until at last a gossip of the ghula sighted them, and taking the matter in Russian fashion, would put her nose in the excrement, and persuaded the ghula that she must be watchful, as Petrosinella was making love with a certain youth, and she suspected that they might go a step forward; because she could see the traffic, and the mosquito flying about; and misdoubted but that they might take flight before May from that house. The ghula thanked the gossip for her good advice, and said that it would be her care to stop the way; and Petrosinella, who kept her ears open, having suspected something wrong, heard her say, 'It is impossible for Petrosinella to escape, as I have charmed her, unless she taketh in her hands the acorns which are hid in the rafter in the kitchen.' When night darkened and starkened, the prince came as usual to his meeting place, and Petrosinella put down her tresses, and he came up, and she told him what had happened, and he searched the beams till he found the acorns, and knowing how to use them, and how she had been charmed by the ghula, he made a ladder with some rope, and both descended, and lifted their heels towards the city. But they were seen by the ghula's gossip, who began howling and screeching until the ghula woke up; and when she heard that Petrosinella had run away, she went down by the same ladder by which the lovers had gone, and set to running after them. When they saw her coming like a wild horse, they thought they were lost; but Petrosinella remembered the acorns, and threw one to the ground, and at once a large dog rose up, terrible of aspect, with mouth open, and barking furiously. And O dear mother, how frightful it was! And the dog flew at the ghula, meaning to make a mouthful of her; but the witch, who was more knowing than the devil, putting her hand in her pocket, drew out a loaf, and threw it to the dog, who put down his tail, and abated his fury; and she began to chase the lovers once more. Petrosinella, who beheld her coming, threw down the second acorn, and behold! a lion, lashing his tail furiously, and shaking his mane, opened his mouth, and got himself ready to make a good meal of the ghula. But the ghula went back and flayed an ass, that was grazing in a field, and putting on his hide, she returned to the lion, who believing her to be a donkey, was frightened so much that he flieth yet.

Therefore having surmounted this second pit, the ghula once more pursued the two lovers, and when they heard her footsteps, and sighted the dust-cloud, which rose to the sky, they supposed that the ghula was once more on their scent, whilst she, thinking that the lion still followed her, had not taken off her ass's hide. And Petrosinella having thrown down the third acorn, a wolf sprang up, who not allowing the ghula to take a new measure of defence, ate her up for an ass, and the lovers thus being saved from further trouble, fared onward very slowly to the prince's realm, where with his father's leave he took Petrosinella to wife. And peace and joy followed, and thus they were happy after so many storms and travails: as saith truly the old saw,

> 'An hour of happiness in safe harbour
> Maketh us forget an hundred years of ill-fortune.'

VERDE PRATO

SECOND DIVERSION

Of the Second Day

NELLA IS BELOVED OF A PRINCE, WHO GOETH TO TAKE JOYANCE WITH HER, PASSING THROUGH A VIADUCT OF CRYSTAL. THIS PASSAGE BEING BROKEN BY ENVIOUS SISTERS, HE IS WOUNDED SORELY, AND COMETH NIGH UNTO DEATH. NELLA BY A STRANGE ADVENTURE OBTAINETH A REMEDY AND APPLYING IT TO THE SICK PRINCE, HE RECOVERETH, AND SHE THUS BECOMETH HIS WIFE.

WITH great zest all listened to Zeza's story, and had it lasted another hour they would have been the better pleased. And it being Cecca's turn to say her say, she began to relate what follows:

It is a great thing to make up accounts in all ways, because with the same wood whereof statues and idols are hewn the beams of the gallows are fashioned, and chairs fit for an emperor, and lids for night-commodes. And yet stranger it seems that from a piece of rag paper is made, that may be used for lovers' letters, which are kissed by beautiful women, or as behind-wipers by country boors; these are things which would cause you and the best astrologer in the world to lose your wits. And the same can be said of a mother who giveth birth to two daughters, the one good, and the other the ruin of her house; one lazy, and the other diligent; one beautiful, and the other hideous; one envious, and the other loving; one chaste, the other unchaste; one with luck, and the other with ill-luck: whereas by reason of their being of the same flesh and blood, both ought to be of the same nature. But let us leave this talk for others that know more of it, and I will bring you an example of that of which I have spoken, in three daughters of the same mother, in whom you will perceive the difference in customs, and manners, and thoughts, which brought the wicked into the pit, and the good upon the wheel of fortune.

Once upon a time there lived a mother who had three daughters, two of whom were so unfortunate that nothing ever came right to them: all that they tried was unsuccessful, and their hopes were blasted and came to naught. But the youngest, Nella hight, brought from her mother's womb good fortune; and I believe that when she was born, things concerted to give her the best of all that they could: the heavens dowered her with their light; Venus with her beauty; love with all his strength; nature with the flower of good manners. She never did a service, but that it came to good ending; never undertook an enterprise, but it was well done; never danced, but every one praised the grace of her movements; and came forth with honour in her every undertaking.

For this reason she was bitterly envied by her own sisters, and beloved of all those that knew her; and the sisters would have liked to see her underground, whilst other folk carried her on the palm of their hands. Now in that country there was a prince who was charmed, and this prince, beholding this sea of beauty, threw forth the bait of the slavery of love, till he caught her and made her his own. And so that they might joy together without the knowledge of the mother, who was of a stern and severe nature, the prince gave her some powder, which built a crystal viaduct from the royal palace to underneath Nella's bed, though it was eight miles distant, saying, 'Every time that thou desirest to feed me as a bird with thy sweet grace, put a pinch of this powder in the fire, and I will at once come through the passage of crystal to enjoy thy dear silvern face.' And having thus agreed, the prince never missed one night to come and go, to enter and go forth through that passage: and the sisters, who were ever on watch to see their sister's doings, observed what took place, and they held counsel together to make her lose such good morsel; and desiring to wreak their wrath upon their love, they brake the passage through and through. And that wretched child throwing the powder into the fire as a signal to the prince that he might come, he, whose fashion it was to come running stark naked, was wounded sorely by the broken glass, so that it caused great distress to see him; and as it was impossible for him to go forward, he retired to his palace all cuts and wounds like a German reiter, and went to bed, and sent for all the doctors and physicians in the city. But as the crystal was charmed, the wounds were mortal, and there was no human remedy that could avail. The king his father, perceiving that his case was desperate, sent the crier to proclaim an edict that whoso could in any way ease the sufferings of the prince and heal him, if a woman, he would marry her to him, if a man, he would give him the half of his realm.

Now Nella, who heard this edict, and was dying with love and sorrow for the prince, bethought herself to try what she could do, and dyeing her face and hands, and disguising herself unbeknown to her sisters, she left the house, thinking that at least she might see him before his death. But as it was the time when the sun's golden balls, with which he plays in the fields of heaven, took their way towards the west, and night darkened and starkened, Nella found herself in a forest near the house of a ghul, where being afraid, and desiring to eschew any danger, she clomb upon a tree.

Now the ghul and his wife were sitting at table, and the windows were open, so that they could enjoy the fresh air whilst they were eating. When they had ended and were satisfied, they began chatting of little and much, and being so very near that place, like as from nose to mouth, Nella could hear what they said; and amongst other things she heard the ghula say to her husband, 'O my hairy beauty, what hast thou heard? What do the folk say in the world?'

And answered he, 'Thou mayest suppose that there is not a foot of ground clean, and everything is going topsy-turvy and crookedly.'

Rejoined the ghula, 'But what is there?'

And the ghul replied, 'There would be great deal to say about all the perplexities, and sayings, and doings which take place. There are matters which when heard would make one jump out of his clothes, jesters prized and regaled, rogues held in high esteem, assassins supported, poltroons honoured, false coiners defended, and good honourable men valued very little, and esteemed less. But as these are matters which annoy one greatly, I will tell thee only what

hath happened to the king's son. He had built a crystal passage from
his palace to the house of a beauteous girl whom he loved, and he
used to go and enjoy her through it, and to depart from the palace
stark naked; and I know not how it occurred, but in making his
way through this passage, he hath been sorely wounded, and before
he will be able to heal so many holes, he will lose his life. And the
king, who loveth him dearly, hath sent an edict, promising great
things to whoso will heal his son; but 'tis all time lost, he may
cleanse his teeth of it; and the best thing he can do is to get ready
the mourning, and prepare the obsequies.' Nella hearing these
words, and thus understanding what was the cause of the prince's
illness, wept with bitter weeping, and said in her mind, 'What accursed being hath done this deed? Who hath broken the passage
wherein flew my sweet bird, so that mine own spirit may take
flight?' But the ghula spake again, and Nella kept silence and
listened, and she heard her say, 'And is it possible, that the world is
lost for this poor young lord? And can no remedy be found for
his sickness? Then thou mayest tell the mediciners that they may
go and bake themselves; and the physicians to hang themselves;
tell Galen and Mesué to return the money to the master, as they
cannot find a recipe to heal the prince.'

Answered the ghul, 'Listen to me, O my dearling, the doctors are
not obliged to find remedies passing the confines of nature. 'Tis
not a cholick, that an oil-bath would cure; 'tis not a wind, that thou
canst chase it with figs, and fingers, and mice's excrement; 'tis not
a fever, that will go by taking medicine and diet; nor are they
ordinary wounds, that with rags and hypericon-oil may be healed:
because the charm which was on the broken glass has that effect
that an onion-juice hath upon iron, by which the wound is becoming incurable: only one thing would do him good and would save
his life; but ask me not to tell thee, as 'tis something I care for.'

Replied the ghula, 'Tell me, O my love, tell me, or I shall die.'

And the ghul rejoined, 'I will tell thee, but thou must promise
never to reveal it to any one living: because it would be the extinc-
tion of our house, and the ruin of our life.'

Answered the ghula, 'Doubt not, O sweet my husband, O beauty, thou shalt sooner see pigs with horns, and apes with tails, and a mole with eyes, than hear one single word out of my lips.'

And swearing an oath, laying one hand upon the other, the ghul said to her, 'Now thou must know that there is naught upon the face of the earth nor in the heavens that can save the prince from death, but by anointing the wounds with our own fat: that would detain the soul, and hinder it from taking flight, and prevent it from forsaking its home, the body.'

Nella, hearing all this talk, gave time to time, so that they should end their chatting; and coming down the tree, heartened her heart, and knocked at the ghul's door, crying, 'O my lord and lady, be charitable, give me an alms, show a token of mercy, have a little compassion upon a wretched creature, an exile, a miserable being banished and badly used by fortune, far from her country, deprived of all human help; night hath surprised her in this dark forest, and she is dying with hunger.' And she continued knocking. The ghula, hearing the words and the continual tapping, was going to throw her half a loaf out of the window, but the ghul, who was a glutton of human flesh, more than the parrot is of nuts, and the bear of doing evil, and the cat of fishes, and the sheep of salt, and the ass of bran, said to his wife, 'Let her come in, poor thing: if she should sleep outside in the forest some wolf might hurt her'; and he said and argued so much, that his wife opened the door at last; and he, with his hairy charity, meant to make four mouthfuls of her.

But one thing thinketh the glutton, and another account maketh the innkeeper; because after having eaten his sufficiency of the supper they had before them, he drank so much that he fell down drunk; and Nella seeing them both fast asleep, took a knife from a cupboard and slaughtered the ghul, and putting the fat in a pot, fared forth on her way to the court and the king's palace. Straightway she demanded to be led to the presence, and when before the king she offered to heal the prince, the king answered her, 'With joy and good pleasure will I take thee to him,' and at once led her in to his son's chamber. And when she came to the prince's bedside she pulled forth the pot, and anointed the wounds with the grease; and it was no sooner done, than just as if she had thrown water upon the fire, the wounds closed themselves, and he was healed. Which wondrous healing was sighted by the king who, turning to his son, spake thus to him, 'This good lady deserveth well the guerdon promised by the edict, and thou shouldst take her to wife.' The prince hearing these words said, 'Tell her to take somewhat else, as I have not in my body a warehouse of hearts, that I may give out to divers folk; mine is already bespoken by another woman and she is mistress of it.' Nella, hearing these words replied, 'Thou shouldst not remember this woman, who was the cause of all thy misfortune.' Said the prince, 'The evil was done me by her sisters, and they shall pay the forfeit.' Nella rejoined, 'Dost thou love her so well?' and the prince answered, 'More than my life.' 'If this be true,' added Nella, 'embrace me, clasp me to thy breast, as I know the fire of this heart'; but the prince beholding her with such blackened face, answered, 'More likely thou shalt be coals, than fire; therefore stand back, or else thou'lt soil me.' But Nella, perceiving he knew her not, asked for a basin of cold water, and she washed her face, and out of the clouds came forth the sun, and the prince knew her, and clasped her to his breast, anod with great pomp, and festivities, and joy, and enjoyance took her to wife. Then he ordered a fireplace to be built, and the envious sisters to be burnt therein: so that like unto leeches they sould purge their blood in the cinders of their wickedness and envy, thus making come true the proverb, that sayeth,

'No evil deed was ever left unpunished.'

VIOLA

Of the Second Day

VIOLA IS ENVIED BY HER SISTERS, AND AFTER A GREAT MANY TRICKS
PLAYED TO AND RECEIVED FROM A PRINCE IN SPITE OF THEM, BECOMETH
HIS WIFE.

THE preceding story was heard with great satisfaction, and the
hearers blessed the prince who had thus punished the sisters of Nella,
and praised a thousand times the great love of the young girl, who
passed such peril in endeavouring to get the salve to anoint the
prince's wounds; till Prince Thaddeus, having made a sign that
they should all be silent, commanded Meneca to proceed with her
say, and she paid her debt, beginning thus:

Envy is a rushing wind which bloweth with such force that it
knocketh down the props which sustain the glory of a good man,
and scattereth to the winds the seed of his good fortunes. But often
Heaven's just punishment reacheth those whose words are this scath-
ing wind that trieth to throw the good with face upon the ground,
but instead is the cause of their reaching to unexpected felicity: as
ye will perceive in this story that I am going to relate.

Once upon a time there lived a man upright and just, Col' Aniello
hight, and he was blessed with three daughters, Rosa, Garofana, and
Viola: and the youngest of these was very beautiful. She was like
syrup which purged the heart from all its cark and care. And
Ciullone, the king's son, burned with a burning fire for the love
of her, and every time that he passed that way and glanced where
the three sisters sat at work together, he would lift his cap, and say
courteously, 'Good morrow, good morrow, sweet Viola,' and she
would answer, 'Good morrow, O our king's son, I am working more
than thou.' And the other sisters were sore envious, and mur-

mured with each other, and said to her, 'Thou art rude, and thou wilt anger the prince'; but Viola noticed not her sisters' words, rather putting them behind her.

Now her sisters, to spite Viola, went to their father, and told him that she was a bold and brazen-faced hussy, who answered pertly to the prince, just as if he were her equal, and one of these days she would be punished, and the just would suffer for the guilty. Col' Aniello, being a wise and good man, sent Viola to stay at the house of her aunt, Cuccepannella hight, bidding her to set his daughter some work to do. Meanwhile the prince tarried every day before the house of his dove, and seeing naught of his heart's desire, passed the days as a nightingale who hath lost her little ones' nest, flying from bough to bough, wofully lamenting. And he pried, and listened, and watched, and looked through keyholes, till at last he knew where they had sent her, and he journeyed to the aunt, and when he reached her house he said to her, 'Dear madam, thou knowest who I am, and if I can do somewhat, and if I am worth somewhat; and all must be between me and thee, and thou must be silent and dumb; thou must do me a favour, and then thou mayest ask of me as much money as thou wilt.' Answered the old woman, 'In all that I can, I am at thy service, command thou me and I will obey'; and the prince, 'I want naught of thee, but only that thou allow me once to kiss sweet Viola, and thou mayest take this money.' And replied the old woman, 'So that I may be of service to thee, I can do naught else than hold the clothes for the bathers: but I may not allow that her innocence be defiled, or the pitcher's handle be broken, or that I hold hand to this infamy, so that my old age be disgraced; nor will I hold the title of the apprentice of a smith who worketh the bellows; but whatever I can do to please thee I will do. Go and hide thyself in the chimney of the little summer-house in the garden, where with some excuse I will send Viola, and as thou wilt hend in hand the cloth and the scissors, if thou do not know how to use of it the fault will be thine.'

The prince, hearing her rede, without any loss of time hid himself in the summer-house, and the old woman pretending that she wanted to cut out some cloth, said to her niece, 'O Viola, go, an thou lovest me, to the garden summer-house, and bring the measure;' and Viola entering the room to obey her aunt's desire, perceived the ambush, and quick as a cat jumped out of the room, leaving the prince heart-sore, and with a lengthened nose for very shame. And the old woman, when she saw Viola coming in such haste, suspected that the prince's ruse had not succeeded, and a little while after said to the girl, 'Go, O my niece, to the summer-house, and bring that ball of thread that thou wilt find upon the table'; and Viola ran to do her aunt's bidding, and slipped like an eel from the prince's grasp. But in a little while the old woman again said to her, 'My sweet Viola, if thou do not go and fetch me the scissors, I shall be ruined;' and Viola went down for the third time, but being quick as a dog, escaped again, and going upstairs, cut her aunt's ears with the same scissors she had brought, saying: 'Here is a good gift to thee for thy romancing: every kind of work hath its reward: a sliding of honour bringeth a loss of ears. I have a mind to cut off thy nose also, but that wouldst smell not the stink of thine own bad fame. Thou bawd, pimp, chickens-carrier, thou canst eat: eat an thou canst, corruption of children.' And leaving her in bad plight, in three minutes was at her own house, leaving her aunt without ears, and the prince full of cark and care.

In a day or two he once more began walking in front of her father's house, and beholding her seated in the same place where she used to work, he began to address her as before, 'Good morrow, good morrow, sweet Viola,' and she at once like a good deacon answered, 'Good morrow, O our king's son, I know more than thou;' but the sisters could not bear to hear this music, and desiring to get rid of her, they canfabulated together how they should best accomplish their purpose; and they bethought themselves of a window in their house which overlooked upon a ghul's garden, and they agreed one with the other that this would be the best means to rid themselves of this hated sister. Therefore, dropping a skain of silk out of this window, with which they were working a piece of tapestry for the queen, they cried out, 'O woe unto us, we are ruined, we will not be able to finish the work in time, if Viola will not help us; she is the youngest and lightest of us, and if she will let us tie a rope round her waist and lower her down, she will be able to pick up the silk.' And Viola, not desiring to see them so sorrowful, offered to descend, and they tied a rope round her, and lowered her down, and then let go the rope.

At the same time entered the ghul for a view of the garden, and the ground being damp he had taken a bad cold and sneezed, and in sneezing he let go wind, so powerful and strong that it sounded like thunder, and Viola, hearing it, screamed with fright, 'O mother mine, help me!' And the ghul, hearing the scream, turned round, and beheld the beauteous child behind him, and remembering that once he had heard a clever student say that the Spanish mares became with foal by the wind, bethought himself that maybe his wind had filled a tree and out of it had come this beautiful child: therefore embracing her with great love he said to her,

'O my daughter, part of this my body, breath of my breath, soul of my soul, who could have told me that a wind could have given life to such a beauteous creature? who could have told me that an effect of a cold would have brought forth such fire of love?' And saying these words, and others of more tender import, he led her to his palace, where he consigned her to three fairies, and bade them take care of her, and entreat her kindly, and give her the best of all things. Such was her case. But the prince who could see nothing of his love, and could hear naught concerning her, neither new nor old, was sorely stricken, and his eyes were swollen for so much weeping, and his face was discoloured, and his lips were whitened, and he could take no food, and his sleep was lost, and he could find no peace. And he searched everywhere, and promised rewards, and sent many of his followers in quest of her, until at last it came to his ears where she dwelt, and sending for the ghul, he said to him, 'I am very ill, as thou canst perceive, and I would ask of thy favour to allow me to dwell for one single day and night in thy garden, as in this chamber I feel suffocating, and I should like to come there to cheer my spirit.' The ghul, being a good liege unto the king, could

not deny the prince so small a favour, and offered him the use of all
his palace if one room did not suffice, and said he would lay down
his life in his service.   The prince thanked him, and was at once
conducted to the ghul's palace, and a chamber was assigned to him
next to the ghul's, where Viola slept in the same bed with him.
And when night came forth to play with the stars the game of
drawing the curtain, the prince finding the door of the ghul's chamber open, it being summer and the heat very excessive, and the ghul
liking to have the fresh air, feeling he was in a safe place he entered
very quietly therein, and going to the side where Viola slept, he
gave her two pinches, and she woke up in affright and cried out,
'O papa, we are full of fleas': and the ghul at once changed place
with his daughter, and sent her into another bed, and when once
more she slept, the prince did the same as before.   And Viola cried
in the same way, and the ghul bade the servants change her bed-
linen and her mattress, and all the night was spent in this traffic,
till with the dawn, the sun finding himself alive came forth, and
the sky shook off its mourning garment.   But as soon as it was day,
the prince walked about in the palace and gardens, and saw Viola
standing at the gate, and said to her as usual, 'Good morrow, good
morrow, sweet Viola;' and she replied, 'Good morrow, O our king's
son, I am working more than thou'; and answered the prince, 'O
papa, we are full of fleas.'

As soon as Viola heard these words, she understood that all the
upset of the night had been a trick played her by the prince, yet she
said naught to him, but went to pay a visit to the fairies, and told
them what had come to pass.   Said the fairies, 'If he hath done this,
we will treat him as a corsair treateth a corsair, and a sailor a galley-
slave; and if this dog hath bitten thee, we will try to get his fur;
he hath played thee a trick, and we will play him a trick and a half:
tell the ghul to make thee a pair of slippers covered with tiny bells,
and after leave all to us, as we will pay him in good coin.'   Viola,
desirous of avenging herself, told the ghul at once to get her these
slippers, and awaiting until the heavens, like unto a Genoese woman,
apparelled themselves with a black veil upon their face, all four

made their way to the prince's palace, where Viola with the fairies entered unseen into his chamber. And as soon as the prince tried to sleep, the fairies made a great noise, and Viola stamped with her feet, and the noise of her heels upon the floor, and the tiny bells ringing, awakened the prince, and he started up in affright, and cried out, 'O mother mine, help me!' and the same was done three times, whereafter Viola and the fairies retired to their home.

Now in the morning the prince was obliged to take lemonade and other drinks to allay his fright, but as usual he made his morning walk, and beholding Viola standing at the gate, since he could not live without a sight of that Viola who so greatly excited his flesh, he said, 'Good morrow, good morrow, sweet Viola;' and Viola replied, 'Good morrow, O king's son, I am doing more than thou;' and the prince said, 'O papa, how full of fleas we are;' and she rejoined, 'O mother mine, help me!' and the prince hearing these words, said, 'Thou hast played me a good trick, thou hast won, I give in, and seeing that in reality thou knowest more than I I will have thee for my wife;' therefore, sending for the ghul, he asked him to give her to him in marriage. The ghul, not desiring to put his hand on other people's property, as in the morning it had come to his knowledge that Viola was the daughter of Col' Aniello, and that his back eye had been deceived to think that this sweetly scented being could be the offspring of a stinking wind, sent for her father, and telling him of her good fortune, with great feasting and enjoyance the prince took Viola to wife, and thus came the proverb true that

'A beauteous girl is married even in the market-place.'

GAGLIUSO

Of the Second Day

GAGLIUSO, HAVING BEEN ABANDONED BY HIS FATHER, BY A CAT'S INDUS-
TRY BECOMETH RICH; BUT SHOWING HIMSELF INSENSIBLE THEREOF, IS
REPROACHED WITH HIS INGRATITUDE.

ALL hearers were delighted to know of the good fortune of
Viola, who by her own hands had thus built a high position in spite
of the envy of her sisters, who were foes to their own flesh and
blood, and had tried in so many ways to bring her to grief; but it
was time that Paola should begin her story, paying from her lips the
golden coins of good words, and thus she discharged her debt:

Ingratitude is a rusty nail, which, nailed to the bark of a tree,
causeth the tree to wither and die; 'tis a broken sink, which soak-
eth up all troubles and afflictions; 'tis a spider's web, which falling
in the pot of friendship, maketh it lose its scent and flavour, as is
seen daily, and as ye will hear in this story which I will relate.
There once lived in the city of Naples a miserly old man, thin, and
tall, and ragged, and tattered, and withered, and wrinkled, so that
he went about as nearly naked as a flea. And as he had reached the
time when the sacks of life are shaken, he called to his side Oraziello
and Pippo his two sons, and said to them, 'I have been sent for to
pay the debt that we all owe to Nature, and believe me, O my
sons, that I would feel most happy to exit from this world of
trouble, this hovel of travail, but for the thought that I leave you,
grown tall and strong as Santa Clara and the five roads of Melito,
without a single coat to your backs, like a barber's basin; sharp as
a drilling sergeant, and dry as a plum-stone; ye are worth not even
as much as a fly would carry tied at its foot; an if we were to run
an hundred miles, ye would not drop a mite: and all this because my

ill-luck brought me all my life where the curs crap; but as thou beholdest, thus thou mayst paint me, and as ye know, I have done many things; and many times I have crossed me, and have gone to bed without cinnamon to my wine; but notwithstanding all this, I desire to leave ye somewhat at my death in sign of my love, therefore, thou Oraziello, who art my first born, take that sieve which thou seest hanging upon the wall, with which thou mayest gain the wherewithal to keep life in thee; and thou Pippo, who are the youngest, take thou the cat, and may both of ye remember your father.' And thus having ended his say, he wept with bitter weeping, and his sons wept with him, and straightway he spake again, and said, 'Adieu, 'tis night,' and died.

Now after Oraziello had had him laid out and buried for charity, he took the sieve, and went about sifting to gain a livelihood: and the more he sifted the more he gained. Pippo, taking the cat with him, said, 'Now behold, what heritage hath my father left me? I have naught to eat for myself, and I will have to think for two. What an heritage is mine! who ever heard of such a gift? Far better had he left me nothing.' But the cat, hearing this repining, said to him, 'Thy lamenting is needless, for thou art the most fortunate: but thou knowest not thine own good fortune, and I shall enrich thee, an I begin my doings.' Pippo, hearing this, thanked the cat, and smoothing her upon the back three or four times, recommended himself to her charge; and the cat feeling great compassion for the sad hearted Gagliuso,* every morning when the sun with his bait of light and gold fisheth the shadows of the night, made her way to the sea-shore at Chiaja, and watching for an opportunity of catching a large gold-fish, she would take it and carry it to the king, saying, 'My Lord Gagliuso, a slave of your highness and a loyal liege, sendeth this fish with his humble greetings, saying, "To a great lord small is the gift."' The king, with a smiling countenance, which he generally wears to those who bring him presents, answered the cat, 'Say to this lord, whom I know not, that I thank him.' Another

* Youngster.

time the cat would run to some marshy ground where the hunters had let fall some pheasants, or wild ducks, or partridges, when she would lift them up, and take them to the king with the same embassy, and for many a day she continued so doing, till one morning the king said to her, 'I feel myself under deep obligation to this thy lord Gagliuso, and I should like to make his acquaintance, so that I may thank him for his offerings, and give him in proof of my gratitude, and do somewhat for him in exchange.' Answered the cat, ' 'Tis the desire of my lord Gagliuso to lay down his life for the weal of thy realm and thy crown, and to-morrow morning unfailingly, when the sun shall have set fire to the ricks of straw in the fields, he will stand before thee to do obeisance.'

Now when the morning came, puss came to the king, and said, 'O my lord, the lord Gagliuso sendeth thee greetings, and wouldst thou excuse him for not coming this morning, as last night some of his varlets took to their heels, carrying with them all my master's wardrobe, and have left him without even a shirt to his back.' The king hearing this, sent to his master of the robes, and ordered that he should forward at once some of his own raiments for the lord Gagliuso.

In two hours' time Gagliuso came to the palace, guided by the cat, and when he stood in the royal presence, the king thanked and complimented him, and made him sit by his side, and then led him to the banquet-hall, where the tables were spread with dainties, and whilst they ate, Gagliuso turned round, and said to the cat, 'O pussy mine, I pray thee watch over those few rags, that they should not go a bad way;' and the cat replied, 'Be silent, hold thy tongue, and speak not of these beggarly objects;' and the king desiring to know what he wanted, the cat answered that he longed for a small lemon; and the king sent at once to the garden to fetch a basketful. Shortly after Gagliuso returned to the same music about his tatters, and the cat bade him again to shut his mouth; and the king inquiring what he wanted, puss had ready another excuse to remedy the vileness and meanness of Gagliuso.

After they had ended eating, and had chatted upon divers subjects, Gagliuso begged leave to retire, and the cat remained with the king, describing to him the prowess, ability, and just judgment of Gagliuso, and above all his great riches, being master of estates near Rome, in the Campagna, and in Lombardy. Saying that he deserved to mate with a king's daughter: and the king inquired if such could be found: and the cat answered, that no account could be kept of the goods, and properties, and houses, and estates of this very rich lord, and it was unknown how much he possessed. But if the king would send forth some of his officers to inquire beyond his kingdom they might have an idea of what he was worth, for no one was so rich as Gagliuso. The king at once sent for some of his most trusty followers, and bade them inquire concerning him, and they departed taking the cat with them as a guide, and she, excusing herself, saying that she would order some food, forewent them, and no sooner were they outside the kingdom than she ran forward. And as she met many flocks of sheep, and cows, and horses, and pigs, she would say to the shepherds and keepers, 'Ho there, keep your brains clear, as a company of robbers is scouring the country, and if ye desire to escape unscathed, and that respect should be shown to your homes and belongings, when they come nigh, say ye to them that all ye hold belongeth to the lord Gagliuso, and no harm shall befall ye.' And she continued so doing in all the farms whereto she came, so that wherever the king's messengers arrived they found a general accord of music, and all things fell into the same reply, that they belonged to the lord Gagliuso. Till being tired of asking more questions, they returned to the king, telling him wonders upon wonders of the great riches of this lord: and the king, hearing this, promised a good present to the cat, if she would manage to bring about this marriage; and the cat, pretending to go and come backwards and forwards, at last concluded the marriage; and Gagliuso came to court, and the king gave him a rich dowry with his daughter in marriage. After a month of high festivities and joy and enjoyance, Gagliuso told the king that he desired to take his bride to his estates, and the king gave him leave, and accompanied him part of the way, and then bade them adieu. Gagliuso continued his journey to Lombardy, where by puss's advice he bought some lands and a palace, and at once became a baron.

Now Gagliuso, finding himself in so much opulence, thanked the cat with deepest gratitude, saying that he owed her his life, and his happiness, and his greatness, since more good had been wrought by the craft of a cat, than by the genius and wit of his father; therefore she could bid and forbid and do whatsoever she chose with his life and his goods; promising faithfully that even if she died in an hundred years, he would have her embalmed, and enclosed in a golden urn, and kept in his room, so as to have ever before his eyes the memory of all her benefits. The cat, hearing this boast, thought she would put it to the test, and three days after she pretended death, and lay stretched out at full length in the garden; and the wife of Gagliuso beholding this sight, cried, 'O mine husband, what a great misfortune hath happened, the cat is dead.' Answered Gagliuso, 'May every evil go with her, better she than ourselves;' and the wife, 'What shall we do with her?' and he 'Take hold of one leg, and throw her out of the window.' The cat, hearing in what way his gratitude was to be shown when least she expected it, cried out, 'These are the thanks I get for the lice I have cleaned from thy neck? This is thy gratitude for ridding thee of thy rags? This is the reward for my spider-like industry in lifting thee up from the dust, beggar, breeches-tearer: thou wert in rags, and tattered, and torn, and full of lice, thou villain, thou scoundrel. Such is the reward of those that wash the ass's head, accursed be all the good I have done for thee, for thou dost not deserve even that I should spit in thy throat: fine golden urn hadst thou prepared for me; beautiful grave, where thou hadst consigned me! Go and serve thou, work and sweat, to receive such fine reward. O wretched is he, that putteth the pot to the fire in hopes that another may fill it. Spake well that sage who said, Whoso goes to bed an ass, an ass riseth again," and "Whoso doeth most expecteth least." But good words and bad deeds deceive the wise and the foolish.'

And saying thus, she jumped off and took to her heels; and although Gagliuso with sweet talk, and omelette in mouth, tried to smooth down her ruffled fur, all was to no purpose, puss would not come back, but running on without turning her head kept saying,

'God guard thee from the rich man who hath become poor,
And from a beggarly clown enriched by fate.'

THE SERPENT

Of the Second Day

THE KING OF STARZA-LONGA WEDDETH HIS DAUGHTER TO A SERPENT, AND DISCOVERING THE SAME TO BE A HANDSOME YOUTH, HE BURNETH HIS CAST-OFF SKIN. THE SERPENT, ATTEMPTING TO ESCAPE, BREAKETH A WINDOW-FRAME, AND ALSO HIS OWN HEAD. THE KING'S DAUGHTER, WISHING TO FIND MEANS TO HEAL THE YOUTH, LEAVETH HER FATHER'S HOUSE, AND BEING TOLD BY A FOX WITH WHAT REMEDY SHE MIGHT EFFECT THE CURE, MALICIOUSLY KILLETH THE FOX, AND WITH THE BLOOD AND THE BLOOD OF DIVERS BIRDS ANOINTETH THE WOUNDS OF THE YOUTH, WHO BECOMETH HER HUSBAND, HE BEING IN REALITY A PRINCE'S SON.

THE cat was compassionated beyond measure, seeing that she had received such unworthy recompense for her well-doing. But there were those who considered she might have found consolation in the thought that she was not alone; for in these days ingratitude hath become a domestic evil, and hath become quite a common disease, like the French sickness, and the horned evil. And there are many who have made and unmade and lost their fortune, and ruined their lives to serve an ungrateful race, and whilst they think of holding a golden cup in their hand, they find themselves decreed to die in the hospital. Meanwhile Popa had prepared herself to speak, and all present were silent, whilst she began as follows:

Whoso seeketh to know through curiosity other folk's affairs usually droppeth the axe on his own feet: as can be instanced by the King of Starza-longa, who for putting his nose in whatso concerned him not, spoiled his daughter's happiness, and ruined his son-in-law; and attempting to break a head, remained with a broken head himself.

There lived a peasant-woman, who longed sorely to have a son, more than a litigant desireth to win his suit, and the sick a glass of water, and the innkeeper his gain. But no matter how much the husband delved all the night long, he could see no sign of her fertility. One day of the days he fared forth to the foot of a mountain to get a fagot of wood, and in bringing it home he discovered a pretty little serpent among the boughs. At this sight Sapatella (thus was the peasant's wife hight) drew a long sigh, and said, 'Even the serpents have their little ones, but I brought ill-luck with me to this world, I have an useless husband, that although he is a gardener, is not capable to engraft a single tree.' And the serpent answered to these words, 'As thou canst have no children, take me, and thou wilt do a good deed, and wilt find thyself contented, and I will love thee better than mine own mother.' Sapatella, hearing a serpent speak, was frightened with sore affright, but after a little while heartened her heart, and said, 'As thou dost desire it, for the loving words thou hast spoken to me, I am content to accept thee just as if thou wert born out of mine own knee;' and thus, taking the serpent home, she found a hole for him to go into, and fed him of whatsoever she possessed with the greatest affection, so that the serpent grew from day to day. And when he had grown large, he said to Cola-Matteo (thus was the gardener hight), whom he treated as his father, 'O my sire, I desire to be married.' Said Cola-Matteo, 'By thy leave, shall we find another serpent like thee, or shall we mate thee with some other race?' Answered the serpent, 'What are thou saying? wouldst thou mate me with serpents, vipers, and others of this kind? go, thou art verily a foolish fellow, and thou makest of all herbs one bunch. 'Tis my desire to wed the king's daughter, and therefore go thou at once to the king's presence, and ask of him his daughter in marriage and tell him that a serpent desireth to make her his wife.' Cola-Matteo, who was a simpleton, and understood naught of these things, went straightway to the king and delivered his message, saying, 'An ambassador is not punished, else there would be many whose backs would be broken. Thou must know that a serpent desireth to wed thy daughter, therefore I was bidden to come, and try if we can engraft a serpent with a dove.' The king seeing that he had to deal with a simpleton, to get rid of him, replied, 'Go and say to this serpent that, if he will make all the fruit in my garden to become gold, I will give him my daughter in marriage.' And so saying, and laughing in his face, he bade him take his leave.

When Cola-Matteo went home and conveyed this answer to the serpent, he said, 'Go early to-morrow morning, and gather all the stones of fruit that thou wilt find in the city, and throw them about the park, and thou wilt behold pearls threaded in gold.' As soon as the sun with his golden besom swept the dust of the shadows of night from the fields watered by the dawn, Cola-Matteo did as he was bid, without asking questions or contradicting anything, and basket on arm, fared on from market-place to market-place, and gathered the stones of peaches, nectarines, cherries, plums, and whatever he found in the streets; and going to the king's park, sowed them as the serpent had directed him. In no time the trees sprang up, and boughs, leaves, buds, and fruit were all sheening gold, at the sight of which the king marvelled with extreme marvel, and was glad with exceeding gladness. But when Cola-Matteo was sent by the serpent to the king to ask him the fulfilment of his promise, the king said, 'Do not go so fast, I must have another gift from thy master, if he desireth to take my daughter in marriage, and 'tis, that he buildeth all the walls, and the ground of the park, with gems and precious jewels.' And the gardener returned and told this to the serpent, and he said, 'Go to-morrow morning, and gather up all the broken bottles and platters and other earthen wares thou canst find, and throw them about in the paths and on the walls of the park, and thus we will reach the end of this lame intent.' And Cola-Matteo, as soon as the night, after protecting with her gloom all thieves and malefactors, went about gathering the fagots of the twilight of heaven, taking a large basket on his head, began to collect pieces of broken pots, and of ewers' handles, and lids of jugs, and bits of lanterns and of night chamber-pots, and slabs, and handles, and all kinds of broken earthenware. And he did with them as the serpent had told him, and all at once the park walls and paths mantled with emeralds, and carbuncles, and sapphires, and diamonds, and rubies, and amethysts, which shone in the sun with glitter enough to blind the sight; and exceeding marvel struck every heart. Whereat the king remained in an ecstasy of amazement, and could not realise what had befallen him. But when the serpent sent for the third time to ask him to fulfil his promise, the king answered, 'That which he hath already done is naught, if he let not' this my palace become all of gold.'

When Cola-Matteo referred this other caprice of the king to the serpent, he thus replied, 'Go and gather several herbs, and anoint with their juice the foundation of the palace, and thus we will try to satisfy this beggar.' Cola-Matteo, obedient to the serpent's orders, went and gathered tender leaves, small radishes, burnet, porchiacca,* rocket, and charvel, and anointing the foundations of the palace with the juice, behold, it at once glistened with gold enough to enrich a thousand houses beggared by fortune. And the gardener returned to the king with the serpent's message, and seeing there was no escape, and that he must maintain his promise, the king sent for his daughter, Princess Grannonia hight, and said to her, 'O my daughter, I have asked gifts and deeds which seemed impossible to me to attain of one who desireth to become thine husband, and whom I liked not, but he hath fulfilled all that I asked, and now I feel obliged to fulfil my promise, and I beseech thee, O my blessed child, not to refuse, so that I may keep my trust, and to try and be content of whatso Heaven hath sent thee, as I am constrained to do.' Answered the princess, 'Do as it please thee, O my sire, I will not gainsay thy will.' The king, hearing these words, sent to Cola-Matteo to bid the serpent come to the presence; and the serpent, hearing the royal command, mounted a golden car, drawn by four elephants caparisoned in jewels and gold, and came to court. But wherever he passed, all folk fled in wild fear, beholding such a large serpent parading the city in a golden car. And when he arrived at the palace, all the courtiers fled, and not even the scullions remained. And the king and queen fled also, and hid themselves in one of the chambers. Princess Grannonia alone stood firmly awaiting his coming. And the father

---

* 'Porchiacca': *portulæa oleracea.* Herb with thick leaves but small, which no sooner springs forth than it dies. It is used for mixed salad, or fried in oil.

and mother cried out to her, 'Fly, run Grannonia, "save thyself Rienzo,"' but she moved not one step, saying, 'Must I run away from the husband that ye gave me?' But no sooner had the serpent entered the room, than he caught the princess by the waist with his tail, and kissed her many times, whilst the king felt the worms dance in him with fright, and if a leech could have bled him in that moment, no blood would have come forth from his veins. And the serpent led the princess into an inner chamber, and bade her shut the door, and shaking off his skin, became a most handsome youth, with an head covered with golden curls, and eyes which caused a thousand sighs; and embracing his bride, he gathered the first fruits of his love. When the king saw the serpent withdraw into an inner chamber with his daughter, and shut the door after him, he said to the queen, 'Heaven give peace to that good soul of our daughter, surely she is dead by this: and that accursed serpent will have swallowed her up like the yolk of an egg.' And going forward, he put his eye to the key-hole, desiring to know what had become of her; but beholding the grace and beauty and comeliness of the youth, and the serpent's skin thrown off on the floor, the king gave a kick to the door, and both he and his wife entered, and taking the skin, threw it into the fire and burned it.

When the youth saw this, he cried, 'O ye renegade dogs, ye have done for me;' and taking the shape of a pigeon, flew to the window. But the windows being closed, he struck his head against the pane of glass and broke it, and he was sore wounded, so that he had no unhurt place on his head. Grannonia, who had been very happy, and beheld herself deprived of all joy, happy and unhappy, rich and poor at the same moment, beat her breast, and buffeted her face, and wept and lamented with her father and mother, upon the trouble that had come upon her, the poison that had embittered her sweetness, and the change of fortune wrought by those who believed to do her service, but instead had brought her evil. And both excused themselves, saying that they had not meant to do harm.

The princess stayed quietly awaiting till the night came forth to light the torches of the scaffold of heaven for the sun's funeral, when, knowing that the folk slept, she took all jewels and gold which were in her desk, and donning a disguise, fared forth from a secret postern, and thought only of wandering about in search of her lover till she found him. And she issued forth from the city, guided by the moon's rays, and she fared on till she was met by a fox, who asked her if she wished for company; and Grannonia answered, 'It will please me very much, O my gossip, as I know not well this country.' And thus they fared on together till they came to a forest, where the trees, playful as children, had built small houses for the shadows to dwell in. And feeling fatigued of their long walk, and desiring to rest, they retired under the shadows of the trees where a fountain played upon the cool grass; and lying down upon this bed of grass, paid the tribute of rest to nature for the wares of ,life; and they stirred not nor awakened till the sun gave the sign with his burning rays to sailors and couriers that they could proceed on their journey. And when they arose, they still remained in the spot to listen to the warbling of various birds, and Grannonia listened with great enjoyance to their singing, and the fox, seeing her pleasure, said, 'Still more pleased wouldst thou be if thou couldst understand what they are saying, as I understand it.' Grannonia, hearing these words, (for all women are as full of curiosity as they are of chatter) begged the fox to relate to her what she heard in the birds' language. The fox, allowing her to beg and pray for some time, so as to provoke the more her curiosity, to give more importance to what she had to tell, at last said that those birds were talking to each other about a great misfortune that had happened to the king's son, who was a very beautiful and graceful youth, because he would not satisfy the licentious desires of an accursed ghula, who had charmed him and given him the curse that he should be a serpent for seven years. And the time had nearly come to an end, when he had fallen in love with a charming damsel, the daughter of a king, and had asked her in marriage of the king her father; and being one day for the first time in a room with his bride, he had left his skin on the floor, and her father and mother out of curiosity rushed in, and seeing the skin on the ground had burned it, whereupon the prince, taking the shape of a pigeon, tried to escape, and in flying out of a window had broken the pane of glass with his head, and wounded himself sorely, so much so that the doctors despaired for his life. Grannonia, hearing thus her sorrows discussed, inquired whose son this prince was, and if there was any hope or remedy for his sickness. The fox answered that those birds were just saying that his father was the King of Vallone-grosso; and there was no other secret to heal those wounds in his head, so that his soul should not come forth, than to anoint them with the blood of those very birds who had related the story. Grannonia, hearing these words, knelt down before the fox, and besought her to do her this kind deed, and to catch those birds for her, to get their blood, and they would afterwards divide the gain. Said the fox, 'Softly, let us await till night darkeneth and the birds are asleep, let thy mother do her will, I will climb up the tree, and I will slay them one by one.' And they passed the day, talking of the youth's beauty, of the mistake of the king, the bride's father, of the misfortune to the youth. And discussing these matters, the time passed, and earth strewed the black pasteboard to gather in all the wax of the torches of night.

The fox, as soon as she beheld the birds fast asleep upon the boughs, clomb up the tree quite quietly, and slew one by one as many bullfinches, swallows, sparrows, blackbirds, larks, chaffinches, woodcocks, wild fowls, owls, crows, magpies, and flycatchers as were upon the tree, and put their blood in a small juglet, which the fox always carried with her to refresh herself by the way. Grannonia was so overjoyed that her feet scarcely touched ground, but the fox said to her, 'Thy great joy is but a dream, O my daughter, thou hast done naught, if thou hast not also my blood to mix with the birds'; and having said these words, she took to her heels. Grannonia, seeing all her hopes fall to the ground, had recourse to woman's art, which is cunning and flattery, and said, 'O my gossip, O fox mine, thou wouldst do well to save thy skin if I were not so much indebted to thee, and if there were no other foxes in the world. But as thou knowest what I owe thee, and thou knowest also that in these woods there is no lack of thy companions, thou mayest rest assured of my faith, and needest not, like the cow, kick the tub when 'tis full of milk. Thou hast done and undone, and thou wilt lose thyself at thy best: stay; believe me; and accompany me to the city to this king's presence, so that he may buy me for his slave.' The fox, never dreaming that the other was a quintessence of foxery, found a woman more a fox than herself; therefore turning back, she walked with Grannonia. But they had not gone an hundred steps when the princess struck her a blow, with the stick which she carried, upon the head, which forthwith stretched her at her feet, and slaughtering her, at once took her blood, mixing it with that of the birds in the juglet. She fared on till she came to Vallone-grosso, and entering the city, went to the royal palace, and sent word to the king, that she had come to heal the prince. The king sent for her to the presence, and marvelled with exceeding marvel to perceive a young damsel undertake to do that in which the wisest doctors in all his kingdom had failed; but as to try doeth no harm, he said that he wished to see the experiment. But replied Grannonia, 'If I succeed in my endeavour, and thou perceive a beneficial effect of my cure, and I fulfil thy heart's desire, thou must promise to give the prince to me in marriage.' The king, believing that his son would certainly die, answered, 'If thou wilt give him to me free and healthy, I will give him to thee healthy and free, as 'tis not such a great gift to give a husband to whoso giveth me a son.' And going to the prince's chamber, the princess stood by the bedside, and anointed his head with the salve, and no sooner had she done so than he rose up in good health, just as if he had never been ill.

When Grannonia beheld the prince hale and strong once more, she bade the king keep his promise, and the king, turning to his son, 'O my son, I gazed upon thee as one dead, and I see thee alive and can hardly believe it. But I gave a promise to this damsel that, if she healed thee, and I beheld thee in health and strength, thou wouldst become her husband, and now that Heaven hath granted this grace, let me fulfil this promise, an thou lovest me: as it is a debt of gratitude which must be paid.' And the prince replied, 'O my lord, would that I could freely do as thou biddest me, and give thee satisfaction, and proof of the great love which I bear to thee; but I have given my faith to another damsel, and thou wilt not ask me to break my troth; and neither will this damsel advise me to act wrongfully and treacherously to one I love, nor can I change my thoughts.' The princess, hearing the prince's words, felt unspeakable joy not to be described, seeing the remembrance of her so deeply impressed in her lover's heart: and the delicate tint of carmine tinging her cheeks, she said, 'But if I could satisfy this young damsel, beloved by thee, and she would willingly give thee up, wouldst thou still be adverse to my desire?' rejoined the prince, 'It shall never be. I can never chase from my mind the sweet image of my love, and in my breast will I keep her enthroned. Let her love me an she will, or chase me from her presence, I will ever remain with the same longing and desire, the same deep affection, and the same thought, and even if I were in danger to lose my life once more, I would never do such a deed, I will never withdraw my plighted troth.'

Grannonia, being unable to resist any more, threw off her disguise, and discovered herself; and when the secret was out, and the prince recognised her, he took her in his arms in deep joy, telling his sire who the damsel was, and what he had done for her sake; and she related to them also what befell her after he had left her, and how through the fox's rede she had been able to heal the prince. And the king sent for the King and Queen of Starza-longa, and all agreed that the marriage-feast should take place at once, and they rejoiced to think how Grannonia had outwitted the fox, concluding at the last that

> ' To the joy of love
> Grief is ever the sauce.'

THE SHE-BEAR

Of the Second Day

THE KING OF ROCC' ASPRA DESIRETH TO TAKE HIS OWN DAUGHTER TO
WIFE. THE PRINCESS, BY THE CUNNING OF AN OLD WOMAN, CHANGETH
HER SHAPE, AND BECOMETH A SHE-BEAR, AND ESCAPETH FROM HER
FATHER'S PALACE. SHE IS TAKEN HOME BY A PRINCE, WHO ONCE BE-
HOLDETH HER IN HER OWN SHAPE IN THE GARDEN, WHERE SHE IS DRESS-
ING HER HAIR, AND FALLETH DEEPLY IN LOVE WITH HER. AFTER MANY
ADVENTURES SHE DISCOVERETH HERSELF, AND TAKETH HER OWN SHAPE
ONCE MORE, AND BECOMETH THE PRINCE'S WIFE.

ALL enjoyed heartily Popa's story, but when she spake of women's
craft and flattery, which were sufficient to outwit a fox, they laughed
till they fell backwards; and truly women are cunning, and their
craftiness is threaded like beads in every hair of their head. Fraud
is their mother; falsehood their nurse; allurement their teacher;
dissimulation their adviser; deceit their companion: and thus they
can turn man round and round according to their liking. But let
us return to Antonella who was eager to begin her story. She stood
a little while as one in deep thought, and at last thus began her say:

Spake well the sage who said that to a command mixed with gall
cannot be rendered obedience sweet as sugar. Man must require
matters justly ordered and rightly measured, if it be his desire to
meet with justly weighed obedience. From undue commands are
born resistance, and rebellion, and evils which cannot easily be remedied: as happened to the King of Rocc' Aspra, who sought from his
daughter an undue thing, thus causing her flight at the risk of her
life and honour.

Now it is said that once upon a time there lived a king of Rocc'
Aspra, who had a wife who for beauty, and grace, and comeliness
exceeded all other women. Truly she was the mother of beauty,
but this beauteous being, at the full time of her life, fell from the

steed of health, and brake the threads of life. But before the candle of life was finally put out, she called her husband, and said, 'I know well, that thou hast loved me with excessive love, therefore show unto me a proof of thy love and give me a promise that thou wilt never marry, unless thou meetest one beauteous as I have been; and if thou wilt not do so, I will leave thee a curse, and I will hate thee even in the other world.' The king, who loved her above all things, hearing this her last will, began to weep and lament, and for a while could not find a word to say: but after his grief subdued, he replied, 'If I ever think of taking a wife, may the gout seize me, and may I become as gaunt as an asparagus; O my love, forget it, believe not in dreams, or that I can ever put my affection upon another woman. Thou wilt take with thee all my joyance and desire.' And whilst he spake thus, the poor lady, who was at her last, turned up her eyes and stretched her feet.

When the king saw that her soul had taken flight, his eyes became fountains of tears, and he cried with loud cries, and buffeted his face, and wept, and wailed, so that all the courtiers ran to his side, and he continually called upon the name of that good soul, and cursed his fate, which had deprived him of her, and tore his hair, and pulled out his beard, and accused the stars of having sent to him this great misfortune. But he did as others do; pain of elbow and of wife acheth much but doth not last. Two, one in the grave, and other on the knee. Night had not yet come forth in the place of heaven to look about her for the bats, when he began to make counts with his fingers, saying 'My wife is dead, and I am a widower, and sad-hearted without hope of any kind but my only daughter, since she left me. Therefore it will be necessary to find another wife that will bear me a son. But where can I find one? Where can I meet a woman dowered with my wife's beauty, when all other damsels seem witches in my sight? There is the rub! Where shall I find another like unto her? where am I to seek her with the bell, if nature moulded Nardella (whose soul rest in glory), and then brake the mould? Alas! in what labyrinth am I! What a mistake was the promise I made her! But what? I have not seen the wolf yet, and am going to fly: let us seek, let us see, and let us understand. Is it possible, that no other she-ass will be found to stable in Nardella's place? Is it possible that the world will be lost for me? Will there be such a misfortune, that no damsel will shoot, or will the seed be lost?' And thus saying, he commanded the public crier to publish a ban that all the beautiful women in the world should come and undergo the comparison of beauty, that he would take to wife the handsomest of all, and make her a queen of his realm. And these news spread in all parts of the world, and not one of the women in the whole universe failed to come and try this venture, and not even flayed hags stayed behind, they came by the dozen, because, when the point of beauty is touched, there is none who will yield, there is no sea-monster who will give herself up as hideous; each and every boasteth of uncommon beauty; and if an ass speaketh the truth, the mirror is blamed, which reflecteth not the form as it is naturally; 'tis the fault of the quicksilver at the back. And now the land was full of women, and the king ordered that they should all stand in file, and he began to walk up and down, like a sultan when he entereth his harem to choose the best Genoa stone to sharpen his blade damascene. He came and went, up and down, like a monkey who is never still, looking and staring at this one and that one. And one had a crooked brow, another had a long nose, one had a large mouth, and another had thick lips, this one was too tall and gaunt, that other was short and badly formed, this one was too much dressed, another was too slightly robed; the Spaniard pleased him not because of the hue of her skin; the Neapolitan was not to his taste because of the way in which she walked; the German seemed to him too cold and frozen; the French woman too light of brains; the Venetian a spinning-wheel full of flax; and at the last, for one reason and for another he sent them all about their business with one hand in front and another behind. And seeing so many beautiful heads of celery turned to hard roots, having resolved to have his will, he turned to his own daughter, saying, 'What am I seeking about these Marys of Ravenna, if my daughter Preziosa is

made of the same mould like unto her mother? I have this beauteous face at home, and shall I go to the end of the world seeking
it?' And he explained to his daughter his desire, and was severely
reproved and censured by her, as Heaven knoweth. The king waxed
wroth at her censure, and said to her, 'Speak not so loud, and put
thy tongue behind thee, and make up thy mind this evening to be
tied in this matrimonial knot, otherwise the least thing that I will
do to thee is that I will have thine ears cut off.' Preziosa, hearing
this resolve, retired within her chamber, and wept and lamented her
evil fate. And whilst she lay in this plight with such a sorrowful
face, an old woman, who used to bring her unguents, and pomade,
and cosmetics, and salve to anoint herself, came to her, and finding
her in such a plight, looking like one more ready for the other
world than for this, enquired the cause of her distress, and when
the old woman mastered it, she said, 'Be of good cheer, O my
daughter, and despair not, as every evil hath a remedy: death alone
hath no cure. Now hearken to me: when thy sire this evening cometh in to thee, and being an ass, would like to act the stallion, put
thou this piece of wood in thy mouth, when at once thou wilt become a she-bear and then thou canst fly; as he being afraid of thee
will let thee go. And fare thou straight to the forest, where 'twas
written in the book of fate, the day that thou wert born, that thou
shouldst meet thy fortune: and when 'tis thy desire to appear a
woman as thou art and wilt ever be, take out of thy mouth the bit
of wood, and thou wilt return to thy pristine form.' Preziosa
embraced and thanked the old woman, and bidding the servants
give her an apron-full of flour and some slices of ham, sent her
away. And the sun beginning to change his quarters like a bank-
rupt strumpet, the king sent for his minister, and bade him issue
invitations to all the lords and grandees to come to the marriage-
feast. And they all crowded thither. And after spending five or
six hours in high revel, and eating out of measure, the king made
his way to the bed-chamber, and called to the bride to come and
fulfil his desire. But instantly putting the bit of wood in her mouth,
she took the shape of a she-bear, terrible of aspect, and stood before

him. And he, frightened at the sudden change, rolled himself up amongst the mattresses, and did not put forth a finger or an eye until the morning.

Meanwhile Preziosa came forth and fared towards the forest, where the shadows met concocting together how they could annoy the sun, and there she lay in unison and in good fellowship with the other animals. When the day dawned, it was decreed by the Decreer that there should come to that forest the son of the King of Acqua-corrente, and he, sighting the she-bear, was frightened with excessive fear; but the beast came forward, and wagging her tail, walked round him, and put her head under his hand for him to caress her. At this sight, which seemed passing strange to him, he heartened his heart, smoothed its head as he would have done to a dog, and said to it, 'Lie down, down, quiet, quiet, ti ti, good beast;' and seeing the beast was very tame, he took her home with him, commanding his servants to put her in the garden by the side of the royal palace, and there to attend to and feed her well, and treat her as they would his own person, and to take her to such a spot that he might see her from the windows of his palace whenever he had a mind to.

Now it so chanced, one day of the days, that all his people had gone forth on some errand, and the prince being left alone, bethought himself of the bear, and looked out of the window to see her, and at that very moment Preziosa, believing she was utterly alone, had taken out the bit of wood from her mouth, and stood combing her golden hair. The prince, beholding this damsel of passing beauty, marvelled with excessive marvel, and descending the stairs, ran to the garden. But Preziosa, perceiving the ambush, at once put the bit of wood in her mouth, and became a she-bear once more. The prince looked about him, and could not discern what he had seen from above, and not finding what he came to seek, remained sorely disappointed, and was melancholy and sad-hearted, and in a few days was taken with grievous sickness. And he kept repeating, 'O my bear, O my bear.' His mother, hearing this continual cry, imagined that perhaps the bear had bit him or done him some evil, and therefore ordered the servants to slay her. But all the servants loved the beast because it was so very tame, even the stones in the roadway could not help liking her, and they had compassion of and could not endure to slay her; therefore they led her to the forest, and returning to the queen, told her that she was dead. When this deed came to the prince's ear, he acted as a madman, and leaving his bed, ill as he was, was about to make mincemeat of the servants; but when they told him the truth of the affair, he mounted his steed, and searched, and turned backwards and forwards till at length he came to a cave and found the bear. Then he took her, and carried her home with him, and putting her in a chamber, said, 'O thou beauteous morsel fit for kings, why dost thou hide thy passing beauty in a bear's hide? O light of love, why art thou closed in such an hairy lantern? Why hast thou acted thus towards me, is it so that thou mayest see me die a slow death? I am dying of despair, charmed by thy beauteous form, and thou canst see the witness of my words in my failing health and sickening form. I am become skin and bone, and the fever burneth my very marrows, and consumeth me with heart-sore pain: therefore lift thou the veil of that stinking hide, and let me behold once more thy grace and beauty; lift up the leaves from this basket's mouth, and let me take a view of the splendid fruit within; lift thou the tapestry, and allow mine eyes to feast upon the luxury of thy charms. Who hath enclosed in a dreary prison such a glorious work? Who hath enclosed in a leathern casket such a priceless treasure? Let me behold thy passing grace, and take thou in payment all my desires; O my love, only this bear's grease can cure the nervous disease of which I suffer.' But perceiving that his words had no effect, and that all was time lost, he took to his bed, and his illness daily increased, till the doctors despaired of his life. The queen his mother, who had no other love in the world, seated herself at the bedside, and said to him, 'O my son, wherefrom cometh all thy heart-sickness? What is the cause of all this sadness? Thou art young, thou art rich, thou are beloved, thou are great; what dost thou want, O my son? speak, for only a shameful beggar carrieth an empty pocket. Dost thou desire to take a wife, choose thou, and I will bid; take thou, and I will pay; canst thou not see that thy sickness is my sickness? that thy pulse beats in unison with my heart? if thou burnest with fever in thy blood, I burn with fever on the brain. I have no other support for my old age but thou. Therefore, O my son, be cheerful, and cheer my heart, and do not darken this realm, and raze to the ground this house, and bereave thy mother.' The prince hearing these words, said, 'Nothing can cheer me, if I may not see the bear; therefore, as thou desirest to see me in good health again, let her stay in this room, and I do not wish that any other serve me, and make my bed, and cook my meals, if it be not herself, and if what I desire be done, I am sure that I shall be well in a few days.' To the queen it seemed folly for her son to ask that a bear should act as cook and housemaid, and she believed that the prince must be delirious; nevertheless, to please his fancy, she sent for the bear, and when the beast came to the prince's bedside she lifted her paw and felt the invalid's pulse, and the queen smiled at the sight, thinking that by and by the bear would scratch the prince's nose. But the prince spake to the bear, and said, 'O mischievous mine, wilt thou not cook for me, and feed me, and serve me?' And the bear signed yes with her head, showing that she would accept the charge. Then the queen sent for some chickens, and had a fire lit in the fireplace in the same chamber, and had a kettle with boiling water put on the fire. The bear, taking hold of a chicken and scalding it, dexterously plucked off its feathers, and cleaning it, put half of it on the spit, and stewed the other half, and when it was ready, the prince, who could not before eat even sugar, ate it all and licked his fingers. When he had ended his meal, the bear brought him some drink, and handed it so gracefully that the queen kissed her on the head. After this the prince arose, and went to the saloon to receive the doctors, and stood under the touch-stone of their judgment. And the bear at once made the bed, and ran to the garden and gathered a handful of roses and orange-blossoms, and came and strewed them upon it, and she delivered herself so well of her divers duties that the queen said in her mind, 'This bear is worth a treasure, and my son is quite right in being fond of the beast.' And when the prince returned to his chamber, seeing how well the bear had acquitted herself of her duties, it seemed like adding fuel to the fire, and if he consumed himself in a slow fire before, he burned with intense heat now; and he said to the queen, 'O my lady mother, if I give not a kiss to this bear, I shall give up the ghost.' The queen, seeing her son nearly fainting, said to the bear, 'Kiss him, kiss him, O my beauteous bear, leave not this poor my son to die in despair.' Then the bear obediently neared the prince, who taking her cheeks between his fingers, could not leave off kissing her on the lips. Whilst thus engaged, I knew not how, the bit of wood fell from Preziosa's mouth, and she remained in the prince's embrace, the most beauteous and ravishing being in the world; and he strained her to his bosom with tightly clasped arms, and said, 'Thou art caught at last, and thou shalt not escape so easily without a reason.' Preziosa, reddening with the lovely tint of modesty and of shame, the most beautiful of natural beauties, answered, 'I am in thine hands, I recommend to thy loyalty mine honour, and do otherwise as thou wilt.' And the queen enquired who was this charming damsel, and what had caused her to live such a wild life; and she related to them all her misfortunes, and the queen praised her as a good and honoured child, and said to her son that she was well satisfied that he should marry the princess. And the prince, who desired for naught else, plighted his troth at once to her, and both kneeling before the queen received her blessing, and with great feasting the marriage took place: and Preziosa thus measured the truth of human judgment that

    'He who doeth good may good expect.'

THE DOVE

Of the Second Day

A PRINCE, BY A CURSE LAID UPON HIM BY AN OLD WOMAN, PASSETH GREAT
TRAVAIL, AND HIS DISTRESS IS INCREASED BY ANOTHER CURSE LAID UPON
HIM BY A GHULA. AT THE LAST, BY THE INDUSTRY OF THE GHULA'S
DAUGHTER, HE ESCAPETH ALL DANGER, AND THEY ARE MARRIED.

WHEN Antonella had ended her story, it was loudly praised as a
pretty and graceful tale, and of great good example for an honoured child; and Ciulla, whose turn it was to say her say, began
as follows:

Whoso is born a prince should not act as an insolent varlet. A
great man must not set a bad example to those below him, for from
the largest ass doth the smallest learn to eat its fodder. It is not
marvellous that Heaven sendeth travail and trouble in abundance
to those that act not in accordance with their birth and position: as
happened to a prince, who had to bear the horse-worms for having
disgusted an old woman, so that he came nigh unto death with sore
travail.

In days of yore, eight miles' distance from Naples towards Astrune,
there grew a forest of fig-trees and poplar-trees, where the sun's
rays hardly penetrated. In this wood there was an old, half-ruined
house, in which dwelt an old woman, who was as light of teeth as
she was burdened with years, and as highly hunch-backed as she
was low of fortune. She had an hundred wrinkles on her face, but
had naught to fill her wrinkles within, and although her head was
covered with silver, yet not a crown piece or a mite could be found
in her pocket to cheer her spirits, so that she went about the neighbourhood begging for alms to keep life in her. But as purses full
of gold are more willingly and easily given to spies and parasites

than half-pence to worthy and really needy persons, so by walking about all day she could hardly get enough to cook herself a dish of beans, whilst there was such abundance in the country that few houses had a closed tomb. But of a truth to an old pot cometh holes, and God sendeth to a lean horse flies, and to a fallen tree the axe.

Thus it was with the old woman, who one day, after cleansing her beans and putting them into a saucepan, laid the pot upon the window-sill, and went forth to gather a few sticks wherewith to cook them. And as she was going and returning, Nard' Aniello, the king's son, who had gone forth a-hunting, passed before that house, and sighting the pot upon the window-sill, he bethought himself of playing a trick, and calling his followers bade them throw stones at it to see who could fling the straightest and strike it in the centre. Then they began to cast stones at the innocent pot, and at the third or fourth throw the prince caught it in the middle, and broke it to bits.

The old woman, arriving just when this bitter disaster had taken place, began to howl and scream, and cried, 'May the accursed stretch his arm, and may this clodhopper of Foggia boast of his chivalrous deed in thus breaking my pot: may this son of a strumpet break the pot of his own flesh, this rustic who hath sown the seed out of season of these my beans; and if he felt no compassion of my misery and want, he might have had respect for his own interests, and not cast down the shield of his house. Nor let things be cast at the feet which should be carried on the head. But let him go, and I pray Heaven on my knees, and with the deepest feelings of my heart, that he may fall in love with the daughter of some ghula, and that she may twist and drag him about in all ways. May the witches torment him beyond measure, so that he may see himself alive, and yet weep as if he were dead, and finding himself shackled by the daughter's beauty and by the mother's charms, may he never be able to take up his saddle-bags and gang his gait, but be obliged to stay, though he should die a subject and a slave of that hideous harpy, who will bid and forbid, order and command him to serve her in all ways, and make him sweat for the bread he eats, so that he may long for the very beans that he hath thrown away for me.'

The curse of the old woman reached the gates of heaven, although there is an old saw which saith that 'Women's curses are sown to the winds;' and, 'An horse accursed fatteneth and getteth a lustrous coat;' but so many times did she continue her song that before two hours were past, being lost in the intricacies of the forest from the view of his people, the prince met a beauteous damsel, who was gathering herbs and slugs, and in playful tone she kept repeating to the slugs, 'Put out thine horns, so that thy mother may not affront thee, and thou wilt be affronted on the Belvidere, for she will tell thee thou art not her son.' The prince, beholding this casket full of the most precious things of nature, this bank rich with the richest trusts from heaven, this arsenal of all the forces of love, knew not what had happened to him, and from that round crystal face shone glances of bright eyes which cost him a thousand sighs, and his heart took fire in an instant and burned as a conflagration, where were baked the bricks of his designs, with which would be built the house of his hopes. Filadoro (thus was the damsel hight) did not pare medlars, as the prince was an handsome youth, who at once pierced her heart through: so that each to the other sought mercy with their eyes, and where the lips were dumb, the eyes spake volumes, like a gaol trumpet, publishing the secret of the soul. Thus they remained for a time unable to utter a single word. At last the prince, heartening his heart, found voice, and spake thus, 'From which garden hath bloomed forth this flower of beauty? from which heaven hath fallen this dew full of grace? from which mine hath come this priceless treasure? O happy woods, O fortunate wilds, that contain this gem, that with its splendour illumineth love's joyances; O forests and woods, where are cut neither broomsticks, nor guillotine boards, nor gibbet beams, nor night-vase lids, but gates for the temple of beauty, and beams for the house of the Graces, and sticks to form the darts of love.' Replied Filadoro, 'Down with thine hands, O Sir Knight mine, praise not so loud, 'tis

thy merits, and not my virtues, to which this epitaph of commenda-
tion should be spoken: I am a woman who can measure my own
worth, nor need I that another should serve me as foot-measure, but
such as I am, either beauteous or hideous, black or white, stout or
thin, warm or cold, hairy or smooth, fairy, doll, or witch, I am thy
slave, ready to obey thy command, as thy fine and manly figure hath
taken my heart, and thy noble mien hath wounded my body through
and through, and thy slave I shall be now and for ever.' These
were not words, but the sound of the trumpet which called the prince
to take his seat at the table of love's enjoyance, and incited him to
mount steed and fare forth to the battle of love; and perceiving a
finger held out to him in love's cause, he took the hand, and kissed
the ivory palm which held his heart in thrall. At this ceremony
of the prince, Filadoro pulled a face à la marquis, or rather as a
painter's palette, where may be seen mixed the vermilion of shame,
and the cerise of fear, and the green of hope, and the cinoper of
desire. And Nard' Aniello was going to repeat the homage, when
the act was stopped midway, and the words cut short on the lips.
In this darksome life there is no wine without its dregs of disgust,
nor is there soup without the fat of discontent, or the froth of disgrace. Whilst they were at their best enjoyance, behold, Filadoro's
mother appeared on the scene, and she was a ghula of most hideous
appearance. Nature had taken her as a mould of deformity. Her
hair stood on end as a knee-holm broom, and it was not made to
cleanse the houses of spider-webs and dust, but to darken the hearts;
the brow was cut out of Genoa stone fit to sharpen the knife of
fear, which sickened all breasts; the eyes were comets, which caused
by a glance a trembling of the limbs, and tightening of the heart,
and ice upon the spirits, sharpening of arms, and looseness of body;
and she brought terror in her face, fear in her eyes, trembling in her
steps, and threats in her words. Her mouth had tusks like a wild
boar's, and was large as a dog-fish's; she stood as one caught by a
sudden stroke, frothing at the mouth like a mule, and from head to
foot thou couldst behold a distillation of ugliness and an hospital
of crooked limbs. The prince must have worn some amulet of the

story of Mark and Fiorella sewn in his coat's lining to prevent himself from crying aloud in terror: and she, stretching her hand, caught the prince by the collar, and said, 'Lift up thine head, thou court bird, thou iron handle.' Answered Nard' Aniello, 'I am your witness; back, canaille!' and laid his hand on the hilt of his sword like an old wolf, but remained as a sheep when it beholds the wolf, and he could not move one step, nor could he speak one word, and thus was he dragged like an ass by the halter to the ghula's house, and as soon as she arrived, she said to him, 'Mind thou workest well, like unto a dog, if thou wilt not die like unto a hog; and for the first work, mind that thou diggest well, and sow the seed in the extent of this orchard; and be careful, that if I come back this evening, and do not find the work done, I will eat thee;' and bidding her daughter mind the house, she went to gossip with her friends, ghulas who dwelt in the woods.

Nard' Aniello, finding himself in such a bad case, began to water his breast with tears, cursing his fate, which had brought him to this pass. And Filadoro consoled him, saying, to hearten his heart, that she would shed her own blood to help him, and that he should not curse the fortune which had brought him to her house, for she loved him with excessive love; and that he shewed but little appreciation of her affection, by standing so in despair of success. And the prince answered, 'I do not grieve at having dismounted from a steed to mount an ass, nor having changed my royal palace for this hut, the banquets of choicest meats for a piece of black bread, the courtiers and servants for orders to dig myself, the sceptre for the mattock, the pride of being the dread of armies for the shame of beholding myself terrified at an hideous ghula. All mishaps I would esteem as ventures, if thou wouldst cheer me with thy presence and lighten me with thy glance; but what woundeth my heart sorely is that I must dig, and spit in my hands an hundred times, I who scorned to spit even on the ground. And what is worse, I have to do what even a pair of oxen could not do in a day, and if I do not finish the task I shall be eaten for supper by thy mother; yet

I would not feel so much the torment of this body, as being torn away from thy beauteous person.'

So saying he sighed a pipe-full and wept a cask-full of tears; but Filadoro wiped his tears away and said to him, 'O my life, do not think that thou wilt be obliged to work in other ground than the orchard of love, and fear not that my mother will hurt one hair of thy head'; thou hast Filadoro by thee, and doubt not, an if thou know it not, I will make thee acquainted with the knowledge that I am charmed, and I can freeze the water and darken the sun; enough therefore, let us be merry for this evening: all will be found as my mother bade, and no one will be able to say one word.' Nard' Aniello hearing these words, said, 'If thou art a fairy as thou hast said, O beauty of the world, why should we not fly from this country, and I will keep thee, and make thee my queen in my sire's house.' And Filadoro replied, 'This is not the time to act this play, as the stars are not propitious: but shortly these trials will end, and we shall be happy.'

In this and other talk the day was spent, and the ghula returning home, called her daughter from the street, saying, 'Filadoro, put down thine hair'; for as the house had no staircase, she always ascended by her daughter's tresses. As soon as Filadoro heard her mother's voice she lowered her hair out of window, thus laying a golden stair for an iron heart; whereupon the old ghula mounted up quickly, and ran to the orchard, and finding the work done, marvelled with excessive marvel, as it seemed impossible to her that such a delicate youth should have done such a dog's work. But no sooner did the sun appear the next morning to dry his garments of the damp he had taken in the Indian river, than the old ghula again descended, leaving word to Nard' Aniello that he should split till the evening six yards of wood, at four to the piece, which were kept in a large room, and if she found not the work done she would make mince-meat of him, and eat him for breakfast. The unhappy prince hearing this command, nearly died of despair; and Filadoro seeing him in this case, said to him, 'What a crap-breeches thou art, I do believe thou wouldst be afraid of thy own shadow.' Nard'

Aniello answered, 'And does it seem to thee a matter of little import, to split six yards of wood, four to each piece, till the evening? Alas! before long I shall be split in two to fill the guts of that hideous old ghula.' Replied Filadoro, 'Doubt not, without any fatigue on thy part thou shalt find the wood split and well done; and meanwhile be cheerful, and cut not my soul with so many doubts, and fears, and lamentations.'

Now when the sun closed the shop of his radiance, refusing to sell the light to the shadows, behold the old ghula returned, and calling for the usual staircase, mounted quickly, and finding the wood split, she suspected her daughter of playing her some trick. The third day she tried him with a third proof, and bade him cleanse the cistern of a thousand casks of water, as she desired to have it filled afresh: and this work must be done by the evening, otherwise she would make smoked meat of him.

As soon as the ghula went forth, Nard' Aniello began again to weep and lament, and Filadoro, perceiving that each trouble became heavier, and that the old ghula acted as an ass to load the unhappy youth with such a heavy load of misery, said to him, 'Be silent and weep not: now is the time past which sequestered mine art, and before the sun saith his evening prayer, we will leave this house, and bid it good eve; and thus my mother will find the country deserted; and I will come with thee, dead or alive.' The prince, hearing these news, was ready to fly for joy, and embracing Filadoro, said to her, 'Thou art the north wind which speedeth my weary bark, O my soul! Thou art the prop of all my hopes.' Now when evening came, Filadoro delved a passage beneath the orchard, and both came forth and fared on towards Naples. But when they came to the grotto of Pozzuolo, said Nard' Aniello to Filadoro, 'O my love, 'tis not convenient that thou shouldst come to the palace decked in this raiment and on foot, therefore wait thou at this tavern, till I return with carriage and horses, and followers and servants, and bring thee fit raiment wherewith to array thyself.' And leaving Filadoro, he made his way to the city. Such was their case.

In the meantime the ghula, when 'twas night, returned home, and

Filadoro not answering at her usual call, she waxed suspicious, and ran to the forest, and making a kind of ladder leaned it against the window, and thus climbing like a cat, went in through the window, and searching inside and out, up and down, high and low, and finding no one, she went to the orchard and espied the passage, and passing through it found that it led to the road going city-wards, and she tore her hair, and buffeted her face, and cursed her daughter and the prince, and prayed Heaven that at first kiss that her lover should receive, he would forget her. Such was her case.

But let us. leave the ghula to say her wild pater nosters, and return to the prince, who as soon as he reached the palace, where they believed him dead, was met by a thousand welcomes, and all the household ran to meet him, crying, 'Here he is safe,' 'Welcome our lord,' 'Thou art well come,' 'How handsome he looks, come back to our country;' and an hundred more endearing terms: and mounting the stairs, he was met at the top by his mother, who embraced and kissed him, saying, 'O my son, O my jewel, O pupil of mine eyes, and where hast thou been, why didst thou delay, causing all such cark and care?' The prince knew not what to answer, as he would have to relate his misadventures, but no sooner had he kissed his mother, than, by the curse of the ghula, all that he had passed went from his memory. Then the queen said to him that to make him forsake this taste for hunting and consuming his life about the wilds and wolds she would give unto him a wife. And the prince replied, 'So be it, here am I ready, and prepared to do whatever my lady mother should desire.' Rejoined the queen, "Tis thus that blessed obedient children act.' And she appointed to bring to the palace the bride in about four days, she having made choice of a lady high in rank and degree, who had come from Sciannena to that city. And great feasting and banquets were ordered by royal mandate.

Meanwhile Filadoro, perceiving that her husband tarried too long, and somewhat of this feasting coming to her ears, watched for the innkeeper's boy, and when she saw him asleep, she took his clothes, which he had laid by the bedside, and disguised herself, and fared city-wards to the royal palace. There the cooks, being in want of help, engaged her as scullion. And the morning appointed for the meeting arose, when the sun showeth upon heaven's bank the privileges of nature sealed by the light, and selleth secrets to clear the sight, and the bride came accompanied by a band of fifes and horns. The tables were spread, and all the grandees and nobles took their places, and the wines went round, and choice dainties were brought. At last the carver carved a large English pasty which had been concocted by Filadoro's own hands, and out of the pasty flew a beautiful dove, and all the guests forgot to eat, and marvelled with exceeding marvel, and gazed at this beauteous bird; and the dove began to say in a sweet pitiful voice, 'Hast thou eaten some cat's brains, O prince, that thou hast forgotten all the love and affection of Filadoro? Dost not remember the services thou didst receive, O thou ingrate? Is it thus thou payest all benefits by thee received? What hath she done to thee, O thou ingrate? She saved thee from the ghula's wrath, she gave thee life, and she gave herself to thee; and is this the recompense thou hast mated to the unhappy child for the great love she bore thee? Say me, is it to be given once, and then to be easily withdrawn? Tell her to feed on this bone until cometh the roast meat: oh, wretched the woman that believeth men's words, they carry in their words direst ingratitude, and to benefits are most unthankful, and of their debts are most forgetful. Behold this unhappy child who thought to cook the pasty with thee, and now she findeth herself divided from thy home; she believed that she would be tied with thee in a knot, and thou instead hast taken to thy heels. She thought of breaking a glass with thee, and now the night-vase is broken. Go thy ways and never mind, thou face of a debt-denier, and may all the curses of that wretched damsel light upon thine head. Thou shalt in time perceive of what account it is to deceive a child, to rail at a damsel, to hoodwink an innocent being doing so fine a deed, putting her behind thee whilst she carried thee on the head; and whilst she served thee so well, thou hast put her where clysters are made. But if Heaven hath not blindfolded its eyes, and if the gods have not stopped their ears, they will see the wrong thou hast done, and when least thou expectest it, the eve and the feast will overtake thee, the lightning and the thunder, the fever and the dysentery. Enough! eat well, enjoy thyself, dance and triumph with thy new bride; whilst the unhappy Filadoro, dying by slow degrees, will leave thee an open field to enjoy thy new wife.' And ending these words, the dove flew out of the window, and was lost to sight.

The prince hearing this long homily preached by the dove, stood wonderstruck: at last he found voice to enquire whence had that pasty come, and who had concocted it, and the carver told him that it had been made by a scullion boy, who had been engaged for the occasion. The prince bade them send him to his presence, and when he came he threw himself at Nard' Aniello's feet, and weeping a torrent of tears, he kept repeating, 'What have I done to thee?' whereupon the prince, struck by Filadoro's great beauty, broke the charm of the ghula's curse, and remembered all that had passed, and his promise and obligation to the court of love: therefore he bade her arise, and seated her by his side. And when he related to the queen the great debt he owed to this beauteous damsel, and all she had done for him, and the promise he had given her, and how it was right it should be fulfilled, his mother, who had no other idol than this son, whom she loved with passing love, said, 'Do as thou wilt, enough that the honour and good taste of this lady whom thou wert going to espouse should not be disgraced.' Said the whilom bride, 'Be not troubled about me, for to speak the truth, I would not willingly stay in this country; and as Heaven hath protected me, I, by your leave, desire to return to Sciannena mine, where I will find the fathers of the glasses which are used in Naples, where, thinking to light a lamp in rightful way, I had nearly extinguished the lantern of my life.' The prince with great joy thanked her, and offered a well-manned vessel for her service, and followers to accompany her to her country, and sending Filadoro to his mother's chamber, bade them array her as a princess, and the banquet continued, and when all had eaten their fill the tables were cleared, and the dancing began, and lasted till evening. And the earth being covered in mourning for the funeral rites of the sun, torches were brought and all the palace illuminated, but behold, a great noise of bells was heard on the stairs; whereat the prince said to his mother, 'This must be an improvised masquerade to honour my bridal feast, truly the Neapolitan cavaliers are very accomplished, and where it is needed they know how to use well cooked meats and raw ones also.' But whilst they thus discoursed, amidst the saloon appeared an hideous mask, which hardly stood three feet high, but it was larger than a cask in diameter, and it came forward and stood before the prince, and said, 'Know Nard' Aniello, that the stones, and thy unworthy behaviour, have brought thy misfortunes upon thine head. I am the ghost of the old woman whose pot thou didst break, and through thy deed I died from hunger; I cursed thee, so that thou shouldest fall into the ghula's hands, and my prayers were heard. But by the strength of this beauteous fairy thou didst escape from thy travails, but the ghula gave thee another curse, and it was, that at the first kiss which thou shouldst receive thou shouldst forget Filadoro: thy mother kissed thee, and Filadoro was forgotten. And now I curse thee again, that in remembrance of the damage thou didst to me, mayest thou ever have before thee the beans which thou threwest away for me, and may the proverb come true in thy case, that "Whoso soweth beans, gathereth horns." ' And having spoken thus, she disappeared like quicksilver, not leaving even smoke behind.

The fairy, beholding the prince, whose colour had yellowed at those words, cheered him, saying, 'Doubt not, O my husband, if 'tis sorcery 'twill not have strength; for I will withdraw thee from the fire.' And the festival being ended, they retired to their chamber, and went to bed in confirmation of the faith they had sworn, they being both witnesses of past travails which made all the sweeter the present joys, thus seeing in the crucible of this world's success that

> ' Whoso slippeth and falleth not
> Forward fareth in his way.'

THE YOUNG SLAVE

EIGHTH DIVERSION

Of the Second Day

LISA BORN FROM A ROSE-LEAF, AND DIETH THROUGH A FAIRY'S CURSE;
HER MOTHER LAYETH HER IN A CHAMBER AND BIDDETH HER BROTHER
NOT TO OPEN THE DOOR. BUT HIS WIFE BEING VERY JEALOUS, WISHING
TO SEE WHAT IS SHUT THEREIN, OPENETH THE DOOR, AND FINDETH LISA
WELL AND ALIVE, AND ATTIRING HER IN SLAVE RAIMENTS, TREATETH HER
WITH CRUELTY. LISA BEING AT LAST RECOGNISED BY HER UNCLE, HE
SENDETH HIS WIFE HOME TO HER RELATIONS, AND GIVETH HIS NIECE
IN MARRIAGE.

'In very sooth,' said the prince, 'every man ought to work at his own craft, the lord as lord, the groom as groom, and the constable as constable; and as a beggar-boy becometh ridiculous when he taketh upon himself the mien and airs of a prince, so it is with the prince who will play the beggar-boy:' and turning to Paola, he added, 'Begin thy say;' and she, sucking her lips and scratching her head, began to relate:

Jealousy is a fearful malady, and (sooth to say) 'tis a vertigo which turneth the brain, a fever burning in the veins, an accident, a sudden blow which paralyseth the limbs, a dysentery which looseneth the body, a sickness which robbeth ye of sleep, embittereth all food, cloudeth all peace, shorteneth our days: 'tis a viper which biteth, a moth which gnaweth, gall which embittereth, snow which freezeth, a nail which boreth you, a separator of all love's enjoyments, a divider of matrimony, a dog causing disunion to all love's felicity: 'tis a continual torpedo in the sea of Venus' pleasures, which never doeth a right or good deed: as ye will all confess with your own tongues on hearing the story which follows.

In days of yore, and in times long gone before, there lived a baron of Serva-scura, and he had a young sister, a damsel of uncommon beauty, who often fared to the gardens in company of other young damsels of her age. One day of the days they went as usual, and beheld a rose-tree which had a beautiful fully-opened rose upon it, and they agreed to wager that whosoever should jump clear above the tree without damaging the rose would win so much. Then the damsels began to jump one after the other, but none could clear the tree; till it coming to Cilla's turn (thus was the baron's sister hight), she took a little longer distance, and ran quickly, and jumped, and cleared the tree without touching the rose, and only a single leaf fell to the ground. She quickly picked it up, and swallowed it before any of the others perceived aught, and thus won the wager.

Three days had hardly passed, when she felt that she was with child, and finding that such was the case she nearly died with grief, well wotting that she had done naught to bring such a catastrophe upon her, and she could not suppose in any way how this had occurred. Therefore she ran to the house of some fairies, her friends, and relating to them her case, they told her that there was no doubt but that she was with child of the leaf she had swallowed. Cilla hearing this hid her state as long as it was possible, but the time came at length for her delivery, and she gave birth secretly to a beauteous woman-child, her face like a moon in her fourteenth night, and she named her Lisa, and sent her to the fairies to be brought up. Now each of the fairies gave to the child a charm; but the last of them, wanting to run and see her, in so doing twisted the foot, and for the anguish of pain she felt cursed her, saying that when she should reach her seventh year, her mother in combing her hair would forget the comb sticking in the hair on her head, and this would cause her to die. And years went by till the time came, and the mishap took place, and the wretched mother was in despair at this great misfortune, and after weeping and wailing, ordered seven crystal chests one within the other, and had her child put within them, and then the chest was laid in a distant chamber in the palace; and she kept the key in her pocket. But daily after this her health failed, her cark and care bringing her to the last step of her life; and when she felt her end drawing near, she sent for her brother, and said to him, 'O my brother, I feel death slowly and surely come upon me, therefore I leave to thee all my belongings. Be thou the only lord and master; only must thou take a solemn oath that thou wilt never open the furtherest chamber in this palace, of which I consign to thee the key, which thou wilt keep within thy desk.' Her brother, who loved her dearly, gave her the required promise, and she bade him farewell and died.

After a year had passed the baron took to himself a wife, and being one day invited to a hunt by some of his friends, he gave the palace in charge to his wife, begging her not to open the forbidden chamber, whose key was in his desk. But no sooner had he left the palace than dire suspicion entered in her mind, and turned by jealousy, and fired by curiosity (the first dower of womankind), she took the key, and opened the door, and beheld the seven crystal chests, through which she could perceive a beauteous child, lying as it were in a deep sleep. And she had grown as any other child of her age would, and the chests had lengthened with her. The jealous woman, sighting this charming creature, cried, 'Bravo my priest; key in waistband, and ram within; this is the reason why I was so earnestly begged not to open this door, so that I should not behold Mohammed, whom he worshippeth within these chests.' Thus saying, she pulled her out by the hair of her head; and whilst so doing the comb which her mother had left on her head fell off, and she came again to life, and cried out, 'O mother mine, O mother mine.' Answered the baroness, 'I'll give thee mamma and papa;' and embittered as a slave, and an-angered as a bitch keeping watch on her young, and with poison full as an asp, she at once cut off the damsel's hair, and gave her a good drubbing, and arrayed her in rags. Every day she beat her on her head, and gave her black eyes, and scratched her face and made her mouth to bleed just as if she had eaten raw pigeons. But when her husband came back and saw this child so badly treated, he asked the reason of such cruelty; and she answered that she was a slave-girl sent her by her aunt, so wicked and perverse that it was necessary to beat her

so as to keep her in order.   After a time the baron had occasion to
go to a country-fair, and he, being a very noble and kind-hearted
lord, asked of all his household people from the highest to the lowest
not leaving out even the cats, what thing they would like him to
bring for them, and one bade him buy one thing, and another
another, till at the last he came to the young slave-girl.   But his
wife did not act as a Christian should, and said, 'Put this slave in
the dozen, and let us do all things within the rule, as we all should
like to make water in the same pot; leave her alone and let us not
fill her with presumption.'   But the lord, being by nature kind,
would ask the young slave what she should like him to bring her,
and she replied, 'I should like to have a doll, a knife, and some
pumice-stone: and if thou shouldst forget it, mayest thou be unable
to pass the river which will be in thy way.'   And the baron fared
forth, and bought all the gifts he had promised to bring, but he
forgot that which his niece had bade him bring; and when the lord
on his way home came to the river, the river threw up stones, and
carried away the trees from the mountain to the shore, and thus cast
the basis of fear, and unlifted the wall of wonderment, so that it
was impossible for the lord to pass that way; and he at last remembered the curse of the young slave, and turning back, bought her
the three things, and then returned home, and gave to each the gifts
he had brought.   And he gave to Lisa also what pertained to her.
As soon as she had her gifts in her possession, she retired in the
kitchen, and putting the doll before her, she began to weep, and
wail, and lament, telling that inanimate piece of wood the story of
her travails, speaking as she would have done to a living being; and
perceiving that the doll answered not, she took up the knife and
sharpening it on the pumice-stone, said, 'If thou wilt not answer
me, I shall kill myself, and thus will end the feast;' and the doll
swelled up as a bag-pipe, and at last answered, 'Yes, I did hear
thee, I am not deaf.'

Now this went on for several days, till one day the baron, who
had one of his portraits hung up near the kitchen, heard all this
weeping and talking of the young slave-girl, and wanting to see to

whom she spake, he put his eye to the key-hole, and beheld Lisa with the doll before her, to whom she related how her mother had jumped over the rose-tree, how she had swallowed the leaf, how herself had been born, how the fairies had each given her a charm, how the youngest fairy had cursed her, how the comb had been left on her head by her mother, how she had been put within seven crystal chests and shut up in a distant chamber, how her mother had died, and how she had left the key to her brother. Then she spoke of his going a-hunting, and the wife's jealousy, how she disobeyed her husband's behest and entered within the chamber, and how she had cut her hair, and how she treated her like a slave and beat her cruelly, and she wept and lamented saying, 'Answer me, O my doll: if not, I shall kill myself with this knife;' and sharpening it on the pumice-stone, she was going to slay herself, when the baron kicked down the door, and snatched the knife out of her hands, and bade her relate to him the story. When she had ended, he embraced her as his own niece, and led her out of his palace to the house of a relative, where he commanded that she should be well entreated so that she should become cheerful in mind and healthy of body, as owing to the ill-treatment she had endured she had lost all strength and healthful hue. And Lisa, receiving kindly treatment, in a few months became as beautiful as a goddess, and her uncle sent for her to come to his palace, and gave a great banquet in her honour, and presented her to his guests as his niece, and bade Lisa relate to them the story of her past troubles. Hearing the cruelty with which she had been entreated by his wife, all the guests wept. And he bade his wife return to her family, as for her jealousy and unseemly behaviour she was not worthy to be his mate; and after a time gave to his niece a handsome and worthy husband whom she loved: which touched the level that

> 'When a man least goods of any kind expecteth,
> The heavens will pour upon him every grace.'

THE PADLOCK

Of the Second Day

LUCIELLA GOETH TO THE FOUNTAIN TO DRAW SOME WATER, AND MEETETH
THERE A SLAVE, WHO TAKETH HER TO A SPLENDID PALACE, WHERE SHE
IS ENTREATED LIKE A QUEEN. BY HER ENVIOUS SISTERS SHE IS AD-
VISED TO LOOK WITH WHOM SHE SLEEPETH AT NIGHT. SHE DOETH AS
SHE IS BID, AND FINDETH THAT HER COMPANION IS A HANDSOME YOUTH,
BUT SHE LOSETH HIS GRACE AND IS EXPELLED FROM THE PALACE. SHE
WANDERETH ABOUT THE WORLD, BUT AT LAST BEING BIG WITH CHILD,
SHE REACHETH, UNKNOWN TO HER, THE HOUSE OF HER LOVER, WHERE
SHE IS BROUGHT TO BED OF A MAN-CHILD, AND AFTER VARIOUS ADVEN-
TURES BECOMETH HIS WIFE.

THE hearts of all were moved to compassion by the sufferings of
Lisa, and four of them had their eyes red with weeping, for there
is naught that touches the heart so much as to behold the innocent
suffer; but it being Ciommetella's turn to mind the wheel and spin
the flax, she thus began:

The advice imparted by envy is always the father of misfortune,
because under the smiling, well-wishing mask is hidden the face
which bringeth ruin. And he that beholdeth in hand the hair of
fortune must expect in all hours a hundred foes to lay snares and
traps to make him fall: as happened to a damsel, who for the wicked
advice of her sisters fell from the top of the stair of happiness; and
it was a mercy of Heaven that in falling she did not break her neck.

Once upon a time there lived a mother who had three daughters,
and misery and want had taken hold of that house (which was the
very sink of all misfortunes), and they went a-begging and gathering cast-away cabbage leaves so as to keep body and soul together.
One morning the old woman had gone forth a-begging at a certain palace, and the cook had given her some greens and a few
things more, therefore she returned home and bade her daughters
to go to the fountain to fetch some water; but one with the other

kept saying, 'Thou go,' and none went, and the cat wagged her tail: till at last the old woman, seeing their unwillingness, said, 'If thou desirest to have anything done, do it thyself:' and taking the juglet, was going to fetch the water, although through her age and infirmities she could hardly put one foot before the other, when Luciella, her youngest daughter, said, 'Give me the juglet, O my mother: although I am not very strong, yet have I strength enough to do this for thee, as I like thee not to do this work,' and taking the juglet, fared forth from the city, whereto stood a fountain, that liking not to see the flowers fade with fear, kept throwing up water in their faces; and Luciella met there a handsome slave, and he said to her, 'Wilt thou come with me, O thou beauteous damsel, and I will take thee to a grotto not very far distant, and I will give thee many pretty things.'

Luciella, who had never met with kindly words and good treatment, answered, 'Let me carry this water to my mother, who is waiting for it, and then will I return to thee;' and carrying the water home, she told her mother she was going a-begging. Returning to the fountain, where she found the slave awaiting for her, they fared on to a grotto all covered by Venus-hair creeper and ivy, and when she entered it he led her to an underground palace, most splendid and shining with gold, where at once a table was laid, covered with all dainties. After she had eaten, two beautiful slave-girls came forth, and taking off the rags she wore, arrayed her in costly raiments: and in the evening they led her to a chamber where stood a bed with coverlets all purflewed with pearls and gold; where as soon as the candles were put out, some one came and slept with her, and this continued for some days.

After this time the damsel felt a longing to see her mother, and she told the slave, and the slave entered an inner chamber and spake with some one, and came forth with a bag full of gold, saying, 'Give thou these to thy mother: and be careful not to forget thy way and come back soon, but do not say where thou comest from, or whither thou goest.' The damsel went home, and the sisters beholding her so well arrayed nearly died with envy. She stayed with them a few hours, and when she desired to go back, her mother and sisters offered to attend her; but she refused their company, and returned to the same palace by the same grotto; and abiding quietly within it for two months, at the last came upon her the same longing as hithertofore, and again she told the slave, and as before was sent home with gifts to her mother. This happened three or four times, and the sisters grew ever more envious. At the last these hideous harpies took counsel together, and decided that they would confer with a ghula whom they knew, and she told them how it was with Luciella. So when the damsel came to visit them, they said to her, 'Although thou wouldst not tell us anything of thy enjoyance, thou must know that we are aware of these, and we know that every night thou sleepest with a handsome youth, whom thou hast never seen because they drug thy drinks, and thou art always fast asleep. But thou wilt always remain as thou art, if thou do not resolve to do the rede that those that love thee will advise. In the end, thou art our flesh and blood, and we only desire thy weal and thy pleasure: therefore, when the evening shall come, and thou shalt go to thy bed, and the slave shall come bringing thee thy night-drink and water to wash thy mouth bid thou him go and fetch thee a towel to wipe thy mouth, and when he is gone on his errand throw the drink away, so that thou mayest remain awake in the night; and when thou perceivest thy husband fast asleep, open this padlock, and thus he will be obliged to break the spell in spite of himself, and thou wilt remain the happiest woman in all the world.' Poor Luciella knew not that under the velvet saddle the thorns were hid, and amongst the flowers the adder slept, and in the golden bowl the poison was prepared. She believed the words of her sisters, and returning to the grotto, went within the palace, and when night came, did as those wretches had told her, and when all things lay still, she struck a light, and lit the candle, and beheld by her side a flower of beauty, a youth like lilies and roses, and sighting so much beauty, said, 'By my faith, thou shalt not escape from my hands, ever;' and taking the padlock, she unlocked it, and beheld some women carrying some skeins of thread on their head. One of these let fall a skein, and Luciella, who was very kind hearted, remembering not where she was, cried out in a loud voice, 'Pick up thy thread, madam.' At the cry the youth woke up; and was so disgusted and an-angered in being seen by Luciella that, at once calling the slaves, he bade them dress her in the same rags that she wore before, and send her home to her mother and sisters.

This they did, and when she stood before them with pale face and sorrow-stricken heart, they bade her go her ways with insolent words; and she, knowing not whither to turn her steps, wandered about the world, and after much travail the unhappy damsel, being big with child, arrived at the city of Torre-Longa, and going to the royal palace, went round to the stables, and sought a place upon the straw wherein to rest. Here one of the court maids of honour found her, and kindly entreated her. So the time for child-bed came, and she was delivered of a son so beautiful that he seemed a golden bough; and the first night he was born, a handsome youth entered the chamber where the mother and babe lay, and going near the child, he took him in his arms, and said, 'O my beauteous son, if my mother knew of thee, in a golden bath she would wash thee, and with a golden band she would swathe thee, and if never a cock should crow, never would I leave thy side;' and whilst he was chanting these words, at the first cock crowing he disappeared as quicksilver. The young maid of honour sat near the bedside, and every night she beheld the youth, who came and took the child in his arms, and chanted the same words, and at the first cock-crow disappeared, so she made her way to the queen's presence, and related to her what she had witnessed; and the queen, as soon as the sun, like a clever doctor, had discharged all the stars from the hospital of heaven, bade the crier publish an edict (which was thought by all folk very cruel) that all the cocks in that city should be slain, thus condemning all fowls to widowhood and wretchedness. And in the evening the queen took the maid's place by Luciella's bedside, and waited in great suspense for the youth's coming, and when he came at the same hour, she recognised in him her own son, and she arose and embraced him; and as the curse which had been cast upon the prince by a ghula was that he should wander about in exile far from his home, till his mother should see him and embrace him, and the cock should not crow, as soon as he was in his mother's arms the spell was broken, and the sad term of exile was ended. Thus the mother found that she had gained a grandson beautiful as a jewel. And Luciella regained her husband, and the sisters after a time having knowledge of her happiness and greatness, came with a brazen face to visit her, but they met with the same reception that they had given her when through their wicked rede she had been cast out from the prince's palace: and thus it was rendered to them evil for evil, and they were paid in the same coin, and in great distress of mind they came to know that

'Son of envy is the heart's disease.'

THE GOSSIP

Of the Second Day

COLA JACOPO HATH A GOSSIP WHO SUCKETH HIM AND LIVETH ON HIM,
AND OF WHOM HE CANNOT RID HIMSELF, NEITHER BY ARTS NOR STRATA-
GEMS. AT LAST, BEING UNABLE TO BEAR IT LONGER, HE PUTTETH HIS
HEAD OUT OF THE BAG, AND WITH A STORM OF INJURIOUS WORDS EXPEL-
LETH HIM FROM HIS HOUSE.

THE preceding story was adjudged truly pretty, and being related
gracefully and with taste, was listened to with attention, so that all
things conspired to give it zest to please. But because every time
that they rested a little in their talk, the slave felt as one on thorns,
Prince Thaddeus solicited Jacoma to take her place at the lathe;
and she put her hand in the cask of prolixity to refresh the desire
of the hearers, and thus began:

The lack of discretion, ladies, maketh the merchant drop the
measure of judgment from his hand, the engineer mistake the compass of good behaviour, and the sailor lose the compass of his reason.
Taking root in the ground of ignorance, it produceth no other fruit
than shame and scorn, as can be seen happening in every-day life:
and it chanced to a certain gossip brazen-faced, as I will relate in
the following story.

Once upon a time there lived a certain Cola Jacopo of Pomeg-
liano, husband of Masella Cernecchia of Resina: a man was he
as full of riches as the sea, nor knew what he possessed. So that
he kept his pigs in stable all day feeding on straw. But, though
he had neither chick nor child, and measured coins by tons, yet he
would fare an hundred miles to save a crown, and lived in a niggardly way the better to put away more of his gold. Nevertheless,
every time that he took seat at his table with his wife to eat his
scanty meals, would come a bad penny of a gossip, who would not

179

let him stir a step without being by his side. Just as if he had a
clock in his body, and a timepiece in his teeth, he unfailingly stood
before the door at each meal hour, so that he could eat with them,
and with a weigher's face there would he stày, and do as they would,
they could not get rid of him. There he remained, counting their
mouthfuls, and saying witty things, till they were obliged to ask,
'Wouldst thou take a bite?' Which invitation he would not let
them repeat, but seating himself between husband and wife, like one
famished he would dart upon the dishes, and cut like a sharp razor,
and like a hunting dog, as if he had a wolfish hunger, with a sharp-
ness and rapidity quite marvellous, as if he had just come from the
mill; he would make use of his hands like a fife-player, and roll
about his eyes like a foreign cat, and use his teeth like a stone
machine, and swallow his food whole, one mouthful awaiting not
for another. When he had stuffed well his guts, and loaded well
his belly, making a stomach like a drum, viewing the dishes empty,
having swept the country without asking by your leave, taking hold
of the wine-flagon, he would blow in it, and sip in it, and empty it,
drinking its contents to the very dregs at one breath, and would not
stop till he could see the bottom, leaving Cola Jacopo and Masella
with a lengthened nose. Perceiving the want of discretion on the
part of the gossip, who, like a sack without a bottom, ate, swallowed,
emptied, cut, wrapped, devoured, planed, combed, shook, disfigured,
and put in order all that lay on the table, they knew not what plan
to adopt so as to be delivered from this leech, this epithema cordial,
this dirt-in-breeches, this August cure, this troublesome fly, this
sticking tick, this spring, this bone-gnawer, this trouble, this continual tax, this many-feet, this heavy weight, this headache; nor
could they sight a time in which they could peacefully eat their
food, without this unsought and unwished for guest to help them.

One morning, at last, they heard that the gossip had gone on some
business out of the city, and Cola Jacopo hearing the happy tidings
exclaimed, 'O may the Sun in Lion be praised, that we will once
be able to move our cheeks, and make good use of our grinders, and
put our meal under our nose without this nuisance; therefore he

will not be able to do me homage, and I will do it myself. In this stinking world, all that one enjoyeth is what he pulleth with his teeth; quick, light the fire, and now that we are free we will have a feast, and will eat some tasty morsel.' So saying, he ran to buy a large swamp eel, and a kilogram of fine flour, and a flagon of good wine, and returned home. His wife at once set to make a fine pizza,* and put it to bake, then fried the eel, and everything being ready, they took their seat at the table. But they had hardly eaten a mouthful, when behold, that parasite of a gossip was heard knocking at the door, and Masella looking out in dismay, and beholding the cause and ruin of their happiness, said to her husband, 'Cola Jacopo mine, 'tis a badly bought pound of meat in the butcher's shop of our relish, if we have the joint of the bone of displeasure. One has never slept yet in the white sheets of satisfaction, without finding some bugs to disquieten one; there never was yet a good lye-washing made, without the rain of dissatisfaction. Behold, thou must drain this bitter drink even to the dregs, and choke thyself with the food in thy throat.' And Cola Jacopo answered, 'Put away these things, clear the table, melt them, disappear with them, stuff them somewhere, hide them, let not a speck of them be seen, and then open the door, and as the village will be plundered and naught will be found, perhaps he will have discretion enough to depart, and thus give us time and place to swallow this poisoned mouthful.' Masella, whilst the gossip rang to arms and chimed to glory, hid the eel in the cupboard, and put the flagon under the bed, and the pizza between the mattresses, and Cola Jacopo scrambled under the table, holding the table cover down, and peeping through a hole.

But the gossip had watched all this traffick from the key-hole. And as soon as the door was opened, he, rather surprised at their proceedings, entered smiling blandly, and inquired of Masella what had happened; saying, 'Thou hast left me so long without, that whilst I was awaiting for the door to be opened by the crow, a serpent came round my feet, and O mother mine, what an hideous

* 'Pizza.' A dough-cake stuffed with cheese, or fish, or ham.

monster! Thou mayst suppose that he was as large as the eel, which thou hast put into the cupboard. I saw myself in bad case, and trembling like a bough shaken by the wind, my limbs quivering with fright, and my body full of worms with fear, I stooped and took up a stone the size of the flagon thou hast just hid beneath the bed, and I threw it on its head and made of it a pizza like the one thou hast hid beneath the mattresses; and when it lay a-dying, I could perceive that it watched me like unto gossip Jacopo who is under the table, and no blood remaineth in my body with excessive fear.' And Cola Jacopo, hearing these words, could no longer stand proof and swallow the sugar, so putting forth his head from under the table, like a jester playing a part, he roared out, 'If it be so, now we will have a pasty, now we will fill the spindle, now we will bake the bread. Now we have won the law-case, see if we owe thee anything, accuse us to the seat of justice; if we have displeased thee, indict us at the mint; if thou feel offended, tie me short; if thou be capricious, cure thyself with the mute; if thou pretend something, pursue us with a fox's tail or put thy nose in Naples. What kind of proceeding is this? When wilt thou put an end to it? It seemeth thou art no soldier of discretion, and thou desirest our goods unceasingly; a finger ought to have been enough, without taking all the hand. Now thou wouldst kick us out of house and home and busiest thyself about it; to him who hath little discretion all the world is his; but who doth not measure himself will be measured, and if thou hast not a yard measure, we have both trepane and plane, and at last thou knowest that it is said, to a fair brow a fair weight; every hedge-hog hath its straw-bed therefore leave us in peace with our troubles. If thou supposest from this day forward to continue this music, thou wilt lose thy footsteps, and thou wilt get nothing for it: thou wilt lose the furniture, as it will not run smooth; and if thou imaginest to lie down on this spring always, thou hast time, and more than time, as March hath shaved thee, and thou canst use the tooth-pick. If thou thinkest that my house is a tavern always open for 'that rotten throat, and when thou comest thou eatest, forget it, take it out of thy head, 'tis lost work, 'tis a thing of wind, there is no more tinder. I care not for thee; thou hadst discovered who would be spited, light had come into thine eyes; for the pigeons thou hadst examined the ass, thou hadst found the happy land; now thou mayest go back, as thou wilt not do it any more; and thou mayest write the name of this house with the pen, as thou wilt never more draw water at this well. Thou art a dinner-spy, a bread-expulser, laying the tables and setting them right, a kitchen-sweeper, a pot-scraper, a bowl-cleaner, a glutton, a sink-throat, a devourer, a wolfish eater, thy body is like the deluge, thy guts are endless, and thou wouldst be a match for an ass, and thou wouldst hold a ship, thou wouldst even eat the prince's bear, and that would not hurt thy digestion. Thou wouldst drink the Tiber dry, and not feel full, and thou wouldst eat even Mariaccio's breeches. Fare to other churches; go and cast thy nets elsewhere; go and gather rags and bones in other dust-holes; go and pick up nails in the torrent; go and gather wax at the obsequies; go and empty the water-closets to fill that belly; and may this house seem fire to thee; for every one has his own troubles, and every one knows what is hid under the surface, and where his stomach aches; and we need not a shoulder shove, nor accounts failed, nor broken lances. Let them be saved who can be saved; 'tis time thou left sucking the breast. Bird who losest thy day, useless being, lazybones. Work! Work! Learn some craft, and find thyself a new master.' The wretched gossip hearing this long oration uttered through the teeth, this dislodging of imposthume, this carding without combing, stood turned to stone, all cold and frozen, like a thief caught in the act, like a pilgrim who hath lost his way, like a sailor whose bark is wrecked, like a strumpet who hath missed accounts, like a child who hath soiled the bed; and with tongue between his teeth, and head bended downwards, beard laid on the chest, and with running eyes, and musty nose, and frozen teeth, and empty hands, sick at heart, and with tail between his legs, cooked and scalded, silent and mute, took to his heels, without ever turning his head to look behind; so that just suited him that time-honoured sentence, which saith,

'Dog not invited to the marriage-feast
Should never go, or else he will be whipped.'

All the company laughed loudly at the scorn received by the gossip, and they perceived not that the sun, having lavished generously his light, had caused his bank to fail, and having thrust the golden key under the door, had taken flight. Cola Ambruoso and Marchionno came forth, robed in leathern tights and serge cassocks, to play the second part, all readily lent a willing ear to the pleasant eclogue which followed.

ECLOGUE

The Dye

Cola Ambruoso and Marchionno

Col. Amid all crafts, O Marchionno,
    To the dye is due, as said
    I know not if a cook or a scullion,
    The first vaunt, and the first place.
Mar. I deny it consequently, O Cola Ambruoso,
    Because 'tis a dirty craft:
    Thine hands are ever
    Amongst vitriol and alum,
    And just varnished like a blackamoor's.
Col. Rather 'tis the cleanest
    Among all exercises;
    'Tis craft fit for a man,
    Who prides himself in cleanliness, and is foul.
Mar. Thou wouldst make me believe
    That 'tis a perfumer's craft,
    Or a purfling business,
    Go thou and turn back: thou art sadly in error.
Col. I will prove to thee
    And maintain it in an oven,

That a dyer's craft
Is work fit for a lord;
In these days 'tis used by all,
With it man lives,
And is kept in great account;
Is he full of perplexities and troubles,
Is he dissolute and full of vices,
With the eye he can hide every fault.

Mar. What have to do the vice and faults of life
With the dye that's used for woollen and silk array?

Col. How easy 'tis to see thou knowest naught:
Thou thinkest that I speak
Of dyeing stockings and old clothes:
The dye of which I speak,
Is not of indigo, nor basil-wood:
'Tis the dye which changeth the folk's face
From dark to white or red carnation.

Mar. I feel as if I were within a sack,
I understand thee not a straw, and this
Thy talk bewildereth me and darkeneth me.

Col. If thou couldst understand me,
Thou wouldst at once be taught to be a dyer,
Or wouldst thou long to know those of the craft,
And wouldst feel rest and pleasure,
In learning this new art that's chosen alway
By the most wary folk:
A craft so disguising all things
That a crab-louse will seem to thee a cat.
Now hearken well, 'tis a gibbet of third rate,
Which sweepeth all that cometh, and all that lighteth,
And lifteth all it sighteth.
Now who knoweth this dye,
Will not give it an infamous name
Of cheat and thief,
But will say, this is a man with sense,

And with his keen judgment, he draweth gold
Even from under ground, he gaineth well,
And could live well even in a wild wold,
And is a clever man and of good worth,
Who can make profit in all things.
A cheat, a tartar, a thief,
And a corsair of first water,
Who loseth not his cap among the crowd,
And useth this dye
So beautiful and gallant:
He is named by folk a prudent man
When he is a rogue and scoundrel.

Mar. Thou fillest my hands with garlic:
This is a most wondrous craft,
But 'tis a craft will not succeed with poor folk:
'Tis only fit for certain rogues,
To whom 'tis granted to name,
Coming from distant parts, in dry cool tones,
Gains their cheats, and fruits their robberies.

Col. Then there is the poltroon, a double-faced man,
A jew, crap-in-breeches, a chicken,
Poor of spirit,
Pullet-hearted,
With a half frightened smile,
Frozen and timorous,
Who trembleth like an aspen leaf,
Always feeleth small,
Is ever full of terror,
Afraid at his own shadow:
If some one glanceth at him askance
He fills a night-vase full of worms;
If some one threaten him, thou shalt see him
Stand like a plucked quail:
He loseth his speech,
Becometh deathly and sallow,

And if the other lifteth a hand,
He taketh to his heels.
But making use of this noble dye,
The folk will take him
For a prudent person,
Staid, and a man of worth,
Who walketh with the lead and with the compass,
Nor taketh excrement on flight,
Nor buyeth with ready money
Any dissension,
Is not a court fire-brand,
But doeth his own business,
Is quiet, and keeps his counsel:
And in such a manner, O my son,
They mistake a rabbit for a fox.

Mar. It seems to me, they understand it well
Who save their own skin,
As I read once
In a fine story, I know not
If written by hand or printed,
That a good flight all bitterness escapeth.

Col. And at the other side
Thou seest a man quite worthy,
Daring, courageous, and tender-hearted,
Who would not flinch before a Rodomonte,
Who can stand hand to hand with a very Roland,
Who can meet in fair fight an Hector,
Who will not let a fly
Pass unhurt before his nose;
And deeds speak for him before his words.
And he maketh his foes stand in order,
And put two feet in one shoe,
Every corner cutter, and part chief
Mixeth well the mixture;
He is a lion-hearted one,

He fighteth even with death,
And never steppeth backward, and hitteth
Always forward like a he-goat;
But let him use this dye
He is held by all
For a break-neck most impertinent,
Rash, and insolent,
Touchy, mad, and brittle,
A tempter, a fire in the house,
Who putteth his foot on every stone,
Who seeketh quarrels with the lantern,
An unreasonable man,
A broken person without bit or bridle;
And no day passeth without some great dissension,
And his neighbours have no peace,
And he is a provocation even to stones in the road:
In fact, a man, whose real worth
Deserveth praise, is not esteemed,
But thought instead to be worthy of an oar.*

Mar. Be silent, they are right,
Because a prudent and praiseworthy man
Commands respect without the need of sword.

Col. And here behold a miser,
One dying with hunger,
One tight in the waist,
An empty purse; a pair of pinchers
Fit for a boiler-maker;
A nail-gnawer,
A Siennese horse,
A dry orange,
A rotten cork, a plum-stone,
An ant out of a miserly crab-apple,
Mother of misery, a beggarly being,
Who, like a kicking horse,

* To be made a galley-slave.

Not only would not give one two small loaves,
But would not part with even an hair of his tail,
A sorrowful figure, a wrinkled face,
Who runneth an hundred miles
To save a mite;
Who will give an hundred bites to a bean,
And will tie in an hundred knots
A half decinco *;
One who never dumps, to save eating.
But this dye covers all his faults,
And he is called a saving man,
Who squanders not what he possesseth,
Who alloweth not his goods
To go down the water side,
And letteth not a crumb fall to the ground;
At last he is called
(But by certain scoundrels)
A man, a very compass: and he is pinchers.

Mar. Oh, what a foul race
This is, their heart is in their coins,
They fast without a doctor's orders,
They dress in an hundred rags,
You see them always sad-faced,
And they bear themselves as servants very humbly,
And die most thin among all this their fat.

Col. But the reverse of this medal
Is he who spendeth and squandereth,
Who would empty a ship of its freight,
And would ruin the mint,
A sack without a bottom,
Throwing away what he holdeth,
And never counting what goods he hath.
Thou seest around him
An hundred sharpers and parasites,

* ' Decinco.' Old coin worth about eleven centesimi.

Without any kind of virtue,
And he bundleth them together
And remitteth to them:
Breaketh without judgment,
Turneth without reason,
Giveth to pigs and dogs,
And squandereth his goods in smoke:
But he useth this dye
He gaineth good opinion,
He is called a liberal soul,
Kind, magnanimous, gentle,
Who would give thee his entrails,
The friend of friends,
The king of kings,
Never refusing to those that ask him,
And with this nice eulogium
Emptieth his chests, and sendeth his home to ruin.

Mar. He lieth in his throat
Who calleth liberal a man like this;
Generous is he who giveth in time and place,
And throweth not his coin about
To folk dishonoured and foolish jesters,
But instead giveth his crowns
To a poor but worthy man.

Col. Thou seest a glutton,
A pot-full, a woolly sheep,
A brainless ram, jumping and butting,
A house with two gates, a shoe-horn,
That cometh from Cornito,*
And hath a house of rest;
A put-things-straight gentleman,
A most original picture
Of infamy, a portrait from the copy:
And when he useth this dye,

* ' Cornito' ancient Roman city.

The folks will call him quiet, a worthy man.
An honest man, a gentleman,
Who mindeth his own affairs,
And is pleasant to all,
And polite, and courtly:
His house is open unto all his friends,
He is not punctilious, ceremonious;
Well-baked as bread,
Sweet as honey,
Thou canst do what thou wilt with him;
And meanwhile, without so much as a blush,
He maketh a good market of the meat
And saveth the bones.

Mar. 'Tis these that live on the fat;
One of these clearly seeth,
If he goeth by night in a tavern,
And, for the bones, giveth light the lantern.

Col. A man liveth quite retired,
And companieth not with false deceitful men,
Escheweth conversations,
Wanteth not an head-ache,
Will not give an account
To the third and to the fourth,
Leadeth a tranquil life,
Is master of himself,
Hath none to awaken him when he sleepeth,
Or to count his mouthfuls when he eateth:
But for all that some one will dye him,
And call him a sophist wild and savage,
The excrement of birds of prey,
Who scenteth not, stinketh not,
A rough and most insipid one,
A stingy, caustic man,
Without any love or taste,
A wretched beastly clodhopper,

A maccarone without salt.

Mar. O most happy he who dwelleth in a desert,
Who seeth not, and butteth not;
Let them say as they will, I find
The old saw in sooth well proven,
'Tis better to be alone than in bad company.

Col. And on the other side
They find a sociable pleasant man,
Who giveth his flesh and shareth it with his friend,
An affable good companion,
Who treateth thee most generously:
And with this dye—who ever would believe it?—
There is found one who cutteth and who sliceth him
Of things, and excuses, and works,
Badly and against the grain,
And judgeth and disputeth his cause
Behind his back;
Calleth him, brazen-faced, froward,
Fart-in-breeches, pointed brow,
Leather-string broken by the dozen,
Impudent, parsley for every sauce,
Who liketh to put salt in all he seeth,
And put his nose in whatsoe'er he heareth,
Busybody, and troublesome,
Lifter of this, and spendthrift: O poor man!

Mar. This is wanted, and worse:
And the Spaniard understood it,
Who said, 'Tis a long while,
And great, since this was all the cause for contempt.

Col. If by chance there is a man,
Who speaketh quickly, chatteth and reasoneth well,
And showeth off his genius, and is eloquent,
And wherever thou touchest him and twisteth him
Thou findest him clever; and he replieth with sense:
This dye will reduce him in such a manner

That he cannot lift his hat,
Without being called by some sink-mouthed wretch
A prattler and a glutton,
Who hath more talk, than a magpie
And would defy in noise even a grasshopper,
Who stunneth thy head, and turneth thy brain,
With many stories, and prolix trifles,
And tales of ghuls,
And troublesome vexation, and bis and vis,
Whenever he putteth that tongue in motion,
With a mouth that goeth like a chicken's arse:
It infecteth thee, it deafeneth and confuseth thee.

Mar. In this, the donkeys' age,
Do as thou wilt, thou always art mistaken.

Col. And if another is ever silent, and mute,
And stoppeth, and speaketh not, nor maketh a sign
And saveth his mouth for the figs,
And thou canst not once hear him whisper:
This dye will change his colour,
And he is called Antony the simpleton,
An ass, a piece of silliness, a mameluke,
Like a block of wood from hell,
Always cold, and ever frozen
Like a bride, may evil happen to him;
So much so, that in this gulf
The north wind I cannot see;
If thou speakest 'tis wrong, and if thou art silent 'tis worse.

Mar. Sooth thou sayest, for in these days,
Thou knowest not what to do,
Thou knowest not how to fish,
And there's no beaten track to those that walk,
And blest is he in this world who can divine it.

Col. But who could ever explain the buzzing
Effects of this dye?
It would require a thousand years unfailingly,

And even a metal tongue it would destroy:
Do as thou wilt,
Treat as thou wilt, in any way,
If the colour is changed, the jester
Is called facetious,
And entertaineth well;
The spy, a clever man,
Who knoweth the ways of the world;
The rogue, ingenious and crafty;
The lazy man, phlegmatick;
The glutton, a bon vivant;
The flatterer, a clever courtier
Who knoweth his master's humour,
And sootheth him in his moods;
The strumpet, a kindly person with good manners;
The ignorant, a simple good-hearted fellow;
And so on from hand to hand,
And discoursing on, and enough:
Therefore 'tis not surprising if at court
The rogue is pampered,
And the upright ill-treated,
Because the lords and nobles
Are misled by this dye in all the colours,
And take one thing for another,
As 'tis always seen,
Leaving the good for the wicked.

Mar. Wretched is he that serveth:
Far better if his mother
Had given him birth still-born,
He leadeth a life of storms, and never **hopeth**
To sight the port.

Col. The court is held alone
For profligate folk and vicious,
And the good are always kept at **distance,**
And shoved away, and kicked,

And butted, and pushed aside;
But let us leave this talk,
For whilst one scratcheth where it itcheth,
Naught would disappear, but be kept in casket.
Therefore let us dot a point, and say farewell,
Now that the sun is playing at hide-and-seek,
And we will do the rest another evening.

They all shut their mouths at the fall of the shadows, and having appointed to return the next morning with a new ammunition of stories, they all made their way to their own houses, filled with words, and loaded with appetite

END OF THE SECOND DAY

THE THIRD DAY OF THE
DIVERSION OF THE LITTLE ONES

No sooner were the shadows delivered by the sun's visit from their durance vile at the judgment-seat of night, than the company, the prince and his wife also, with the women, returned to the same place, to spend cheerfully those hours between breakfast and dinner-time. They sent for the band of music, and began to dance with great zest and pleasure, and to play games, such as, 'Roger,' 'The Young Peasant Girl,' 'The Story of the Ghul,' 'Stefania,' 'The Crafty Peasant,' 'All the Day with the Dove,' 'Tordiglione,' 'The Nymph's Ball,' 'The Gipsy,' 'The Whimsical One,' 'My Bright Star,' 'My Sweet Amorous Flame,' 'The One I am Seeking,' 'The Weeping One and the Little Weeper,' 'The Peace-maker,' 'High and Low,' 'The Clearing with the Foot-Point Cutter,' 'Behold with Whom I Fell in Love,' 'Extort, for 'tis Useful,' 'The Clouds Flying in Air,' 'The Devil in his Shirt,' 'Living in Hope,' 'Change Hands,' 'Cascarda,' * 'The Little Spaniard.' And they ended the ball with 'Lucy the Bitch': all this to please the slave. And the time sped on, and they took no note of its flight till the meal hour came, when all kinds of dainties were brought, as if from Heaven, and so tasty were they that the company is still eating; and the tables were cleared, and Zeza, who sat on thorns ready to relate her story, began in this way:

* ' Cascarda.' A popular dance common in Naples, accompanied by singing.

CANNETELLA

Of the Third Day

CANNETELLA IS UNABLE TO FIND A HUSBAND TO HER TASTE, BUT FOR
HER SIN SHE FALLETH INTO THE HANDS OF A GHUL, WHO MAKETH
HER LEAD A BAD LIFE. SHE IS SAVED AT LAST BY A LOCKSMITH, HER
FATHER'S VASSAL.

LADIES, 'tis a bad thing to seek for better bread than that of wheat-flour, because in the end one cometh to long for that which he hath thrown away. Each should content himself with what is honest and right: for whoso loseth all, and whoso walketh on the tree-tops, hath as much madness in his brains as danger under his heels: as befell to a king's daughter, which hath given matter for this story that I now relate.

In days of yore, there lived a king of Bel-Puojo, and he longed to have an heir more than the porters long for funeral rites that they may gather the wax. And he at last made a vow to the goddess Serenga that, if she would vouchsafe to him the blessing of a daughter, he would name her Cannetella, in remembrance of the goddess who had transformed herself in a cane. So long did he pray and beseech that the grace was granted him, for his wife Renzolla presented him with a beauteous woman-child, whom he named as he had promised. Now the child grew foot by foot till she was as tall as a crane, when the king said to her, 'O my daughter, thou art now, Heaven bless thee, grown as tall as an oak, and it is time thou shouldst company with a husband worthy of thy beauteous face, to maintain and multiply the seed of our house. Therefore, as I love thee better than mine own entrails, and desire to please thee, I would that thou wouldst say what kind of an husband thou wouldst like. What manner of man would be to thy taste? wouldst thou

have him a wise man of letters, or a swordsman? young, or somewhat old? dark, white, or fair? a tall mosquito, or a sprig from the
vine fit for a rush basket? small of waist, or round as an ox?
Choose thou, and I will consent.' The princess, hearing these offers
from her sire, replied that she had vowed her virginity to the goddess Diana, and would not take herself an husband. But the king
urged and implored till at last she said, 'As I do not desire to show
myself ungrateful to thy great love, I will obey and fulfil thy wants,
but thou must find such a husband for me that there shall not be
another in the world like unto him.' The father, hearing this answer, with great joy agreed to please her, and from morn till eve
he stood at the window, looking, measuring, weighing, and observing the menfolk as they passed that way. And when a handsome
and pleasant man came in sight, the king said to his daughter 'Run,
Cannetella, and look out of the window, and see if this youth meet
thy requirements.'

On one occasion Cannetella called the youth upstairs, and the
king ordered the table to be spread for a great banquet, and all kinds
of food to be brought, leaving naught to be desired: and whilst eating, an almond fell from the mouth of the youth, and he, stooping
down, dexterously picked it up, and laid it under the table-cloth.
The eating having ended, he went his ways: and after he was gone,
said the king to Cannetella, 'How dost thou like the youth, O my
life?' And she replied, 'Make him disappear from my sight, the
clownish boor: a man so tall and big as he is, to allow an almond to
drop from his mouth!' The king hearing this answer again went
to the window, and watched till he beheld another youth cast in a
graceful mould, when he called his daughter, and enquired if this
other met her approval. Cannetella replied, that he should be invited upstairs. Then the king ordered another feast to be spread,
and when all had eaten their fill the youth went his ways, and the
king demanded of his daughter, whether this one pleased her, and
she answered, 'And what am I to do with such a miserable fellow?
He ought to have brought at least two valets to help him to take
off his cloak.' 'If this be all, 'tis a patty,' said the king: 'these are

the excuses of a bad pay-master. Thou art picking up down from the cloth, so as not to give me this satisfaction: thou hadst better resolve, as it is my will to marry thee, and thus find root enough to rear upon the sprouting the succession of mine house.' At these angry words of her sire, Cannetella replied, 'To speak sooth, dear my lord and sire, out of my teeth, and as I feel it, thou art digging in the sea, and art counting badly on thy fingers: as I will never submit to the will of any man living, if he hath not a golden head and teeth.' The unhappy king, perceiving that his daughter was headstrong as a mule, sent the crier to publish a ban throughout the city that whosoever in his kingdom suited the desires of his daughter should come forward, and he would give him Cannetella to wife, and he should be made king.

Now the king had a bitter foe, Scioravante hight, most hideous to behold, so that if he had been painted on the wall none could look at him. Scioravante, hearing this edict, and being a clever necromancer, well versed in the art of sorcery, called to his aid a company of those who are best away, and commanded that they should at once make him a golden head and teeth of gold; and they answered that they could hardly do him this extravagant service, and much sooner would they give him horns of gold, for the latter were more fashionable and in use. But forced by the power of charms and spells, at last they did what he required. And when he beheld himself with head and teeth of twenty-carat gold, he paced up and down under the king's windows, and the king, sighting the very man he was seeking, called his daughter, and she as soon as she perceived him, said, 'Now this is the one, and he could not be better, even if I had kneaded him with mine own hands.' And the king sent for him, and well entreated him, and Scioravante arose to go his ways, when the king said to him, 'Await a little while, O my brother, do not be in such haste; thou must be hot at thy back; or it seems, as if thou hast a pledge at the jew's, or that thou hast quicksilver in thy behind, or a bit of wood under thy tail. Easy, for now I will give thee luggage, and followers to company thee, and my daughter, whom 'tis my desire thou shouldst take to wife.' Said Scioravante,

'I thank thee for nothing: it is enough if thou wilt give me a steed, so that I may seat her before me, and carry her home with me, where there is no lack of servants and followers, and furniture as much as there is sand in the sea.' And having contested the point for some time, at last Scioravante won his way, and mounting steed, and putting his wife before him, he departed.

In the evening, when the red horses retire to give place to the white oxen, they arrived at a stable-yard, and leading Cannetella to the stable, where some mares were feeding, Scioravante said to her, 'Keep thy brains about thee. I must go to mine house, and it will take me seven years to get there, therefore be thou careful and await for me in this stable, and go not out, nor let any one see thee: an if thou disobey me, I will make thee remember whilst thou art green and alive.' To which Cannetella made answer, 'I am thy liege, and will do thy commandment even unto the fennel: but I should like to know what thou wilt leave me to live upon.' And Scioravante replied, ' 'Twill be enough for thee, to eat of what remaineth of the fodder eaten by these mares.'

Now ye must consider what heart did poor Cannetella make in hearing this, and if she cursed the hour and the moment when ever a word was spoken. And she remained cold and frozen, and had no other food to sustain her but her tears, cursing her fortune, and the stars which had reduced her from the palace to the stable, from the perfumes to the stink of dung, from the mattresses of barberian wool to the bed of straw, and from the daintiest of food to the leavings of the mares. Thus she passed two months in this hard life, eating the corn that was left by the mares, whose mangers were filled every morning by invisible hands, and thus she sustained her life. But at the end of that time she perceived a little hole, and gazing through it she observed a beautiful garden, with avenues of orange-trees, grottoes surrounded by citrons, squares of flower-beds, fruit-trees, and vines which it was a pleasure to behold: and she, sighting these things, longed for a bunch of grapes, and said in her mind, 'I will issue forth quite quietly, and let come what will, even if the heavens fall, I will eat thereof. What can it matter in another hundred years? Who can or will tell my husband? And even if, by an unfortunate chance, he should come to know of it, what can he do to me? It is but a bunch of grapes, and not horns.' And thus saying, she went forth, and gladdened her soul, which had failed her for want.

After a little while, and before the established time, her husband returned, and one of the mares accused Cannetella of having stolen the grapes. And Scioravante became exceeding wroth, and drawing from his belt a knife, he would have slain her. But she knelt down before him, and wept, and prayed him to hold his hand, for it had been hunger which had chased the wolf from the forest, and she said, and prayed, and besought so much, that Scioravante said to her, 'I forgive thee for this time, and I give thee thy life as an alms: but if another time the evil one tempt thee, and I come to know that thou hast been seen in the sun, I will make mince-meat of thy life: therefore keep thy brains steady, as again I am going away, and will stay away in very truth seven years this time. Walk straight, for thou shalt not succeed again, and I should make thee pay for the old and the new.' Thus saying he departed, and Cannetella wept a river of tears, and beating hand against hand, and striking her breast, and buffeting her face, and pulling her hair, she said, 'O would that I had never been born to pass such bitter venture! O my father, O how thou hast smothered me! But why do I reproach my sire, if I myself have done the damage? I am the builder of mine own evil fortune. I desired a golden head, to fall into the molten lead, and die in irons. O how I flew to gain the golden teeth, so that I might grow teeth of gold; this is the just punishment of Heaven. I ought to have done as my sire desired me, and not to have had so many whims and impossible fancies: and whoso hearkeneth not to the father and mother walketh a road which he knoweth not.' And not a day passed but that she wept, and wailed, and thus addressed herself: so that her eyes had become two fountains, and her colour had yellowed, and her face was pinched, and she inspired compassion to the beholder. Where were those eyes darting love glances? where all her gentleness and sweetness? where the smile of those lips? Her own sire would not have known her.

Now after a year had gone by, by chance passed that stable the king's locksmith, and he being recognised by Cannetella, she called him, and issued forth. Hearing some one uttering his name, and not recognising the poor child, for she was so much changed, he marvelled with excessive marvel; but when she told him who she was, and how she was changed, partly in pity of her troubles, and partly to gain the king's grace, he bethought himself to save her, and putting her within an empty cask which he was carrying on the top of his load, on the back of a mule, he trotted towards Bel-Puojo, and he arrived there at four o'clock in the morning, and straightway entered the king's palace. He knocked at the gate, and the servants looking out of window, and hearing that it was the locksmith, began to abuse him grossly, calling him an animal without discretion, coming at such an hour to disturb and awaken the whole household; adding that he would escape cheaply, if they did not throw something at him, or let go a large stone at his head. But the king, hearing all this noise, and one of his valets telling him who it was, bade them lead the locksmith to the presence, considering that if he had come at such unusual hour, and had taken the liberty to awaken all the king's household, it must be that some great matter had occurred. And when the locksmith came to the presence, he unshipped his load, and uncovering the cask, out stepped Cannetella. But more than words had to be brought to bear witness before the father could recognize his daughter; and had it not been for a wart which she had on her right arm, she could have gone back whence she came. But being certified of her identity, he embraced her, and kissed her a thousand times; and sending her at once to the bath, to be cleansed, and arrayed in befitting garments, the king led her to breakfast, which she sorely needed as she was dying of hunger. And the father said, 'Who could have told me, O my daughter, that I should meet thee in such a plight? What face is this? Who hath brought thee to such a pass?' And she answered, 'And so it is, O my lord! That barbarian Turk hath made me suffer great ill-usage, and at all hours

I have been ready to give up the ghost; but I will not tell thee what I have passed, because it far surpasseth what 'tis possible for human beings to endure, and 'tis impossible for man to believe it. Enough, O my father, I am here, and I will never more move one step away from thy footsteps, and I would rather be a servant in thine house than a queen in any one else's home, and I would rather have a napkin where thou art, than a golden mantle far from thee, I would sooner turn the spit in thy kitchen, than hend a sceptre under the dais of any one else.' Such was her case.

In the meanwhile Scioravante had returned from his journey, and the mares had told him what had taken place, that the locksmith had carried away Cannetella inside the cask; and he hearing this, feeling overwhelmed with shame, and heated with wrath, hastened towards Bel-Puojo, and finding an old woman who dwelt opposite to the king's palace, said to her, 'How much wilt thou have, O madam mine, if thou wilt let me behold the king's daughter?' And the old woman asked of him an hundred ducats. Scioravante put his hand in his hunting bag, and counted out the golden pieces one after the other, and she having taken them, bade him mount to the terrace, and from thence he beheld Cannetella out in her own terrace, drying her hair; and her heart spake to her, and turning that way, she perceived the ambush, and running down the stairs, she flew in the presence of her father, crying 'O my lord, if thou wilt not build me a chamber this very moment with seven iron doors I am lost.' 'Will I lose thee for so little?' said the king. 'Let even an eye of the head be spent to give satisfaction to my beauteous daughter.' And at once the doors were made; and Scioravante, hearing of this, returned to the old woman, and said she to him, 'What dost thou want with me?' Said he, 'Go to the king's palace with the excuse of selling a bowl of red colour, and entering where the daughter is, put carefully amongst the mattresses this paper, saying whilst thou put it there, between thy teeth: "may all the folk be fast asleep, and Cannetella alone be left awake."' The old woman agreed for another hundred ducats, and served him right well. O unfortunate is he who alloweth these hideous women to enter his home with the excuse of mending things and carrying manure, for they mend and manure only his honour and his life!

Now no sooner had the old woman done this good deed, than a heavy sleep seemed to overtake all the folk in the house, and they were like dead. Cannetella alone stood with eyes wide open: and being awake, she heard the doors shaken, and she began to scream, but there was no one that could come to her aid. Meanwhile Scioravante had thrown down the seven doors, and entering the chamber, caught hold of Cannetella and was carrying her away with the bed: when as her good luck would have it, the paper that the old woman had put amongst the mattresses slipped to the ground, and the powder within it fell out, and all the folk sprang up awake, and hearing Cannetella's screams, they ran to her assistance, even the dogs and cats, and seizing the ghul they made mince-meat of him. Thus was he caught in the snare which he had prepared for the luckless Cannetella: proving to his own cost that

'There existeth not worse grief and pain
Than his, who of himself his love hath slain.'

PENTA THE HANDLESS

SECOND DIVERSION

Of the Third Day

PENTA SCORNETH TO WED HER BROTHER, AND CUTTING OFF HER HANDS,
SENDETH THEM TO HIM AS A PRESENT. HE COMMANDETH THAT SHE
SHOULD BE PUT WITHIN A CHEST AND THROWN INTO THE SEA. THE
TIDE CASTETH HER UPON A SEASHORE. A SAILOR FINDETH HER, AND
LEADETH HER TO HIS HOME, BUT HIS WIFE THRUSTS HER AGAIN INTO
THE SAME CHEST AND INTO THE SEA. SHE IS FOUND BY A KING, AND
HE TAKETH HER TO WIFE; BUT BY THE WICKEDNESS OF THE SAME
WOMAN, PENTA IS EXPELLED FROM THAT KINGDOM. AFTER SORE TROU-
BLES AND TRAVAIL SHE IS RECOVERED BY HER HUSBAND AND HER BROTHER.

HAVING heard Zeza's story, the company were of the mind that
Cannetella deserved what befell her and more, because she sought
for an hair within an egg: yet they felt pleased when they beheld
her saved from so much sorrow, and there was matter for reflection
in that, knowing how all men were dirt for her, she was reduced
to the pass of humbling herself and bowing down before a locksmith, so that he might save her from so much travail. But the
prince signed to Cecca to begin her story, and she did not delay in
speaking, proceeding thus:

Virtue is tried in the crucible of troubles, and the candle of goodness shineth the more where it is darkest, and fatigue begetteth
merit. Who sitteth idle triumpheth not, but whoso turneth the
ladle, as did the daughter of the King of Preta-secca, with sweat of
blood and danger of death, buildeth for himself the house of contentment, like unto the fortunes I am going to relate.

The King of Preta-secca having been bereft of his wife, the
evil one entered his head, and suggested that he should take his sister
Penta to wife. For this reason, sending for her one day, he met
her alone, and said, ' 'Tis not a matter, O my sister, to be done by
a man with sound judgment, to let the good which he hath in his
own house depart; and besides one knoweth not how it will be,

when one alloweth strange people to put their feet in one's house; therefore having well digested this business, I came to the resolution, and I purpose to take thee to wife, because thou art made of mine own breath, and I know thy nature. Be thou content therefore to be tied in this knot, to be set in this setting, to join this partnership, to enter into this *uniantur acta,* this mixture, *et fiat potio,* and let it be done, as both of us will do a good day's work.'

Penta, hearing this thrust in filth, stood nearly out of her mind, and her colour came and went, and she could scarce believe her own ears, thinking it impossible that her brother could jump to this height, and try to sell her a pair of rotten eggs when he needed an hundred fresh ones. Remaining silent for a while, thinking how she should answer to such an impertinent question, and out of purpose, at last, unloading the fardel of patience, she said, 'If thou hast lost thy wits, I will not lose my shame. I am in a transport of surprise at thee, that thou allowest such words to escape thy mouth, which if said in joke befit an ass, and if in earnest stink of lecherousness. I regret that, if thou hast tongue to speak such outrageous language, I have not ears to hearken thereto. I thy wife? Yes 'tis done for thee: oh, smell thy fill: since when dost thou these foul tricks? this olla podrida? these mixtures? and where are we? in the ice? His sister, O baked-cheese! Ask thy priest to correct thee, and never allow such words to escape thy lips, or else I will do incredible things, and whilst thou esteem me not as a sister, I will not hold thee for what thou art to me.' And thus saying, she departed, and entering a chamber, locked and bolted the door, and saw not the face of her brother for more than a month, leaving the wretched king, who had listened with an hardened brow, to tire out the shot, scorned as a child who hath broken the juglet, and confounded as a cook-maid when the cat hath stolen the meat.

After some days were past, the king again gave vent to his licentious desires, and she desiring to know what had caused her brother such great longing, and what was in her person that should put such a thought in his head, came forth out of her chamber, and went to him, and said, 'O my brother, I have admired myself and looked at myself in the mirror, and I cannot find anything in my face which could deserve and inspire such love as thine, as I am not such a sweet morsel to cause folk to pant and long for me.' And answered the king, 'Penta mine, thou art beauteous and accomplished from head to foot, but thine hand is the thing which above all others causeth me to faint with excessive desire: that hand is the fork which extracteth from the pot of this breast my heart and entrails: that hand is the book which lifteth from the cistern of my life the pail of my soul: that hand is the pincers wherein is held my spirit whilst love is filing it. O hand, O beauteous hand, spoon, which administereth the soup of sweetness: nippers, which nip my longing and desire: shovel, which casteth dust within my heart!' And he would have said more, but Penta replied, 'Thou mayest go, I have heard thee; we will meet again;' and entering her chamber, she sent for a witless slave, and giving him a large knife and an handful of coins, said to him, 'Ali mine, cut off mine hands, I wish to make them beautiful in secret, and whiter.' The slave, believing he was doing her pleasure, with two blows cut them off. Then she had them laid in a faenza basin and sent them covered with a silken napkin to her brother, with a message that she hoped he would enjoy what he coveted most, and desiring him good health and twins, she saluted him.

The king, beholding such a deed, was wroth with exceeding wrath, and he waxed furious, and ordered that a chest should be made straightway, well tarred outside, and commanded that his sister should be put therein, and cast into the sea. And this was done, and the chest sailed on battered by the waves until the tide projected it upon a sea-shore, where, found by some sailors who had been casting their nets, it was opened, and therein they beheld Penta, far more beautiful than the moon when it riseth after having spent its lenten time at Taranto. Masiello, who was the chief and the most courageous of those folk, carried her home, bidding Nuccia his wife to entreat her with kindness. But no sooner had her husband gone forth, than she, who was the mother of suspicion and jealousy, put Penta again within the chest, and cast her once more into the sea, where beaten by the waves, and buffeted here and there, it was at last met by a large vessel, on board of which was the King of Terra-Verde. Perceiving this chest floating about, the king instructed the sailors to strike sail and lay to, and ordering the small boat to be lowered, sent some of the sailors to pick up the chest. When they brought it on board, they opened it, and discovered therein the unhappy damsel, and the king, beholding this beauty alive within a coffin for the dead, believed that he had found a great treasure, although his heart wept because the casket of so many gems of love was found without handles. Taking her to his realm, the king gave her as maid of honour to the queen; and she did all possible services to the queen, as sew, thread the needle, starch the collars, and comb the queen's hair, with her feet, for which reason, no less than for her goodness, youth and beauty, she was held dear as the queen's own daughter.

Now after a month or so was past, the queen was called to appear before the judgment seat of destiny to pay the debt to nature, and she asked the king to her bed-side, and said to him, 'But a short while can my soul remain till she looseth the matrimonial knot between herself and the body: therefore hearten thy heart, O my husband, and strengthen thy soul. But if thou lovest me, and desirest that I should go content and consoled and comforted into the next world, thou must grant me a boon.' 'Command, O mine heart,' said the king, 'that if I cannot give thee proof whilst in life of my great love, I may give thee a sign of the affection I bear thee even after death.' Replied the queen, 'Now listen, as thou hast promised. As soon as mine eyes will be closed in the dust, thou must marry Penta, although we know not who she is, nor whence she came: yet by good breeding and fine bearing is known a steed of good race.' Answered the king, 'Live thou an hundred years; but even if thou shouldst say good-night to give me the evil day, I swear to thee that I shall take her to wife, and I care not that she is without hands and short of weight, for of the bad ones one must always take the least.' But these last words were uttered in an undertone so that his wife should not hear them. And as soon as

the candle of the queen's days was put out, he took Penta to wife;
and the first night that he lay with her she conceived. But after a
time the king was obliged to sail for the kingdom of Anto-scuoglio,
and farewelling Penta, he weighed anchor.

The nine months being over, Penta brought to the light a beauteous man-child, and all the city was illumined and tables spread in
honour of the new-born babe, and the ministers and counsellors
quickly dispatched a felucca to advise the king of what had taken
place. Now the ship met stormy weather on the way, so that one
moment it seemed as if she would meet the stars, and another moment that she would plunge into the very bottom of the ocean. At
last, by the grace of Heaven, she went ashore in the same place
where Penta had been found, and had met with kindness and compassion from the chief of the sailors, and had been cast again into
the sea by a woman's cruelty. As ill-fortune would have it, the
same Nuccia was washing the linen of her child at the sea-shore,
and curious to know the business of other people, as 'tis the nature
of women, enquired of the felucca's master whence he came, and
whither he was bound, and who had sent him. And the master
answered, 'I come from Terra-Verde, and am going to Anto-
scuoglio to find the king of that country, to give him a letter, and
for this I have been sent on purpose. I believe 'tis his wife that
hath written to him. But I could not tell thee clearly what is the
message.' Replied Nuccia, 'And who is the wife of this king?'
and the master rejoined, 'From what I have heard said, she is a
beauteous young dame, and she is hight Penta the Handless, as she
hath lost both her hands. And I have heard them saying that she
was found within a chest in the midst of the sea, and by her good
fortune and destiny she hath become the king's wife, and I know
not why she is writing to him in such haste that I needs must run
against time and tide to reach him quickly.' Hearing these words,
that jewess of a Nuccia invited the master to come and drink a
glass in her house, and she plied him with liquor till he was dead
drunk, and then taking the letter out of his pocket, she called a
scribe and bade him read it. All the time the man read, she was

dying with envy, and every syllable made her sigh deeply, and at the last she bade the same scribe to falsify the writing, and write to the king that the queen had given birth to a dog, and they awaited his orders to know what they should do with it. After it was written they sealed it, and she put it in the sailor's pocket, and when he awakened and beheld the weather changed, he weighed anchor, and tacked the ship, and fared with a light wind for Anto-scuoglio. Arriving thereto, he presented the letter to the king, who, after reading it, answered, that they should keep the queen in cheerful spirits, so that she should not be troubled at all, for these things came through Heaven's commandments, and a good man should not rebel against the stars' decree.

And the master departed, and in a few days arrived at the same place, where Nuccia met him, and entreating him with exceeding great kindness, and giving him wine of extra good vintage, he fell to the ground intoxicated once more. And he slept heavily, and Nuccia putting her hand in his pocket found the answer; and calling the scribe bade him read it, and again bade him falsify a reply for the ministers and counsellors of Terra-Verde, which was, that they should burn at once mother and son. When the master got over his drinking bout, he departed; and arriving at Terra-Verde, presented the letter to the counsellors, and they opened it. When they had mastered its contents, there was a murmuring and whispering among those old sages; and they conversed at length about this matter, and concluded at last that either the king must be going mad, or that some one had cast a spell upon him, for when he had such a pearl of a wife and a gem of an heir, he ordered to make powder of them for death's teeth. So they took the middle course, and decided to send the queen and her son away from the city, where no news could ever be heard of them: and so, giving her some money so as to keep body and soul together, they sent out of the house a treasure, and from the city a great light, and from the husband the two props unlifting his hopes.

The unhappy Penta, perceiving that they had expelled her, although she was not a dishonest woman, nor related to bandits, nor a fastidious student, taking the child in arms, whom she watered with her tears, and fed with her milk, departed, and fared towards Lago-truvolo where dwelt a magician, and he beholding this beautiful maimed damsel who moved the hearts to compassion, this beauty who made more war with her maimed arms than Briareus with his hundred hands, asked her to relate to him the whole history of her misadventures.   And she related to him how her brother, because she would not satisfy his lust of her flesh, sent her to be food for the fishes, and she continued her story up to the day in which she had set her foot in his kingdom.   The magician, hearing this sad tale, wept with ceaseless weeping; and the compassion which entered through the ear-holes issued in sighs from the mouth; at last comforting her with kind words, he said, 'Keep a good heart, O my daughter, for no matter how rotten is the soul's home, it can be supported with the props of hope; and therefore let not thy spirit go forth, as Heaven sometimes sendeth great trouble and travail, so as to make appear all the greater the marvellous coming of success.   Doubt not, therefore, thou has found father and mother here, and I will help thee with my own blood.'   The sad-hearted Penta thanked him gratefully, and said, 'I care not now for aught.   Let Heaven rain misfortunes upon my head, and let a storm of ruin come, now that I am under thy shelter I fear naught as thou wilt protect me with thy grace as thou canst and wilt; and I feel like under the spell of childhood.'   And after a thousand words of kindness on one side and thanks on the other, the magician allotted her a splendid apartment in his palace, and bade that she should be entreated as his own daughter.

The next morning he sent for the crier and commanded that a ban should be published, that whosoever would come and relate at his court the greatest misfortune, he would present them with a crown and sceptre of gold, of the worth of a kingdom.   And the news of this edict flew to all parts of Europe, and to that court came folk more than broccoli to gain such great riches, and one related that he had served at court all the days of his life, and had found that he had lost the water and the soap, his youth and health, and had been paid with a form of cheese. And another, that he had met with injustice from a superior, which he could not resent; and that he had been obliged to swallow the pill, and could not give vent to his anger. One lamented that he had put all his substance within a vessel, and owing to contrary winds had lost the cooked and the raw. Another complained that he had spent all his years in the exercise of his pen and had had so little fortune, that never had it brought him any gain, and he despaired of himself, seeing that matters of pen and ink were so fortunate in the world, whilst his only failed. Such was their case.

In the meanwhile the King of Terra-Verde had returned to his kingdom; and finding this fine sirup at home, he became frantic, and acted as a mad unchained lion, and would have slain all the ministers and counsellors, if they had not shown him his own letter, and perceiving that it had been counterfeited, he sent for the ship's master, and bade him relate to him what had occurred in the voyage. And the king keenly divined that Masiello's wife must have worked him this evil; and arming and equipping a galley, he departed and sailed for that coast, and arriving there he sought and found the woman, and with kindly words he drew out from her the whole intrigue, and thus ascertaining that envy and jealousy had been the cause of this great misfortune, he commanded that the woman should be punished: and they well anointed her with wax and tallow, and put her among a heap of wood, setting fire thereto. And the king stood and watched till he beheld that the fire with its red tongues had licked up that wretched woman. He then ordered the sailors to weigh anchor and depart. And whilst sailing amid the sea, his craft was met by a large vessel, and on enquiry being made he found that on board of it was the King of Preta-secca. They exchanged a thousand ceremonious compliments, and the King of Preta-secca informed the King of Terra-Verde that he was sailing towards Lago-truvolo, as the king of that kingdom had published a certain ban, and he was going to tempt his fortune, as he did not yield to any in misfortune, being the most sorrow-stricken man in all the world. Answered the King of Terra-Verde, 'If 'tis for such case thou goest, I can surpass thee, or at least equal thee, and I can give fifteen for a dozen, and excel the most unfortunate, whoever he be, and where the others measure their cark and care with a small lantern, I can measure it even to the grave. Therefore I will also come with thee, and let us act as gentlemen, each one of us, and whoso shall win of us two shall divide the winnings with the other, even to a fennel.' 'I agree to it,' answered the King of Pretta-secca, and plighting their word between them, they sailed together for Lago-truvolo, where they disembarked, and fared to the royal palace, and presented themselves before the magician. And when he knew who they were, he entreated them with honour as due to kings, and bade them be seated under the dais, and said, 'Well come, and a thousand times welcome!' And hearing that they also had come to the trial of wretchedness and unhappiness of men, the magician enquired what great sorrow had subjected them to the south wind of sighs. And the King of Pretta-secca first began to tell of his love, and the wrong done to his own flesh and blood, and the honourable deed of a virtuous woman done by his sister, and his own dog-heartedness in shutting her up in the chest, and casting her into the sea. And he grieved with exceeding grief as his conscience reproached him of his own error, and his sorrow was great, passing all distress, for the loss of his sister. In one way he was tormented by shame, in the other by the great loss: so that all the cark and care of the most great affliction in others was in him like hell compared to a lantern, and the quintessence of sorrow was as naught, compared with the anguish which gnawed at his heart. Having ended his say, the King of Terra-Verde began to relate, saying, 'Alas! thy sorrow and trouble are like small lumps of sugar, and cakes, and sweetmeats compared with mine, because that very Penta the Handless of whom thou hast spoken, and whom I found in that chest, like a Venice wax torch to burn at my funeral, I took to wife. And she conceived, and bare me a son of passing beauty, and by the envy and malignity of an hideous witch, both had nearly been slain. But, O sore nail to my heart, O anguish and sore affliction, I can never find peace and rest in this world! They were both expelled from my kingdom: and I have taste for naught, and I know not how under the heavy load of such cark and care, doth not fall the ass of this weary life.'

The magician, having heard both their say, understood at once from the points of their noses that one of them was the brother, and the other the husband, of Penta, and sending for Nufriello the son, said to him, 'Go and kiss thy sire and lord's feet;' and the child obeyed the magician, and the father seeing the good breeding and beauty and grace of the child threw a gold chain round his neck. And this done, the magician said again to the child; 'Go and kiss thy uncle's hand, O beauteous boy mine,' and the child obeyed at once. The uncle marvelling with exceeding marvel at the wit and spirit of the little one, presented him with a valuable gem, and enquired of the magician if he were his son, and he answered that they must enquire of his mother. Penta, who had been hid behind a curtain, and had heard the whole business, now came forth, and like a little dog who, having been lost, and after some days finding his master again, barks, and wags its tail, and bounds, and licks his hand, and gives a thousand signs of its delight: thus it was with her, now going to the brother, and then to her husband, now clasped by the love of the one, and then drawn by the blood's instinct of the other, she embraced first one, and then the other, and their delight, and joy, and happiness knew no bounds. Ye must suppose that it was a concert in three of broken words and interrupted sighs; but having ended this music, they then returned to caress the child, first the father, and then the uncle, clasped him, and kissed him, and embraced him. After that from both sides all was said and done, the magician concluded with these words, 'Heaven knoweth how this heart fluttereth with joy in beholding the happiness of all, and the lady Penta comforted, who for her own good deeds deserveth to be held in the palm of the hand, and by this scheme I tried to draw to this kingdom her husband and her brother, and to one and the other I submit myself their slave; but as man bindeth himself with words, and the ox is bound by the horns, and the promise of a worthy man is his bond, judging that the King of Terra-Verde

was in sooth the one most likely to burst with grief, I will maintain
my promise to him, and therefore I give him not only the crown
and sceptre as hath been published by the ban, but my kingdom also.
And as I have neither chick nor child, by your good grace I desire
to take as my adopted children this handsome couple, husband and
wife, and ye will be dear unto me as the eye-ball of mine eyes; and
because there should be naught left for Penta to desire, let her put
her maimed limbs between her legs, and she will withdraw them
with a pair of hands more beauteous than she had before.' And
this being done, and all happening as the magician had said, the joy
was great: they were out of mind with delight.   The husband
esteemed this the greater good fortune, more than the other kingdom
given to him by the magician; and for a few days there were great
joyances and feasting, and then the King of Pretta-secca returned
to his kingdom, and the King of Terra-Verde sent his brother-in-
law to his realm, bidding his younger brother take his place, and he
and his wife remained with the magician, forgetting in joy and
delight the past travail, and taking the world to witness, that

> ' There is naught sweet and dear
> Unless one hath been first tried by the bitter.'

THE FACE

Of the Third Day

RENZA IS SHUT IN A TOWER BY HER FATHER, IT HAVING BEEN FORETOLD
THAT SHE WOULD DIE THROUGH A BIG BONE. SHE FALLETH IN LOVE
WITH A PRINCE, AND WITH A BONE BROUGHT TO HER BY A DOG, SHE
BORETH A HOLE THROUGH THE WALL, AND ESCAPETH. BUT BEHOLDING
HER LOVER, WHO IS WEDDED TO ANOTHER, KISSING HIS BRIDE, SHE
DIETH OF A BROKEN HEART, AND THE PRINCE, UNABLE TO ENDURE HIS
ANGUISH, SLAYETH HIMSELF.

WHILST Cecca with great effect related her story, one could observe an olla podrida of pleasure and disgust, of comfort and affliction, of smiles and weeping. The company wept for Penta's misfortunes, but laughed to hear the end; they were afflicted to behold her passing so much trouble, but they felt comforted that she was saved at last in such great honour; they were disgusted at the treachery done to her, but they were pleased at the vengeance which followed. Meanwhile Meneca stood ready with the match at the powder-train of chatter, and laid her hands on the irons, beginning thus:

It chanceth ofttimes, that when a man believeth himself to eschew an ill adventure, 'tis then that he meeteth it in full. Therefore a wise man must know how to lay in the hands of Heaven all his interests, and not put his trust in the circle of the magician or in the lies of the astrologer because otherwise in seeking to prevent all danger as a prudent man, he falleth within the ruins like a beast: and that this is truth ye will now hear.

Once upon a time there lived the King of Fuosso-stritto, who had a beautiful daughter, and desiring to know what was written in the book of fate for her, he sent for all the magicians, and astrologers, and gipsies of the country, and they came to the royal court, and looking at the lines in the hand, and the marks in the face, and the movements of the person of Renza (thus was the damsel hight), each said their say. But most of them concluded, that she stood in great danger of losing her life through a master bone. The king hearing this, and wishing to wend forward so as not to fall, ordered that a tower should be built, wherein he placed his daughter with twelve damsels and a housekeeper to serve her, and commanded, under pain of death, that all the meat should be served to her without bone, so as to escape the decree of this false planet.

Renza grew up like a full moon. One day as she stood at the lattice-window, there passed that way Cecio, the son of the Queen of Vigna-larga, and beholding such a beauteous face, he at once took heat, and saluted her, and perceiving that she returned his salute, and smiled sweetly the while, he took courage, and going under the window, said, 'Adieu, O thou protocol of all the privileges of nature, archives of all the concessions from heaven: adieu, universal table of all the titles of beauty.' Renza, hearing this praise, reddened with shame, thus becoming even more beautiful, and adding fuel to Cecio's burning fire. She threw, as it is said, boiling water upon the burning flesh; and desiring not to be surfeited by Cecio's courtesy, answered, 'Mayest thou be welcome, O thou dispenser of the food of the graces; O thou magazine of all the stores of virtue; O custom-house of love's traffick.' But Cecio replied, 'How comes it that the castle of the strength of Cupid is enclosed within a tower? How is it that thus is imprisoned the enslaver of all hearts? How is it that imprisoned behind these iron rails is this golden apple?' And Renza related to him how matters stood. Cecio said to her that he was the son of a queen but a vassal of her beauty, and if she would be pleased to escape and wend with him to his kingdom, he would set a crown upon her head.

Renza, who felt as if stinking of mould, having been shut within four walls, and who desired and longed with great longing to inhale the sweet scent of liberty, accepted the offer, and begged Cecio to return in the morning when the dawn calleth the birds to witness of the bad deed done to it by Aurora, and then they would fly together; and putting a flower-vase upon the window, she retired, and the prince returned to his lodging.

Meanwhile Renza stood thinking which would be the best way to file off and trick the damsels, when a certain dog, which the king kept on guard before the tower, entered within her chamber with a large bone in his mouth, and hid under the bed, and there lay eating. Renza, lowering her head, beheld the dog feasting; and it seemed to her that, as chance and luck would have it, it had been sent for her need. Driving the dog out, she took up the bone, and telling the handmaidens that her head ached, and that she desired to be left alone to rest, she locked her door, and began to work in good earnest with this bone, knocking down a stone, and pulling down the mortar. She worked and worked, she dug and levelled, till at last she had made a hole in the wall large enough for her to pass without trouble. Tearing a pair of sheets and twisting them like a rope, when the curtain was lifted from the shadows of the scene of heaven for Aurora to come forth and act the prologue of the tragedy of night, and hearing Cecio whistling, she attached the end of the rope to a post, and slid down into Cecio's arms. He seated her upon an ass, with a saddle covered by a carpet, and they faced on towards Vigna-larga. But towards evening they arrived at a place called Viso, and there finding a beautiful palace, Cecio remained to take possession of his amorous charge: but as it is the trick of Fortune ever to spoil the thread, and upset all games, and to put her nose in the good dreams of all lovers when they are at the best of their enjoyment, a courier arrived with a letter from Cecio's mother, in which she wrote that if he did not hurry back to her, he would not find her alive, because she felt like reaching the end of her vital alphabet. Cecio, hearing these bad news, said to Renza, 'O my heart, the business is important, and I must depart in all haste to arrive in time; therefore stay five or six days in this palace, for I will return, or will send at once to fetch thee.' Renza, hearing this, began to weep and said, 'O wretched fortune mine, O how soon must I drain the dregs from the cask of my enjoyance! O how soon have I reached the bottom of the pot of my pleasure!

How hath it reached me this nail in the heart of my contentment!
O wretched Renza, my hopes have fallen into the cistern, my designs are upset, my satisfaction has ended in smoke: hardly have I
put my lips to this royal sauce, than the mouthful choketh me:
I have no sooner put my mouth to this fountain of sweetness, than
it hath embittered my taste: I have just seen the sun appearing, when
I may say good night, uncle's nest.' These and many other words
issued from the Cupid's bows of those lips, darting barbed arrows
into Cecio's heart, when he rejoined, 'Be silent, O beautiful pole
of my life; O clear lantern of mine eyes; O hyacinth and comfort
of mine heart, I shall soon return, and no one from miles of distance will make me ever go the distance of one foot from thee;
and time will have no power to erase thee from my memory; be
still, rest thy brain, dry thine eyes, and keep me in thine heart.'
Thus saying, he mounted steed and galloped towards his kingdom.

Renza, remaining awhile planted like a cucumber, ran quickly
after Cecio's footsteps, and untethering a horse which she found
in a pasture ground, galloped after him; and in her way she met
with a lay-brother, and she reined in her steed, and bade him give
her his garments, whilst she, giving the man her own raiments
which were all purflewed with gold, put on his woollen robe and
girded the cord round her waist, which held the arms and snares
of love, and mounting steed pursued her route, spurring on her
horse, so that in a short time she came up to Cecio, and said to him,
'Well met, O my gentleman,' and Cecio answered, 'Well come,
O my father, whence comest thou, and where art thou going?' and
Renza replied:

> ' I come from a place, where ever there is weeping:
> There dwelleth a woman, who saith, "O my white face,
> Alas! who hath caused thee to leave my side?" '

Hearing these words, Cecio said to her, whom he believed to be a
boy, 'O my handsome youth, thy company is dear to me; therefore
I pray thee (and take my entrails if thou wilt) leave not my side,
and now and then repeat to me these verses, for thou touchest my

heart with them.' And thus with the fan of chat fanning the heat of the way, they reached Vigna-larga. Here they found that the queen had wedded Cecio to a lady of high degree, and the letter he had received had been only a trick to hasten his return; and the bride stood awaiting his orders; and when Cecio arrived, he begged his mother to well entreat and detain in the house this youth who had kept him company in the way, and to use him as his brother. The queen being pleased and consenting, the prince seated him by his side, and also at table with the bride.

Now ye may suppose what heart could Renza make, and if she could swallow a mouthful: but for all that now and then she kept repeating the verses, which so much pleased Cecio; but the tables being cleared, and the bride and bridegroom retiring in an alcove to speak one with other, Renza, being left to herself, had time to alleviate the anguish and passion of her heart, and entering an orchard which was past the garden, near the saloon where the revels had been held and retiring under a plum-tree, thus began to lament, 'Alas! cruel Cecio, these are the thanks thou givest me for my great love! this is the gratitude for my deep affection! this is the sweet beverage thou holdest to my lips in exchange for my strong devotion! Here have I left my sire and my home, tainted mine honour and given myself into the hands of a heartless dog, that hath cut my way, and shut the door in my face, and hath lifted up the bridge, when I believed I was going to possess such a beautiful fortress. Alas, that I should sight myself written in the excise book of thy black ingratitude, whilst I thought of staying quietly in the height of thy grace; that I should see myself treated like a child, and playing at the game of "Ban and Cammandment, by Master Clement," when I believed I would have played at "Nicholas" with thee! Have I sown my hopes to gather cheeses? Have I been casting nets of desires, and caught within them the sand of ingratitude? Have I been building castles in the air, to drop with a crash all the building? This is the change and exchange that I receive: this is the double point that is given to me: here is the payment that I receive. I have lowered in the well the pail of my amorous desires, and the handle is left in mine hands; I have put my washing to dry in the sun, and it has been raining heavily; I have put upon the fire of my desires the pot which containeth my thoughts, and whilst cooking the spider's web of my misfortunes, I have fallen within it. But who could believe, thou turn-coat, that thy faith should be like unto fame? and that the cask of thy promises should empty itself to the dregs? and the bread of thy bounty should be musty? Fine deed of a worthy man, fine proofs of honoured folk, fine ending for the son of a king, to laugh at me, and trick me, and deceive me, and make me wear a large mantle so that my skirt should appear shorter; promising a sea of pleasure and a world of enjoyment, only to cast me within a darksome grave; washing my face so that I should find my heart blackened. O promises thrown to the winds, O words of bran, O vows of fried spleen! here am I an hundred miles afar when I believed I had reached the baron's home: verily 'tis perfectly true, that the wind carrieth away words said in the evening. Alas! when I believed I should have been one flesh with this cruel man, I shall be with him as dog and cat. When I imagined to eat with the same spoon with this ungrateful dog, I shall be with him like serpent and toad, because I shall not be able to endure that another with a fifty-five of good fortune should snatch from my hands the first number of all my hopes. I shall be unable to bear to be check-mated: O ill-guided Renza, trust thou, and fill thyself with words from lawless men, without any loyalty; unhappy is she who doth trust them, sad-hearted is she who loveth them, wretched whoso lieth in the large bed they make for her. But do it not, for thou knowest that whoso tricketh children dieth the death of the cricket: thou knowest, that even in heaven's bank there are tricking clerks, who will upset the carts: and when least thou expectest it, will come thy day, having done this hand-play to whoso hath given herself to thee on trust, to receive this evil satisfaction in ready coin. But can I not see that I am telling my reasons to the winds? that I am weeping and lamenting to myself empty sighs and lost sobs? He will this evening square up accounts with the bride, and break the measure; and I shall square up my accounts with death, and will pay my debt to nature. He will lie in a perfumed bed of white linen, and I shall be laid on a darksome and stinking bier. He will play at "Emptying the cask" with the bride, and I, "O comrade mine, I am wounded:" I shall strike myself with a poignard through the ribs, and thus end this wretched life.' And after speaking these and other words full of anguish and sorrow, the meal time being near, she was sent for, and the dainties and delicacies were arsenic and bitters, and her head was full of something else than the desire of eating, and she felt no appetite to fill that stomach. Cecio, beholding her so full of thought and sad of face, said to her, 'What is the meaning of this, and why dost thou not honour these drinks? What is the matter with thee, of whom dost thou think, how dost thou feel?' Answered Renza, 'I am not well, and I know not if it is a vertigo or an indigestion.' Replied Cecio, 'Thou doest well in losing one meal, for diet is the best cure for every sickness; but if thou needest the advice of a doctor we will send for a water doctor, who will look only at thy face, without feeling the pulse, and will know at once the infirmity of the person.' Rejoined Renza, 'Mine is not a sickness that requireth a prescription, as no one knoweth the vexations of the pot but only the spoon that wadeth in it.' Said Cecio, 'Go out a little while to breathe the fresh air.' And Renza replied, 'The more I see, the more my heart is breaking.'

Meanwhile all had ended their eating, and the time for retiring had come; and Cecio, desiring to hear continually Renza's verses, bade her sleep on a couch within the same chamber where he was going to sleep with the bride, and now and again he called her to repeat her verses, which were as many knife thrusts in the heart of Renza, as of annoyance in the ears of the bride, so that the latter at last puffed out, 'Ye have broken me with that white face: what kind of music is this? is it dysentery that it lasteth so long? A little of it is quite enough, what in the world can ye find in always repeating the same thing? I believed I would lie with thee to listen to a music of instruments, and not to a bewailing of voices; and ye have taken it in a fine way to touch always on the same mat-

ter. Please let it cease, O mine husband, and do thou allay thy
thirst for garlic, and let us rest a while.' Answered Cecio, 'Be
quiet, O my wife, for now we will break the thread of speech:'
and thus saying, he gave her a loud kiss that could be heard from the
distance of a mile; and the noise of their lips was like a clap of
thunder for Renza's breast, and she felt such anguish that all the
spirits ran to render help to the heart, and it chanced as 'tis said,
that a surfeit in the pot breaketh the pot and the lid; for the rush
of blood to the heart was so great, that she stretched her feet.

Cecio, after playing a few tricks with the bride, called Renza in
a whisper, and bade her repeat those verses which pleased him so
much, but not receiving any reply, he besought and prayed again
that she would oblige him by fulfilling his desire. Hearing not a
word, he arose lightly and pulled her by the arm; and the other
answering naught, he laid his hand upon her face, and on touching
the cold nose, perceived that the heat of the fire of that body was
put out for ever. And he stood stunned and affrighted, and rang
for candles, and uncovering Renza, he recognised her by a patch
that she had between her breasts, and crying with a bitter cry, he
began to say: 'What dost thou behold O wretched Cecio? What
hath happened to thee? What a spectacle is before thine eyes?
What ruin hath fallen upon thy head? O my sweet flower, who
hath gathered thee? O my light, who hath put thee out? O pot
of my love desires, how hast thou overflown? Who hath over-
thrown thee, thou beauteous home of all my happiness? Who hath
torn thee, O thou free paper of my pleasures? Who hath foun-
dered thee, O thou beauteous vessel of the enjoyments of this heart?
O my love, when thou hast closed thine eyes, the magazine of all
beauties hath failed; all business hath ceased for the graces; and
love is gone to cast bones into the sea. At the departure of thy
beauteous soul hath departed the seed of all beauty, the mould is
broken of thy graceful form, nor can the compass be found of all
the sweetness of love. O evil irreparable, O anguish without compare, O immeasurable ruin. Go and stretch thine arm, my mother,
thou hast done a fine deed to smother me, thou hast made me lose

this fine treasure! What will become of me, stripped of all pleasure, light of taste, without consolation, without satisfaction, without enjoyance; believe it or not, O my life, that I will remain in this world. I will follow thee, and take thee by siege wherever thou goest, in spite of death's jaws. We shall be united, and if I had taken thee as companion of my bed by affection, I shall be thy companion in the grave, and the same epitaph shall speak of both and our unhappy fate.' And as he ended speaking he snatched a nail and plunged it under his left breast, and thus bereaved himself of life, leaving the bride cold and frozen with fright. As soon as she could find tongue to speak she called the queen, and the queen came in haste with all her court, and beholding the dreadful catastrophe of Renza and her own son, and hearing the cause of this deed, she tore her hair, and buffeted her face, and beat her breast, and knocked herself about like a fish out of water, calling the stars cruel for pouring such direful misadventure upon her house, and cursing her dark old age in which it had been decreed that such a tragedy should chance. After weeping, and wailing, and crying, and moaning, she commanded that both should be laid in the same grave. And the history of their fortunes was written and stored in the archives.

In the meanwhile there arrived the king, sire of Renza, who had gone round the world in search of his daughter who had run away. He was met in his way by the monk who was selling her clothes, and he related to him his adventure: and the king arrived when the wheat was gathered and the sheaves of their young ears were ready to be laid in the grave; and sighting her, and knowing her, and sighing for her, he cursed the bone which had fattened this soup of roses, for it had been found in his daughter's chamber, and recognised as the instrument which caused this bitter blow, and thus had verified this crime in its gender, or rather the sad presage of those sorcerers, who had said that by a bone she should die, and in this can be clearly seen that

> ' When an evil chooseth to come,
> It will enter by the key-hole.'

SAPIA THE GLUTTON

FOURTH DIVERSION

Of the Third Day

SAPIA WITH HER ABILITY MAINTAINETH HERSELF IN ALL HONOUR, IN
SPITE OF THE BAD EXAMPLE OF HER SISTERS, THEIR FATHER BEING AWAY.
SHE LAUGHED AT HER LOVER, AND FORESEEING THE DANGER WHICH OVER-
SHADOWETH HER, SHE SURPASSETH IT; AND AT LAST THE KING'S SON
TAKETH HER TO WIFE.

THE enjoyment of listening to the other stories was darkened
by the sad end of the two unfortunate lovers, and the company
stood silent for a while, just as if a daughter had been born. Thereupon the king said to Tolla that she should relate some pleasant tale,
to moderate the affliction caused by the death of Renza and Cecio,
and she, obedient to the command, ran on in the manner which followeth:

Man's good judgment is like unto a good lantern, which lighteth
the night of the world's travail, and by its light deep chasms are
passed without danger, and darksome passes without fear. Therefore it is better to have sound sense than money, for the last comes
and goes, whilst the first is ready when most needed: of which
thing ye will perceive a great experience in the person of Sapia the
Glutton, who with the sure North wind of her judgment came forth
in safety from the great gulf, and reached in security good port.

In times long gone before, there lived a very rich merchant,
Marcone hight, who was blessed with three beautiful daughters,
named Bella, Canzolla, and Sapia the Glutton. One day of the
days he had to fare forth for certain merchandise, and well knowing that the eldest daughters were unruly and great flirts, he nailed
down the windows, and gave rings to each, which possessed gems set
in them that whosoever wore them on their fingers and behaved
unseemingly the gems would change colour, and become like so

many patches. No sooner had the father left behind him Villa-aperta (the land thus being hight), than they began an attempt to open the windows, and to look out of the small wickets, although Sapia the Glutton, who was the youngest, scolded, and cried that their house was not the abode of bad women, nor an orange store, nor a chamber-pot, to play these tricks and coquet with the neighbors.

Now vis-a-vis stood the palace of the king, and the king was blessed with three sons, Ceccariello, Grazullo, and Torre hight, who beholding these young damsels, began to sign with their eyes. From signs they came to handkissing, and from handkissing to words and from words to promises, and from promises to facts, so that one evening when the sun, unwilling to contest with night, retires with his income, the three sons scaled the walls and entered the house where the sisters dwelt, and the two elder brothers taking the two elder sisters retired, and Torre was seizing Sapia the Glutton, when she slid from his hold like an eel, and shut herself up within a chamber, bolting the door in such fashion that it was impossible to open it. The unhappy boy was constrained to count his brothers' mouthfuls: and whilst the two loaded the sacks at the mill, he held the mule. But when morning came, and the birds, trumpeters of the dawn, blew the up-in-saddle, so that the hours should mount the steed of day, the two elder brothers departed highly pleased and cheerful, having satisfied their desire, but the younger fared forth disconsolate at having spent so bad a night.

Now the two sisters became with child and had an ill time, and Sapia the Glutton reproached them severely, as they grew rounder from day to day. She puffed out to them from hour to hour, always coming to the conclusion that their drum-like bellies would bring unto them ruin and war, and that when their sire should return there would be a fine sheep-dance. In the meanwhile Torre's desire grew, partly for Sapia's beauty, and partly because he felt spited and ashamed, and he took counsel with the elder sisters, and they agreed to concert a device together so as to cause her to fall in the trap set for her, when least she expected it. They would have brought her to the pass of seeking for him even in his own house.

Therefore one day calling Sapia, they said to her, 'O my sister, what is done cannot be undone, and if advice were paid for, it would cost more, and would be more esteemed. If we had but listened sagely to thy words, we would not have ruined the honour of our house, nor filled our bellies, as thou hast seen; but to what is done there is no remedy, and the knife hath entered up to the handle. Things have gone too far, the goose's beak is made; but nathless we cannot suppose that thine anger will be so great as to desire us out of the world; and if not on our account, at least for the sake of these unborn creatures that we bear in our womb, thou wilt be moved to compassion of our sad state.' 'Heaven knoweth,' answered Sapia the Glutton, 'how my heart doth weep for this error ye have done, thinking of the present shame, and of the trouble which awaiteth you when our father shall return and find this wrong done in his house; and I would give a finger of mine hand, that such a thing should not have happened. But as the devil hath blinded you, I will try and do what I can. Enough that my honour is safe, as blood cannot be changed into milk or water, and, after all, the flesh draweth me to pity your case, and I would lay down my life to remedy this deed.' When Sapia ended speaking, the sisters replied, 'We desire naught else as a token of thine affection, but that thou gain for us some of the bread eaten by the king; because we long for it with such longing, that if we do not satisfy this our want, we fear that a loaf may be found on the nip of our children's noses when they be born; therefore if thou art a Christian, to-morrow morning, when 'tis yet dark, we will lower thee through the window whence came up the king's sons, and we will disguise thee as a beggar, and thou shalt not be known.' Sapia the Glutton, feeling compassion for the little ones, donned a ragged raiment, and slinging a linen bag across her chest, with a comb hanging behind her, when the sun lifteth the trophies of light in sign of the victory gained against the night, was lowered through the window, and she wended towards the king's palace and begged some bread, and when she had received the alms and was ready to retire, Torre, who was in the secret of this trap, knew her at once and tried to seize her, and she turning her back, his hand struck against the comb, and he tore and scratched his hand, so that he was maimed for a few days.

The sisters, having received the bread, had assuaged their desire for it. But hunger gnawed the vitals of the wretched Torre, and they conferred together once more, and in two or three days again the sisters turned to Sapia, telling her that they longed for two pears from the king's garden, and the good sister, arraying herself in another disguise, went to the royal gardens, where she met the king's son. Sighting her and hearing what she sought, he himself climbed the tree, and cast down some pears to Sapia. But when he was going to descend to get hold of her, she withdrew the ladder from under the tree, leaving him to keep company with the owls, and if a gardener had not chanced to pass that way to gather a couple of cabbage-lettuces, and perceiving what had happened, helped him to descend, he might have stayed there all night, for which reason he bit his nails and threatened to avenge himself, in great wrath.

Now as Heaven would have it, the two sisters of Sapia were brought to bed, and they gave birth to two beauteous boys, and they sent for Sapia and said to her, 'We are ruined, O our beautiful sister, if thou resolvest not to help us; because our sire cannot tarry long now in his return, and finding this bad service in the house, the least that he will do, is to cut our ears; therefore do thou fare below, and we will lower the two children in a basket, and thou shalt carry them to their sires, so that they may take every care of them.' Sapia the Glutton had a tender heart full of love, and although she thought it hard to do this work for the stupidity of her sisters, still she allowed them to persuade her to go down, and then they lowered the children, and she carried them to the princes' chambers. The fathers not being there, she laid a child upon each bed, and having discovered which was Torre's chamber, she laid a large stone upon his bed, and then returned home. When the princes came to their chambers, and found these charming children with the names of their sires written on a slip of paper and sewn upon the breast, they were pleased and joyful, and Torre was annoyed and vexed, because he had not been thought worthy to have an offspring. And when he retired to rest he threw himself upon the bed, and knocked against the stone in such a way that he gained a good contusion. Such was their case.

Meanwhile the merchant, returning from his travels, and looking at the rings he had given to this daughters, perceived that the two of the elder sisters were soiled and darkened, and he was wroth with exceeding wrath, and did most wild deeds, and was about to lay hand upon sword to torture and beat them well, so as to discover the truth, when the king's sons demanded the daughters in marriage. Not knowing what had taken place between them, he believed himself scorned. At last he heard what had passed, and of both of the children, and held himself happy and fortunate that it had come to a good ending. And the night was appointed for the bridal. Sapia, knowing the cark and care that she had caused to Torre, although he had asked her hand in marriage with great eagerness, and that all herbs are not mint, and that the mantle is not hairless, at once made a beautiful statue of pastry and sugar, and laying it within a basket, covered it with some raiment. In the evening there being festivals, and balls, and joyances, she sought an excuse, and retired to rest before the others, saying that she was over tired, and she went to the bedside, and bidding them bring her the basket, saying that it held a change of raiment, bade them retire, and when she was alone, she took out the statue, and laying it between the sheets, she hid herself behind the screen awaiting the issue of events. The hour came at last when the brides and bridegrooms retired to their chambers, and Torre, coming to his bed, and believing that Sapia was lying in it, said, 'Now shalt thou pay me, O ungrateful bitch, for all the anguish and heart-sore thou hast caused me; now shalt thou perceive what it is for a cricket to compete with an elephant; now shalt thou pay for all, and I will make thee remember the comb in the linen bag, the ladder taken from under the tree, and the other tricks thou hast played me.' And saying thus he drew a poignard from his side, and struck the statue through and through, and not satisfied with this, said, 'And I will even drink thy blood.' And withdrawing the poignard from the statue, he laid it on his mouth and licked it, and tasting its sweetness, and the scent of musk which came from it, he repented that he had been so cruel as to slay such a sweet damsel, and he began to weep and lament for his fury, speaking words which would have melted a stone; saying that his heart must have been made of gall, and the knife a poisoned one, which could have wounded such a beautiful being. After lamenting, and crying, and weeping, driven by despair he raised the same weapon to slay himself; but Sapia quickly came forward and held his hand, saying, 'Hold thine hand, O Torre, here is a slice of the one thou art weeping for, here am I alive, and in perfect health, and desiring to see thee alive and green. Take me not for a ram's hide. If I have annoyed thee and caused thee displeasure, it was only to try thy constancy, and prove thy truth; this last deceit was done to remedy the furies of thine angered heart, and therefore I beg thee to pardon me for my past deeds.' Torre embraced her with great affection and love, and made her lie by his side, and they made their peace, and their enjoyance was all the sweeter after the past travail, and he esteemed the more the retirement of his wife than the overmuch readiness of his sisters-in-law, because, as saith the poet,

> 'Nor naked Venus, nor Diana dressed,
> The middle course is ever prizèd most.'

THE LARGE CRAB-LOUSE, THE MOUSE, AND THE CRICKET

FIFTH DIVERSION

Of the Third Day

NARDIELLO IS SENT THREE TIMES BY HIS FATHER TO BUY SOME WARES
WITH AN HUNDRED DUCATS EACH TIME. THE FIRST TIME HE BUYETH
A MOUSE, THE NEXT A LARGE CRAB-LOUSE, AND THEN A CRICKET, AND
BEING EXPELLED BY HIS FATHER FOR THIS, HE REACHETH A CITY
WHERE BY MEANS OF HIS PURCHASES HE CURETH THE KING'S DAUGH-
TER, AND AFTER VARIOUS ADVENTURES BECOMETH HER HUSBAND.

THE prince and the slave praised highly the good judgment of
Sapia the Glutton: but they commended Tolla the more for the way
in which she related the story, for she made it seem as if they had
been present, and because, following the order of the list, it came to
the turn of Popa to speak, she behaved as a very Roland, saying in
this way:

Fortune is a captious woman, who escheweth all sages, because
they make more count of the turning of a paper than the wheeling
of the wheel. She standeth the more willingly by the ignorant, and
unworthy; and objecteth not to plebeian honour, nor to divide her
goods with boors, as I will relate to you in the story which followeth.

Once upon a time there dwelt at Vommaro a very rich farmer,
Miccone hight, and he had a son named Nardiello, who was the
most wretched good-for-nothing to be met with amongst all the
good for naught. The life of the unhappy father was embittered
and darkened through his son's folly, and he knew not what to do,
nor how to set him straight, nor how to make him do things as they
ought to be and in good order. If he went to the tavern to eat his
surfeit, he was sure to choose the most treacherous companions to
quarrel with; if he had anything to do with fast women, he was
sure to take hold of the worst flesh and pay for the best; if he went

to a gambling-place, they would trick him, and putting him between them, they would pluck him well from right to left, so that in this way he had cast away half of his father's goods, for which reason Miccone was always up in arms, swearing, scolding, threatening, and saying, 'What dost thou think of doing, thou spendthrift? dost thou not perceive that my goods are going from high to low tide? Leave these accursed taverns, which begin with the name of foes and end with an evil signification: leave them, for they are a migraine of the brains, dropsy of the throat, and dysentery of the purse! Leave this accursed play, where thou endangerest thy life, and thy goods are eaten up, and thy monies are lost, and thy happiness is gone, and the stones bring thee to naught, and the words bring thee down to a pill. Leave the bad whoredom and that evil race, the daughters of sin, where thou spillest and spendest, and for a common fish consumest thy substance, and for some rotten flesh thou sickenest, reducing thyself over the bone that thou art gnawing: not a prostitute, but the Thracian sea, where thou art taken by the Turks; fly from the occasion, and thou shalt lose the vice; remove the cause, 'tis said, and the effect is removed. Therefore take these hundred ducats, and go to the fair at Salern, and buy some calves, and in three or four years they will become oxen; and we will sow a field of wheat, and when the wheat becomes ripe, we will gather it, and turn corn-merchants, and if a scarcity should come, then we will measure the crowns with the corn measure; and when there is naught more to do, I will buy thee a title with the fief of some land of a friend of ours, and thou also shalt be titled like so many others; therefore listen thou to me, O my son, as every head lifteth thee higher, and whoso beginneth not cannot go forward.' Answered Nardiello, 'Leave it to me, now I shall keep proper accounts, and I have done with all other matters.' Replied the father, 'And thus I like it to be,' and handing him the money, Nardiello farewelled him, and fared to the fair.

Now he had hardly reached the waters of Sarno, that lovely river, from which the ancient family of Sarnelli taketh its name, when in an avenue of elm-trees, at the foot of a large stone which was watered continually by the fresh water, and had covered itself with a covering of creeping ivy, he beheld a fairy, who was amusing herself with a crab-louse, which played a small guitar, so that had a Spaniard heard it, he would have said that it was a most surprising and wonderful thing. Nardiello, sighting this sight, stood still, like one in a spell, to listen, saying that he would have given anything to be the owner of such a clever beast, and the fairy answered that if he would pay for it an hundred crowns, she would give it to him. Answered Nardiello, 'Never was there a better time than this, as I have them ready for thee'; and thus saying he threw down the one hundred crowns, and taking the crab-louse, which was laid inside a small box, ran to his father in great glee, happy even unto the marrow of his bones; saying, 'Now shalt thou see, O my lord, if I am a man of genius, and if I know how to do mine affair, because without even tiring myself till the evening I have found midway my fortune, and for an hundred crowns I have had such a gem.' The sire, viewing the small case, held for certain that he had bought a rough diamond, but opening the box, and beholding the crab-louse, his contempt, and anger, and vexation for the loss were as bellows puffing him with wrath, and making him swell like a toad.

Nardiello desired to relate the truth about the crab-louse and its ability, but it was impossible for him to do so, for his father would not allow him to speak one word, saying continually, 'Hold thy tongue, be silent, shut thy mouth, speak not, do not even whisper, thou seed of a mule, sense of a horse, head of an ass, and at this very moment go and take back the crab-louse to whomsoever sold it to thee. Here are another hundred crowns, I give them to thee, buy calves, and return at once; and mind not to be blinded by the evil one, or else I will make thee bite thine hands.' Nardiello took the money, and fared towards the tower of Sarno, and arriving at the same spot, he met the fairy who was now amusing herself with a mouse, which was dancing the most pretty figures of dances that ever could be seen. Nardiello stood sometime with mouth wide open, staring at the bows, and jumps, and turnings, and twistings of the animal, and he wondered with excessive wonder, and enquired of the fairy if she would sell it, for he would give her an hundred ducats. The fairy accepted the offer, and took the monies, and handed him the mouse within a small box, and he returned home, and shewed to the wretched Miccone the fine wares he had bought. Again the father waxed wroth with excessive wrath, and did things out of mind, stamping about like a fantastical horse; and if it had not been for a gossip who happened to be at the show, the son would have received good measure for his hump. At last Miccone, who was in great wrath, took another hundred ducats, and said to him, 'Be careful and do thy fine tricks no more, for the third will not succeed. Go to Salerno and buy the calves, for by the soul of my dead, if thou playest me another trick, wretched will be the mother that gave thee birth.' Nardiello, with his head bowed downwards, slunk towards Salerno, and arriving at the same place, he was met by the fairy who was amusing herself with a cricket, which sang so sweetly that the folk fell asleep with the sound. Nardiello, who heard this new style of nightingale, at once longed to buy it for his wares; and agreeing to pay the hundred ducats, he laid the cricket in a small cage hollowed out of a vegetable marrow and bits of wood. Thus he returned to his father, and the latter, beholding this third bad service, lost all patience, and taking up a stump, laid it about his shoulders in bad manner, like a Rodomonte.

Nardiello, when he could escape from the claws, took up the three little animals, and left the country, and fared towards Lombardy, where lived a high and mighty lord, Cenzone hight, and he was blessed with an only daughter, named Milla, who for a certain sickness from which she suffered had become melancholy, so much so that for the space of seven years no one had seen her smile. And her sire, being in despair, had attempted a thousand remedies, and spent the cooked and the raw, and at last commanded the crier to publish a ban, that whosoever would cause the lady Milla to laugh, he would give her to him in marriage. Nardiello having heard the ban, the whim seized him to tempt his fortune, and going before

Cenzone, he offered to make Milla smile, to which offer answered the lord, 'Be careful, O my comrade, for if the trial be not successful, the mould of thy hood shall pay for it.' Answered Nardiello, 'Let the shape and the shoe go, I will try it, and let happen what will happen.'

The king sent for his daughter, and seating her under the dais, and taking seat himself, Nardiello came and stood before them, and taking out of the boxes the three animals, put them before them, and they played, and danced, and sang with such grace and sprightliness, that the princess laughed heartily. But the king wept within his heart, because by virtue of the ban, he was obliged to give a jewel of a woman to the dregs of humanity to wife. Yet as he could not withdraw his promise, he said to Nardiello: 'I will give thee my daughter in marriage and my estates as a dowry, if thou wilt agree, that if thou do not consummate within three days the act of matrimony, I will send thee to be food for the lions.' 'I am not afraid,' said Nardiello, 'for in that time I am man enough to consummate the marriage of thy daughter and of all thine house. Slowly we will go on, said the flame: at the trial are proved the melons.'

The marriage feast was spread, and the guests ate and enjoyed their sufficiency, and when the evening came, when the sun, like unto a thief, is carried with the hood over against the jail of the west, the bride and bridegroom went to bed.

Now the king had maliciously given Nardiello some opium, so that all night he did naught else but snore loudly, which thing continued to the second and third day, when the king bade that he should be cast in the lions' den, where Nardiello finding himself in such a strait, opened the boxes which contained the three animals, saying, 'As my evil fate has brought me to such a dark pass, as I have naught to leave you, O my beautiful animals, I give you your freedom, so that ye may go whither ye please.' The animals, as soon as they were free, began to antic about, and dance, and play in such manner, that the lions remained like statues watching them.

Meanwhile the mouse spake to Nardiello, whose spirit was ready to take flight, saying: 'Hearten thine heart, O our master, that although thou hast given us our liberty, we will be thy slaves, more than ever, because thou hast fed us with so much love, and preserved us with great affection; and at the last thou hast shown unto us signs of such passionate love as to give us our freedom; but doubt not that who doeth good good expecteth. Do a good action and forget it. And thou must know that we are charmed; and to let thee see if we can and will help thee, follow us, and we will save thee from this danger.' And Nardiello followed them, and the mouse at once bored a hole the size of a man, cut stair-wise, by which they went upstairs quite safely, and they led him to an hayloft, and they said to him that he should command whatever he should desire, since they would not leave a thing undone to please him. Said Nardiello, 'The thing that would please me most, is that if the king hath given another husband to Milla, ye would oblige me, if he were not to allow him to consummate this marriage, because it would be a consummation of this wretched life.' Answered the animals, 'That which thou requirest and naught is all one, hearten thine heart, and await for us in this hayloft, and now we will go to chase away all rottenness.' And they fared toward the court, where they found that the king had wed his daughter to an English lord, and that very night the cask would be open. When they heard this, the animals entered dexterously into the newly wedded couple's chamber, awaiting for the evening, and as soon as the banquet was ended, when the moon cometh forth to feed the chickens with the dew, the pair retired to rest. The bridegroom had loaded his gun, and bent the bow, and taken too much paper, so that as soon as he lay within the sheets, he fell asleep, as one dead. The crab-louse, hearing the snoring of the bridegroom, gently and slowly crept up the bedpost, and slid under the blanket, and quickly crawled to the bridegroom, serving him as a support in such guise, that he opened the body in such wise that he could have said with Petrarca,

' From love it extracted thence a subtle liquid.'

The bride hearing the grumbling of the bowels, and the zephyr, the odour, the comfort, and the shade, awakened her husband, who, beholding with what a perfume he had incensed his idol, was ready to die with shame and to burst with wrath. Rising from bed, and washing all his body, he sent for the doctors, and they said that the cause of this mishap was due to the disorder of the past banquet.

When the following evening came, again taking counsel with the valets, they one and all advised him to cover himself well, to remedy some other inconvenience; which thing being done, he went to bed, but again falling asleep, the crab-louse returned to its duties, but found the way stopped. For which reason it returned unsatisfied to its companions, saying how the bridegroom had put on repairs of bindings, a bank of ribbons, and a trench of rags. The mouse hearing this, said: 'Come with me, and thou shalt see if a good sapper can cut the way;' and reaching the place, he began to gnaw at the rags and clothes, and to make a hole in level with that other hole. Again the crab-louse entered, and gave him another medicinal dose, in such a guise that a topaz sea came forth, and the Arabian perfumes infected the whole palace. The bride being tainted with such odor awoke, and sighting the orange deluge which had coloured the white Holland sheets to Venetian tabby, holding her nose, flew to the chamber of her handmaidens. The wretched bridegroom, calling the valets, loudly and at length lamented his misfortune, that through a lax foundation the greatness of his house would be closed. His followers and servants comforted him, and advised him to be careful the third night, and related to him the story of the sick man, and of the mordacious doctors, the former allowing foul wind to escape him, the doctors speaking to him in a learned language, said, 'Sanitatibus,' and the other letting out another, replied, 'Ventositatibus,' but a third following, he opened his mouth widely, and said, 'Asinitatibus.' 'Therefore,' continued they, 'if thy first mosaic work made in the nuptial bed was blamed upon the disorders of the banquet, the second upon the bad condition of the stomach, and this had caused the motion, the third will be imputed to natural looseness, and thou wilt be expelled, in a disgraceful and shameful manner.' Said the bridegroom, 'Doubt not, as to-night, were I even to burst, I will keep watch, not allowing sleep to overcome me; and besides this, we will think of what remedy we can use to stop the master conduct, so that no one should say,

> 'Three times he fell, and at the third lay still.'

Having agreed thus, when the following night came, he changed room and bed, and calling his comrades, he sought their advice so as to stop up the third relaxation of the body, so that he should not be tricked for the third time. As for his remaining awake, not all the poppies in the world would make him fall asleep. Amongst his servants there was a youth whose craft was to make bombards; and as every one speaketh of his craft, he advised the bridegroom to have a wooden stopper made, as it is done for the mortars, which thing was at once done, and put in place as it should be, and he went to bed, not touching the bride, being afraid of doing mischief and of disarranging the new invention; closing not his eyes, so as to be ready, at every move of the body, to jump out of bed. The crab-louse, who saw that the bridegroom fell not asleep, said to its companions, 'Alas, this time we will fail, and our ability will be for naught; as the bridegroom sleepeth not, and giveth me no time to follow my enterprise.' Said the cricket, 'Wait a moment, and I will serve thee;' and he began to sing sweetly, and after a little while the bridegroom fell asleep; and the crab-louse perceiving it, crept at once to its duty as a syringe. But finding the door bolted, and the way stopped, it returned in despair, and confusion to his companions, relating what had happened.

The mouse, which had no other end in view but to serve Nardiello and please him, at once fared to the pantry, and sniffing about from place to place, it came at last to a pot of mustard, wherein dipping its tail, it returned to the bridegroom's bed, and anointed the nostrils of the unhappy Englishman, and he began to sneeze so loudly and strongly, that the stopper came forth in a fury, and as he lay with his back turned to the bride, it struck her mid-breast with such a blow that it nearly slew her. And she screamed and screeched, and at her screams the king ran in, and enquired of her what ailed her. She told him that a petard had been shot at her breast. And the king marvelled with excessive marvel at such a folly, and wondered how with a petard on her chest she could speak; and lifting the bed-clothes, he found the bran mine, and the petard's stopper which had hit the bride, and made a good mark in her breast; although I know not which caused her more disgust, the stink of the powder, or the blow from the ball. The king, beholding such a dirty sight, and hearing that it was the third liquidation of this instrument which he had done, expelled the bridegroom from his estates; and, considering that all this evil had happened to him through the cruel treatment used to Nardiello, he struck his breast with repentance; and whilst he lamented what he had done, the crab-louse appeared before him, saying, 'Despair not, as Nardiello liveth, and for his good qualities deserveth to be the son-in-law of thy magnificence; and if thou art pleased that he should come, we will send for him at once.' Answered the king, 'O thou most welcome with the happy tidings, O my beautiful animal. Thou hast saved us from a sea of trouble, as I felt a pricking at mine heart, because of the wrong I had done to that unhappy youth. Therefore bid him come, for I long to embrace him as my son and give him my daughter in marriage.' The cricket hearing this, jumping and dancing, went to the hayloft where was Nardiello, and relating to him what had happened, led him to the royal palace, where he was met and embraced by the king, and the king led Milla to him, and the beasts gave him a spell, and by its power he became a handsome youth, and they sent for his father from Vommaro, and they all lived happily together, proving after a thousand troubles and heart-aches that

'More will happen in an hour than in an hundred years.'

THE WOOD OF GARLIC

Of the Third Day

BELLUCCIA, DAUGHTER OF AMBRUOSO DE LA VARRA, BEING OBEDIENT TO
HER FATHER, AND ACTING PRUDENTLY IN HIS COMMANDS, BECOMETH
THE WIFE OF A RICH YOUTH, NARDUCCIO HIGHT, THE FIRST-BORN OF
BIASILLO GUALLECCHIA. HER SISTERS, BEING POOR, ARE DOWERED BY
BIASSILO, AND GIVEN IN MARRIAGE TO HIS OTHER SONS.

The company laughed heartily, not so much at the expulsion of
the bridegroom, as at the trick played him by the mouse; and they
would have laughed till the next morning, if the prince had not
bade them be silent, and let Donna Antonella speak, who was ready,
and thus she began to relate:

Obedience is a sure merchandise which bringeth gain without
danger, and is such a possession that in every season it rendereth good
fruit: as will be shown to you by the daughter of a poor farmer,
who by being obedient to the behests of her father, not only opened a
good way for herself, but also for her sisters, who married well.

Once upon a time there lived in the village of la Varra a rustic,
Ambruoso hight, and he was blessed with seven daughters. But all
that he possessed to maintain and bring them up to the honours of
this world was a forest of garlic. The worthy man was bound in
the strongest bonds of friendship to another farmer, Biasillo Guallecchia of Resina hight, who possessed good funds, and who was
blessed with seven sons, of whom Narduccio, the first born and his
right eye, fell sick of a dangerous sickness. No remedy could be
found to cure him, although his sire's purse was always open. And
one day of the days Ambruoso paid him a visit, and Biasillo enquired of him how many children he had, and Ambruoso, feeling
ashamed to tell him that he had brought into the world so many
chatterers, said, 'I am blessed with four sons and three daughters.'

Replied Biasillo, 'If it be so, send one of thy sons to converse and cheer my son, and thou wilt confer upon me a great favour.' Ambruoso, who saw himself taken at his word, knew not what answer to give, therefore he made a sign with his head accepting the invitation, and returning to la Varra was ready to die with sadness, knowing not how to present himself before his friend. At last calling his daughters one by one, from the eldest to the youngest, he asked them which of them would like to cut her hair, and array herself in male attire, and feign herself a youth, so as to converse and keep company with the son of Biasillo, who was sick. At these words the eldest daughter Annuccia, answered, 'Since when is my father dead, that I should shear myself?' Nora the second answered, 'I am not married yet and thou wouldst see me in sad plight?' Sapatina, the third, said, 'I have always heard it said that women should never wear breeches.' Rosa, the fourth, answered, 'Miaou, miaou, thou shalt not fish me to go and seek what the chemists have not, for the entertainment of a sick man.' Cianna, the fifth, said, 'Tell this sick man that he may cure himself, and endeavour to get better, for I would not give a thread of mine hair for an hundred threads of men's lives.' The sixth, Sella, said, 'I was born a woman, I live as a woman, and I will die as a woman; and I will not disguise myself as a man, and lose the name of good woman.' The last, a shy, retired damsel, Belluccia hight, seeing that the father, at every answer of her sisters, sighed deeply, answered, 'If 'tis not enough to disguise myself in male attire, I will even take the form of a beast, and make myself small to please thee.' Said Ambruoso, 'Mayest thou be blessed, O my daughter, as thou hast given me new life for the blood that I gave thee. Now let us lose not a moment, at the lathe is the work quickly made;' and cutting her hair (the golden ropes of the bailiffs of love), and robing her in an old raiment, they fared to Resina, where they were received with the greatest of welcomes by Biasillo and his son, who was abed.

Ambruoso, taking his departure, wended home, leaving Belluccia to serve Narduccio, the sick youth, who watched her, and could see such a light shine among those rags, and such beauty as to spellbind the beholder, and gazing again and again, and observing her well, he said in his mind, 'If mine eyes deceive me not, this youth must be a woman: the sweetness and tenderness of the face betray her, and her manner of speech confirms it, and her graceful movement proves it, and my heart tells me of it, and love discovers it. It is a woman unfailingly; and perchance she came disguised as a man to lay snare to take and wound this heart.' Losing himself deeply in this thought, great sadness overcame him, and the fever strengthened, and the doctors found him in bad plight: and his mother who burned with a deep love for her son, said to him, 'O my son, light of mine eyes, prop and tongs of mine old age, what is the reason and right cause that instead of strengthening thyself thou art worse in health; and instead of going forwards thou goest backwards, like skin upon the burning coals? Is it possible that thou wilt make thy mother disconsolate without telling her the cause of thy sickness, so that we may cure it? Therefore, O my jewel, ease thy mind, let thy words rush forth, speak, tell me quickly, what dost thou need? and whatever is thy want, let Cola do it for thee, and I will not fail to fulfil all thy desires, whatsoever they be.' Narduccio, encouraged by these kind words, spake in language of fire, and confessed the hot passion of his soul, explaining to his mother that he held for certain that Ambruoso's supposed son was a woman; and if they would not give her to him to wife, he had resolved to cut short the thread of his life. Said his mother, 'Softly, O my son, to quieten this fancy which hath taken hold of thy brains, we will try some device, and will discover if it be a woman or a youth, if it be a cropped country or a country well filled with trees. We will send the youth to the stable, and bid him mount the wildest pony there: if it be a woman, the women have not spirit enough, and thou shalt see her change colour and be nigh fainting, and at once we shall discover the weight of the goods.' The son was pleased with this thought, and sent Belluccia to the stable, and they handed her a devil of a pony, and saddling him, she mounted him, and with the spirit of a lion began to promenade up and down, enough to keep the gazers wonderstruck, walking the pony in manner enough to stun, and making it whirl round enough to marvel, and pushing it forward so that folk stood in ecstasy, and curvetting and careering in surprising manner: for which reason said the mother to Narduccio, 'Drive out of thine head, O my son, such frenzy; for this youth stood firm in his saddle, better than the oldest crap-in-saddle of Porta-reale.' But for all that proof Narduccio continued to say that it was a damsel, and that not even Scannarebecco would drive it from his head. The mother, to erase from his mind this desire, said to him, 'Softly, O my blackbird, we will devise a device a second time, to clear this matter;' and calling for a gun, sent for Belluccia, bidding her to load and shoot. And she lifted the weapon, and put the powder in the cane and the powder of desire in the body of Nardiello, and set the match to the matchlock and the fire in the heart of the sick youth, and discharging the gun, loaded the breast of the wretched Narduccio with longing and desire.

The mother, who beheld the grace, and dexterity, and charming mien of the seeming youth in shooting, said to her son, 'Drive out of thy mind such thoughts, and think well that a woman cannot do so much.' But Narduccio stood firm in his belief, and could find no peace, and would have staked his life that this beauteous rose had no bud, and kept saying to his mother, 'Believe me, mother mine, that if this beautiful tree of all graces and love will give a fig to thy sick son, thy sick son will show the figs to all the doctors; therefore let us try every means to ascertain the truth: if not I shall fail daily in my strength, and because I cannot find my way to a pit, I shall fall in another and deeper pit.' The unhappy mother, who beheld his obstinacy, and having put his feet on ground, signed scissors, scissors ever, said to him, 'If thou wouldst ascertain thyself of the truth, take the youth with thee to swim and bathe, and thou shalt see if 'tis a happy arch or an imperfect bay; if 'tis a large square or a little fork; if 'tis a supreme circus, or a Trajan column.' Answered Narduccio, 'Bravo, naught can be said to that, thou hast caught in point: to-day will be seen if 'tis a spit or a frying-pan, a roller or a sieve, a spindle or a small ditch.' But Belluccia scented the snare laid for her, and sent at once for one of her father's apprentices,

who was a very sharp and clever youth, and she tutored him, and
bade him that he should keep watch and as soon as he saw her near
the shore undressing ready to go a-bathing, he should come forth
from his hiding place, and bring her the bad tidings that her father
lay a-dying, and would like to see her before his soul should take
flight. And the youth did as he was bid, and no sooner did he behold Narduccio and Belluccia at the sea-side beginning to cast off
their garments than, according to his agreement, he served her at
the first cut; and she hearing the news took leave of Narduccio, and
fared towards la Varra; and the sick youth returned to his mother
with head bent downwards and rolling eyes, yellow of colour, and
with white lips, and related to her that the business had failed; and
for the mishap which had happened he could not do the last trial.
Answered his mother, 'Despair not, we must catch the hare with
the cart. Fare thou at once to the house of Ambruoso, and call thou
the son, and whether he come down quickly or delay, thou shalt
clear this ambush, and discover the intrigue.' At these words the
cheeks of Narduccio became of a more natural hue, and the following morning, when the sun taketh up the rays and chaseth away the
stars, he fared straight to the house of Ambruoso, where calling him,
he said that he desired to speak on an important matter to his son,
who could not be seen neither long nor short. The farmer bade
him wait a while, and he would send his son to him; and Belluccia,
not wishing to be found in *flagrante delicto*, divested her gown,
and donned the breeches and the male attire; but her hurry was
such that she forgot to take her earrings from her ears, which was
sighted by Narduccio: as by the ears of a donkey one can foretell bad
weather, so by Belluccia's ears he ascertained his desire. Catching
her in his arms like unto a Corsican dog, he said, ' 'Tis my will that
thou shalt be my wife in despite of the envious, and in annoyance of
fortune, even against death.' Ambruoso perceiving the good intention of Narduccio, said, 'Enough that thy father is satisfied, and if
he will consent with one hand, I will with an hundred;' and thus
they with one accord fared to Biasillo's house, where the mother and
father of Narduccio, desiring to see the happiness of their son, re-

ceived with great pleasure their daughter-in-law, and desiring to know why Ambruoso had played this trick, and sent her to their house arrayed in male attire, and hearing that the cause had been not to discover that he had been such an ass to give life to seven daughters, Biasillo said, 'As Heaven hath given thee so many girls, and to me so many boys, we will have one journey to seven services. Go thou and bring them all hither, for I desire to dower them, as, praise be to Heaven, I have enough and more than sufficient for all these mixtures.' Ambruoso hearing this, put his best foot forward, and went to fetch his daughters, and brought them to Biasillo's house, where there was a bridal-feast with seven weddings, and the music and the dance reached the seventh heaven, and there they are now enjoying themselves mightily, and 'tis clearly seen that

' The divine grace ne'er cometh late.'

CORVETTO

Of the Third Day

CORVETTO, FOR HIS VIRTUOUS QUALITIES, IS ENVIED BY ALL THE COUR-
TIERS OF THE KING, AND IS SENT UPON SEVERAL DANGEROUS EXPEDI-
TIONS, BUT ISSUING FORTH WITH HONOUR IN DESPITE OF HIS FOES,
IS MARRIED TO THE PRINCESS.

THE listeners marvelled so in hearing the deeds of Belluccia recounted, that when they were told of her marriage, they were as
pleased, and joyous, as if she had been their own child. But the
desire to hear Ciulla made them pause in their applause, and strain
their ears at the motion of her lips, which spake thus:

I once heard it said that Juno to find the lie fared to Candia.
But if some one enquired of me where in very sooth fraud and deceit would be taught, I could point out to them no other place than
the court, where they knew how to hide under the mask of levity
the murmurs of malcontent, to conceal slander with comic jest, and
treachery with jokes, and roguery with Punch-like tricks: where at
the same time 'tis cut out and sewn, 'tis pricked and anointed, 'tis
broken and plastered up again: of which matters I will show you a
netful in the story that ye will listen to.

Once upon a time there lived in the service of the King of
Sciummo-largo a right worthy youth, Corvetto hight, who through
good conduct and excellent behaviour was held dear in his royal
master's heart, and therefore hated and held in dislike by the courtiers; who were very bats of ignorance, and could not endure to
gaze upon the light of Corvetto's virtue, since with ready money and
with a good end in view he had gained his master's good graces.
The zephyr of the king's favour to Corvetto was as a sickening
easterly wind to the envious courtiers, and they did naught else at the
corners of the palace but murmur, and chatter, and whisper, and

cut, and slice, and backbite the poor youth, saying, 'What spell hath this good-for-naught cast upon the king, that he loves him so well? What great fortune is his, that not a day passeth without some favour is shown to him? We are always stepping backwards like unto rope-makers and we lose our connections, though we work like dogs, and sweat like diggers, and run like deer, so as to divine the king's pleasure. Truly one must be born lucky in this world; and whoso is unlucky, 'tis best for him to cast himself into the sea: at the last must we look on and burst.' These and other words came forth like poisoned darts from the bow of their lips to be shot at the target of Corvetto's ruin. O wretched is he who is condemned to the hell of a court, where fawning flattery is sold by the dozen, and malignity and bad actions are measured to the grave, and deceit and treachery are weighed by the ton. But who can say what machinery of melon's parings is laid under the feet to cause one to fall? Who can tell what a quantity of the soap of falsehood was anointed in the ladder of the king's ears, to cause Corvetto to slip down and break his neck? Who can relate what pits of deceit were dug within the brains of the master, and the cover laid over the snares of good zeal, to make him fall? But Corvetto was charmed, and perceived the snares set for him, and discovered the traps, and knew the skeins, and could understand the intrigues, and the ambush, and the conspiracies, and the troubles of his adversaries. He kept his ears open, and his eyes on watch, so as not to mistake the thread, knowing that fortune is inconstant to all courtiers. The higher the youth stepped, the louder became the slander and the discoveries of his foes, till at last, knowing not how to drive him from their feet, because their evil speaking was not listened to, they thought to upset him by praising him very highly, so as to make him fall into a deeper chasm (this art was invented in the hot-house, Hell, and re-fined at court), which matter they attempted in the manner which follows.

There lived about ten miles distance from Scotland, where this king's realm was, a ghul, the most savage and brutal that ever lived in Ghul-land. As he was persecuted by the king, he had strengthened himself within a desert-forest on the top of a high mountain, where not even the birds would fly: and it was such a wild and intricate place, that a sight of the sun was never seen there. The ghul had a beautiful steed, which seemed painted, and among other beauties it had the gift of speech, because by a charm it spake like ourselves.

Now the courtiers knew how wicked was the ghul, and how wild was the forest, and how high was the mountain, and how wonderful was this horse, so they went to the king, and descanting minutely upon this steed's perfections, they said that it was worthy of so great a king, and that some means must be found to take it from out of the clutches of the ghul, and that Corvetto would be the very one to take hold of it, as he was a youth of great spirit and firm courage, and good to come forth from burning fire. The king, who knew not that under the flowers of these words the snake lay hid, called Corvetto to him, and said, 'An thou lovest me, leave no means untried to get for me the steed of my foe the ghul, and thou wilt be happy and satisfied of having rendered me this service.' Corvetto understood at once that this drum had been beaten by those who wished him evil; but in obedience to the command of the king, he fared mountain-wards, and entering softly the stable, he saddled the ghul's horse, and mounted, and firmly setting his feet on the stirrups, spurred the steed homewards. The horse feeling the spur, and perceiving that it was leaving the palace, cried out, 'Be on guard, for Corvetto is taking me away.' The ghul hearing the cry rushed out with all the animals which served him, on this side ye could see a monkey, on the other side a bear, on this side a lion, and on that side a wolf, ready to make mince-meat of him. But the youth spurred on, and galloped down the mountain, and fared city-wards, and safely arrived at court, where presenting the steed to the king, he stood before him, and the king embraced him like a son and drawing out a purse, he filled Corvetto's breeches with gold pieces, thus increasing the envy and hatred of the courtiers, whose flame of ire, like unto a candle before, now burned like a conflagration, beholding that the way they had chosen to throw down Corvetto's good fortune only served to pave the way to a higher good.

But they knew that not at the first attack in war is the fortress taken. They desired to try a second time, and they said to the king, 'It hath come in good time the beautiful steed, which will in sooth be an honour to the royal stable, but if thou hadst the bed-cover of the ghul, which is a wonderful thing, thy fame would spread all over the country, and in all the fairs, and no one could boast of greater riches or greater treasure than thine, and no other than Corvetto, who is a clever hand at these matters, could help thee to it.' The king who danced at every sound, and of these bitter fruits sugared over ate only the paring, called Corvetto, and begged him to get him the ghul's bed-cover. Corvetto answered not a word, but fared to the mountain, and entering the ghul's chamber unseen, and looking, where he slept, he hid himself under the bed, and awaited there till the night, to make the stars laugh, maketh a carnival book of the heavens, when the ghul having gone to bed with his wife, Corvetto came forth quite quietly, and desiring to pull off the bed-cover from the bed, began to draw it down very gently. But the ghul awoke, and bade his wife not to pull so much, because she would leave him naked, and he would catch a pain in his bowels. ' 'Tis thou who uncoverest me,' answered the ghula, 'I have not even a rag left on.' Replied the ghul, 'Where the devil is the blanket?' and putting down his hand it touched Corvetto's face; and the ghul cried out, 'The little monk, the little monk, folk, candles, run'; and at these cries all the house turned topsy-turvy. But Corvetto, who had thrown everything out of window, jumped down upon them, and making them up into a parcel, fared city-wards; where the king met him, and entreated him with the highest favour, and all the courtiers were nigh to burst with rage and envy. But nathless they made up their minds to fall upon Corvetto with the rearguard of roguery, finding the king in high glee for the gift of the bed-cover, which was of silk purflewed with gold, whereon were chronicled a thousand feats, and whims, and thoughts. Among the rest, if I remember rightly, there was a cock in the act of crowing at the dawn, which it beheld coming forth, saying with the old Tuscan saw, ' 'Tis enough to behold thee,' and also yet a faded flower, with a Tuscan proverb, 'At sun-set.' And so many and numerous were they that it would need a long memory and more time in which to relate them. They found (as I said before) the king in high glee and joyance, and said to him, 'As Corvetto hath done so much in thy service, it would not be a matter of great importance, if he would also let thee have the ghul's palace, which is fit for an emperor. It has so many apartments and chambers, inside and outside, that it can lodge an army: and thou canst not imagine how many courtyards, and supporters, and lodges, and passages, and water-closets it contains, and what chosen architecture and fine arts shine in it, and how nature joyeth there, and how marvel shaketh one there.' The king, who was endowed with a prolific brain, called Corvetto, and told him that he longed for the ghul's palace, and that after having fulfilled so many of his wants, if he would join this one to them, he would write it with the crayon of gratitude upon the tablets of his memory. Corvetto, who was all fire, and could go an hundred miles an hour, at once lifted his heels, and soon arrived at the ghul's palace, and reaching there found that the ghula had given birth to a handsome little ghul, and her husband had gone to invite their friends and relatives. The ghula, having left her bed, was busy getting ready the banquet, and Corvetto, entering with a brazen face, said, 'Well met, O worthy woman and beauteous housewife, why dost thou use ill thy life and squander thy health so? Yesterday thou wert brought to bed, and now thou workest: hast thou no pity upon thine own flesh?' Answered the ghula, 'What dost thou want that I should do, when I have nobody to help me?' Replied Corvetto, 'Here I am to help thee for bites and kicks.' Said the ghula, 'Mayest thou be welcome, and as thou hast come to offer thyself with such deep affection, help me to chop those four blocks of wood.' Rejoined Corvetto, 'By thy grace, if four be not enough, I will chop five;' and seizing an axe newly sharpened, instead of hitting the wood, he struck off the ghula's head, which fell on the ground with a thud; and running to the entrance gate, he dug a deep pit before it, and covering it with boughs and sod, hid himself behind the door. When he beheld the ghul coming with his kith and kin, he went in the courtyard and screamed out, 'I am thy witness, half-excrement! Hurrah for the King of Sciummo-largo!' The ghul, hearing this bravado, ran toward Corvetto to seize him and make mince-meat of him, and he ran with such fury under the portal, that he put his foot in the pit, and fell headlong in it, and Corvetto cast stones at him till he had crushed him like a cake. Then locking the palace gate, he took the key to the king, who, perceiving of what priceless worth was this youth against the teeth of fortune, and despite all envy and the jealousy of the courtiers, gave him his daughter in marriage, so that the beams of envy became the phalanx whereon stood the vessel of his life launched into the sea of greatness, and his enemies remained confused and crushed, and went to bed without a candle, for

'The punishment due to a wicked man
May be delayed, but faileth not to strike.'

THE IGNORANT YOUTH

Of the Third Day

MOSCIONE IS SENT BY HIS FATHER TO BUY SOME GOODS IN CAIRO, TO
WEAN HIM FROM THE PATERNAL ROOF, WHERE HE WAS EXCEEDINGLY
IGNORANT. FARING CAIROWARDS, HE MEETS IN HIS WAY SEVERAL VIRTU-
OUS FOLK WHO TAKE HIM WITH THEM, AND THROUGH THEM HE
RETURNETH HOME LOADED WITH SILVER AND GOLD.

COURTIERS were not wanting, among those who surrounded
the prince, who would have shown their anger, if their art had not
been dissimulation, for they had been touched to the quick: nor
could they have told you, if they felt more hurt at having thrust
under their noses their chicanery and falsehood, or by their envy of
Corvetto's happiness. But as Paola began to speak, she drew forth
their souls from the deep well of their passion with the hook of
these words:

An ignorant man has always been more praised by consorting
with virtuous men than a sage who joineth company with folk of
small worth; because as much competency and greatness as one may
gain from the former, so much goods and honour one may lose
through the latter: and as with the wooden peg the ham is tried, so
by the tale that I am going to relate you will perceive if my proposi-
tion be true.

Once upon a time there lived a father who was as rich as the sea;
but as happiness is not to be had in this world, he had a son so
ignorant and stupid that he hardly knew a fritter from a cucumber.
So, being unable to bear any more with his folly, his sire gave him a
well-filled purse, and sent him to trade in the east, well knowing
that travel wakeneth the mind, and that consorting with divers peoples sharpeneth the judgment, and maketh man expert.

Moscione (thus was the son hight) mounting steed, fared towards

253

Venice, the arsenal of the wonders of the world, intending there to take ship for Cairo.

When he had fared one day's journey, he met a youth standing against a poplar-tree, and he said to him, 'O my youth, what is thy name? Whence comest thou? What is thy craft?' and the other answered, 'My name is Furgolo, I come from Saetta, and I can run as fast as lightning.' Replied Moscione, 'I should like to see thee run;' and Furgolo said, 'Wait a moment, and thou shalt see if it is gun-powder or corn-flour.'

And they stood still a moment, when behold a hind came bounding before them, and Furgolo, letting her pass a good way, set to run, and he was so light of foot that he might have stepped upon a field bestrewed with flour and left no footprint marked thereon, and in four jumps he came up with her. And Moscione, marvelling with exceeding marvel, said to him, 'Wilt thou stay with me, an I will pay thy wage?' and Furgolo agreeing, they fared on together. But they had not journeyed four miles when they met another youth, and Moscione said to him, 'What is thy name, comrade? Which country is thine? And what is thy craft?' and the other answered, 'My name is Hare's Ear, I come from Valle-curiosa, and when I lay my ears on ground, without moving from the place I can hear what is done in the world, what is monopolized, what is conferred, what the craftsmen do to raise the price of things, what bad services are done by courtiers, what wicked advice is given by pimps, what appointments are made by lovers. I can hear the plots of rogues, the lamentations of servants, the reports of spies, and Luciano's cock saw not so much with the aid of the Frank's lantern, as can these ears of mine observe.' Answered Moscione, 'If thou speakest sooth, tell me, what are they talking about in mine house?' and Hare's Ear, laying his ears on ground, said, 'An old man is speaking to his wife, and saith, "May the sun in Lion be praised, that I have rid mine eyes from the sight of that Moscione, that face of an old jar, that nail of mine heart, for I hope at least that in going about the world he will become a man, and will not be such a beastly ass, such a knave, such a good-for-naught."' Cried Moscione, ' 'Tis enough, 'tis enough, thou speakest sooth, I believe thee; therefore come with me, for thou hast found thy good fate.' Said the youth, 'I will come;' and thus they fared together, and they had gone about ten miles, when they met another youth to whom Moscione said, 'How callest thou thyself? Where art thou born, O my worthy man? And what canst thou do in this world?' and he answered, 'My name is Hit Straight, I am from Castiello-Tira-giusto, and I can shoot with the crossbow and hit an apple in the centre.' Replied Moscione, 'I should like to see a proof of it,' and the other charged his crossbow, pulled the string, and hit a bean on the top of a stone, whereupon Moscione took him also into his company. And they continued wayfaring another day's journey till they came to some men who were building a pier in the scorching heat of the sun, so that they could have said, with truth, 'Frying-pan, put water to the wine, for my heart is burning.' And Moscione felt pity for them, and said to them, 'O my masters, how can ye stand this burning heat, where a buffalo would be roasted?' And one of them answered, 'We are as cool and fresh as a rose, because we have behind us a youth who blows at us in such a manner, that it seems as if all the west winds were blowing.' Said Moscione, 'Let me see him, and God guard thee'; and the builder called the youth, and Moscione said to him, 'How do they name thee, thou priest of thy fellows? From which land comest thou? And what is thy profession?' and the other answered, 'I am hight Sciosciariello, I come from Terra-Ventosa, and I can imitate with my mouth all the winds which blow from Posilippo towards evening;' and turning all at once towards certain plum-trees, he blew such fury of winds that it uprooted the fruit-trees.

When Moscione saw this, he took him also for companion, and they fared as long a way again, when they were met by another youth, to whom Moscione said, 'What is thy name, and let it not be an order? Whence dost thou come, can it be known? And what is thy craft, if the question may be asked?' And the other answer, 'My name is Forte-Schiena, I come from Valentino, and I have a gift that I can carry a mountain up my back, and it seems to me the weight of a feather.' 'If this be true,' said Moscione, 'thou deservest to be king of the custom-house, and thou wouldst win the prize on the first of May; but I should like to see the experiment.'

Then Forte-Schiena began to load himself with large stones, trunks of trees, and so many other weighty things that a thousand carts could not have borne them; which when Moscione saw, he bade the youth to stay with him. Thus they fared toward Bello-sciore, the king of which place had a daughter who could run like the wind, and if she ran upon a broccoli field she was so light of foot that she would not damage a single flower; and the king had issued an edict, that whoso could overtake her when she ran, he would give her to him in marriage, but whoso remained behind should lose his head.

When Moscione arrived in this land, and heard of this royal mandate, he fared to the royal presence, and offered to run with the king's daughter; making the agreement, that either he would run well or lose his head. The race was appointed for the next day, but when morning dawned, he sent a message to inform the king that a bad dysentery had seized him, and as he could not run in person, he would send another youth to take his place. 'Let come who will,' answered Ciannetella, thus was the daughter hight, 'I care not one straw, and there is enough for all.'

Thus all being settled, the square was filled with people come to see the race, insomuch that the men folk swarmed like ants, and the windows and belvideres were full like eggs. Furgolo appeared, and stood at the top of the square, awaiting his fair antagonist. And behold Ciannetella appeared, arrayed in a short skirt which reached above the knee, and with small thin shoes, pretty and tight-fitting. Then setting shoulder to shoulder, they awaited for the tarantara and tu-tu of the trumpet, when they darted off running at such speed that their heels touched their shoulders. Ye may suppose that they looked like hares pursued by the greyhounds, horses escaped from the stable, dogs with bladders tied on their tails, asses with sticks in their behinds. But Furgolo true to his name left her behind him, and reached the goal before her! and you should have heard the cries, the screams and public reports, and whistling, and hissing, and beating of bands, and stamping of feet, and the folk crying, 'Hurrah, hurrah, viva for the foreigner!' whereat Ciannetella's face turned crimson, like the behind of a school-boy who hath just received a beating, as she felt scorned and affronted by her loss. But the race was to have a second trial, and she bethought herself how she should avenge this affront, and going to the palace, she enchanted a ring, so that whosoever wore it on his fingers his legs would fail beneath him, and he would not be able to walk, much less to run; and she sent it as a gift to Furgolo, so that he should wear it for her sake.

Hare's Ear, who heard this talk between father and daughter, kept silence, awaiting for the result of this business. And as soon as the awakener of the birds, the sun, scourged the night, riding the ass of the shadows, they returned to the field, and the usual sign being given, they lifted their heels. But Ciannetella seemed a second Atalanta, whilst Furgolo had become a heavy donkey, and a lame horse, and he could not move a step, but Hit Straight, who saw his companion's danger, and hearing from Hare's Ear how stood the matter, took up cross-bow, and drew the string, and hit Furgolo on the finger, splitting the ring just where the charm lay hidden; whereupon Furgolo's legs straightened, and in four steps, like a goat, he leaped past Ciannetella, ond won the race.

The king, beholding that the race was won by a slipshod, and the victory given to a clodhopper, and a triumph vouchsafed to a good-for-naught, thought deeply in his mind of what he should do, and if he should give him his daughter in marriage; and he sent for the sages of his realm, and asked their counsel, and they answered, that Ciannetella was no morsel for a penniless beggar, an idle bird; and that without dishonour for his failing to keep his promise, he could make him a compensation in golden ducats, which would be more satisfactory to the ugly beggar than all the women in the world.

The king was pleased with this rede, and sent a message to

Moscione, asking him how much gold and silver would satisfy him
in exchange for the wife who had been promised him.   Then Moscione taking counsel with the others, answered, 'I should like thee
to give me as much silver and gold as one of my companions can
carry on his back.'   The king agreed, whereupon they sent for
Forte-Schiena, and they began to load him with bags full of golden
ducats, and sacks of copper monies, and purses full of silver, and
casks full of small coins, and caskets full of gold chains, and rings;
but the more they loaded him the firmer he stood, just like a tower,
and the royal treasury did not suffice, nor the banks, nor all the
money-changers in town; and the king sent to all his knights and
noblemen to borrow their candlesticks, and basins, and ewers, and
cup-holders, and plate, and trays, and baskets, and even to the silvern
chamber-pots and night vases; and yet 'twas not enough to make
the weight right.   At last they took leave and departed, not suf-
ficiently loaded, but satisfied, and weary of waiting.

When the king's counsellors beheld these youths carrying off all
the wealth of the realm, they said to the king, that it was a great
piece of stupidity to allow them to take away all the riches of his
kingdom, and therefore it would be advisable to send a company
of soldiers to lighten the load of this new Atlas, who was carrying
on his shoulders a heaven of treasures.   The king, bending to this
rede, at once sent armed men, foot and horse, after them, but
Hare's Ear, who had been listening to this rede, informed his
companions, and whilst the dust rose high in the air from the footsteps of the coming host which came to unload this rich farm,
Sciosciariello, who saw matters in bad plight, began to blow in such
a way that not only did he overthrow all the foes, but with the
strength of the southern winds which blow in that country he sent
them flying more than a mile distant.   And having no other impediment in their journey, they fared on and all arrived at the house
of Moscione's father, where he divided his gain with his companions
(because it is said: to whoso helpeth thee to gain a patty, give him
in exchange a rotten leaf, and whoso helpeth thee to gain a block

of wood, give him a chip), and he sent them away happy and satisfied; and he remained with his father rich in all, just like an ass
loaded with gold, giving not the lie to the ancient say,

'Heaven sendeth biscuits to the toothless.'

ROSELLA

NINTH DIVERSION

Of the Third Day

A SULTAN IS RECOMMENDED TO BATHE IN THE BLOOD OF A GREAT LORD,
AND HE SENDETH HIS FOLK TO SEIZE A PRINCE. HIS DAUGHTER FALLETH
IN LOVE WITH THE PRISONER, AND THEY FLY TOGETHER; HER MOTHER
FOLLOWETH THEM, AND HER HANDS ARE CUT OFF. SHE DIETH WITH
GRIEF, CURSING HER DAUGHTER, SO THAT THE PRINCE FORGETTETH HER.
AFTER VARIOUS RUSES AND TRICKS PLAYED BY HER, HER HUSBAND RE-
MEMBERETH HER ONCE MORE, AND THEY LIVE AND ENJOY THEMSELVES
HAPPILY TOGETHER.

THE story related by Paola was heard with great gladness, and
all said that the father was right in his desire to have a virtuous
son, although the owl sang for him, and if the others kneaded the
dough, he cut the macaroni. But it now being Ciommetella's turn
to say her say, she spake thus:

Whoso liveth badly cannot die well; and if any one escapeth
from this sentence, he is a white chow, because whoso soweth oil
cannot gather wheat, and whoso planteth tomatoes cannot gather
broccoli. And this tale that I am going to relate will not give me
the lie: pay me, I pray you, by opening well your ears and your
mouths, and I will make an effort to give you satisfaction.

In days of yore there lived a sultan who was afflicted with leprosy,
and no remedy could be found to cure him. The doctors, not knowing what to do to rid themselves of the importunity of the sick man,
proposed to him an impossible thing, telling him that if he desired to be cured there was no other remedy but that he should
bathe in the blood of some great prince. The sultan, hearing this
wild prescription, and longing to regain his health, sent off a large
fleet to scour the seas, so that by means of spies, and rich gifts, and
promises of higher things, they might meet with some city where
they could find some famous prince ready at hand. And the ves-

sels coasted along the Fonte-Chiaro Seas until they met a small boat, sailing slowly on. Seated therein was Paoluccio, son of the king of that country, and they took him prisoner, and carried him straightway to Constantinople. The doctors, hearing of this, made effort to lengthen the business, not so much in pity or compassion for the unhappy prince, as for their own sake, since the bath could not cure the sultan, and they would have to pay the forfeit. They therefore induced the sultan to believe that this prince was wroth at having lost his liberty, and in consequence thereof his blood was troubled, and if the sultan were to bathe therein, it would do him more harm than good; and it was necessary that the remedy should be suspended for a while, till the melancholic mood of the prince had given way to a brighter and more pleasant one. And moreover they should keep the prince in good humour, and feed him with substantial food, so that he should make good blood. The sultan hearing this, thought that he would try to make him cheerful, and he sent him into a beautiful garden where it was ever spring. Fountains played and disputed with the birds and the cool zephyrs as to whoso could murmur best, and the sultan, sending his daughter therein to keep the prince company, promised him that he would give her to him to wife. Rosella (thus was the daughter hight), when she saw the beauty of the prince, was strongly tied by the rope of love, and uniting her desires with those of Paoluccio, they bound themselves with one ring and in the same thought.

But the time came when the cats go in search of adventures, and the sun plays at ram-butting with the celestial ram, and this being spring-time, and the blood of the prince being now of better quality, the doctors were unable to procrastinate the bath any longer, and were about to slay Paoluccio, to please the sultan. But although her sire had kept these matters hidden from Rosella, she had discovered the treachery by means of the art of geomancy taught her by her mother, and giving her lover a sword, she said to him, 'O my beauteous muzzle, an thou desire to be free, and to save thy life which is so dear to thee, lose no time; run like an hare to the sea-side, where thou shalt find a boat, enter therein and wait my coming, for by the virtue of this charmed sword thou shalt be received by the sailors like an emperor.' Paoluccio, seeing open to him such a good way to liberty, took the sword, and fared to the seashore, where he found the boat, and he was received therein with great respect by those a-board of it.

In the meanwhile Rosella cast a spell upon a paper, and slid it unseen into her mother's pocket, so that she fell asleep at once, and slept in such a manner that she could hear naught, neither head nor foot; and after this Rosella collected a large bundle of jewels and other valuables, and ran to the boat, and they set sail. But the sultan coming to the garden, and finding neither his daughter nor the prince, did things to frighten all the world, and ran to find his wife, but he could not awaken her, neither by shouting, nor screaming, nor pulling her nose. And he thought that she must be in a fit, and calling the handmaidens, bade them undress her. As soon as they slid off her skirt, the spell was at an end, and she woke up, crying, 'Alas, my treacherous daughter hath played me this trick, she hath taken flight with the prince; but it matters not, I will serve her out and put her way straight.' Saying thus, she ran to the sea-side and threw a tree-leaf on the sea, which became at once a felucca, finely pointed, and it cut the waves and speedily ran behind the fugitives. Rosella, although her mother was not visible, yet with her magic art could see what betided, and turned to Paoluccio, and said to him, 'Quick, O mine heart, hend thy sword, and stand at the vessel's stern, and when thou hearest the noise of the clanging chains, and the hiss of the hooks thrown to grapple the ship, cut, and slash, and hit with eyes shut, and spare none, and who is hit, let him be hit, and let their warmth be cooled, or we are lost, and our flight is useless.' And because the prince feared to lose his own skin, he followed the advice, and when the sultana's vessel came alongside and threw the grapple-hooks, he began to cut and slash in all sides, and luckily at a single stroke he cut off the sultana's hands, and she shrieking like a damned soul, cursed her daughter, and wished that the prince, at the first step he walked in his own land, might forget her. And returning to Turkey with her stumps running

blood, she presented herself before her husband, and showing him
the painful spectacle, said to him, 'Behold, O my husband, we have
both played at Fortune's table, I and thou, and we have lost, thou
thine health, and I my life.' And when she ended speaking, she
gave up the ghost, and went to pay her wage to the teacher who had
taught her the black art. And the sultan, drowned in the sea of
despair, followed his wife's footsteps, and fared cold as ice to the
hot-house. Such was their case.

Now Paoluccio, as soon as he arrived at Fonte-Chiaro, bade
Rosella await in the vessel, so that he might lead her in triumph
to his own house. But no sooner did he put his foot on ground,
than he forgot Rosella, and arriving at the royal palace, was received with caresses from his father and mother. Ye cannot imagine the welcomes and festivals and illuminations done in his
honour. And Rosella awaited three days in suspense for Paoluccio,
when she remembered her mother's curse, and bit her lips, for she
had not thought before to remedy it; therefore like a woman driven
to despair she left the vessel, and fared on city-wards, and hired a
palace opposite the palace of the king, wherein to contrive some
scheme by which the debt of gratitude he owed her should be
brought in remembrance before the prince's mind. The nobles and
lords of the court, who are always desirous to put their noses everywhere, sighting this new bird come to the palace vis-à-vis, and contemplating such beauty, which ravished all hearts, and passed all
bourns, and caused great marvel and exceeding wonder, began to
buzz round it like mosquitoes, and not a day passed but that they
were seen promenading and curvetting before the house. Sonnets
flew right and left, and serenades and music enough to deafen.
And the hand-kissing, and great nuisances, and behind-annoyances
went on; and the one knew not of the other, and they all shot at
the same target, and sought in the inebriation of love to drink out
of that cask. And Rosella, who well understood where to anchor
the ship, was pleasant to all, and entertained all, and gave hopes to
all. At last, desiring to tighten the strings, she agreed secretly with
a cavalier of high standing at court that if he brought her a thou-

sand ducats and a complete raiment, when night darkened and starkened, she would give unto him a proof of her affection. The wretched window-gazer, who was blinded by his passion, went and borrowed the money at high interest, and taking on trust from a merchant, whom he knew, a rich raiment, impatiently awaited the hour when the sun changed with the moon, to gather the fruit of his desires. When night came, he fared secretly to Rosella's house, and found her lying in a rich bed, and she looked like Venus in a flower-garden, and with charming grace she asked him not to come to bed without shutting the door. The cavalier thinking it but a small service to please such a beautiful jewel, turned to shut the door, but no sooner did he shut it than it opened again. Again he shut it, and again it opened, and all night he continued thus till the sun sowed with its golden rays the fields which the aurora had furrowed. Having thus seen how long was the night, and being unable to use the key of that accursed door, to make matters worse he caught a good dressing from Rosella's tongue, who called him a dark creature, not good enough to shut a door, but with presumption enough to open the casket of love's enjoyments. The wretched man, confused and scorned, went his ways hot on head and cool on tail.

The second evening she gave appointment to another baron, and bade him bring another thousand ducats and another dress, and he pledged all his silver and gold to the jew money-lenders, to satisfy the desires which carrieth at the end of pleasure repentance, and when the night like a shameful beggar covereth her face with her mantle and asketh for alms in silence, he came to Rosella's house, and found her in bed. And she said to him, 'Put out the candle, and come to bed.' And the baron doffed his sword and his raiment, and began to blow at the candle, but the more he blew, the more it burned, for the wind that came out of his mouth had the effect of the bellows blowing the fire of the smithy. So he spent all the night in trying to put out the candle, and to put out a light he melted himself like wax. But when night, not to behold the divers mad feats of mankind, hideth her face, the unhappy and despised baron received a volley of injurious epithets, like his predecessor, and went his ways. When the third night came, the third lover arrived with another thousand ducats taken from a jew at high percentage, and with a raiment spunged out of some one. Mounting the stairs quietly, he entered Rosella's chamber, and she said to him, 'I will not go to bed without combing my hair'; 'Let me do it for thee,' answered the nobleman, and bidding her sit down and to hold her head straight, thinking that he was going to steal French cloth, he began to comb out the knots with an ivory comb. But the more he tried to comb them out the more knotted they became; and he spent all night in knotting, and unknotting, and trying to put things right, till he spoiled and put the hair in such disorder that he was fit to knock his head against the wall, and as soon as the sun came forth to listen to the latest news sung by the birds, and with the spreading of his rays to give a good beating to the crickets infesting the school of the fields, with another double-soled scolding, frozen and cold, he fared forth out of the house. But this nobleman conversing one day in the king's ante-room with other noblemen, where they cut, and slice, and speak of matters that sad-hearted be that mother who chanceth to have a daughter, where the bellows of flattery blow about, and the webs of deceit are woven, and the keys of murmuring are deftly touched, and the melons are cut to prove their ignorance, related what had happened to him, whereupon the second answered, 'Be silent, if Africa wept, Italy doth not smile. I have also gone through this head of a needle, and therefore be comforted, for a common trouble is half enjoyment.' And the third replied to this, 'We are all plastered with the same tar, and we can touch our hands without envying one another, this treacherous damsel hath treated us all alike, and stroked our fur the wrong way; but it is not right that we should swallow such a pill without avenging ourselves; we are not men to be despised and put in a sack; therefore we must devise a device to punish this barbarous woman, this cheat.' And they agreed together to go to the king, and relate to him what had taken place. And the king sent for Rosella, and said to her, 'Where didst thou learn to cheat and make fools of my courtiers? Dost thou not think that I will have thee written in the excise book, vile woman, strumpet, lewd piece?' And Rosella, without a change in her colour, answered, 'What I have done, O my lord, hath been to avenge a great wrong wrought upon me by one of thy court, although there is not a thing in the world which can compensate me for the injury I have suffered;' and the king commanded her to relate to him this offence. And she related to him, without naming the offender, what she had done in the behalf of the prince, and how she had freed him from slavery, and saved him from death, and made him escape the danger of the sorceress, and brought him safe and sound in his own native land, only to be repaid by the basest ingratitude, with a back turned, and a form of cheese: a thing not due to her estate, as she was a lady of high descent, and the daughter of kings. The king, hearing this, at once entreated her with high honour and respect, and seated her under the dais, and begged that she would discover to him the name of the ungrateful knave who had done such a deed. Taking off a ring from her finger, she said, 'The one whose finger this ring fitteth is the unfaithful traitor who hath done me this deed;' and throwing the ring it went straight to the prince's finger, who was present. The virtue of the ring flying at once to his head, his memory returned, he opened his eyes, the blood coursed freely, and his spirits returned, and he ran and embraced Rosella, and he was not satisfied to hold her within his arms, but he kissed her over and over again, asking her to forgive him for the trouble he had caused her, and she answered, ' 'Tis needless to ask forgiveness for errors unwillingly committed. I know the reason that made thee forget thy Rosella, as my mother's curse has not escaped my mind, therefore I excuse thee and pity thee;' and a thousand loving words followed. The king, hearing under what deep obligation his son lay to the princess, desired that they should be united in marriage, and baptizing Rosella in the Christian faith, they were married, and lived highly satisfied, more than any who had worn the matrimonial yoke, and they beheld at last that

> ' Ever with time and straw
> Thou mayest see the medlar ripen.'

THE THREE FAIRIES

Of the Third Day

CECELLA, ILL-TREATED BY HER STEPMOTHER, IS WELL ENTREATED BY
THREE FAIRIES. HER ENVIOUS STEPMOTHER SENDETH HER OWN DAUGH-
TER TO THEM, AND SHE IS SCORNED BY THEM, FOR WHICH REASON SHE
SENDETH HER STEPDAUGHTER TO WATCH PIGS. A GREAT LORD FALLETH
IN LOVE WITH HER, BUT THROUGH THE CRAFT AND WICKEDNESS OF
THE STEPMOTHER, THEY GIVE HIM THE UGLY DAUGHTER IN EXCHANGE,
AND SHE PUTTETH HER STEPDAUGHTER IN A CASK READY TO POUR BOIL-
ING WATER UPON HER. THE LORD DISCOVERETH THE TREACHERY, TAKETH
OUT CECELLA, AND PUTTETH THE HIDEOUS DAUGHTER IN HER PLACE;
AND THE MOTHER COMETH, AND SCALDETH HER WITH BOILING WATER,
AND FINDING OUT HER ERROR, SLAYETH HERSELF.

THE story of Ciommetella was esteemed one of the prettiest
which had been related, and Ghiacova perceiving that all were silent
with exceeding wonder, said:

If I were not obliged to obey the command of the prince and
princess, which acteth like a crane to a cart and draggeth me along,
I would end here all my prattling; as it seemeth to me too much to
bring aught forth out of the blunderbuss of my mouth, in comparison with the sweetness of Ciommetella's words. But, as it is the
will of my lord, I will make an effort, and I will relate a story
concerning the punishment given to an envious woman who, desiring to push down her stepdaughter, instead lifted her to the stars.

In the village of Marcianese lived a widow, Caradonia hight,
who was the mother of envy, and she never looked with kindness
on any of her neighbours. If she heard of good chancing to some
acquaintances, it was gall and bitterness for her, nor did she ever
see man or woman happy without being ready to burst with jealousy.

Now this woman had a daughter, Grannizia hight, and she was
the quintessence of hideousness, and the first cut of a sea-ghula,
and a pattern for a flattened cask. Her head was full of lice, her

hair was unkempt, she had swollen eyes, a thick round nose, teeth full of slime, a mouth like a dog-fish, a chin like a wooden shoe, a neck like a magpie, and breasts like two saddle-bags. She was round-shouldered, and had thin long arms, crooked legs, and heels like a cheese farm; and in very sooth, from head to foot she was an hideous witch, a fine pest, an ugly piece, a naught, a pig's hide. But nathless all these combined graces of this crab-louse, her mother thought her a beauty worthy a painter's brush.

Now it chanced that this widow married a certain Micco Antuono, a very rich farmer from Pane-cuocolo, who had been twice elected bailiff and mayor of that village, and he was respected and held in high esteem by all the Pane-cuocolesi. Micco Antuono had also a daughter named Cecella, whose beauty was the most wonderful and marvellous in the world. She had eyes which drew one's heart away, a small sweet mouth, fit for kisses, which would send one into ecstasy, a sweet white throat which sent lovers into despair, and she was so graceful, caressing, playful, affable, mild, and kind, and so charming, with bewildering smiles, that she drew all hearts to her. But enough of this. My praises run short. She was a model fit for a painter's brush, and he would have found no blemish in her. But Caradonia, beholding that her daughter suffered by the comparison with Cecella, like a kitchen duster near a velvet cushion, or like the bottom of a greasy saucepan, or the muzzle of a Venetian ass, as harpy compared to a Fairy Morgana, began to look upon her with envy and despite. And 'twas not long before the imposthume at her heart burst forth, and being unable to hang herself any longer on the rope without breaking out, she began to torment and worry the wretched child openly. She arrayed her daughter in a fine woollen skirt all purflewed around, and in a bodice of chenille, and the stepdaughter in the worst rags she owned. Her daughter ate of the whitest bread of the finest quality, and the stepdaughter of the hardest lumps of black bread. The daughter was kept like the Saviour's vial, and the stepdaughter had to run to and fro to sweep the house, wash the dishes, make the bed, do the washing, feed the pigs, tend the ass, and empty the slops, may ye well digest it.

Which matters the good obedient damsel did well and quickly, sparing no fatigue to please the wicked stepmother. But as her good luck would have it, one day of the days, the unhappy damsel went at a distance from the house in a steep broken-down place to cast away the filth and dust, and the large basket she held slipped from her grasp and fell down the chasm, and she gazed after it thinking how she might more easily fish it out, and whilst she was looking, behold, an hideous sorcerer appeared, and ye could not have said whether he was the original of Æsop, or a copy of the ugly beggar. He was a ghul, and his hair stood up like an hog's bristles, black and stiff, sinking to the very marrow of the bones; the forehead was full of wrinkles, so that it seemed furrowed by the plough; he had shaggy brows, crooked eyes sunk deeply into their orbits, and filled with what do ye call it, and they looked like shops under the eyelashes' heavy gutter; he had a crooked, frothing mouth, out of which protruded a pair of tusks, like a wild boar's; his breast was full of bumps, and covered with hair enough to stuff a mattress; and above all he was hunchbacked, round-bellied, and had thin legs, and crooked feet. His appearance was such, that it would make you twist your mouth with fear: but Cecella, although she beheld an evil spirit enough to frighten her out of all mind, heartened her heart, and said, 'O my worthy man, couldst thou hand me up that basket, which fell out of my hands? and mayst thou be married to a rich spouse;' and the ghul answered, 'Come down, O my daughter, and take it up;' and the good child, taking hold of the roots and stones, slowly went down, and when she reached the ground (a thing hardly worth belief) she found three fairies, each handsomer than the other. Their hair was threads of gold; and their faces like the moon in her fourteenth night; they had speaking eyes, and mouths that invited the most sweet kisses. What more? A slender white throat, a round breast, a delicate hand, a small foot, and an undulating grace which was like a gilded frame to this painting of perfect beauty. And Cecella was entreated kindly by them, and they kissed and caressed her; and taking her by the hand, led her to a house under the rubbish, fit for a king to dwell in. And as soon as they reached there, they sat down upon Turkish carpets, with velvet cushions thereon, and leaning their heads towards Cecella, the fairies bade her comb their hair, and whilst she, with great gentleness, did her work with a buffalo-horn comb, one of the fairies asked her, 'Beauteous child, what dost thou find on this head of mine?' and she very gracefully replied, 'I find small nits, and little lice, and pearls, and garnets.' Her good behaviour pleased exceedingly the three fairies, and after she had plaited their hair, which was thrown about the shoulders, they led her round this enchanted palace, and she saw beautiful desks with fine chestnut-trees engraved thereon, and caskets covered with leather, with brass corners, and walnut tables so bright that ye could gaze at yourselves therein. There were cupboards with polished rests which dazzled the sight, and table-covers of green cloth adorned with flowers, and chairs of horse-leather high-backed, and many other luxuries that whoso saw them would be surprised. Cecella gazed at the splendid elegance of the house, but did not go into raptures about it, as all ill-mannered folk would have done.

At last they led her to a wardrobe full of rich raiments, and they showed her the Spanish camorra,* and long robes with wide velvet sleeves, purflewed with gold, and bed-covers of cataluffo,† and taffeta mattresses, and natural-flower pillows, and charms in half-moon shape and in the shape of the tongue of a serpent, and playthings of blue crystal and white, and gems in the shape of an ear of wheat, and lilies, and feathers to wear on the head, and garnets encrusted with enamel and silver, and necklaces, and jewelry, and a thousand other things, and they bade Cecella choose what she wanted, and take the prettiest of those things. But Cecella, who was humble as oil, leaving the most precious things, took only an old skirt of very little worth. And the fairies watched her, and said, 'O my love, by which gate wilt thou go forth?' And she

---

* 'Camorra' (Sp. *chamarra*). An ancient texture highly prized, and from it the dress was called ' Gamurra.'

† 'Cataluffo.' A kind of precious stuff purflewed with bits of enamel and gems.

bowing to the ground said, ' 'Tis enough for me to issue from the stable door.' And at those words the fairies embraced her, and kissed her, and doffing her old raiments, they arrayed her in sumptuous robes, all purflewed with gold, and they put on her head a Scotch cap, and tied her hair with ribbons, and then accompanied her to the large gate, which was of solid gold, with the frame all encrusted with carbuncles, and they said to her, 'Go Cecella, may we see thee well married; fare thy ways, and when thou art outside this gate, look up, and see what there is above.' The damsel, gracefully bending to them, took her leave and departed, and when she came under the gate, she lifted her head, and a golden star fell upon her forehead, which was a most beautiful thing to behold, and starred like a steed, and light, and gentle, she stood before her stepmother, and related all that happened to her. But this story was not a story for that envious woman, but a rope twisted round her neck, and she could not rest till she knew the place where the fairies dwelt, and she sent to them the ugly daughter, who came to the enchanted palace, and found the three beauteous fairies. Leading her in, the first thing they bade her do was to comb their hair, and enquiring of her what she found there, she answered, 'Lice as large as beans, and nits as large as spoons.' The fairies were wroth at the lack of tact and courtesy of that hideous rustic, but they dissembled, and knew the bad day from the morning, and when they led her into the sumptuous chambers and bade her take what she liked, Grannizia, seeing that a finger was offered her, took the whole hand, and she asked for the finest raiment she saw in the wardrobes. The fairies, beholding this act, and seeing that she filled her hands with all kind of goods, yet said naught, but enquired of her, 'By which gate wouldst thou like to go forth, O handsome maiden, by the golden gate or by the garden gate?' And she with a brazen face replied, 'By the best that there is.' But the fairies, seeing the presumption of this good-for-naught, said not a word, and sent her away, saying, 'When thou comest to the stable door, lift up thy face to heaven, and see what will come to thee.' And she went forth amid the dung, and when she reached the stable door, she lifted up

her face, and upon her forehead fell something, which sticking to
the skin, looked like somewhat for which her mother longed when
she bare her; and with this fine gain, softly and quietly she returned
to Caradonia.

When Caradonia saw what had taken place, she became angry
like a bitch watching her pups, and bidding Cecella doff her clothes,
she just covered her middle and behind with a rag, and sent her to
guard pigs, dressing with her garments her own daughter. And
Cecella with great phlegm, and with a patience worthy of a Roland,
supported this wretched life. O cruel deed, enough to move to compassion the very stones in the road. That sweet mouth worthy of
love's conceptions was obliged to blow the pipe, and cry out 'Cicco,
Cicco,' 'Enze, enze.' That great beauty was lost amongst pigs, and
living amongst pigs, that hand worthy of drawing to her an hundred weapons, was obliged to chase with a wand an hundred sows;
and a thousand times accursed be the wickedness which sent her to
these forests, where under cover of the shadows stood fear and
silence sheltering themselves from the sun. But Heaven, who
crusheth the presumptuous, and upraiseth the humble, sent before
her an high and mighty lord, Cuosimo hight, who beholding amid
the mire such a jewel, among pigs such a Phœnix, and amid the
broken clouds such a beauteous sun, was caught at once in love's
meshes, and he sent to enquire who she was and where she dwelt,
and he spake with the stepmother, and asked her to wife, promising
to endow her with an hundred thousand ducats. Caradonia opened
wide her eyes, and thought of what a good thing it would be for
her daughter, and bade him to return at night, for she desired to
invite her kith and kin. Cuosimo, quite happy and contented, departed, and the time till the sun went to sleep in the silvern bed that
the moon prepareth for him seemed to him long as a thousand years,
till he could go and sleep with that sun that burned his heart.

In the meanwhile Caradonia had placed Cecella within a cask,
and covered her up, designing to throw some boiling water upon
her, and to scald her to death. As she had forsaken the pigs, she
was going to pickle her like a pig with hot water, but dusk crept on,

and the heavens became like a wolf's mouth, and Cuosimo, who had
fits of impatience, and was dying with the longing to clasp that
beauty within his arms, to lighten his heart from the oppressive load
of his love, with great joy fared towards the house of his beloved,
saying, 'This is the appointed hour, when I must go to engraft the
tree that love hath planted within my breast, to suck from it the
manna of amorous sweetness; this is the time to go and dig up the
hidden treasure, that Fortune hath promised me; therefore lose no
time, O Cuosimo: when the suckling pig is promised to thee, run
with the rope.   O night, O most happy night, O thou friend of the
enamoured lover, O souls and bodies, O spoon and platter, O Love,
run, run quickly, because under the tent of thy shadow I can shelter
myself from the heat that consumeth me.'   And thus saying, he
arrived at Caradonia's house, and found Grannizia instead of
Cecella, an owl instead of a bullfinch, a wild herb instead of a rose:
for although she had arrayed herself in Cecella's raiments, and it
could be said of her 'dress thou a block of wood, and it will look
like a baron,' yet withal she looked like a crab-louse within a golden
net.   Not all the powders, cosmetics, and pomades that her mother
had used could rid her of that beauty amid the brows, the swollen
eyes, the freckled face, the dirty teeth, the warts in the throat, the
saddle-bags in the breast, and the flat heels; and the stink of that
sink could be smelt from afar.   The bridegroom, perceiving this
ugly creature, could not think what had happened to him, and drawing back just as if he had seen the one that melteth, said in his mind,
'Am I awake, or have I put a blind over my eyes, or do I look the
other side?   Am I myself, or not myself; what dost thou perceive,
O thou most wretched Cuosimo?   Is not this the face which
yesterday morning took me by storm; is not this the image carved
within mine heart?   What is this, O fortune?   Where is the
beauty?   Where is the hook which caught me, the crane which
lifted me up, the dart which passed mine heart?   I knew that neither
women nor linen must thou buy by the light of a candle, but this
one I bargained for in the light of the sun.   Alas! the gold of
this morning hath turned to brass, the diamond to glass, and the

beard to bristles.' These and other words he muttered and grum-
bled between his teeth.   At last, constrained by necessity, he gave
a kiss to Grannizia; but just as if he were kissing an antique vase,
he neared and withdrew his lips three times before he touched
the lips of the bride, and when at last he drew near, it seemed
to him to be on the sea-shore at Chiaja, in the evening when those
worthy dames brought the tribute to the sea of other than Arabian
perfumes.   But when Heaven, desiring to look young, had darkened the colour of his white beard, the estates of the lord Cuosimo
being far distant, he was obliged to take her to a house near Pane-
cuocolo for that night; where laying a sack upon two chests, he
lay down with the bride.

But who can tell of the bad night spent by each of them?   Although it was summer, and the night was not longer than eight
hours, it seemed to them one of the longest winter nights.   The
bride, having a cold, coughed, and sneezed, and blew her nose, and
kicked, and sighed, and with silent words sought for the wage of
the house now let; but Cuosimo pretending to snore, withdrew himself as far as possible in the hard bed, so as not to touch Grannizia,
and missing the sack and the chest, tumbled on the top of the night-
chamber, and the matter ended in stink and shame.   How many
times the bridegroom cursed all the sun's dead, for being so slow to
appear, so as to keep him longer in that plight! and how he prayed
that the night might break her neck, and the stars might sink, to
take away from his side, with the coming of day, that bad day!
But no sooner had the dawn come forth to chase out and awaken the
cocks and the fowls, than he jumped out of bed, and buttoning up
well his breeches, raced to the house of Caradonia, wishing to re-
nounce her daughter, and pay her the scant use he had made of her
with the broomstick.   Entering the house he found her not, for she
had gone to the forest to gather a fagot of wood so as to get ready
the boiling water to scald the stepdaughter, who was enclosed in that
Bacchus's tomb, whilst she was worthy to be drawn within love's
gondola.   And Cuosimo, seeking Caradonia, and finding her not,
began to cry out, 'Ho there, where art thou?' and behold, a Persian

cat cried time upon time, 'Miaou, miaou, thy wife is within the cask, miaou, miaou.' So Cuosimo went near the cask, and heard a dull lamenting, and a weeping in whispers, and taking up an axe from near the fireplace, he brake the cask, and when the pieces fell, it seemed like the lifting of the curtain when a goddess is discovered to begin the prologue. I know not how at sight of all this splendour he did not fall dead; but the bridegroom stood, and looked, and looked again, like one who hath seen the little monk, and after a while, coming to himself, he ran and embraced her, saying, 'Who hath put thee in this wretched place, O jewel of mine heart? Who had stolen thee from me, O thou hope of my life? What thing is this? The dove within this wooden cage? And the bird of prey coming to my side? How was this done? Speak, muzzle mine, comfort my spirit, let my breast be broadened.' And Cecella answered to those words by repeating all the facts, without leaving out one word, how much she had suffered in her stepmother's house since she had put her feet in it, till in order to deprive her of life Caradonia had buried her in the cask. Hearing this, Cuosimo bade her dress, and hide herself behind the door, and putting the cask together again, sent for Grannizia, and shoving her therein, said to her, 'Stay here quietly like a lamb, as I am going to have a spell made for thee, so that the evil eye may have no strength against thee.' And covering well the cask, he embraced his wife, and putting her on the back of a horse, they fared quickly to Pascarola, this being the name of the lord Cuosimo's estate. And Caradonia came home shortly after with a large fagot of wood, and she lit a large fire, and putting on a caldron of water, as soon as it began to boil she threw it within the cask, thus scalding her own daughter, who closed her teeth, just as if she had been eating Sardinian grass. And the skin rose up, like the snake when it casteth off its skin; and when she thought that Cecella had caught the fish and straightened her feet, the old witch brake the cask, and found (O terrible sight!) her own daughter, cooked by a cruel mother. And she tore her hair, and buffeted her face, and beat her breast, and struck palm against palm, and knocked her head on the wall, and stamped with her feet, and wept, and lamented, and cried, and screamed, so that all the folk in the village ran to see what had happened. And after doing and saying things of the other world, as no pity could comfort her, nor advice soften her, she ran to a well and cast herself therein, and broke her neck: showing by this how very true is the sentence that

'Who spitteth to heaven on his face receiveth the spittle.'

The story ended, and following the orders given by the prince, all at once there appeared before the company Giallaise and Cola Jacopo, the one the cook and the other the cellar-keeper of the court, dressed in old Neapolitan costumes, and they recited the eclogue which followeth:

ECLOGUE

THE STOVE

Giallaise, and Cola Jacopo

Gial. Well met and well found, O Cola Jacopo.

Col. Well met and well come, O Giallaise.
    Tell me whénce comest thou?

Gial. From the stove.

Col. With this heat near the stove?

Gial. The hotter it is the better.

Col. And dost thou not burst?

Gial. I would burst, O my brother, if I went not.

Col. And what pleasure canst thou find in it?

Gial. The pleasure to moderate
    The sorrows of this world
    Where one must swell with rage,
    As all things in these days go the wrong way.

Col. I believe thou laughest at me:
    Thou thinkest me a sweet marrow,
    And that I never angle to the bottom;

What hath the stove in common with the world?

Gial. When thou thinkest thou art angling thou fishest least;
Dost thou think that I speak to thee
Of such a stove, where thou keepest near
Within a chamber without moving foot,
And roastest thyself and diest with heat?
No, no, I speak of that
In which, speaking sooth,
Is ended every grief
Of this most anguished life.
And all that I behold
Filleth me with the same thought.

Col. I hear new matters,
Thou surprisest me indeed:
Thou art not an ass,
As seemed to me at first.

Gial. Thou must know, O my brother,
That this world is a stove,
Wherein floweth evil combined with good.
Hast thou joyance and pleasure in large fagots,
Hast thou greatness and honours enough to satisfy thee,
All things will weary thee and surfeit thee;
And that this is true, open thine ears, and hear me,
And be thou comforted,
For every human joyance and delight
Will most unfailingly come to this pass.

Col. In very sooth thou dost deserve a gift:
Speak on, that I may hear thee
In open-mouthed wonder.

Gial. Thou shalt behold, *verbi gratia,*
A virtuous young damsel
Just suited to thy taste;
Thou sendest a mediator
To treat about the marriage;
Ye agree, a notary is sent for,

To draw and complete the settlements;
Thou wendest up the stair, and kissest the bride,
Who is decked in sumptuous array, with gems and charms.
Thou also like a prince
Arrayest thee in new garments:
A band of musicians is called,
A banquet is spread, and dancing is begun,
And with more longing and desire
Thou waitest for the night,
As longeth the true sailor for fair winds,
The writer for a rumour,
The thief for a crowd, and the doctor for a quarrel.
Behold here cometh the night,
Night of bad omen,
That bringeth darksome mourning
Whilst liberty (O unhappy one!) lieth in death.
Thy wife doth clasp thee with her arms,
And thou seest not that thou art bound
With chains, like unto a convict's chains;
But just three days last
The caresses, and whims,
And amiable acts;
And thou hast not yet reached the fourth day,
When already thou art wearied,
And cursest the day when the word was spoken;
And cursest the cause a thousand times!
And if thy wretched wife speaketh one word,
Thou glarest at her,
And wearest a sulky face, and art stern, severe;
And when thou liest with her, 'tis in the style
Of the double-headed eagle;
And thou turnest thy head away if she try to kiss thee,
And from thine house all good and joy escape.

Col. An unfortunate gardener is the one that marrieth,
For only one night he soweth the seed of contentment,

And after endureth a thousand days of dread torments.

Gial. And now a father will behold
A beauteous child brought for him to the world:
How happy is he, how great his joy,
He getteth a silken cover for the cradle,
And he loadeth his son, like unto a weigher,
On neck and shoulders, with a wolf's tooth,
Figs, crescents, and coral, and little pigs,
And he looketh exactly
Like a buyer of saffron:
He findeth him a nurse,
He seeth not from other eyes,
He speaketh to him in whimpering tones,
'How dosh zhou do, my pretty boy?
I love zhee bery much;
Zhou art zhy papa's heart,
Sweet tit-bit of zhy mamma.'
And while he standeth in wonder
With his mouth wide open,
Listening to 'Cacca,' and Ppappa,'
He gathereth with gusto what from the other escapeth.
Meanwhile he groweth like a wild nettle,
And shooteth up like unto a broccolo,
Papa sendeth him to school,
And expendeth upon him his coins of gold;
And when he hath counted upon
Seeing him a wise doctor of law,
Behold he escapeth from his hand,
Taketh to evil ways,
Gets mixed up with light women,
Treats with knaves and rogues,
And companies with brigands, and either giveth or taketh;
Is always quarrelling with barbers and with clerks;
And for this cause he is stoved
By his worthy sire, who kicketh him out,

Or curseth him,
Or to put straight
The brainless youth,
He hath him sent to prison in tower or castle.

Col. Imprison, as thou wilt, a wicked son,
Yet with the change of moon,
He is born to take the oar, or for the halter cast.

Gial. What more wilt thou have?　The food,
A necessary thing of life,
Also becometh nauseous:
Eat, swallow, munch, crush, plane and comb,
Ruminate, gormandize, put thy cheeks in motion,
Put it under thy nose, stuff well thy guts
With sweet things, and sour, and lean, and fat;
Give to thy jaws enough to do;
Give work to thy valiant teeth;
For at the last
Thou shalt be overcome by indigestion;
Thou causest the tomb with pride to swell;
Thou belchest rotten eggs,
Thou losest appetite,
And for this reason thou art surfeited.
The meat stinketh for thee,
The fish is nauseous,
The sweetmeats tasteless, or bitter like gall;
Wine is thy foe,
And what maintaineth thee alive, is what thou sippest up.

Col. Would 'twere not true
That a bad rule
Sendeth to more than one a dysentery,
And every sickness beginneth with gluttony.

Gial. If thou playest at cords or dice, or at nine-pins,
At oranges, or chess, or farinole,*

* 'Farinole.' Dice, small forms bearing the signs of the game on only one side.

One spendeth all his time there,
Risketh his life and soul,
Compromiseth his honour and reputation,
Loseth his goods and monies,
Loseth his friends and friendship;
His sleep is never restful,
He eateth not a mouthful;
In peace, always his mind is filled
With thoughts of this cursed vice,
Where two agree to put him in their midst,
And pluck him well, and then divide the spoil;
And when at last he can perceive
That he loveth his loss, and cheats despoil him
On all sides, then he is wroth;
But weary of all his losses,
When he beholdeth ever any games
He sighteth just the fire and the flames.

Col. Blessed is he that flieth all games,
And far be it from me, I'll guard my legs,
For one may lose his days, if not his monies.

Gial. And the entertainments
Which are less risky, and bring more enjoyance;
They weary thee also:
The farce, the comedy, and the clowns,
The woman who jumpeth upon a rope,
The other with a beard,
And the other who seweth with her feet,
And the marionettes, and the juggler,
The goat which standeth upon the reels:
But to be brief, are wearisome all pleasures,
And jesters, and merry folk, and fools, and madmen.

Col. And therefore gossip Junno used to sing
There is no lasting pleasure in this earth.

Gial. Then there is music, a ting which penetrates
Within the marrow of thine every bone

With great variety of sounds, and fashions,
Of trills, and runs, and fast, and slow,
And quavers, and semiquavers,
And false treble, and counter-point,
Solos, or duets,
With melancholic, or cheerful voice,
Or serious, or comic,
Low, or high treble, or tenor,
With stunning keys, or stunning voice,
And with cords of metal or of catgut;
Still everything wearieth,
And if thou feelest not in the humour,
Thou carest not to fill thy lungs with air,
And mindest not if the trumpets all were broken.

Col. When the mind is filled with care,
Sing, and jest, and do as thou wilt,
Let a star sing, or a jackass,
A symphony is worse than a lament.

Gial. Of dancing I say naught to thee:
Thou seest round-going, and jumping,
And hopping, and capers, and slower
Than a doe,
And bows, and runs.
For a little while it may please thee,
And thou mayest enjoy it;
But 'tis an August cure;
Four changes of figure weary thee,
And thou longest for the moment,
When beginneth the dance, with torch and fan,
To disappear; ended the ball,
Thou art tired of foot, and light in thine head.

Col. In very sooth, 'tis time lost,
Aid for a noisy dance
One weareth out much, and naught gaineth.

Gial. Conversazioni and parties,

Amusements and friendly meetings,
Drinking and swallowing in taverns,
Rambling in bad corners,
Making tumults in the public places
With old rotten rubbish and night-stool covers;
Never at rest,
With the brain flying and lifting like a crane,
And the heart like an engine going ahead,
And past the time
When the blood is boiling,
Thou art weary more than ever;
And lowering down thine head,
And hanging up to the smoke thy playthings,
Thou wisely retirest from all turmoil,
And lookest to thine affairs,
Weary of those years,
Which take their pleasure in shadows,
And drink the beverage of anguish.

Col. All that which pleaseth mankind
Is but a fire of straw,
Which passeth, burneth, flareth up, and melteth.

Gial. There is not a sense within the head
Which is not full of whims;
But very soon they weary:
The eyes, of gazing at
Beautiful painted things,
Splendour, beauty, pictures,
Spectacles, gardens, statues, and fine buildings.
The nose, of smelling
Pinks, violets, roses, and lilies,
Ambergris, musk, and civet,
Ox-tail soup, and roast beef;
The hand, of touching
Soft things and tender;
The mouth, of tasting

Good, tasty morsels and dainties;
The ears, of hearing
The latest news and gossip.
Therefore if thou keepest account,
All that thou dost, and seest, and hearest,
Becometh nauseous, both joys and pain.

Col. Man would feel too much engrafted to this earth,
Whilst he is made alone for heavenly rest,
If he had what he wanted,
And was in all things satisfied;
But thou hast thrust within thy mouth
Anguish and troubles without end,
And pleasures in a limited strain.

Gial. There is only one thing
Which never wearieth thee,
But ever cheereth thee,
And always maketh thy days
Happy and comforted;
And this is wisdom, and the ducat;
Therefore did the Greek poet say to Jupiter,
With warmest prayers poured forth from out his heart,
'Give me, O my lord, virtue, and gold pieces.'

Col. Thou hast a ton and a half of reason,
As one hath never enough of the one, or the other,
Who hath sour grapes and salt;
For the gold is great, and the virtue immortal.

This eclogue was so full of good taste, that all the company, charmed and well pleased, hardly perceived that the sun, tired of playing the canary all day in the fields of heaven, having chased out the stars to the torch ball, had retired to change his shirt: therefore seeing the twilight of the skies, the prince ordering that they should return as usual, they retired to their own homes.

END OF THE THIRD DAY

FOURTH DAY OF THE

DIVERSION OF THE LITTLE ONES

A SHORT time before the dawn had come forth to seek a beverage after all the labour, and just as the sun was peeping forth, the white prince and the black princess went to the meeting-place, where were already assembled the ten women, who having filled their bellies with red mulberries, and made their mouths and hands like unto a dyer's, had taken seat together by the side of a fountain which served as basis to some orange-trees whose branches were interlaced above their heads so as to blind the sun. Now the women had taken counsel together how to pass the time in some manner until the hour came in which they had to move their jaws, so as to give pleasure to Thaddeus and Lucy; therefore they began to discuss if they should play at 'Brick-drying,' 'Head or Cross,' 'Sweet or Wind,' * 'Mallet or Switch, † 'Mora at the Bell,' at 'Narorchie,' ‡ 'the Castle,' 'Nearer to the Ball,' or at 'Nine-pins.' But the prince, who was tired of so many games, ordered that some instruments of music should be brought, and that something should be sung. At once the attendants brought calascioni, tambourines, lyre, and harp, chin-chiaro, fire-thrower and chio chio, § and zu zu, and having played a

---

* 'Cucco o viento' = sweet or wind, childish game, in one fist is held tight a confetto (sweet) or something else, and in the other fist nothing, and then both are held to the companion in the game who must guess when asked: Is it 'cucco o viento?' = 'Is it sweet or wind?' in which of the two hands the sweet or other may be found, and if he cannot guess then he loses the same quantity of whatever the hand may enclose.

† 'Mazza o pinzo' = mallet or switch. Game for youths in which a rod is sent backwards and forwards by blows from a switch with which the two players are provided.

‡ Card game.

§ 'Chio chio.' Onomatopœa of the song of some birds, especially of a turkey-cock.

fine symphony, in the style of Abbé Zefiro, and some jocular pieces, and the ball of Florence, a handful of songs were sung of those good times which we may sooner weep for than find; and amongst others they sang:

> Stop at that, thou little Margaret. Thou art over-scandalous,
> As for every little thing thou wilt have the gown before thee;
> Stop at that, thou little Margaret.

And that other:

> I would, thou cruel one, slowly return, and stay under that foot; even if I knew that I should be always ill-used would I run to thee.

And after this followed:

> Come forth, come forth, thou sun, and give warmth to the emperor.

And then, 'My Little Silver Stool,' 'Worth Four Hundred, Four Hundred and Fifty,' 'All the Night it Sings,' 'Sing with Viola,' 'The Master of the School':

> O master, master, send us forth soon,
> For the head-master will come down with lance and with sword.

By the handmaidens followed:

> Play, play, thou little bag-pipe,
> And I will buy thee a gown, a gown of scarlet;
> And if thou wilt not play, I will break thine head.

Not forgetting the other:

> Rain not, rain not, as I desire to stir,
> To stir the grain of Master Julian;
> Lend me a lance, as I wish to go to France,
> From France to Lombardy, where dwelleth Madame Lucy.

Now whilst they were in the midst of their best singing, the viands were brought in and laid upon the table, and all ate their sufficiency: and Thaddeus bade Zoza to head the entertainment, beginning the day with her song; so she in obedience to the prince's command began thus:

THE COCK'S STONE

Of the Fourth Day

MINIC' ANIELLO, BY VIRTUE OF A STONE FOUND IN THE HEAD OF A COCK, BECOMETH YOUNG AND RICH: BUT BEING CHEATED OF IT BY TWO MAGICIANS, RETURNETH TO BE OLD AND A BEGGAR. HE GOETH ABOUT THE WORLD SEEKING FOR IT, TILL HE COMETH TO THE REALM OF MICE, WHERE HE HEARETH NEWS OF THE STONE, AND ASSISTED BY TWO MICE, HE RECEIVETH IT BACK AGAIN, AND RETURNETH TO HIS PRISTINE ESTATE, AND TAKETH REVENGE OF THE CHEATS.

THE wife of the thief does not always laugh. Who weaveth a fraud, deviseth his own ruin; there is no deceit which is not discovered, nor treachery which cometh not to light; the walls are spies for the rogues; even the ground will open and speak of theft and whoredom: as ye will hear from what I am going to relate, if ye will stay with your ears at home.

Once upon a time, in the city of Grotta-negra, lived a certain man, Minic' Aniello hight, who was so persecuted by fortune that all the good he owned up and down was a little cock, which he had fed and reared upon crumbs. But one morning, finding himself in sore straits and distressed with appetite (as hunger chaseth the wolf out of the forest), he bethought him to sell the cock and take some coppers for it: and carrying it to market, he met two old magicians, with whom he came to agreement, and sold it for half a ducat; so they told him to carry it to their house, and they would count him out the coin. In such case the magicians fared forward, and Minic' Aniello, following them, overheard them speak softly to each other, saying, 'Who could have told us, that we would find such a good occasion, O Jennarone? this cock unfailingly will be our good fortune, for cause of that stone, of which thou wottest, and which he holdeth in his head; we will have it set at once in a ring, and thus we shall have all that we know how to demand.' 'Hold thy tongue,

Jacovuccio,' answered Jennarone, 'I see myself rich already, and can hardly believe it; and I wish for the hour to come in haste so that I may cut this cock's throat, and give a kick to all beggary, and stretch my stocking in the sun, because, in this world, without any tornesi * the virtues are held as feet-rags, and as thou goest, so art thou held.' When Minic' Aniello, who had travelled many countries, and eaten bread from divers bakers' shops, heard this talk, he turned his back, and took to his heels down the dusty road. And running home, he twisted the cock's neck, and cutting open his head, found the stone, which he at once had set in a brass ring. Desiring to try the power of its virtue, he said, 'I should like to become a youth eighteen years old.' Hardly had he spoken these words, when the blood coursed hotter through his veins, the nerves became stronger, the legs stood firmer, the flesh smoother, the eyes more full of fire, the silvery hair became of a golden hue, the mouth, which had been a devastated village, became peopled with pearly teeth, the beard, which had been a preserved forest, turned to newly sown ground; in fact he was changed to a most handsome youth. Then he said, 'I should like to have a sumptuous palace, and be related to the king.' And lo! a palace of unparalleled beauty stood before him, with chambers marvellous to see, with wondrous columns, and perfect paintings to daze and amaze the beholder; silver plentifully strewn around, gold overflowing; and jewels with their sheen and shine blinding the gazer; and servants swarming around; horses and carriages were there, numberless; in brief, it was so rich and lordly a mansion, that the king opened his eyes wide with wonder at the sight of it, and willingly gave his daughter Natalizia in marriage to the owner thereof.

In the meanwhile the two magicians, as soon as they discovered the good fortune of Minic' Aniello, bethought themselves how to take out of his hands his great wealth; so they made a beautiful doll, which played and danced by means of counterpoise, and disguising themselves in merchants' gear, they fared to seek Pentella, Minic' Aniello's daughter, with the pretence of selling her the doll. When

* Neapolitan coin.

the child saw the beautiful thing, she said, 'What is the price?' and they answered that no amount of money could buy it, but that she could become the owner of it, if she would but grant them their request, which was, to let them see the setting of the ring her father possessed, so that they might take a pattern of it, and have one made like it, and they would give her the doll without any payment. Pentella, who had never heard the proverb, 'Of cheap things think before thou buyest them,' instantly accepted their bargain, saying, 'Return ye in the morning, and I will ask my sire to lend it to me.' And the sorcerers fared forth, and as soon as her father came home, she fluttered around him lovingly, and caressed him with charming and alluring flattery until he granted her her wish, and lent her the ring, finding as excuse, that she was straitened of heart, and that it would cheer her to play with the ring. When the following day came, as soon as the sun with the small straw broom sweepeth away the dirt of the shadows in the squares of heaven, the two magicians returned; and no sooner had they the ring between their hands than they made their escape, melting like the one of whom it is said, 'that not even smoke is seen of him,' so that the wretched Pentella had like to have died with grief.

Now when the magicians came to a forest where the branches of the trees interlaced thickly overhead, forming a dense archway, and others stood playing at hot bread between themselves, they demanded of the ring that it should lay waste the doings of the old man made young. And the words were hardly spoken when Minic' Aniello, who was standing at that very moment before the king, was seen to get older, and grey-haired, the white forehead to furrow with lines, the brows and eye-brows to harden like bristles, the eyes to get blood-shot, the face to be covered with wrinkles, the mouth to become toothless, the beard to become thinner, the back to rise up to a hump, the legs to tremble, and above all things the sumptuous robes to change to the former rags. The king, beholding this hideous beggar sitting in conversation with him, ordered him to be instantly turned out, with blows and hard words; and Minic' Aniello, finding himself fallen so low, fared to his daughter, weeping sorely, and asking from her the ring, so that he might be able to remedy this evil disorder. But when he heard of the cheat practised upon him by the two false merchants, he nearly cast himself out of the window in his despair, cursing a thousand times the ignorance of his daughter, who, for a wretched doll, had caused him to become as an hideous gnome, an accursed goblin; and for a thing made out of rags, had reduced him to doings fit for madmen, adding that he was resolved to wander through wilds and wolds, and take no rest till he had gained some information of the two false merchants. So saying he threw a fishing-net and a pair of saddle-bags across his shoulders, donned rustic attire, drew sandals on his feet, hent staff in hand, and leaving his daughter cold and frozen, he fared away in his despair, and never ceased faring until he came to the realm of Pertuso-cupo, inhabited by the mice. When the mice beheld him, they supposed him to be a spy of the cats, and they seized him, and carried him before Rosecone their king, who asked him, 'Who art and whence comest thou, and what art thou doing in these parts?' Minic' Aniello, presenting first to the king, in sign of tribute, a piece of lard, related to him all his misfortunes, concluding, that he would so long wear and tear that miserable body of his, till he gained news of those damned souls, who had deprived him of a jewel so dear, robbing him at once of the flower of youth, and the fount of all his riches, and the prop of his honour. At these words King Rosecone felt himself gnawed with pity, and desiring to console the poor man, sent for all the elder mice to hold council together, asking their rede about Minic' Aniello's disaster, and commanding them to make all diligence and speed in seeking out some news of these false merchants, if it were possible to get any.

Now amongst these, so it fortuned, stood two of the elder mice, Rudolo and Saltariello hight, well versed and expert in the matters of the world, who had spent six years of their lives in a road-side tavern, and they said, 'Be of good cheer, O our comrade, as matters will be much better than thou thinkest. Now thou must know that we happened to be one day of the days within one of the chambers of the Horn Tavern, where are wont to lodge and enjoy themselves the highest, and noblest, and most esteemed men in the world, when two men from Castle-Rampino passed that way, and entered, and took seat, and ordered some viands to be brought, and when they had eaten their sufficiency, and seen the bottom of the pitcher, they began to converse one with the other of the good trick they had played to a certain oldster of Grotta-negra, having despited him and outraged him by taking from him a stone possessed of great virtue, 'Which (said one of the two, who was hight Jennarone) I will never draw off from my finger, as hath done the daughter of this grey-beard.' Minic' Aniello, hearing these words, said to the mice, that if they would feel confident to accompany him to these rogues' country, and be the means of his recovering the ring, he would present them with a whole cheese and a piece of salt pork, so that they might take their sufficiency, and enjoy it, together with their lord the king. The mice, hearing that their hands would be anointed, offered their services, and promised to do wonderful deeds, and cross seas and mountains to fulfil their enterprise. Thereupon they craved leave of the mousish crown to depart, and fared forth, and never ceased wending till they came after long travel and travail to Castle-Rampino, where the mice bade Minic' Aniello take rest under some trees on the bank of a river which like a leech sucked the blood of the able workers and cast it into the sea, whilst they should go and seek the dwelling-place of the two magicians. And the two mice wended forward and found the house of the sorcerers, and perceiving that Jennarone never drew the ring from his finger, thereupon they sought to gain this victory by stratagem. So awaiting till the night darkened, clouding with its murk the face of heaven which had been burned by the sun, and the magicians had gone to their couches, Rudolo began to gnaw at the finger on which the ring was, and Jennarone feeling the pain took the ring off, and laid it on a table which stood near the bedside. As soon as Saltariello saw this, he quickly jumped upon the table and put the ring in his mouth; and both ran back to Minic' Aniello, who in gazing at it felt more joy than a man condemned to be hanged feeleth when the grace reacheth him; and as soon as Minic' Aniello held it in his hand, he bade the two magicians to be turned into the shape of two asses, upon one of which he laid his cloak, jumping upon his back like a handsome noble, and loading the other with lard and cheese, fared forward Pertuso-cupo-wards, where gifting the king and his counsellors, he thanked them for all the good they had done to his cause, and for all the benefits received, praying Heaven that never trap or snare should cause them damage or hurt, and never cat should do them harm, nor arsenic cause them displeasure. Then farewelling them, he departed from that country, and wended onwards till he came to Grotta-negra, handsomer and more sumptuously arrayed than erst he had been, where he was received by the king and his daughter with the greatest caresses in the world. And bidding the two asses to be cast down a mountain, he joyed with great joyance in union with his wife, never again taking the ring from his finger, so that he might not be the cause of more ruin or destruction, for

> ‘The dog who is scalded by hot water
> Feareth even the sight of cold water.’

THE TWO BROTHERS

Of the Fourth Day

MARCUCCIO AND PALMIERO ARE BROTHERS, ONE RICH, AND CORRUPT, AND VICIOUS, AND THE OTHER POOR, BUT VIRTUOUS. THEY MEET AFTER VARIOUS VICISSITUDES, BUT THE POOR BROTHER IS DRIVEN AWAY BY THE OTHER; AFTER A TIME THE RICH BROTHER FALLETH INTO POVERTY AND IS DRIVEN NEAR THE GIBBET, BUT AT LAST, RECOGNISED TO BE INNO-CENT, IS SAVED BY HIS BROTHER, WHO HATH BECOME RICH AND A BARON, AND WHO GIVETH HIM A SHARE OF HIS GOOD.

THE case of Minic' Aniello gave great satisfaction to the prince and princess, and they blessed a thousand times the mice by whose aid the poor man regained the stone, and rejoiced that the magicians got a broken neck for the circle of a finger. Cecca, having set herself in position to begin her chattering, thus barricaded with the bar of silence the gate of their words, and in this fashion began to relate:

There is no better shield against the assaults of fortune than virtue, which is a counter-poison of all misfortunes, a prop against all ruin, a safe harbour for all travails. It chaseth thee from the fire, protecteth thee from the storms, guardeth thee from every adversity, comforteth thee in every evil betiding thee, helpeth thee in every necessity, and giveth thee peace in the hour of death: as ye will hear from this tale which I hold in the tip of my tongue ready to relate to you.

Once upon a time there lived a father who had two sons, Marcuccio and Palmiero hight; and he, being on the point to settle his accounts with nature, and to tear up the account-book of life, called them to his bedside, and said to them: 'O my blessed sons, but a short time may the bailiffs of time still delay to come and break down the door of my years, to make execution against the constitution of this kingdom upon the dowered good of this life for that which I owe to the earth; and therefore loving you as mine own entrails, I must not depart from you without leaving you some good remembrance, so that ye may sail with the north wind of good counsel in this gulf of travail, and thus reach good port. Then open well your ears, that if what I give you seems nothing to you, ye must know that it is a treasure that will not be stolen from you by robbers; a house that no earthquake can destroy; a possession that cannot be consumed by dissipators. Now first and foremost be fearful of Heaven, for every thing comes from Heaven: whoso mistaketh that road has fried the liver. Do not let laziness cut your throats, growing up like pigs in the stye; whoso curries his own horse cannot be called a groom; one must help oneself with kicks and bites, for whoso worketh for others eateth for himself. Be saving when ye have goods; whoso saveth gaineth; by small coins is made the ducat; whoso putteth away findeth; whoso hath from women gathereth a good leaf; put away and thou shalt eat; do naught for which thou needest be ashamed; good is the house where there are friends and relations; sad is the house which is empty; whoso hath money buildeth; whoso hath fair wind saileth; and whoso hath no money is an hobgoblin, an ass, that every moment is caught by a spasm. And therefore, O thou my kindest friend, as thou hast the income, so do thou expend behind as large as thou mayest cover it, and grind as much as thou canst smell: as thou feelest, so do thou make use of thy teeth, for a small kitchen maketh the house large. Do not be over-talkative, as the tongue hath no bone but breaketh the bone; hear, see, and be silent; if thou desirest to live peacefully, whatso thou seest see, whatso thou hearest hear, little of meat little to speak; is there warmth of clothing, it never did hurt anything; whoso often speaketh often maketh a blunder. Be satisfied with little, for 'tis better to have beans which last than sweets which end; 'tis better to joy a little than to be for ever bewailing; whoso cannot eat the meat, let him drink the broth; whoso can do naught else lieth down with his wife; what will be will be; patch thyself up as best thou can; whoso may not eat the flesh must gnaw at the bone. Frequent and unite yourselves with your betters, and pay the expenses; tell me with whom thou goest; and I will tell thee what thou doest; whoso walketh with the lame at the end of the year will walk lame himself; whoso sleepeth with dogs will not arise without fleas; to the rogue give thou thy goods and let him go, as bad company bringeth man to the gibbet.

'Think before, and act after, as it is a bad thing to shut the stable-door when the oxen are gone; when the cask is full draw to thy will, but when it is empty there is naught to draw from it; chew well first and swallow after, for the she-cat in her hurry brought out her kittens blind; whoso fareth slowly doeth a good day's journey. Fly all disputes, and company not with licentious youths, putting not thy foot upon every stone; for whoso jumpeth over many stakes will fall on one upon his hind parts; a horse apt to kick receiveth more than he giveth; whoso with hook woundeth by sword dieth; the pitcher goeth to the well till it leaveth its handles there; the gibbet is built for the unfortunate; do not make an ass of thyself with pride; there is need of something more than a white table cloth upon the table; be humble and correct thyself; never hath the house been good which is filled with smoke; a good alchemist passeth whatso he distilleth through the ashes, so that it should not be smoked; and the man o' weal must ever keep in his memory that he must return to dust all the proud thoughts, so that he should not be smoked by his own presumption. Take not the thought of the red-haired, for whoso intermingleth in the business of other folk, hindereth himself; and it is matter for a lazzarone to put a tariff upon the cucumbers and salt within the pot. Do not mingle with the great, but rather go and cast thy net, than serve at court. Love of the great is wine of flask, which in the morning is good and in the evening hath turned sour; from them thou canst only get good words and rotten apples; where thy services are barren, thy designs rotten, thy hopes fruitless, thou sweatest without compassion, runnest without rest, sleepest without repose, doest a deed of nature without light, and eatest without taste. Take care of a rich man become poor, of a peasant become rich, of a beggar in despair, of a petted servant, of an ignorant prince, of a mercenary judge, of a jealous woman, of a man of to-morrow, of a court flint-stone, of a beardless man, of a woman with beard, of a quiet river, of a smoky chimney, of bad neighbours, of a child that always weepeth, and of an envious man. And constrain yourselves to understand that whoso hath a craft hath a part; and whoso hath salt in his head will live even in the wood, and hath grown his wisdom-tooth, and changed his first ears: for to a good horse no saddle is wanting.

'I should like to tell you a thousand other things, but the agony of death is coming near me, and my breath is failing me.' Thus ending his say, he had just the strength to lift up his hand and bless them, when, furling the sails of this life, he entered into the harbour, leaving all the vexations of this world.

As soon as the sire departed, Marcuccio, who had engraved his words deep amiddlemost his heart, gave himself up entirely to study in school, and to the academies, and to disputes with the students, and the discourse of virtuous matters; so much so, that in a very short time he became the first wise man of that country; but as poverty is a sticking tick upon virtue, and from the man anointed by Minerva, the goddess of wisdom, it sucketh out the water of his good fortune, this poor man was always despised, always penniless, ever clean-hearted and burning with desire. Oftentimes he found himself full on empty vessels, and greedy of licking the frying-pan, tired of studying counsels, and beggared of help, working upon indigestion, and finding himself always fasting.

Now it was the opposite with Palmiero. He gave himself up to drinking in high excess, and heedlessly gambling one way, and tavern-going the other, growing up in height, without any single virtue in the world; and for all this, by riffe, and raffa,* and knaving, and tricking, he raised good straw under himself, and Marcuccio seeing this repented himself of having followed the advice of his sire and thus mistaking the road; wherefore the gift naught proper had given him, but the cornucopia had reduced him to such' want. And his just dealing had brought him naught within his

---

* Prov. phrases, "riffe and raffa" knavery and trickery.

saddle-bags, whilst Palmiero with the entertainment of bones made good flesh, and with playing with his hand had filled his guts. At the last, unable to stand firm against the importunity of need, he fared to his brother, beseeching him that, as fate and fortune had made him son of the white fowl, he should remember that he also was of his own flesh and blood. Now Palmiero in the heyday of his affluence had become stingy, and therefore said to him, "O thou who wouldst follow the studies and thy father's rede, and hast always cast in my face the conversations and play, go and gnaw thy books and leave me in peace with my misfortunes, as I am not able to give thee even salt, as well have I to work hard to get these few coppers that I have; thou hast age and judgment, and whoso knoweth not how to live, all the worse for him; every man for himself and God for all. If thou hast money, cast them above. An thou art hungry, bite thy legs; an thou art thirsty, bite thy fingers;' and having said these and other words, he turned his back upon him. Whereupon Marcuccio, his mind turned to the direst despair, seeing his own brother use him so badly, with a steadfast spirit and with the strong waters of a desperado resolved to separate the gold of the soul from the earth of the body; therefore he fared forth towards a very high mountain which stood as a spy from the earth to see what was doing high on air, or rather like a sultan of all the mountains, with a turban of clouds upon his forehead, raised up to heaven, ready to light up the moon. And mounting up, and climbing up, and crawling up, by a very narrow steep way Marcuccio reached the summit, whence he beheld a great precipice. Turning the key of the eye-fountain, and weeping, and lamenting, and bewailing his lot, he was about to cast himself down, head foremost, when a beauteous damsel, arrayed in green raiment, with a laurel wreath upon her golden hair, caught him by the arm, and said, 'What art thou doing, O my poor man? where dost thou let thy evil thoughts carry thee? art thou a virtuous man, and hast thou burnt much oil, and lost much of thy sleep in studying? art thou one who, to spread abroad thy fame like unto a careened galley, hast been so long under the careen, and now losest thyself at the best, and usest not those

weapons which thou hast tempered at the forge of thy studies?
Knowest thou not that virtue is a mighty remedy against the poison
of poverty; a good snuff against the catarrhs of envy; a powerful
prescription against the infirmities of time? knowest thou not that
virtue is a compass by which to regulate ourselves to the winds of
misfortune, a flambeau by which we light out way in the murk of
our discontent, a strong archway able to resist all the earthquakes
of travail?   O thou unhappy one, be thyself once more, and turn
not thy back to whoso can give thee courage in dangers, strength in
disasters, phlegm in despair.   Art thou aware that Heaven sent thee
to this mountain so difficult to climb, where dwelleth Virtue herself,
so that she, blamed wrongfully by thee, should save thee from the
wicked intention which blinded thee?   Therefore awake, be comforted, change thy thoughts; and so that thou mayest perceive that
virtue is ever bountiful, ever worthy, ever useful, take this small
packet of powder, and wend to Campo-largo, where thou wilt find
the daughter of the king of that realm nearly at the last gasp, and
no remedy can be found for her grievous sickness.   Let her take this
within a new-laid egg, and thus thou wilt at once give a patent of
dislodgment to her ailment, which, like a soldier who surrenders
himself at discretion, will leave her, whilst now 'tis sapping her
life; and thou wilt gain a prize for it that will chase away thy poverty, and thou shalt be able to live as beseemeth to such as thee,
and thou wilt need no help from that other.'

Marcuccio at once knew the speaker by the point of her nose to
be Virtue herself, and casting himself at her feet, besought her forgiveness for the error that he had designed to commit, saying, 'I
lift up the veil from before mine eyes, and recognise thee by the
wreath that crowns thee, that thou art Virtue, praised by all, and
followed by few; Virtue, that knowest how to sharpen the intellect,
strengthen the mind, refine the judgment, embrace all honourable
fatigue, and put on wings so as to enable us to fly to the celestial
spheres.   I know thee, and I repent of having used so badly the
weapons which thou hast given me; and I vow thee from this day
forth to charm myself so well with thy counter-poison, that not

even a March thunder-clap will hurt or move me.' And he stooped
to kiss her feet, when she disappeared from sight, leaving him comforted like a poor sick man, to whom after the accident is past is
given the bitter root with cold water. Then sliding down the
mountain, Marcuccio fared Campo-largo-wards, and reaching the
palace of the king, sent word that he had come to heal his daughter
from her sickness; and the king hearing this, entreated him with
great honour, and brought him to the chamber of the princess, where
he found that unhappy damsel lying in a perforated bed, so much
consumed and grown so thin, that she was only skin and bones: the
eyes were so deeply sunken in their orbits, that one would have
needed Galileo's glasses to see the eye-balls, the nose was so sharply
defined that it might have usurped the office of the supposed form,
the cheeks were so thin and drawn that she seemed like the death of
Sorrento, the under-lip fell back upon her chin, the breast was flat
down like unto the breast of a magpie, the arms were like the shin-
bone of a lamb, bared of the flesh; in brief she was a transformed
being, who with the cup of pity drank a toast to compassion. And
Marcuccio, beholding her in such plight, wept, and the tears rained
down his cheeks at the weakness of our nature subjected to the
murthering of time, and to the revolutions of complexion, and to
all the ills of life. So he asked for a new-laid egg of a young
fowl, and making the princess swallow it when it was just warmed
up, first putting the powder within it, he heaped up four blankets
upon her, and left her. But Night had not yet entered port and
set up her tent, when the sick damsel called her handmaidens, and
bade them change her bed, which was soaked in sweat, and when
they had changed her, she felt refreshed, a thing that in seven years
of infirmity had never happened, and she sought somewhat of food;
so that they had fair hopes, and they gave her something to sip.
Thus every hour she gained strength, and every day her appetite
increased, and not a week went by without she recovered, and her
health returned, and she left her bed. Seeing this, the king thought
Marcuccio the god of leechcraft, and he endowed him with lands
and fiefs, and made him a baron, and prime minister of his court,

and married him to a lady the wealthiest in that country. Such was his case.

In the meanwhile Palmiero was lightened of all that he had; as gambling money comes, so it goes, and the luck of the gambler, when it is at its highest point, is sure then to turn. When he beheld himself in such a beggarly plight and so unhappy, he resolved to wander unceasingly, so that perhaps in changing place he might change fortune; either he would free himself of the load of his life or better his position, and he fared on through wilds and wolds, and passed cities, and crossed seas, for the full length of time of six months, till he came to Campo-largo, so weary and tired that he could hardly stand on his feet, and perceiving that he could not find a place wherein he could lay himself down and die, and hunger gnawing his vitals, and his raiment falling in rags from his back, despair seized him, and sighting an old house outside the walls of the city, he entered it, and taking off his garters which were made of cotton and thread, tying them together made a noose, which he fixed to a beam. Then mounting upon a heap of stones which he had heaped together, he placed his neck in the noose: but by decree of the Decreer, it happened that the beam was old and rotten, so that with the weight it brake asunder, casting Palmiero alive upon the heap of stones, thereby hurting his ribs, which made him suffer for a few days. Now when the beam breaking came to the ground, some golden chains, and necklaces, and rings fell down with it; which had been put within the cavity of the wood, and amongst other things, a leathern purse containing some golden crowns. And Palmiero with a kick in the air jumped over the pit of poverty, for if before he had hanged himself through despair, he was now up-lifted with joy, so that his feet hardly touched ground, and picking up this gift of good fortune, he fared quickly to the tavern to gain the spirit which just now had failed him.

Now two days before, some thieves had stolen these things from that very same tavern keeper, to whom Palmiero had gone to take his sufficiency of viands and drink, hiding them as they thought safely within that beam, well knowing that they could take them one at a time, and dispose of them quietly. Palmiero, having now fulfilled his belly, pulled out the leathern purse to pay, which the tavern-keeper no sooner sighted than he knew it, and calling some men who were in the tavern, he had Palmiero arrested. With fine ceremonies he was led before the judge, who commanded that he should be searched, and upon his person was found the evidence of his crime; thereupon he was convicted and condemned to play the game of three and the handmill with his feet in the air. The wretched man who found himself in such plight, feeling that the eve of a garter was to be followed by the feast of a rope, and the trial on a rotten beam to be followed upon a new gibbet bar, began to buffet his face, and pluck his hair and beard, and weep, and wail, and cry that he was innocent, and that he appealed against his sentence. Whilst he was so crying, and looking up and down the road, and saying that there was no justice, that poor folk were never heard, and that decrees were issued and matters done in a blind sort of way, and because he had not oiled the judge's hand, spoken to the clerk, given a good handful to the magistrate, and a good measure to the attorney, he was to be sent to work in the air to the widow teacher, he accidentally met with his brother, who was a counsellor, and chief of the wheel, whereupon he tried to stop the sentence, and make the court understand his reasons, and he related all that had occurred.

Marcuccio answered him, saying, 'Be silent, for thou knowest not thy good fortune, because doubtless thou, who at the first trial hast found a chain three feet long, wilt find at the second a rope three yards in length. Fare thou joyfully onward, for the gibbet is thy very own sister; and where the others lose their lives, thou fillest thy purse.' And Palmiero hearing him give him a double weight of words thus answered him, 'I came hither for justice and not to be jeered at, and know thou that of this matter of which I am accused my hands are clean, as I am an honoured man, although thou beholdest in me a beggar in rags, for thou knowest that the cowl makes not the monk. And because I would not hearken to my sire Marchionno, and my brother Marcuccio, I am passing through this

trial, and I am on the point of singing a madrigal in three under
the hangman's feet.' Marcuccio, hearing the name of his father
and his own, felt his blood warm towards him, and glancing fixedly
upon Palmiero, he seemed to know him, and at last discovering him
for his brother, his feelings contended with each other, shame and
affection, flesh and honour, justice and pity; and he blushed to
avow himself a brother to such an impudent-faced man. It grieved
him overmuch to see his own flesh and blood in that plight, and the
flesh drew him like an hook to remedy this matter, and his honour
drew him back, as he felt unwilling to dishonour himself in the
sight of the king by a brother convicted of theft; justice ordered
that satisfaction should be given to the offended party, but pity inclined him to seek the safety of his own brother. But whilst his
brain weighed on the scales the pros and cons of the case, not knowing what best he could do, behold, there came one of the doorkeep-
ers of the judge, with his tongue protruding one foot out of his
mouth for his running haste, who was crying with a loud voice,
'Stop, stop the work of justice; stay, stay, slowly, await.' 'What
is the matter?' said the minister; and the other answered, 'Something very marvellous, by decree of the Decreer, and the good fortune of this youth. Now so it chanced that two rogues fared to the
old house to take therefrom some monies and gold, which they had
hidden within the rotten beam, and they found naught, and each one
thought that his companion had done the cheat and taken the whole,
thereupon they came to high words, and from words to blows, until
they both fell wounded even unto death; and the judge was sent
for, and they confessed at once their deed, by which confession the
innocence of this poor youth is at once established, and I was sent to
stay the hand of justice, and save the youth, who is faultless.' Palmiero, hearing this, grew a foot taller, where he had been afraid to
go an arm's length. And Marcuccio, seeing his brother freed from
the blot, and his good fame restored to him, lifting up the mask
of disguise, discovered himself to him, saying to Palmiero, 'O my
brother, if thou knowest well what is vice, and that vice and
gambling are the cause of thy ruin, know thou now the worth of

virtue and the enjoyance of all good. Come thou freely to my house, where thou shalt enjoy with me the fruits of that virtue, which thou didst hold in great disdain and didst abhor, whilst I, forgetting all thy former contempt, will hold thee in love and honor within these eye-balls.' And thus saying, he led him to his house, and arrayed him in sumptuous raiment from head to foot, making him understand that in all trials, everything is wind, and that

'Virtue alone maketh man blessed.'

THE THREE ANIMAL KINGS

THIRD DIVERSION

Of the Fourth Day

CIANCOLA, SON OF THE KING OF VERDE-COLLE, FARETH TO SEEK HIS
THREE SISTERS, MARRIED ONE WITH A FALCON, ANOTHER WITH A STAG,
AND THE OTHER WITH A DOLPHIN; AFTER LONG JOURNEYING HE FINDETH
THEM; AND ON HIS RETURN HOMEWARDS HE COMETH UPON THE
DAUGHTER OF A KING, WHO IS HELD PRISONER BY A DRAGON WITHIN
A TOWER, AND CALLING BY SIGNS WHICH HAD BEEN GIVEN TO HIM BY
THE FALCON, STAG AND DOLPHIN, ALL THREE COME BEFORE HIM READY
TO HELP HIM; AND WITH THEIR AID HE SLAYETH THE DRAGON, AND SET-
TETH FREE THE PRINCESS, WHOM HE WEDDETH, AND TOGETHER THEY
RETURN TO HIS REALM.

MORE than four of the ladies were much affected to hear of the
compassion of Marcuccio for Palmiero his brother, and all confirmed the truth that virtue giveth sure riches which neither time
consumeth, nor storm carrieth away, nor tick gnaweth, whilst on
the contrary the other goods of this world come and go, and that
which is evilly begotten not even the third heir can enjoy. At last
Meneca, to unite the related success, brought forward upon the table
of trifles the story which follows:

In the days of yore there lived a king of Verde-colle, who was
blessed with three daughters, each of whom was a gem of rare
worth. For these three damsels were consumed with love-longing
the three sons of the King of Bello-prato. But as these three princes
had been ensorcelled by a fairy into the form of animals, the King
of Verde-colle disdained to give his daughters in marriage to them;
therefore the first, who was a beautiful falcon, by witchcraft called
the birds to come to take counsel together, and behold chaffinches,
wrens, bullfinches, fly-catchers, screech-owls, larks, cuckoos, magpies,
and all the gender pennatorum flocked at his call, and he bade them
spoil the flowers upon the trees at Verde-colle. And they did his
bidding, leaving neither leaf nor flower upon them. The second,

who was a stag, called to his side the rams, goats, hares, rabbits, porcupines, and the other animals of that country, and bade them destroy the seeds and the young growths, and they did his bidding, laying waste the land, and leaving not a single blade of grass. The third, who was a dolphin, taking counsel with an hundred seamonsters, brought upon that coast such a fearful storm that not a ship nor a boat was left whole. The King of Verde-colle, seeing that matters took a bad turn, and were made worse, and that he could not remedy the damage done him by these three wild lovers, resolved to save himself from this trouble and give to them his daughters in marriage; and they, not desiring marriage-feasting, nor any other joyance, carried the daughters away from that kingdom. When the brides were ready to depart, Grazolla, the queen their mother, gave to each daughter a ring exactly alike, saying that should they be divided and after some time meet again, or meet some one of their own blood, by means of those rings they would be able to recognize each other. And thus they took their departure and went their ways, and the falcon carried Fabiella, the eldest sister, upon the top of a very high mountain, so high that its confines touched the clouds, reaching with dry top where rain never falleth, and there leading her to a magnificent palace, entreated her, and kept her like a queen. The stag carried Vasta, the cadette sister, into an intricate forest, in which the so-called night-shadows knew not how to come forth and pay their homage to her; where, in a sumptuous mansion, surrounded by gardens the like of which had never been seen, he kept her as was suitable for the daughter of a king. The dolphin swam with Rita, the youngest sister, sitting upon his back amid the sea, till they came to a beautiful rock upon which was built a marvellous palace, where could have dwelt three crowned kings.

In the meanwhile Queen Grazolla had given birth to a man-child, whom they named Titone, and when time passed, and he came to the age of fifteen, hearing his mother often bewail and lament the loss of three daughters married to three animals, of whom she had never heard news since they left her, he felt a longing to fare over the

world until he could discover his sisters; and begging his sire to grant
him leave to wend and seek for them, after a time the king granted
his request, and the queen giving him a ring in the same way as she
had given rings to her daughters, they farewelled him, having first
equipped him with everything that was needful, and a suite to company him as a prince of his condition should possess. And he left
not a hole unseen in Italy, nor a subterraneous hiding-place in
France, nor was there a place throughout Spain which he left un-
explored, and he passed through England, and visited Slavonia, and
travelled to Poland, and in brief fared from east to west, till having parted with his retinue, some at taverns and some at the hospitals,
he at the last found himself, without even a suit of clothes, on the
top of the mountain where dwelt the falcon and Fabiella. When
he came before the palace, he stood gazing at it and its wonderful
beauty in a transport of amazement, beholding the corners of porphyry, the walls of alabaster, the windows of pure gold, and the entrance gate of pure silver; and while thus he stood gazing, Fabiella
sighted him from one of the windows, and sent for him to come
to her presence, and when he came she asked, 'Who art thou, and
whence comest thou, and what good fortune hath brought thee in
these parts?' Titone told her the name of his country, and of his
side, and of his mother, and his own name; and Fabiella recognized
him for her own brother, and after they had confronted the rings
which they wore upon their fingers, she was sure of it, and she embraced him with great joy, and fearing that her husband might not
be pleased to hear of his coming, she bade him hide himself. So
when the falcon came home, Fabiella began to say to him that she
longed with excessive longing to see her parents once more; and
the falcon answered, 'Let thy longing cease, O my wife, as it may
not be, until I am in an humour to carry thee there.' 'At least,' said
Fabiella, 'send for some one of my relations to console me;' and
the falcon replied, 'And who will come to see thee in such a distant
place?' 'And if some one did come,' retorted Fabiella, 'wouldst
thou be displeased?' 'And why should I be displeased,' answered the
falcon, ' 'tis enough that he be of thine own flesh and blood for me

to set him within mine eyes.' And Fabiella, hearing this, heartened her heart, and bade her brother come forth, and presented him to the falcon; and he said to Titone, 'Five and five make ten, love showeth through a glove, and water cometh forth from the boot; mayest thou be welcome; thou art master of this house; command and thou shalt be obeyed; and do whatso thou wilt.' And thus say·· ing the falcon gave orders to his household that they should honour Titone, and serve him as his own person.

After a fortnight of his stay upon the mountain had gone by, a longing seized him to fare forth and look for his other sisters, and he sought leave to depart, which was granted to him, the falcon giving him one of his feathers, saying, 'Take this, O Titone mine, and hold it dear, because if thou ever hast a need, thou wilt esteem it as a treasure; enough, take every care of it, and if thou desirest something very sore, throw it on the ground and say, "Come, come" and thou wilt praise me.' Titone wrapped carefully in paper the feather, and put it safely in a purse, and after a thousand cere- monies, and leave-takings, and farewellings, he departed. He fared through wilds and wolds for a length of time, till at last he came to the forest where dwelt the stag with Vasta, and being an-hun- gered, he entered a garden to gather some fruits, and he was per- ceived and recognized by his sister in the same way as he had been recognized by Fabiella. She brought him before her husband, who bade him welcome with the best of welcomes, treating him truly as a prince, and he stayed a fortnight also with them and after that time had elapsed he desired to go forth and seek the other sister. Then the stag gave him one of his hairs with the same words as had been spoken by the falcon, and with as many more from the stag as he had had from the other, and farewelling them, he wended on his journey, and he journeyed so long as to reach the extremes of the earth, and the sea stood before him, and he took ship with the design to seek in all the islands for some news; and spreading the sails in the wind, he wandered and sailed about from place to place, till at last he came to the island whereon dwelt the dolphin with Rita. As soon as he landed, his sister saw him, and knew him in

the same way as the two others had done, and he was welcomed
by his brother-in-law with a thousand welcomes, and when he wished
to depart after such a long time to fare to his mother and the sire,
the dolphin gave him one of his scales with the same words as the
others had said; and he farewelled them, and then took horse and
fared homewards.

Now he had not gone half a mile from the sea-shore, when he
came to a forest which was the dwelling of the shadows and the
free ladder of fear, where was a continual night of murkiness and
affright, and there he perceived a tower built amid a lake, that kissed
the trees' feet, so that they should not allow the sun to see their
hideousness; and at one of the windows he beheld a beauteous damsel
sitting at the feet of an hideous dragon who was fast asleep; and
when Titone sighted her and she beheld him, she broke out in a
melodious plaintive voice, 'O beauteous youth mine, sent perhaps to
me by Heaven to console and comfort me in my misery and
wretchedness, in this place where I never sight the face of a Christian; deliver thou me from the hands of this serpent tyrant, who
bare me away from the King of Chiara-Valle who was my sire, and
brought me in this darksome tower, where I am in misery slowly
dying of heartache, and becoming rank and rusty.' 'Alas!' answered
Titone, 'what can I do to serve thee, O thou beautiful damsel mine?
Who can ford this lake? Who can mount to this tower? Who can
come near that hideous dragon, whose sight terrifieth one, and soweth the seed of fear, and causeth looseness to the beholder? But
softly, stay a little while, we will try to chase away this serpent with
other help: step by step, said Gradasso: we shall soon see if it is
sweet or wind;' and so saying, he cast on the ground the feather,
the hair, and the scale that had been given to him, saying, 'Come,
come,' and hardly were the words spoken, when from the earth,
that like drops of water in summer giveth birth to the frogs, appeared the falcon, the stag, and the dolphin, and each and all cried,
'Here we are, what dost thou command?' Titone, seeing this, joyed
with great joy, and answered, 'I do not wish for aught else, but that
this unhappy damsel may be freed from the claws of that dragon,

and be brought out of this tower, and that a heap of ruins may be made of this place, and this beauteous damsel be taken by me to wife and carried home.' 'Hush,' said the falcon; 'when least thou expectest it there springs up the bean; this very moment we will twist it for thee on the top of a carlino *; and it is our will that he should have scarcity of ground.' 'Do not let us lose any time,' said the stag, 'disasters and macaroni must be eaten warm;' and thus saying, the falcon called to his side a quantity of griffins, who flew to the window of the tower, and lifted up the young lady, and carried her to the lake side, where stood Titone with his brothers-in-law, and if he thought the damsel from afar looked like the moon, when she was near he esteemed her a sun in beauty and comeliness. But whilst he clasped her to his heart, and spake sweet words to her, the dragon awoke from sleep, and casting himself out of the window, was swimming to where stood Titone, to devour him. When his brother-in-law the stag saw this, he called to his aid a squadron of lions, tigers, wolves, wild cats, and other animals, and they cast themselves upon the dragon, and made mince-meat of him with their claws.

When this was done, and Titone was ready to fare homewards, said the dolphin to him, 'And I also will do somewhat for thee, and in thy service;' and bade the sea cover the tower and all that surrounded it, so that not even the memory of such a murksome and accursed place should remain; and Titone, having witnessed these deeds, thanked his brothers-in-law as much as he could and knew, bidding the bride to do the same, as but for their aid she had not come forth safe from the danger. And they answered, 'It is instead our duty to thank this beauteous lady, since it is she who is the cause of our returning to our pristine forms; through the curse of a fairy, because of something done to her by our mother, we were to remain in the shape of animals from our birth until we should save from great danger the daughter of a king; and behold the time hath come for which we have longed so much; behold this

* A silver coin struck by Charles I of Angio, from whom it received its name 'carlino.' Worth 43 centesimi.

bunch of sorb-apple, 'tis ripe, and already we feel in our breasts a
new spirit, and new blood in our veins.' When they ended their
words, they became three handsome young men, and one after the
other embraced with great affection their brother-in-law, and
clasped the hands of their new relatives, who had fainted for joy.
And Titone seeing this, sighed heavily, and was nigh a-swooning,
and when he recovered said, 'O my Lord God, why have my father
and mother no share in this great delight? They would have
melted to see before them such graceful, comely, and beauteous
sons-in-law.' 'It is not night yet,' answered the brothers-in-law:
' 'twas the shame to behold ourselves so transformed that reduced us
to fly from the sight of men; but now that we may, through the
grace of Heaven, appear before folk, we will retire under the same
roof with our own dear wives, and live cheerfully. Now let us fare
on quickly, because before the sun to-morrow morning unpacks
the merchandise of its rays from the custom-house of the east, we
shall be together with you and our wives.'

And when they had ended their say, so that they should not wend
a-foot, there being naught of conveyance but a small boat which had
brought Titone, they bade appear a splendid carriage drawn by six
lions, and the five took place within it and they fared the day, and
in the evening they came to a tavern, and while they got ready the
viands, they passed their time reading many of the witnesses of
men's ignorance written on the walls by those who had stopped at
the place. At last they ate their sufficiency, and retired to their
beds, but the three youths pretending to go to bed, when the others
slept, fared onwards through the night, so that in the morning,
when the stars timid and shamefaced like newly made brides, do
not desire to be seen by the sun, they found themselves at the same
tavern with their wives, where when they met there was a great deal
of embracing, and joyance, and delight, passing all bounds. After
a time the eight entered the same carriage, and wended their ways,
and after faring for a length of time they arrived at Verde-colle,
where the king and queen gave them the warmest and fondest of
welcomes, and having gained the capital of three daughters, whom

they had believed lost, and the shield of three sons-in-law, and a daughter-in-law (who were the four columns of the temple of beauty), and sending messengers to the kings of Bello-prato and Chiara-valle, informing them of their sons' success, they both came to the joyance and feasting, and there was great rejoicing, refilling all with the fatness of delight in the married pot of their enjoyance, forgetting past grief and sorrow, but remembering that

' An hour of happiness causeth forgetfulness of a thousand years of torments.'

THE SEVEN PIECES OF PORK-SKIN

FOURTH DIVERSION

Of the Fourth Day

AN OLD WOMAN, A BEGGAR, GIVETH A GOOD BEATING TO HER DAUGHTER
FOR HER GLUTTONY, SHE HAVING EATEN SEVEN PIECES OF PORK-SKIN,
AND MAKETH A MERCHANT BELIEVE THAT SHE HAD DONE THIS, BECAUSE
SHE HAD WORKED TOO MUCH IN FILLING SEVEN SPINDLES. THE MER-
CHANT TAKETH HER TO WIFE, BUT SHE WORKETH NOT; BUT BY GIFT
OF THREE FAIRIES THE HUSBAND ON HIS RETURN FROM A JOURNEY
FINDETH THE PIECE OF CLOTH FINISHED, AND BY ANOTHER RUSE OF THE
WIFE HE RESOLVETH NOT TO ALLOW HER TO WORK ANY MORE, FOR
FEAR THAT SHE SHOULD FALL ILL.

ALL blessed Meneca's mouth for relating with so much taste her
story, which put before the eyes of the hearers doings that had happened so far away in such a manner that it caused envy to glow in
Tolla's breast, so that it made her wish from the marrow of her
bones to excel and surpass Meneca; therefore, having first well
cleared her throat, she began thus, in a clear voice:

Not a word is spoken which, if not all true, is not half true, and
this is the reason that some one said, Crooked face and straight venture; and he knew the things of this world, or perhaps he had read
the history of Antony and Palmiero, who had no eyebrows, and
without birdlime caught Becafico. It is by experience that this world
is the true portrait of the Cuccagna, land of pleasure and felicity,
where who works most gaineth least; where he hath the best who
taketh things as they come, and expecteth not that macaroni will
fall down his throat; as is truly known, and one touches it with
hands, that plunder and the spoils of fortune are gained and won,
not by the full-sailed galley, but by the darksome sailing boat, as
ye shall hear from what I am going to relate.

Once upon a time there lived a beggarly old woman, who with
distaff in hand, dabbling folk with her spittle on the way, used to

step from door to door, begging alms, and since by craft and deceit one lives half the year round, she made some women, who were tender of lungs and easy of faith, believe that she was going to do I know not what to fatten a very thin daughter she had. By thus begging, she gained the gift of seven pieces of pig's lard with the skin, which she took home with a quantity of straw and small bits of wood she had gathered by the way. Giving them to her daughter, she bade her cook them, whilst she went and begged of some gardeners an handful of greens to cook with them, and thus to make a tasty dish of food. The daughter took the pieces of skin, and burning off the bristles, put the skins in the pot, and began to cook them. But not so much did they boil in the pot, as they boiled in her throat, because the smell which came forth therefrom was a mortal defiance to taste its flavour in the field of appetite, and an immediate summons to the bank of gluttony, so much so, that after resisting for some time the temptation, at the last provoked by the natural odour that came forth from the pot, and drawn by her natural greed, and pulled by the throat by the hunger which gnawed at her entrails, she let herself slip, and tried a little of it, and the flavour being good, she said to herself, 'Let him that feareth become a bailiff; I am in it for this time; let us eat, and let it come of clay, or nails, or other, 'tis but a pig's skin. What will it be? Whatever may it be? I have good skin upon my shoulders to pay for these skins;' and thus saying, she put down the first, and feeling her stomach gnaw the more, took up the second; and afterwards she ate the third, and thus, one after the other, until she had eaten them all. Now having done this bad service, thinking of the error, and dreaming that the skins would stick in her throat, she bethought herself to blind her mother, and taking an old shoe, cut the sole in seven pieces, and put it in the pot.

In the meanwhile her mother returned with a bunch of greens, and cutting them up in small bits with all the suckers, so as not to lose a crumb, when she saw that the pot boiled, she put all the greens therein, together with a quantity of lard, that a coachman, who had it left from greasing a carriage, gave her in alms. Then she bade her daughter lay a coarse cloth upon an old box of poplar-wood, and bringing forth from a pair of saddle-bags two pieces of stale bread, and taking from a shelf a wooden basin, she cut up the bread within it, and threw upon it the greens with the old shoe-leather, and began to eat. But at the first mouthful she perceived that her teeth were not for shoe-leather, and that the pig's skins, by a new Ovid's transformation, had become the gizzard of a buffalo. Therefore she turned to her daughter, and said, 'Thou hast done me brown, this time, thou whore accursed, and what filthiness hast thou put in the pottage? Has my belly become an old shoe, that thou shouldst provide me with old leather? Quick, do thou confess this moment, how this was done; or say naught, and I will not leave thee a whole bone in thy body.' Saporita (thus was the girl hight) be-gan to deny, but the old woman's vexation increasing, she blamed the smoke which had entered the pot and came forth from it, which had blinded her and caused her to do this evil deed. And the old woman, seeing her food poisoned, and taking hold of a broomstick, began to work in good earnest, and more than seven times did she take it up and let it down, hitting anywhere as it fell. And the daughter shrieked with loud shrieks, and at her cries a merchant who was passing by entered, and seeing the dog-like treatment dealt by the old woman to her daughter, he took the stick from her hand, and said to her, 'What hath this poor child done to thee, that thou hast a will to slay her? Hast thou found her running a lance or breaking money-boxes? Art thou not ashamed to treat thus a wretched child?' 'Thou knowest not what she hath done to me,' answered the old woman, 'the shameless chit, she can see that I am a beggar, and she hath no consideration, and she would like to see me ruined by doctors and druggists: because having commanded her now that it is hot weather that she should not work so much, so that she should not fall sick, as I have naught with which to feed her, the presumptuous creature, in my despite, would fill seven spindles, risking by doing this to have some bad disease of the heart, and re-main some two months in a bed of sickness.' The merchant, hear-ing this, thought that the cleverness and industry of this damsel could make his house into a fairy's kingdom; therefore he said to the old woman, 'Leave off thine anger and cast it on one side, for I will deliver thee from this danger in thine house by taking this daughter of thine to wife, and lead her to my home, where I will entertain her as a princess, as by grace of Heaven I bring up mine own fowls, and fatten mine own pigs, and keep pigeons, and I can hardly turn round in my house because of its fulness; may the heavens bless me, and the evil eye have no power over me, for I have my casks full of corn, my press full of flour, my pitchers full of oil, my pots and bladders full of lard, and hams and salt provisions hanging by the roof beam, and the rack full of crocks, and heaps of wood, and mounds of coal, and safes of linen, a bed fit for a bridegroom: and above all, from rents and interests, I can live like a mighty lord; and besides, I gain safely in these fairs some ten ducats, and if business always went full sail I should soon be rich.' The old woman, beholding this good fortune raining upon her when least she dreamt of it, taking Saporita by the hand (in the Neapolitan custom and fashion), consigned her to him, saying, 'Here she is, may she be thine for many happy years with health and fine heritage.' The merchant threw his arms round Saporita's neck, and carried her home, and he was very anxious for the day to come when he would fare to the market to buy some flax for his wife to spin.

When Monday came he arose early in the morning, and wending where the country-women came, he bought twenty dozens of flax, and taking it to Saporita, said to her, 'If thou hast a will to spin, be not afraid, as thou wilt not find another so madly enraged as thy mother, who used to break thy bones, if thou filledst the spindle; whilst I, for every ten spindle-full will give thee ten kisses, and for every distaff-full I will give thee mine heart; work thou then with a good will, and I will wend to the fair, where I shall tarry some twenty days, and when I return from the fair, do thou let me find these ten dozen of flax all ready spinned, and I will buy thee a fine pair of sleeves of Russian cloth trimmed with green velvet.' 'Thou mayest go an thou art ready,' said Saporita to herself, 'thou hast filled my spindle, yes, run and light the fire. An thou expectest a shirt out of my hands, thou canst provide thyself from this moment of blotting-paper; thou hast found her, and 'twas milk of the black goat, to spin twenty dozens of flax in twenty days. May evil happen to the boat that brought thee in this country. Go, for thou hast the time, and thou shalt find the flax spun when the liver groweth hair, and the ape a tail.'

In the meanwhile her husband fared on his journey, and she, who was as greedy and gluttonous as she was lazy, did not wait long before she began to mix flour, and take the oil, and cook fritters, and make cakes, and from morning till night she did naught else, but gnaw and munch like a mouse, and eat like a pig. But now when the term arrived of her husband's return, she began to spin very fine, considering the noise and great fracas that would occur when the merchant came back and found the flax untouched, and the press and pitchers empty; and therefore, taking a long perch, wound round it a dozen of the flax with all the tow and the rest, and hanging upon a big fork an Indian vegetable marrow, and tying the perch at one side of the wall of the terrace, she began to lower this father abbot of spindles down the terrace, keeping by her side a cauldron full of macaroni broth instead of the saucer full of water, and whilst she spinned like a ship's rope, every time she dipped her fingers in water she played a carnival game with the passers-by. Now passed that way three fairies, and they enjoyed so much the sight of this ugly vision, that they laughed till they fell backwards: and for this cause they cried, 'May all the flax in that house be found spun, and made into cloth, and whitened,' which thing was done at once, and Saporita swam in the fat of enjoyance, sighting this good venture raining upon her from heaven. But so that no more of this kind of enjoyance should befall her from her husband, she let him find her in bed, having first spread on it a measure of hazel-nuts; and when the merchant arrived, she began to lament, and turning first one side then the other she cracked the nuts, which made a sound as if the bones unhinged one from the other; and her husband asking of her how it was with her, she answered him with a very melancholic voice, 'I cannot be much worse, than I am now, O my husband, I have not a whole bone in my body; and what does it seem to thee but a little grass for the sheep, to skin twenty dozen of flax in twenty days, and to weave the cloth also? Wend thy ways, O my husband, for thou hast not paid my mother, and discretion has been eaten by the ass; when I shall be dead, my mother will not give birth to another like me, and therefore thou wilt not catch me any more at these dog's works; and I do not wish to fill so many spindles that I break the spindle of my life.'

The husband made her a thousand caresses, and said to her, 'Be thou well once more, O my darling wife, as I desire much more this beauteous loving frame than all the cloths in the world; and now I know that thy mother was right in chastising thee for so much work, because thou losest thine health. But be of good cheer. I shall spend an eye of my head to get thee back to health, and wait a while, I shall go at once for the doctor;' and thus saying, he went at once to call Messer Cattupolo. Whereupon Saporita ate up all the nuts, and threw the shells out of the window, and when the doctor came, feeling her pulse, and observing her face, and looking in the chamber-pot, and smelling in the night-vase, he concluded with Galenus and Hippocrates that her malady was superfluous blood, and from doing naught; and the merchant, thinking he heard nonsense, putting a carlino in his hand, sent him off warm and stinking; and wanting to go for another physician, Saporita told him that there was no need, because the sight of him only had cured her; and so her husband embraced her, and said that from that time forth she should enjoy herself without work, because it was impossible to have a Greek and cabbages,

'The cask full, and the slave-girl drunk.'

THE DRAGON

Of the Fourth Day

MIUCCIO PASSETH THROUGH MANY DANGERS, BY THE DEEDS OF A QUEEN
WHO IS A SORCERESS, BUT WITH THE HELP OF A CHARMED BIRD, HE
COMETH FORTH WITH HONOUR OF THEM ALL. IN THE END THE QUEEN
DIETH, AND HE IS DISCOVERED TO BE THE SON OF THE KING, AND
MAKETH THEM DELIVER HIS IMPRISONED MOTHER, WHO BECOMETH
THE KING'S WIFE.

THE story of the seven bits of pork's skin had with so much taste
been chattered out by Tolla that it seasoned well the pottage of
the prince's appetite so that the fat ran out, hearing the ignorant
malice and the malicious ignorance of Saporita; but Popa, unwilling
to yield even a crumb to Tolla, embarked in the sea of trifles with
the story which followeth:

Whoso seeketh to do harm to others findeth his own damage; and
whoso layeth traps to catch the third and the fourth by treachery
and deceit often falleth into the traps himself: as ye will hear of a
queen, who built with her own hands the trap wherein she was
caught by the foot.

It is said that once upon a time there lived a king of Alta-
marina, who, for his tyranny and hard-heartedness, was dethroned
from his royal seat whilst he was away with his wife at a castle far
from the city, and his realm was occupied by a certain woman a
sorceress. Whereat he had prayers recited to a certain wooden statue
of a serpent, which gave wise answers; and it told the king that he
would recover his estate only when the sorceress lost her sight.
Now this witch, besides being well guarded, knew by their noses
the folk sent by him to do her hurt, and she used against them a
brutal injustice, so that he being in despair to revenge himself of
the sorceress, so many women that came from that place as he

caught, so many he dishonored and then slew; and he did thus to hundreds and hundreds, whom their evil destiny had sent there to be robbed of honour and deprived of life.

There arrived one day of the days a damsel, named Porziella, who was the most beauteous being that could be seen upon earth. Her hair was as the handcuffs of the bailiffs of love; her brow a table, whereupon was written the tariff of the shop of all the graces; her eyes were two signal lights, whose beams ensured the vessels from being wrecked against the port of enjoyance; her mouth a bee-hive full of honey, amid two hedges of roses. And this damsel fell into the hands of the king, and having passed the same ordeal as the others, would have been slain, but that at the same time in which the king lifted the poignard, a bird letting fall I know not what upon his arm, caused it to tremble so, that the weapon fell from his hand. Now this bird was a fairy, who a few days before had fallen asleep in a forest, where sheltering under the tent of the shadows of the trees, she played off the heat to the galley of affright, and whilst a certain satyr desired to do her some bad things, Porziella awakened her. For this service the fairy followed the steps of Porzeilla so as to render her back her benefice. The king seeing this, thought that the beauty of that face had seized his arm, and enchanted his poignard, so that he was unable to slay her as he had done to so many others; therefore he bethought himself that a madman would be quiet enough in his own house, and that it was useless to dye with blood the implement of death as he had done the instrument of life, but that he would have her die built up in a garret of his own palace. This in very deed he had done, and they built up the loved but wretched one between four walls, without any food or drink, so that she should die a slow death. The bird, seeing her in such bad plight, with kindly human words consoled her, saying that she should be of good cheer, and keep her eyes cool and clear, since to return to her the good she had erst done for her, the bird would help her even by shedding her own blood, and Porzeilla besought the bird to tell her who she was. But the bird would not do so, saying only that she was under an obligation to her, and that she would leave naught undone to serve her; and seeing that the unhappy damsel was an-hungered, she flew out, and shortly returned with a sharp pointed knife in her bill which she had taken from the king's buffet. Then she told Porziella, to make a hole in a corner of the flooring, which responded in the royal kitchen, and from thence she would always be able to take something so as to maintain life. And Porziella obeyed the bird's rede, and worked with a good will till she made a hole large enough for the bird to pass through, and watching for the opportunity, the bird, beholding the cook to go with a pail for some water at the fountain, flew through the hole, and lifted up a fine pullet, and warm as it was carried it to Porziella; and not knowing how to remedy her thirst, as the bird knew not how to carry aught to drink, she flew to the pantry, where were hung up a number of bunches of grapes, and carried up a fine bunch to Porziella; and thus did the bird for some days.

After a time Porziella, who had conceived by the king, was brought to bed of a man-child beauteous as the moon; and she nursed him and brought him up with the help of the bird; but when he grew up, the fairy advised the mother to make the hole a little larger, and to lift up of the slates from the floor, enough for the child to pass through, and after she would lower down by ropes, which the bird brought, little Miuccio (so was the child hight), and this done, she would replace the slates in their former places, so that it should not be seen from whence he had come. Porziella did as the bird bade her, and commanded her son not to say whence he had come, nor whose son he was, and when the cook had gone forth on some errand, she farewelled him and lowered him down. And when the cook returned, and beheld so beauteous a child, he asked him who he was, and whence he came, and what he had come to do; and Miuccio, remembering his mother's rede, answered that he had lost himself, and was seeking for a master. At that very moment entered the king's equerry, and seeing the pretty child, so full of life and spirit, bethought him that he would be a very graceful page for the king, and therefore he led him to the royal chambers; and when the child stood in the presence, and the king beheld him, so comely, and graceful, and bright, a pure gem, the king was pleased with him, and he took him in her service as page, and he entered his heart as a son, and therefore he had him instructed in all manly exercise and chivalry, and educated as a true cavalier should be. As he grew in age, so he excelled in virtue, and became one of the ablest and most virtuous at court, and the king loved him with great love, and looked upon him with deeper affection than his step-son; because of which the queen had him in dislike and despite. And the more accomplished he became, envy and malevolence grew upon the queen and gained ground, and as Miuccio grew more in honour and favour and grace with the king, the greater became the hatred of the queen, and she took thought how she should soap well the ladder of his fortune, so that from the top he should slide down to the bottom.

One evening, whilst they had accorded their instruments together, they made a music of conversation, and the queen said to the king that Miuccio had boasted that he would build three castles in the air, and the king, since he felt rather confused, and desired to please his wife, when in the early dawn the moon, mistress of the shadows, giveth an holiday to her pupils so as to leave the place clear for the sun's festival, he sent for Miuccio, and commanded him, by every means, to build the three castles in the air as he had promised, otherwise he would cause him to kick the air. When Miuccio heard this he retired to his own chamber, and began sorely to weep and lament, and seeing by this how brittle is a prince's favour, and how short-lived are his graces, he increased his weeping and lamenting, and whilst he was in this plight, behold, the bird came and said to him, 'Hearten thine heart, O Miuccio, and doubt not, whilst thou hast this body by thy side, for I can draw thee even out of the fire,' and saying thus, the bird ordered him to take some paste-board, and glue, and making three large castles, called three big griffins, and tied a castle upon each bird, and then bade them fly; and when they flew in air, Miuccio called the king, and he came with all his court to behold this spectacle, this marvellous sight, and perceiving Miuccio's craft, held him in firmer affection, and honoured him, and largessed him, and caressed him more than ever:

for which matter, fuel was added to the queen's envy, and jealousy and ill-will to her disdain, and she resolved to make new attempts, but naught that she devised fulfilled her desire, and she took no rest, nor days nor nights, and sleep failed her, and if she slept she dreamed of some way by which she could rid herself of this eye-sore, this peg in her eyes: and, after a few days were past, she said to the king, 'O my husband, now is the time to return to thy former grandeur, and to thy sumptuousness of years gone by, because Miuccio has offered to blind that sorceress, and with the plucking of a pair of eyes make thee win back thy lost realm.' The king, feeling this touch upon what pained him most, sent for Miuccio, and said to him, 'I am surprised with great surprise, and wonder with great wonderment, that when I love thee so well, and thou canst replace me in mine own seat whence I fell, thou passest thy time unmindful, and thinkest not to save me and uplift me from so much misery, seeing me the while reduced from a kingdom to a forest, from a city to a miserable castle, and from bidding and forbidding a quantity of folk, to be served of a few bread-and-share carvers and broth-suckers; an if thou wilt not have my misfortune, run thou this moment and blind the sorceress, who keepeth from me all my goods; and thus closing her shops thou wilt reopen the bazaar of my greatness; putting out those lights thou wilt light the lamps of mine honour, which have been darkened and extinguished, and cause me great wretchedness.' Miuccio, hearing this proposal, was going to answer that the king had been misinformed and was mistaken, and that he was not a crow to go and pull out eyes, nor a scavenger that he should cleanse dirty holes, when the king interrupted him, saying, 'No more words; this is my will and it must be done: bethink thyself that in this brain of mine I have set the scales of justice; this side is the reward if thou doest what it is thy duty to do, the other side is the punishment if thou doest not my bidding.' Miuccio, who could not knock his head against the stone, and had to deal with a man, that wretched was the mother who had given him her daughter, therefore wended his ways in a dark corner, and began to weep and wail, when the bird flew to him, and said, 'Is it possible, O Miuccio, that thou always drownest thyself in a glass of water? If I had been killed, then thou mightest have done all this confusion and weeping and wailing. Knowest thou not that I have more thought for thy life than for mine own? Hearten thine heart, and follow me, and thou shalt see what Meniello can do.' And the bird began to fly and stopped in a forest, where she began to whistle, and at once a number of birds came at her call and flew around her, and she enquired which of them would be able to pluck out the witch's eyes, for to him she would give a safeguard against the claws of the vulture and the hawk, and a free pass against guns, bows, and cross-bows, and the net and the bird-lime of the fowler.

Now among these was a swallow, who had built her nest in a beam of the royal palace, and she hated the sorceress because, in doing her accursed sorcery, many a time had she driven her to fly away from her chamber with the fumigations; partly for this desire of revenge, and partly to gain the promised reward, she offered her services to the bird, and thereupon took her flight citywards, and entering the palace, found the sorceress lying upon her couch, and two handmaidens fanning her. When the swallow arrived, she flew straight upon the witch's eyes, and thrusting her bill and claws, plucked them out; and the witch, seeing at midday the night, and knowing that the loss of her sight was the shutting of the custom-house for the merchandise of the kingdom, cried aloud with the cries of a damned soul. Then she renounced the sceptre, and fled, and hid herself in a cavern, where beating her head against the walls, she ended her days.

When the sorceress was gone, the counsellors and grandees of the realm sent forth messengers to the king bidding him come and enjoy his own once more, since the blindness of the sorceress had been the means for him to see such a joyful day; and when these arrived, Miuccio also arrived, and the latter, being taught by the bird, said to the king, 'I have served thee with good coin: the witch is blinded, the realm is thine; therefore if I deserve any reward for this service, I desire no other than that thou wilt leave me in peace with my misfortunes, without sending me forth again to meet these dangers.' The king embraced him with great affection, and made him put on his cap and sit by his side; and Heaven may tell ye if the queen swelled with wrath, and at the rainbow which showed in her face could be supposed and could be understood the wind of all the ruin that she devised in her heart against Miuccio.

Now at no great distance from this castle dwelt a most ferocious dragon, which had been born at the same time as the queen had seen the light, and when they sent for the father of astrologers to draw his calculation and say what it portended, he replied that the child that was born would live as long as the dragon lived, and when the one died, the other would die also; one thing only could save the queen, and that was that they should anoint the temples, and the chest bone, and the nostrils, and the wrists with the blood of that same dragon. Now the queen knew of the fury and strength of the animal, and she thought of sending Miuccio to be caught in his clutches, well sure that it would make a mouthful of him, and he would have been like a strawberry in a bear's throat, so turning towards the king she said, 'In very sooth, Miuccio is the treasure of thine house, and thou shouldst be ungrateful if thou didst not love him, and much more so, as he hath given us to understand that he will slay the dragon for which, although he is my brother, as he is thy direst foe I shall be glad, as I love an hair of an husband more than an hundred brothers.' The king hated with deadly hatred this dragon, and knew not what to do to rid himself of the sight of him, and therefore as soon as he heard her words he sent for Miuccio, and said to him, 'I know that thou puttest thy sleeve where thou desirest, and therefore, now that thou hast done so much, thou must do me yet another kindness, and thereafter thou mayest turn me as thou wilt. Do thou go forth this very moment, and slay for me the dragon, and thou wilt have done me a great service, and I shall be grateful and give thee due reward.' Miuccio, at these words, went nigh out of his senses, and when he recovered himself, and could utter his words plainly, he answered the king, 'Now, this is a bad headache, thou hast taken to wearing me out. Is my life the gift of a black goat, that thou weariest it out in this way? This is not a matter of "a peeled pear, fall down my throat," 'tis a dragon which with its claws tears you to pieces, with its tusks pierces you through, with its tail crushes you, with its eyes transfixes, and with its breath slays. And now how wilt thou send me to death? Is this the dead place thou givest me, in exchange for having given thee a kingdom? What accursed soul hath put these dice upon the table? Who hath been the son of Satan to put thee up to this jumping, and given thee to understand these words?' The king, who was easily led, and like to a balloon, which is light to make it leap, but was headstrong and harder than a stone to move in maintaining what he had once said, put his feet down, saying, 'Thou hast done so much, and now thou losest thyself at thy best? Therefore, no more words, go, rid my kingdom and the world of this scourge, if thou wilt not that I rid thee of life.' Thus the wretched Miuccio saw himself well favoured first and threatened after, this moment a caress upon the face, another instant a kick on the hind-parts, now warm, then cold; he could reflect how unstable and changeable are the fortunes of the court, and he wished in his heart that he had been fasting of the king's friendship; but knowing well that to reply to the behests of great men is idle, just like plucking off the beard of a lion, he retired to a darksome place, cursing his fortunes, which had reduced him to be at court so as to shorten the hours of his life; and whilst sitting upon a doorstep, leaning his head between his hands, and his elbows upon his knees, washing his shoes with his tears, and warming up with the counter-poise of sighs, behold, the bird came with a branch of some herb in his bill, which she threw to Miuccio, saying, 'Rise up, Miuccio, and reassure thyself, thou shalt not play at unloading the ass with thy days, but at getting rid of the life of the dragon; therefore do thou take this herb, and when thou reachest the cave where dwelleth this hideous animal, throw it within, and he will be caught by a deep sleep, when thou, with a fine large knife, canst cut him in twain, and at once do thou make him the feast, and return, as matters will prosper better than thou supposest. Enough, I am doing well what I carry underneath, and we have more time than money, and whoso hath time hath money and life.' And when she had ended speaking, Miuccio arose, and putting a large carter's knife underneath his vest, and taking up the herb, fared to the dragon's cave, which was under a mountain of such a great growth that the three mountains, which were used as ladders by the giants, would not have reached its waistband. When he arrived, he threw the herb within the cave, and the dragon fell asleep at once, and Miuccio went in and began to cut him in pieces. But at the same time that he sliced up the dragon, the queen felt that her heart was being cut up also, and seeing that she was coming to a bad end, understood her error, and that she had bought death for herself, in ready money; and calling her husband to her side, said to him that the astrologer had foretold that upon the dragon's life depended her life, and as she doubted not that Miuccio had slain the dragon, she therefore was slowly sliding to the end; and the king rejoined, 'If thou knewest that the dragon's life was the prop of thine own, and the root of thy days, why didst thou bid me send Miuccio to slay the dragon? Who is at fault? Thou hast done the evil and thou shalt weep for it; thou hast broken the glass and thou shalt pay for it.' And the queen answered, 'I never could have believed that a bit of a chit could be so crafty and have such strength as to cast to the ground an animal which thought slightly of a whole army, whilst I believed that he would leave there his rags; but whereas I made up the accounts without the host, and the boat of my design is gone wrong, do me at least a favour, an thou lovest me. As soon as I shall be dead, bid a sponge be brought full of the dragon's blood, and anoint with it all the extremities of my person before I am buried.' 'This is but small matter for the love I bear thee,' answered the king, 'and if the dragon's blood is not enough, I will give of mine own to please thee'; and the queen desiring to thank him, her spirit flew forth with her words, because at that very moment Miuccio had ended making mince-meat of the dragon.

When Miuccio stood before the king to give him proofs of the deed, the king commanded him to go back and bring some of the dragon's blood. But the king being curious to see the deed done by

Miuccio's hand, followed him, and whilst Miuccio came forth from the palace gate, the bird met him and asked him, 'Where art thou going?' and Miuccio answered, 'I am going to do the king's bidding, for he is pleased to make me go to and fro like a weaver's shuttle, he does not let me rest an hour.' 'To do what?' enquired the bird; and Miuccio replied, 'To take some of the dragon's blood;' and replied the bird, 'O thou wretched one, this dragon's blood will be an ox's blood for thee, which will burst within thee; and with this blood will be strengthened that wicked woman, who hath been the cause of thy passing so many dangers and travails, because it was she that sent thee ever to new perils, hoping that thou shouldst leave thy life therein; and the king who alloweth such an hideous witch to blind him, sendeth thee about like a thrower to risk thy person, which is of his own pure flesh and blood; it is a true sprig of that shrub; but the unhappy man knowest thee not; although he should have understood that a strong intrinsic affection is a spy to the relationship, so that the real services thou hast rendered to this thy lord, and the gain he hath in such a beauteous heir, should have strength to make that unhappy Porziella thy mother enter into grace, as now 'tis fourteen years that she lives buried alive within a garret, wherein is seen a temple of beauty built within a small chamber.' And whilst the fairy spake thus, the king, hearing every word that was spoken, came forward so that he could understand the matter better; and hearing that Porziella had conceived Miuccio by him, and that she yet lived within that garret-chamber, the king summoned the workmen and bade them immediately knock down the wall which had been built, and bring Porziella before him; and they obeyed his bidding, and she came and stood before him, and he gazed at her and found her handsomer than erst she had been, because of the good treatment she had received from the bird, and he embraced her with great love, and he never tired of embracing first the mother and then the son, and he begged her to forgive him for the ill-treatment she had received at his hands, and his son for the dangers he had passed through his commands. Then bidding the handmaidens array her in the richest raiments of the dead queen, he took her to wife; and knowing that she lived, and his son had been saved from so many perils and travails, because the bird had provided the one with provaunt, and the other with wise rede, he offered the bird his goods and his life; but the fairy answered that she would not have any other reward for her services than Miuccio for her husband; and thus saying, she became a beautiful young damsel, and she, with great pleasure from the king and Porziella, was given in marriage to Miuccio. So, whilst the dead queen was cast in the grave, the two couples of brides and bridegrooms gathered enjoyance and content by tons; and to have the festivities greater, they fared to their realm, where they were expected by the nobles, and grandees, and all the lieges, with great desire, recognizing that this good fortune had come to them from the fairy, for the good deed done to her by Porziella, because after all

‘ The doing of a good deed is never lost.’

THE THREE CROWNS

S I X T H D I V E R S I O N

Of the Fourth Day

MARCHETTA IS STOLEN BY THE WIND, AND CARRIED TO THE HOUSE OF A
GHULA, WHENCE, AFTER VARIOUS ACCIDENTS, RECEIVING A BUFFET, SHE
GOETH FORTH DISGUISED IN MAN'S CLOTHING. SHE WENDETH TO THE
PALACE OF A KING, WHERE THE QUEEN BECOMETH ENAMOURED OF HER,
AND BECAUSE HER LOVE MEETETH WITH NO CORRESPONDING FEELINGS,
ACCUSETH HER HUSBAND OF HAVING TEMPTED HER TO A DEED OF SHAME.
THEREUPON MARCHETTA IS CONDEMNED TO BE HANGED, BUT BY THE
VIRTUE OF A CHARM THAT HAD BEEN GIVEN TO HER BY THE GHULA,
SHE IS SAVED, AND AT LAST BECOMETH QUEEN.

THE story of Popa well satisfied the hearers, who rejoiced to
hear of the good fortune of Porziella. Yet not one envied her this
fate, which was bought at the price of so many travails, since, to
arrive at the royal estate, she had nearly lost her personal real
estate. But Tolla, perceiving that the misfortunes of Porziella
had troubled the souls of the prince and princess, desired to raise
their spirits, and thus began speaking:

The truth, O my lord, and ladies, is like oil which always swim-
meth on the top, and the lamp is a fire that cannot be hidden, but
rather is it a modern gun, which slayeth whoso fires it, nor is it
above calling him a liar whoso is not faithful in words; it burneth
and consumeth not only the virtues and the good that are carried
within the breast, but even the very purse which containeth them:
as I will cause you to confess by this story that ye will hear.

In days of yore there lived a king of Valle-tescosse, who was
not blessed with children; and at all hours, wherever he found
himself, he would say, 'O Heaven, send me an heir of the estate,
that I may not leave desolate mine house.' And one time of the
times, when, finding himself within a garden, he cried aloud the
same words, he heard a voice coming out of the bushes, which said:

> ' O king, what dost thou want before thee?
> Daughter, that will fly thee?
> Or son, that will destroy thee?'

The king was confused at this proposal, and knew not what answer
to make, and he bethought him to take counsel with the sages of
his court.   Returning at once to the palace, and retiring within
his apartments, he summoned his counsellors, and when they stood
before him, he commanded them to discourse upon this matter.
Some answered that honour should be thought more of than life
and others that life should be thought more of than honour as an
intrinsic matter of real good, whilst honour was but an exterior
matter and therefore to be held of less worth; one said that life
being but water which passeth away, it mattered little the expense to
lose it; and thus all things are the columns of life laid upon the
unstable wheel of fortune; but honour being a durable matter,
which leaveth the footsteps of fame, and is a signal of glory, must
be guarded jealously, and kept with love; another argued that life,
by which the race is preserved, and wealth, by which is maintained
the greatness of the house, are to be held dearer than honour, because honour is but an opinion, by reason of virtue, and to lose a
daughter through ill-fortune does not prejudice the father's virtue,
nor carry filthiness to the honour of the house; but above all there
were some who concluded that honour did not consist in a woman's
petticoat, in other way than as a just prince ought to look more
readily to the common weal than to his own particular interests;
and that a woman given to lewdness would cause but little scorn in
the sire's house, whilst a wicked son would set fire to his own house,
as well as to the realm.   Therefore as the king longed for a child,
and to him had been proposed these two divided courses, let him ask
for the female, who could not endanger the life and the estate.

   This rede pleased the king, and he returned to the garden, and
again crying out his plaints as before, and hearing the same voice,
he answered, 'Woman, woman.'   And returning home in the evening, when the sun invites the hours of the day to take a view of the
small ill-made folk of the Antipodes, he lay with his wife, and at

the end of nine months she was brought to bed of a beauteous female child. As soon as the child was born, he bade them take her and shut her up in a palace with wet-nurses, and nurses, and good guards, using all possible diligence, so as not to leave for his own part anything undone which could remedy the bad influence under which she was born; and he had her brought up with care, and taught all virtues which sit well in a race of kings. When she had grown up, he treated to marry her to King Pierdisenno, and having concluded the compact, he brought her forth from that palace, which she had never before left, to send her to her husband. But a strong wind arose, and she was lifted up, and swept away, and no more seen. The wind, carrying her in air for a space of time, at last set her down before the house of a ghula, within a forest which had banished the sun, as one struck down by plague because he had slain Pitone the infected; here she found an old woman, whom the ghula had left to guard her goods, and the old woman said to her, 'Oh! bitter be thy life, and where hast thou set thy foot? O unhappy thou, if the ghula, mistress of this house, should come, I would not pledge thy skin for three coppers, for she feedeth on naught else but human flesh, and my life is sure only because the need of my services detains her, or because this wretched shellful of syncope, heart-disease, flatulency, and sand is declined by her tusks. But knowest thou, what is best to do? here is the key of the house, do thou enter within, set to rights the chambers and clean everything, and when the ghula shall come, hide thyself that she see thee not, and I will not let thee want in food; meanwhile who knows? Heaven helpeth; time may bring to pass great things; enough, be wise and patient, and thou shalt pass every gulf, and overcome the storm.'

Marchetta, thus was the girl hight, making a virtue of necessity, took the key, and entering the chamber of the ghula, and seizing a broom, swept the house so clean that one could have eaten maca-roni from off the flooring; with a piece of lard she rubbed so well the walnut presses and chests, and made them so bright, that one could have looked in them as in a looking-glass; and afterwards she made the bed; and when she heard the ghula come in, she entered a cask, which had been full of corn. The ghula, finding such unusual event, was pleased and calling the old woman, said to her, 'Who hath put things in order so well?' and the old woman answered that it had been herself; and rejoined the ghula, 'Whoso doeth for thee whatso he doeth not usually, hath either cheated thee or will deceive thee. In very sooth thou mayest put the stopper in the hole, seeing that thou hast done a most unusual thing, and therefore thou deservest a fat pottage.' And saying this, she ate, and after she had taken her sufficiency, she fared forth, and when she returned, she found the beams swept clean of spiders' webs, and the copper utensils made bright and hanging symmetrically upon the walls, and the dirty linen put in soak; and the ghula was pleased with exceeding pleasure, and she blessed a thousand times the old woman, saying to her, 'May Heaven prosper thee always, Madam Pentatola mine, mayest thou ever reign and go forward, for thou dost fill me with joy, and my heart overjoyeth to behold this fine putting in order, so that I see a house fit for a doll, and a bed fit for a bride.' And the old woman was glad with exceeding gladness to have won the good opinion of the ghula, and repaid Marchetta for her pleasure with good mouthfuls, feeding her and stuffing her like a young capon. And when the ghula fared out again, the old woman said to Marchetta, 'Be silent, and we will try to reach this lame matter and tempt thy fortune; therefore make something nice with thine own hand, which should suit the ghula's taste, and if she take an oath by the seven celestial matters, believe her not, but if she should swear by her three crowns, then thou mayest come forth and let her see thee, for the matter will succeed, and then thou wilt acknowledge that my rede hath been the rede of a mother.' Marchetta, hearing this, slew a fine fat goose, and from the giblets she made a stew, and then stuffing the goose well with cut-up lard, and onions, and garlic, put it on the spit, and providing a few priest-chokers * on the bottom of a basket, she laid the

---

* Strangola-preti: 'gnocchi,' a kind of home-made macaroni, to be eaten with gravy or butter and cheese.

cloth upon the table and then filled it full with roses and orange leaves.

Now when the ghula came home and found these preparations, she nearly went out of her clothes with joy, and calling the old woman, said to her, 'Who hath done this good service?' 'Do thou eat,' answered the old woman, 'and do not seek for other; 'tis enough that thou hast one who serveth thee and giveth thee satisfaction.' The ghula, whilst eating, felt the good morsels going down to the marrows of her bones, and began saying, 'I swear by the three words of Naples, that if I knew who hath been the cook of this good repast, I would give him my eye-balls;' and she added, 'I swear by the three bows and arrows, that if I knew him, I would enshrine him within my heart; I swear it by the three candles, which are lit when a deed or a will is written by night; by the three witnesses, who cause a man to be hanged; by the three feet of rope that twist the man that is hanged; by the three things that chase a man from his house, stink, smoke, and a wicked woman; by the three things which wear out a house, fritters, warm bread, and macaroni; by the three women and a goose which make up a market; by the three F's of fried fish, cold fish, and stewed fish; by the three first singers of Naples, John de la Carrejola, Gossip Junno, and the king of music; by the three S's which are needful to a lover, solitude, solicitude, and secrecy; by the three things which are needful to a merchant, credit, spirit, and fair fortune; by the three sort of folk to whom the whore holds, the boasters, the beauteous youths, and the spiteful; by the three things most important to the thief, eyes to lighten well, claws to grapple well, and feet to disappear well; by the three things which are the ruin of youths, gambling, women, and taverns; by the three virtues necessary to a bailiff, sight, speed and success; by the three things useful to a courtier, deceit, phlegm, and fortune; by the three things needful to a pimp, large heart, great prattling, and small shame; by the three things which are observed by a doctor, the pulse, the face, and the night-vase.' But the ghula might have spoken from to-day till to-morrow, for Marchetta would not have moved from her hiding place. But hearing her say at last, 'By my three crowns, if I ever know the industrious good housewife who hath done me such good service, I will do her more caresses and kindnesses than she can imagine,' she came forth, and said, 'Here am I;' and when the ghula beheld her, she answered, 'Thou shouldst give me a kick, for thou hast known more than I; thou hast done a masterly matter, and hast safely guarded thyself from being baked in this my body; but as thou hast known to do so much, and hast pleased me, I will keep thee by me as my own daughter; therefore here are the keys of all the chambers, and be thou mistress, and faculty, and most arbitrary power; only one thing I reserve for myself, and that is, that on no account must thou open the door of the last chamber, which this key fitteth, because then thou wouldst make the mustard rise to my nose; therefore mind thy housework, and blessed be thou, and I promise thee by my three crowns to marry thee to a rich mate.' Marchetta kissed her hand, and thanked her gratefully, and promised to serve her more than a slave.

Now when the ghula went forth, great curiosity got hold of Marchetta to see what was within that forbidden chamber, and she opened the door, and found therein three damsels arrayed in golden raiments, seated upon three imperial seats, and seemingly fast asleep. And these damsels were the daughters of the ghula, and had been ensorcelled by their mother, because it had been foretold them that they should have to pass a great danger if a king's daughter did not come to awaken them; and therefore she had ensorcelled them and shut them up in that room, to save them from the risk they ran, which was threatened by the stars. Now when Marchetta entered therein, the noise she made with her feet roused them, and they awoke and asked for food, and Marchetta took three eggs for each, and laid them to cook under the ashes, and when they were done she gave them each three, and they ate, and their spirit returned to them. Then they wished to go forth and breathe the fresh air, and they entered the saloon. But when the ghula came back and found them there, she was so much distressed and wroth, that raising her hand she dealt Marchetta a buffet, and

the damsel felt such shame for such treatment, that there and
then she begged leave of the ghula to depart, and to go forth a
wanderer through the world, seeking her fate and fortune. So
the ghula sought to pacify her with kind words and kinder deeds,
saying that she was but trifling, and that she would not touch her
again; but all was in vain, she could not be persuaded to stay; and
therefore the ghula was obliged to allow her to depart, but before
leaving, she gave her a ring, and told her to wear it always but
to turn the stone, which was set in it, within the hand, and think
of it only when she found herself in some great strait, and heard
her name repeated by the echo; moreover she gifted her with a
sumptuous suit of man's clothes that Marchetta had asked of her;
and arraying herself in it, the damsel fared forth, and she wended
onwards till she came to a forest, where the night was going to
gather wood to warm herself from the frozen time past; and there
Marchetta met a king who had gone an-hunting, and he, seeing
this handsome youth (for thus she seemed), enquired whence he
came, and whither he was going, and what he was doing in those
parts; and she answered that she was a merchant's son, whose
mother had died, and that, because of his step-mother's ill-treatment, he had run away from home. The king was pleased with
the readiness and fluency of speech of Marchetta, and took her
with him as page, and he led her to his palace, and when the queen
sighted him, she felt taken by the grace and beauty of the stranger,
and all her desires were sent high in air. And although for a few
days, partly from fear and partly from pride, which have always
been encased with beauty, the queen sought to subdue her flame
and to constrain the pricking of love under the tail of desire; nathless, being short in heels, she could not stand firm against the meetings of the unbridled and licentious desires; and therefore she called
Marchetta aside, one day of the days, and began to discover to her
all her suffering and longing; and to tell her what a weight of
cark and care she bare upon her since the day that she had beholden
his beauty, grace, and comeliness; so that if he would not resolve
to give water to the grounds of her desires, she would dry up with-

out any other hope of life. And she praised the manifold beauties
of his face, putting before his eyes that ill would it suit a scholar
in the school of love to make a daub and a mistake of cruelty within
a book of so much grace, and that he would afterwards have the
horse * of repentance; to the praise she added prayers, beseeching
him by all the celestial spheres not to be so hardened as to behold
within a furnace of sighs, and amid a mire of tears, one who held as
ensign at the shop of her thoughts his beauteous vision; thereafter
followed offers, promising him for every finger's depth of enjoyment a foot of benefits, and for ever to keep open for him the
bazaar of her gratitude to every pleasure of so fine account. At
last she made him remember that she was a queen, and when she
had entered the ship he must not leave her amid the gulf without
some help, because she would surely wreck upon the rocks with his
damage. Marchetta, hearing these tender and loving words, these
promises and threats, these face-washings and takings-off of hoods,
would have answered, that to open the door of her pleasures and
joyments the key was wanting; she would have revealed that to
give her the peace she desired she was not Mercury, and she carried not his caduceus; but not wishing to unmask herself she answered that she could not believe that the queen would have
wrought crooked spindles to a king of such great merit, like unto
her husband; but even if she was ready to put aside the reputation
of her house, she could not and would not do this wrong to a master
that loved his page so well.

The queen, hearing this first reply to the intimation of her desires, said to her, 'Now without delay walk straight, and think well
that my peers, when they beseech, then they command, and when
they kneel, then they kick thee down the throat; therefore do thou
make well thine accounts, and see how may succeed for thee this

---

* In the Neapolitan schools the 'horse' means that when a boy is disobedient
or fails to do his lessons, the teacher calls two of the elder boys and the culprit
out, and then one of the boys makes the culprit get upon his shoulders, horse
guise, but with his face lying upon the shoulders and his behind up, and the
other boy canes him well till the teacher bids him stop; and this is called
a 'horse.'

merchandise; enough and sufficient, as I will tell thee clearly one thing more, and then I will depart, and 'tis this, that when a woman of my degree remaineth scorned, she taketh care to wash with the blood of the offender the smear from upon her face.' And thus saying, with a wrathful face, she turned her shoulders, leaving poor Marchetta confused and frozen. But for a few days more the queen continued to assault this beautiful fortress, and seeing at last that her work was useless, and was scattered to the winds, and that she sweated in vain, and cast her words to the wind, and the sighs in emptiness, she changed her register, dissolving love in hatred, and the desire to joy with the beloved object in a desire for revenge. And with this thought, feigning the tears filling the eyes, she fared to her husband, and said to him, 'Who would have told us, O my husband, that we should cherish a serpent in our sleeve? Who could ever have imagined it, that a little, wretched, idle bit of goods could have such daring? But the fault lies in all the kindness and caresses which thou hast dealt to him; to the peasant if one holds out a finger, he will take all the hand; in conclusion, we all desire to piddle in the urinal; but, an thou punish him not as he deserveth, I will return to my sire's house, and will never see thee again, nor hear thee named.' 'What has he done to thee?' answered the king; and the queen replied, 'A mere nothing. The little rogue wished to exact from me the matrimonial debt that I have with thee; and without any respect, and with no fear, and shameless, he had the face to come before me, and tongue to seek from me the free pass to the territory, where thou hast sowed in honour.' The king hearing this fact, without seeking any further witnesses, not to prejudice the faith and the authority of his wife, had Marchetta caught and pinioned by the country folk, and there and then, without giving her time for defence, condemned her to see how much the hangman statue could carry around the neck; and she was carried to the place of punishment, knowing not what had happened to her, nor what crime nor evil deed she had committed, and she began to cry aloud, 'O Heaven, what have I done, to deserve the funeral of this wretched neck, and the obsequies of this miserable body? Who could have told me that, without absenting myself from the place, under the standard of rogues and highwaymen, I should enter on guard in this place of death, with three paces of rope round my throat? Alas! who will console me at this my extreme pass? who will help me in this great danger? who will save me from this gibbet?' 'Ibbet,' answered Echo, and Marchetta, hearing that she was answered in this manner, remembered the ring which she wore upon her finger, and the words of the ghula when she departed; and glancing at the stone, at which she had never glanced before, behold, a voice was heard three times in the air repeating, 'Let her go, she is a woman'; and it was so terrible that neither policemen, nor soldiers, nor shopkeepers remained in the place of justice; and the king hearing these words, which made the palace tremble from the foundation, bade them bring Marchetta before him; and when she stood in his presence, he bade her tell the truth, and relate who she was, and how she had come in that country. And she, forced by necessity, related to him all that had occurred in her life, how she was born, how she had been kept shut up in that palace, how the wind had carried her away, how she was deposited before the gate of the ghula's house, how she departed and what the ghula had told her, and she related also what had passed between her and the queen, and how, not knowing in what she had erred, she beheld herself in danger to row with her feet in the three-beamed galley. The king, hearing this story, and comparing it with one that in past times had happened to the King of Valle-tescosse, his friend, recognised Marchetta for who she was in reality; and knew also the malignity of his wife, who had cast such an infamous calumny upon the innocent; for which matter he commanded that she should directly have a weight tied to her feet, and be cast into the sea; and he sent messengers to invite the sire and the mother of Marchetta, and he took her to wife, which made clear the problem that

'For a ship in distress
God findeth safe harbour.'

THE TWO CAKES

MARZIELLA, BY SHOWING KINDNESS TO AN OLD WOMAN, IS ENDOWED
WITH A CHARM; BUT HER AUNT, ENVIOUS OF HER GOOD FORTUNE, CAST-
ETH HER INTO THE SEA, WHERE SHE IS KEPT PRISONER BY A MERMAID;
SHE IS DELIVERED BY HER BROTHER, AND BECOMETH A QUEEN, AND THE
AUNT BEARETH THE PUNISHMENT DUE FOR HER ERROR.

SURELY the prince and princess would have said that this story of Antonella won the battle of all those which had been related, if it had not been for disheartening Ciulla, who had already set the lance of her tongue in rest, and entered the ring of Thaddeus' and his wife's pleasure in the manner which followeth:

I have always heard it said that whoso doeth a pleasure himself findeth pleasure; the bell of Manfredonia saith, 'Give me, and I will give thee'; whoso putteth not the bait of kindness in the hook of affection, will never catch the fish of favour: and if ye will see the truth of this, listen to this story, and after ye will say if the miser does not lose more than the man who is generous.

It is related that once upon a time there lived two sisters, Lucetta and Troccola hight, who had two daughters, named Marziella and Puccia. Marziella was as charming and beauteous of face as she was beautiful of heart; whilst on the contrary Puccia, by the same rule, had a face of ugliness and an heart of pestilence; and the damsel resembled her parent, for Troccola, her mother, was an harpy within and a bawd without.

Now one day of the days so it fortuned that Lucetta had a few carrots to warm up in order to fry them with some green sauce, so she said to her daughter, 'Marziella mine, go, my dearling, to the fountain, and bring me a pitcher of water.' 'With good will, O my mother,' answered the daughter, 'but, an thou lovest me, do

339

thou give me a cake, that I may eat it near the fountain, and drink some fresh water after it.' 'Willingly,' said the mother; and from a basket which depended upon a hook from the roof beam she took a fine cake, which she had baked the day before with the bread, and gave it to Marziella, who put the pitcher on a pad upon her head, and fared to the fountain, which, like unto a charlatan, upon a stone or marble bench, to the music of the falling waters, was selling secrets to drown thirst. And whilst her pitcher was filling, up came an old woman, who upon the scaffold of a great hump represented the tragedy of time, and she, beholding the nice cake, which Marziella was just putting to her mouth for a bite, said 'O my beauteous child, may Heaven send thee a good lot and fortune, give me a morsel of that cake.' Marziella, who was in her ways a queen, answered 'Take it all, and eat it, my good woman; and I regret, that it is not made of sugar and almonds, for I would even so give it to thee with all my heart.'

The old woman seeing the loving kindness of Marziella, said to her 'Go, and may Heaven always prosper thee for this thy goodness which thou hast shown to me, and I pray all the stars that thou mayest be ever happy and content; that when thou breathest, from thy lips may come forth roses and jasmines; when thou combest thine hair, may ever from thine head drop pearls and garnets; and when thou settest thy foot upon the ground, may there spring up under thy step lilies and violets.' The damsel thanked the old woman for her good wishes, and went her way home, where after the mother had cooked the dinner, and given satisfaction to the natural debt of the body, they spent that day in their usual way. When the next morning came, and at the market of the celestial fields the sun made show of his merchandise of light which he brought from the east, Marziella began to comb her hair, when she saw a rain of pearls and garnets fall around her, whereupon calling her mother, with great joy they put the gems into a large basket, and Lucetta fared forth to a banker friend of hers to sell him some.

In the meantime arrived Troccola to visit her sister, and finding

Marziella busy gathering those pearls, she asked her how, when, and where she had gotten them? But the damsel, who knew not how to trouble water, and perhaps had not heard that proverb, 'Do not all thou canst do, eat not all thou canst eat, spend not all thou hast to spend, and tell not all thou knowest,' related the whole affair to her aunt, who no longer cared to await for her sister, for the time till she reached home again seemed to her a thousand years. Then giving a cake to her daughter, she sent her to the fountain, where Puccia found the same old woman. And when the old woman begged of her a small piece of cake, the damsel, who was greedy and selfish, answered, 'Have I naught else to do than give the cake to thee? dost thou take me for an ass, that I should give thee whatso belongeth to me? Go thy ways, for our teeth are nearer than our relatives.' And thus saying, she ate up the cake in four mouthfuls, playing for spite of the old woman, who, when she saw the last piece disappear, and her hopes of a bite buried with it, exclaimed with great wrath, 'Go thy ways, and when thou breathest, mayest thou send forth froth, like a doctor's mule; when thou combest thine hair, may the lice fall from thine head in heaps; and wherever thou steppest may there spring forth wild herbs and prickly ferns.'

Puccia took her pitcher, and returned homewards, where her mother impatiently waited for the hour to comb her hair; and putting a fine towel upon her knees, she laid her daughter's head upon it, and began to comb her hair, when, behold, there fell a flood of alchemist animals, which stopped even quicksilver; at the sight of which her mother to the snow of her envy added the fire of her wrath, casting forth flames and smoke from mouth and nostrils.

Now it chanced after a time that the brother of Marziella, Ciommo hight, was at the court of the King of Chiunzo, and the discourse turning on the beauties of several damsels, he stood before the king unmasked, and said that all the beauties mentioned and unmentioned could go fare and pick up bones at the bridge, if his sister appeared, for beside the grace, and beauty, and comeliness which were a counterpart of her soul she possessed a great virtue in her hair, in her mouth, and in her feet given to her by a fairy. The king, hearing these praises, told Ciommo to bring his sister before him, and if he found her to be as he had boasted, he would take her to wife. Now Ciommo thought that this was an opportunity too good to be lost; so he forthwith sent a messenger to his mother, relating to her what had occurred, and beseeching her to come at once, in order not to let her daughter lose such good fortune. But Lucetta, who was lying ill at the time, recommended the sheep to the wolf, and begged her sister to accompany Marziella to the court of Chiunzo, whereupon Troccola, seeing that the matter fell nicely into her hands, promised her sister to carry Marziella safe and well to the hands of her brother, and embarking on board a ship with Marziella and with Puccia, sailed away. When they were amiddlemost the main, and the sailors were asleep, Troccola threw Marziella into the sea, and just as she was drowning there came a beautiful mermaid, who held her up by an arm, and carried her away. Such was her case.

Now when Troccola arrived at Chiunzo, Puccia was received by Ciommo, who had not seen his sister for so long a time, and thus could not recognise her, as if she had been Marziella; and instantly he led her before the king. But no sooner did she stand before the king, than he bade the handmaidens to comb her hair, and when they obeyed him, behold there rained a shower of those animals which are such great foes to truth, that they for ever offend their witnesses; and when the king looked at her face, he saw that as she breathed hard from the fatigue of her wayfaring she made quite a lather at her mouth which seemed a boat of soapy clothes; and lowering his glance to the ground, he beheld a field of stinking herbs, the sight of which turned the stomach sick. Thereupon he drove away Puccia and her mother, and to punish Ciommo for his boast, sent him to guard the geese of the court.

And Ciommo was in despair for this business, not knowing what had happened to him; and he followed the geese in the fields, and allowed them to feed as they liked and to go their way along the shore, whilst he entered a hayloft, and wept, and wailed, and lamented therein his bad lot and fortune. Now whilst the geese ran about the shore, the mermaid and Marziella came forth from the waters, and fed them with sweet pastry, and gave them rose-water to drink, so that the geese after a time grew as large as rams, each one, and they could hardly see out of their eyes, and when at night they came to a small orchard which was under the king's window, they began to sing,

> Pire, pire, pire,
> Very beautiful are the sun and the moon,
> But much more beautiful is she who feedeth us.

The king, hearing this goose-music every evening, sent for Ciommo, and asked him the meaning of this song, and where, and how, and of what food he fed his geese. And Ciommo answered, 'I do not let them eat aught but the fresh grass from the fields.' But the king, who did not like the answer, sent a faithful servant behind him, to watch where he drove the geese. Then the man followed his footsteps and saw him enter the hayloft, and leave the geese alone to go their way; and when they arrived at the shore, Marziella came forth from the sea (and I do not believe that so beauteous a being came forth of the waves in the mother of that blind god, who, as a poet said, will take no other alms than tears). The king's servant, beholding this sight, was out of himself with wonder and surprise, and ran to his master, and related to him the wonderful sight he had witnessed upon the sea-shore.

The curiosity of the king was aroused by what the man told him, and a great longing and desire seized him to go himself and behold this enchanting view, so in the morning, when the cock, chief of the bird-folk, awakens them all to arm the living against the night, Ciommo having gone with the geese to the usual place, the king followed him, never for a moment losing sight of him, and when the geese reached the sea-shore without Ciommo, who had remained in the same place as usual, the king beheld Marziella come forth from the water. And after giving the geese a quantity of pastry to eat, and a kettle full of rose water to drink, she seated herself upon a stone and began to comb her hair, from which fell pearls and garnets in handfuls; and at the same time from her mouth came forth clouds of flowers; and under her feet was formed a Syrian carpet of lilies and violets. When the king beheld this sight, he sent for Ciommo, and showing Marziella to him, said, 'Dost thou know this beauteous damsel?' And Ciommo recognized her, and ran to embrace her, and in the presence of the king she explained the treachery done by Troccola, that hideous pestilent creature, who had caused this beautiful fire of love to inhabit the waters of the sea. The joy felt by the king in having become the owner of such a rare gem is not to be told; and turning to her brother, he said that he had right to praise her, and indeed that he found her two-thirds more beautiful than he had described; he thought her, therefore, the more worthy to become his wife, if she would be content to accept the sceptre of his kingdom.

'Oh, if the sun in Lion would let me,' answered Marziella, 'and I could come and serve thee even as thy slave, and servant of thy crown. But seest thou not this golden chain which holdeth me by the foot, by which I am kept a prisoner by the mermaid; and when I tarry too long to breathe the fresh air, or to sit by the sea-side, she draweth me within the main, keeping me in rich captivity chained with a golden chain.' 'What remedy can there be,' enquired the king, 'to enable us to withdraw thee from the grasp of this mermaid?' 'The remedy would be,' answered Marziella, 'to file with a soft file this chain, and thus could I make my escape.' 'Expect thou me to-morrow morning,' replied the king, 'and I will come with all the matter ready, and I will lead thee to my house, where thou shalt be my right eye, and the eye-babe of mine heart, and the entrails of my soul.' And thus, plighting their love with a clasping of hands, she withdrew within the main, and he within the fire, into such a fire indeed that he found no rest all that day, and when the murk of night came forth to play and dance Tubba Catubba,* with the stars, he never closed his eyes, but kept ruminating with the jaws of memory the beauty, grace, and comeliness of

* A Moorish dance, introduced by the Spaniards.

Marziella, discoursing within his mind of the marvellous hair, of the wonderful mouth, of the astounding feet, and applying the gold of her graces to the touchstone of judgment, he found them of twenty-four carat gold. And he disliked the night for tarrying so long at her embroidery of stars, and cursed the sun for his slowness, which arrived not soon with his coach full of light to enrich his house with the longed-for good; to enable him to carry in his chambers the mint of gold, which casteth pearls, a quail of pearls, which casteth flowers. But as he was lost in a sea of thoughts of the one that lived in the sea, behold, the sappers of the sun straightened the road whereon he should pass with the army of his rays. Then the king arose, and arrayed himself, and with Ciommo wended towards the seashore, where they found Marziella, and with the file they had brought the king filed with his own hand the chains from the foot of his beloved; all the while forging another and a stronger chain within his heart; and at last lifting on his horse's crupper the one who rode upon his heart, he fared towards the royal palace, where Marziella found all the handsomest women of that country assembled to receive her as their mistress by order of the king. And with great joyance, and feasting, and burning of casks for illumination, the king ordered that the person of Troccola should be included amid the fire, so that she should pay for the deceit which she had practised upon Marziella; and sending for Lucetta, he gave her and Ciommo enough to live upon as rich folk; whilst Puccia, sent forth from that kingdom, went about as a beggar; and because she would not sow a small piece of cake had now to suffer a famine of bread, for it is the will of Heaven, that

'Whoso hath no pity, findeth none.'

THE SEVEN PIGEONS

Of the Fourth Day

SEVEN BROTHERS FARE FORTH FROM THEIR HOME, BECAUSE TO THEIR
MOTHER WAS NOT VOUCHSAFED A DAUGHTER; AFTER A TIME SHE BRING-
ETH ONE TO THE WORLD, AND THE BROTHERS, WHO WERE EXPECTING
THE NEWS, RECEIVE THE SIGNAL; BUT THE MIDWIFE MAKETH A MISTAKE
IN THE SIGNS, BY WHICH REASON THEY GO FORTH AS WANDERERS
THROUGH THE EARTH. THE SISTER GROWETH UP, AND GOETH TO SEEK
THEM; SHE FINDETH THEM, AND AFTER MANY ADVENTURES THEY RETURN
HOME WEALTHY.

THE story of the two cakes was truly a full cake which pleased
the taste of every one, and they are still licking their fingers of it.
Paola having donned the corselet in readiness to relate her story, all
tongues were silenced by command of the prince, and thus she began
to say:

Whoso doeth a kindness always findeth kindness; and a benefit
is the hook with which friendship is drawn, and love is caught;
whoso soweth not reapeth not; and as Ciulla hath given you the first-
course of examples, I will bring forth to you the dessert, if ye will
remember what Caro said, 'Speak but little, when at a banquet.'
And therefore be ye kind enough to lend me an ear; and may
Heaven lengthen your ears, to enable you to listen to matters satisfactory to your taste.

There was once in the country of Arzano a good woman, who
every year brought into the world a man-child, until the number of
them had reached seven, and ye beheld in them the siphon of the
god Pan with seven tubes, one larger than the other. And when
the sons had cast their first ears, they said to Jannetella their mother,
who was full with child, 'Know, O our mother, that an thou, after
having so many sons, have not a daughter, we have resolved to
leave this house, and wander through the world like sons of exile

346

wandering on ruthlessly.' The mother, hearing this their decision, prayed Heaven to drive out of their minds such desire, and to save her from the anguish of losing seven such precious jewels as were her sons. The time drew nigh when she expected to be delivered, and the sons said to Jannetella, 'We will withdraw, and fare to that height which faces us; if thou givest birth to a man-child, put an ink-case and pen upon the window-sill; and an thou givest birth to a female-child, put a spoon and a distaff in the same place; so that if we behold a sign that a female is born to us, we will return home to spend the rest of our lives between thine hands; but an we perceive the sign that a male-child is born to thee, thou mayest forget us, and thou canst name him Pen.' When her sons had departed, the hour came in which, by the will of Heaven, Jannetella was delivered of a beauteous daughter, and she bade the midwife give the signal to the brothers, but the woman was so stupefied and out of her wits, that she put the ink-case upon the window-sill instead of the distaff. As soon as the brothers beheld the sign, they departed in haste, and fared on, and wandered over wilds and wolds until, after journeying three years, one day of the days they arrived at the opening of a forest, where the trees danced to the music of a rivulet which played its counter-points upon the pebbly shore. Within this forest stood the house of a ghul, whose eyes had been poked out by a woman while he was fast asleep, and therefore he felt a deep hatred for the whole sex, and was their foe, and as many as he could meet or find he made a meal of.

Now when the seven youths arrived at the ghul's house, weary of their journey and an hungered, they besought him if he would in compassion give them a bittock of bread: and the ghul answered them that he would keep them, and give them wherewith to maintain themselves, if they would serve him, and they would have naught else to do but to watch him and tend him each in turn, as if he were a small pet dog. The youths upon hearing this were pleased, for it seemed to them as if they had found mother and father; so they agreed and remained in the ghul's service, who having learned their names by heart, one moment called Giangrazio, and another Cecchitello, now Pascale, and then Nuccio, this time Pone, and after Pezzillo, and Carcavecchia, for thus were the brothers hight; and appointing for their use part of the ground-floor of his house, and giving them of food and provaunts till they were satisfied, they passed pleasantly their days. Such was their case.

In the meanwhile their sister, having passed a length of years, had grown up, and hearing that she had seven brothers who, by forgetfulness of the midwife, were wandering through the world, and that no news of them had reached their mother's ear, she longed with sore longing to fare on to seek them; and she prayed, and besought, and supplicated her mother, and said and did many things to her, and at last, being tired of listening to her lamentations, she gave her leave to depart, making her don the attire of a pilgrim. Then the maiden fared on her journey, enquiring from place to place whoso had seen seven brothers pass that way, and she wandered through many countries, and cities, and villages, till at last, coming to a tavern, she heard some news of them. And bidding the folk show her the way to that forest, where one morning the sun with the penknife of his rays was scraping away the mistakes made by the night upon the paper of heaven, she found herself in that place, where with great joy she was recognized by the brothers, who cursed that ink-case and that pen for writing falsely so many misfortunes for them. Loading her with caresses, they warned her to remain hidden within that chamber, so that the ghul might not scent her; bidding her besides, that whatsoever dainty or any other food should be brought to her, she should give a share of it to a cat, which was within the chamber, otherwise the animal would do her some harm. Cianna, thus was the sister hight, wrote these redes in the writing-book of the heart, and of everything she had she shared in good fellowship with the cat, making share and share alike, saying, 'This for me, this for thee, and this for the daughter of the king,' giving the cat her equal share, even to a caraway-seed and small fennel.

Now it so fortuned that one day of the days the brothers had gone forth to chase and hunt in the service of the ghul, and they left their sister a small basket full of beans that she might cook them, and while she was picking and cleansing them she found, unfortunately for her, amongst them a hazel-nut, which became the stone of scandal whereupon her peace was shattered, because on seeing it she cracked it, and putting the kernel in her mouth, ate it without giving the cat her share, and that brute in spite went and piddled upon the fire, thus putting it out. Cianna, perceiving this, and knowing not what to do, fared forth from the chamber against the commands of her brothers, and entered the ghul's apartment to seek somewhat to light the fire. The ghul, hearing a woman's voice, said, 'Well come, and fair welcome, my master, wait a while and thou shalt find the thing thou art looking for.' And so speaking, he seized a genoa stone, and anointing it well with oil, he fell to sharpening his tusks upon it. And Cianna perceiving which way the cart would drive, caught hold of a fire-brand, and ran back to her own chamber, and shutting the door, pushed behind it bars, chairs, tables, chests, and bedsteads, and everything that the chamber contained.

As soon as the ghul had ended sharpening his tusks, he ran to the chamber, and finding the door fastened, began to kick and beat at it, trying to break it down. And while this turmoil was taking place, the seven brothers returned, and the ghul hearing them began to reproach them as traitors, seeing that their chamber had become the asylum of his foes; but Giangrazio, the elder brother, who had more sense than the others, seeing the matter taking a bad course, said to the ghul, 'We know naught of this, and it might be that this accursed woman did enter this chamber while we had gone forth to the chase; but as she hath entrenched herself within, come with us, and we will lead thee by a way whence we will fall upon her, and she will be unable to defend herself.' And hending the ghul by hand, they led him to a deep pit, and giving him a push they made him fall within it; and picking up a mattock, which they found lying on the ground, they filled up the pit with earth. Then they bade the sister to open the door, and reproached her severely for her error, and for the danger in which she had fallen, saying that for the future she should be careful, and beware of gathering the grass from around the place where the ghul was buried, because if she did so, they would become pigeons. 'Heaven guard me of this,' answered Cianna, 'and that I should cause you such damage and foul wrong.' After this they took possession of the ghul's goods, and of all which the house contained, and so they spent their days in enjoyment, awaiting until the winter should be past, when the sun would offer in gift to the earth for having taken possession of the Bull's house, a green skirt, purflewed with many coloured flowers; then they would fare on their journey homewards.

Now one day of the days it so fortuned that the brothers had gone forth to the mountain side to gather some wood, wherewith to make a fire to shield themselves from the cold, which became greater from day to day, when there arrived in those wilds a pilgrim who, in his way, had beheld a monkey sitting upon a tree, and he had made mock at him, and the beast had cast a nut upon the pilgrim's head, which had caused it to swell in a large bump, and the wretched man was in great pain, and cried with loud cries, like unto a damned soul. Cianna hearing those cries came forth, and her heart softened with pity at his suffering, and she ran at once to gather some rosemary which had grown on the top of the ghul's grave, and with bread-crumbs and salt made up a poultice which she applied to the wound; then she got ready some food, and gave him his breakfast, and he departed. Now when Cianna was preparing the midday meal, and laying the cloth, awaiting for her brothers, behold, seven pigeons flew upon the table, and they said to her, 'O thou the cause of all our woe, it would have been far better if thine hands had been palsied, than that thou hadst gone to gather that cursed rosemary, which causeth us to wander restlessly by the shore. Hast thou eaten cat's brains, O our sister, that thou hast not called to mind our rede to thee? Behold, we have become birds, subjected to the claws of the eagle, the hawk, and the vulture; behold, we have become the companions of sea-gulls, bull-finches, screech-owls, gold-finches, magpies, crows, white-tails, wild cocks and wild fowls, chaffinches, larks, sparrows, swallows, turtle-doves, fly-catchers, robins, black-hoods, red-breasts, black-birds, nightingales, and thrushes. Thou hast done a good deed; we have now gone back to our country, so that we may behold nets and bird-lime spread for us; to heal the head of a pilgrim unknown thou hast broken the head of thy seven brothers, and there is no remedy to our evil if thou findest not the mother of Time, who will teach thee the way by which to pull us out from this dire sorrow.'

Cianna turned towards her brothers like a plucked quail, and besought them to forgive her for the error she had committed, and promised to wander through the world until she found the dwelling of the old woman. And begging them not to stir from home till she returned, for fear that some misfortune should happen to them, she fared forth, and wandered on her journey without ever tiring; and although she fared on foot, the desire to help her brothers served to push her on like a racing mule, faring at the rate of three miles an hour. And she never ceased faring until one day of the days she reached the shore, where the sea with its waves beat the rocks because they answered not to the Latin it had taught them, and there she beheld a large whale, who spake to her thus, 'O beauteous young lady, what mayest thou be doing?' and she, 'I am seeking for the house of the mother of Time.' 'Dost thou know what is best for thee to do?' replied the whale. 'Fare thou ever in a straight direction along this shore, and the first river thou reachest, walk thou on the heights above it, and there thou shalt find one who will lead thee on thy way; but when thou shalt meet this good old woman, do me a kindness, ask her a boon in my name, and that is, that she should devise me a device, and find me a remedy, so that I may tread securely in my way, and not always get caught amongst rocks and buried sand.' 'Let this body do thy bidding,' said Cianna, and thanking her for her kindness in showing her the way, she fared onwards along the shore, and after journeying for a length of time, she arrived at that river side, which, like a fiscal's com-missary, disbursed silvern monies in the bank of the sea. She made her way to the heights, and reached a beautiful meadow, which

aped the heavens, in showing its green mantle purflewed with starry
flowers, and there she was met by a mouse, who said to her, 'Where
art thou going thus, alone, O beauteous damsel?' and she replied,
'I seek the mother of Time.' 'Thou must fare yet a long way,'
rejoined the mouse, 'but do not be disheartened; every matter hath
an ending; do thou fare on towards those mountains, which, like
the owners and lords of these fields, entitle themselves highnesses,
and there shalt find better news of that which thou seekest; but
do thou oblige me with a favour: when thou shalt reach the house
thou art looking for, do thou ask of this good old woman what
remedy we could use to deliver ourselves from the tyranny of the
cats, and after do thou ever command me, and I shall be thy slave.'
Cianna, after promising to do his bidding and farewelling him,
fared on towards the mountains, which, although they appeared
near, seemed never to be reached. But having at length come to
the end of her journey, and being excessively fatigued, she sat upon
a stone; and whilst thus sitting, she beheld an army of ants, which
were carrying their corn provisions into their granaries; and one
of them, perceiving Cianna, said, 'Who art thou, and whither art
thou going?' and Cianna who was kind to all, answered, 'I am a
most unfortunate damsel that, for a matter which concerneth me
much, have wandered through wilds and wolds, seeking the house
of the mother of Time.' 'Fare on,' answered the ant, 'and in one
of the outlets of those mountains thou shalt perceive a wide space,
and there thou wilt hear some more news; but do me a great kindness, try to find out from this old woman what we ants should do
to live some time longer, because it seems to me a great madness of
the earthly matters to work and toil so much, to gather together
such a quantity of provaunt for a life so short, which, like a magician's candle, when at the best offer of years, goes out.' 'Be at
rest,' said Cianna, 'and I will return thee thy courtesy.' Then she
fared on and passed those mountains, and arrived at the wide plain,
and she wayfared for a time until she sighted a large mulberry-
tree, a witness of antiquity, sweetmeats of that bride who found
happiness, and mouthfuls given by the time, in this bitter age of

all lost sweetness; and he, forming lips of the bark and tongue of the sap, said to Cianna, 'Whither, oh whither, art thou hurrying, O my daughter? Come and rest under my shadow;' and she thanked him, but excused herself from staying, because she hurried to find the mother of Time. And when the mulberry-tree heard her words, he answered, 'Thou art not far from her, and thou shalt not fare more than a day's journey, when thou shalt sight a house on a mountain-top where thou shalt find what thou seekest; but an thou art as kind as thou art beauteous, try to learn for me what I could do to gain back my lost honour; as from the post of a great man I am become food for pigs.' 'Leave the thought of it to me,' answered she, 'and I will see how best to serve thee;' and she journeyed on, and taking no rest, ceased not faring till she reached the foot of the mountain, spoiler of rejoicing, which with its head annoyed the clouds, and there she found an old man, who had cast himself upon some hay, for great weariness. When he looked upon Cianna, he knew her at once for the damsel who had poulticed the bump on his head, and on hearing whom she sought, he said to her, that he was taking the rent to Time for the letting of the ground which he had sown, and that Time was a tyrant who had usurped all the goods of the world, and exacted a tribute from all, but particularly from a man of his age, and as he had received a benefit from the hands of Cianna, he would return it to her an hundred-fold, giving her good rede on her coming to this mountain, where he could not accompany her, because his age condemned him to descend, and not to ascend, and obliged him to remain at the foot of those mountains to settle accounts with the clerks of Time for the labours and travails, the disgusts, and grievances, and infirmities of life, and to pay the debt to nature.

And thereupon he continued, 'Now, O my beauteous daughter, do thou hearken well to my say. Thou must know that on the top of that mountain thou shalt find an old broken-down house, which remembereth not the days when it was built; the walls are cracked, the foundations are rotten, the doors are worm-eaten, the furniture ancient, and everything therein is timeworn, and consumed, and de-

stroyed; here thou shalt see broken columns, there broken statues,
nothing being entirely whole, but only the coat of arms upon the
gate, where thou shalt behold a snake biting its tail, a stag, a crow,
and a phœnix; and when thou shalt enter within, thou shalt perceive lying about the floor soft files, saws, scythes, and mattocks,
and hundreds on hundreds of kettles full of ashes, and thereupon
labels as on chemists' jars, with names written upon them, where
one can read the names of Corinth, Troy, Carthage, and a thousand
other cities which have turned sour; and these are kept in remembrance of their grandeur, magnificence, and enterprise. Now when
thou art near this house, hide thyself till Time goes forth, and when
he is gone, do thou enter within, and there thou shalt find a very
old, old woman, with a long, a very long, beard reaching the
ground, and with an hump which reacheth to the heavens, and hair
to her heels like the tail of a horse; the face is like unto curly
greens, for furrows and lines, with the wrinkles of many long ages;
and she is always sitting upon a clock which hangeth on the wall;
and because of her eyelashes, which are so long, she will be unable
to see thee. When thou enterest, at once withdraw the weights
from the clock, and after this is done call the old woman, and beseech her to give thee satisfaction in that which thou desirest; and
she will cry a loud cry, and call her son, and bid him eat thee; but
because the weights are wanting to the clock upon which sitteth his
mother, he will be unable to walk, and therefore she will be obliged
to give thee whatso thou wantest. But believe not any oath that she
may swear to thee, unless she nameth and sweareth by her son's
wings; then mayest thou believe her, and do thou whatsoever she
biddeth thee, for thou shalt be satisfied.' And so saying the poor
man fell in a heap quite undone, and like unto a dead body, enclosed in the tomb, when the light and air fall upon it, crumbled
into dust. Cianna gathered up those ashes, and shedding a small
measure of tears upon them, delved a pit, and buried them within
it, and prayed upon them to Heaven to give peace and rest unto
them.

Then she fared up the mountain, and the way wearied her exceedingly, and when she came to the house, she waited till Time went forth, and he was a very old man, with a very long beard, and he wore a very old mantle covered with small cards, upon which were inscribed the names of numberless people; he had large wings, and ran so swiftly that he was soon lost to sight. Cianna thereupon entered the house of the mother, and smiled in beholding that wretched being; and snatching off at once the weights from the clock, related to the old woman what she desired, and the old woman cried with a loud cry, and called her son, but Cianna said to her, 'Thou mayest knock thy head against the wall, for thou shalt certainly not see thy son, while I hold these weights within mine hands'; and the old woman, perceiving that her way was stopped, began to coax her and flatter her, saying, 'Let them go, O my love, do not hinder my son in his race, a thing which no man living in the world ever did; let them go, and may God guard thee. I promise thee and swear to thee by the strong water with which my son destroyeth all things, that I will do thee no harm'; 'Thou art losing time,' answered Cianna, 'far better say, if 'tis thy desire that I let them go.' 'I swear to thee, by those teeth that gnaw all mortal things, that I will tell thee all that which thou desirest to know.' 'Thou wilt do naught of it,' replied Cianna, 'and I wot well thou mockest me and deceivest me;' and the old woman, 'Now I will speak to sooth, I swear to thee by those wings which fly everywhere, that I will give thee more pleasure than thou canst imagine;' and Cianna, hearing this, let go the weights, and kissed the hand of the old woman, which smelt strongly of mildew and mustiness, and she, beholding the good behaviour of the damsel, said, 'Hide thyself behind that door, and when Time cometh, I will enquire of him whatso thou desirest to know. And when he goeth forth once more, because he never remaineth long in one place, thou mayest wend thy ways; but do not let him see thee or hear thee, because he is a great glutton, and eateth even his own children, and if all fails, he eateth even himself, and after springeth up again.'

Cianna did as the old woman bade her; and behold, Time appeared, tall and light, and he gnawed all that came to his hand, even to the plaster on the walls, and when he was ready to depart, his mother told him everything she had heard from Cianna, and besought him by the milk he had sucked from her to answer and tell her clearly of each thing she asked; and the son, after a thousand prayers, answered, 'Let it be told to the tree, that he will never be dear to the folk, whilst he holds treasures buried under his roots. And to the mice, that they will never be safe from the cat, unless they tie her a little bell on the leg, to hear when she is coming. And to the ants, that they will live an hundred years if they can do without flying, because when the ant desireth to die she groweth wings. And to the whale, that she should be cheerful and friendly with the sea-mouse, and he will guide her, and she will never go astray again. And to the pigeons, that when they fly and rest upon the column of riches, they will return to their pristine forms.' And having ended his say, Time began to run his usual race, and Cianna, taking leave of the old woman, came down the mountain, at the same time that the seven pigeons, following her footsteps, had reached their sister, and being very tired of flying for so long, they rested upon the horns of a dead ox. But no sooner had their feet rested thereon, than they became beauteous youths, as erst they were, and wondering with exceeding wonder for this marvellous deed, they understood and comprehended, that the horn, being a symbol of the cornucopia, was the column of riches mentioned by Time, and joying with exceeding joyance with their sister, they fared onwards behind Cianna by the same road they came. And after a time they came to the mulberry-tree, and relating to it what they had heard from Time, the tree besought them to withdraw from beneath it the treasure that was the cause of the fruit's dishonour: and the seven brothers found a mattock amid an orchard, and they dug so deep, until they found a large vase full of golden coins, and they divided it in eight parts between them and their sister, so that they could carry it with them with more easiness. But being very tired of their journey, and of the weight they carried, they lay themselves down near a hedge, and a company of marauders came to that place, and seeing the wretched brothers and sister sleeping with their heads upon the money parcels, they bound them hand and foot to some trees, and taking the gold from them, went their ways; leaving them weeping sorely and lamenting not only the loss of their wealth, but the danger to their lives, that without hope of help were threatened by death from hunger, or else to satisfy the hunger of some wild beast.

Whilst they thus bemoaned their fate, arrived before them the mouse, who after hearing the message they had brought from Time, in gratitude for the service they had rendered him gnawed all the ropes which bound them, and gave them their freedom. And they fared on, and after wending for some length of time they met the ant, and when she heard Time's advice, sighting Cianna, who stood sad and silent, whilst her colour had faded and yellowed, she asked her the cause, and the damsel related to her what had passed between them and the thieves; and the ant answered her, 'Be silent, I think I have in my hands the means by which thou mayest be quits with them, and thus enable me to show thee my gratitude for the service received; thou must know that whilst I was carrying a load of provaunt to my granary underground, I sighted a place wherein these dogs and assassins had hidden their hoards; and they have made under an old building some cavities where they put out of sight the stolen goods, and now that they have gone forth to another expedition of plunder and foray, I will lead thee to the place, so that ye may recover all that ye have lost.' And thus saying she wended on, and led the seven brothers to some old broken-down houses, where she pointed out to them a pit, and Giangrazio, being the bravest of them, went down into it, and therein he found the monies which had been taken from them, and calling his brothers, they took them, and farewelling and thanking the ant, went their ways. And they fared on towards the shore where they were met by the whale, to whom they related the good rede given for her by Time, who is the father of redes, and whilst they were conversing together, the brothers relating to her their adventures, behold, the marauders, who had followed in the wake of their footsteps, appeared armed to the teeth; and when the brothers sighted them, they cried, 'Alas! this is the time that not even a fragment will be left of us, because now the thieves are coming with armed hand, and they will slay us alive.' 'Be not afraid, and doubt not,' said the whale, 'I am able to save you from the fire, besides I desire to give back to you, the good deed of love that ye rendered me, and therefore mount ye upon my back, and I will immediately carry you to a secure place.' The unhappy youths, who beheld the foe at the back and the waters in front, mounted upon the back of the whale, who, distancing the rocks, carried them in sight of Naples, where, not trusting to disembark the youths where the sea was rough, she enquired of them, 'Where wish ye that I should leave you, on the coast of Amalfi?' and Giangrazio answered, 'See if thou canst do without it, O my beauteous fish, because in no place can I disembark content, because of Massa 'tis said "salute it, and pass on"; of Sorrento, "tighten thy teeth"; of Vico, "carry all with thee," and of Castellamare, "neither friend nor gossip."' And the whale, to please the brothers and sister, turned her back, and swam towards the Salt Rock, where she left them, and they hailed the first fishing smack that passed, and bade the fishermen set them ashore, and returning to their country healthy, beautiful, and rich, thus consoling their mother and father, they joyed a happy life through Cianna's goodness, which showed the truth of that ancient say,——

'Always, when thou mayest, do good and forget it.'

THE CROW

Of the Fourth Day

JENNARIELLO, DESIRING TO PLEASE HIS BROTHER, MILLUCCIO, KING OF
FRATTA-OMBROSA, GOETH FOR A LONG JOURNEY, AND BRINGETH BACK
WHAT HIS BROTHER LONGED FOR, TO SAVE HIM FROM DEATH. UPON
HIS RETURN, JENNARIELLO IS CONDEMNED TO DEATH; AND DESIROUS
TO PROVE HIS INNOCENCE, BECOMETH BY A STRANGE ADVENTURE A MAR-
BLE STATUE; AT LENGTH HE RETURNETH TO HIS PRISTINE SHAPE, AND
ENDETH HIS DAYS IN HAPPINESS.

If I had an hundred throats of cane, and a bronze breast, and a
thousand steel tongues, I should fail to explain how much the story
of Paola entertained the hearers; they were pleased that none of
the good deeds remained unrewarded; and the dose of prayers had
to be doubled to persuade Ciommetella to relate her story, since she
felt almost unable to draw the cart at the prince's command; but
as she could do naught but obey, so as not to spoil the game, she
began as follows:

It is a truly great proverb which saith, 'We see wrongly, but
we judge rightly;' but it is a saying difficult to make use of, because
few men in their judgment hit the nail on the head; rather is it
within the sea of human matters, that most are fishermen of sweet
waters who catch crabs; and whoso thinketh of taking, the just
measure is surest to be mistaken; for which reason it ensueth that
all run in the dark, and work blindly, and think in a way to choke
themselves, and act foolishly, and judge unwisely, and most times,
by an ill decision, resolve to do some foolish act, and thus they
purchase for themselves an everlasting repentance of good sense:
as it happened to the King of Fratta-ombrosa, whose adventures you
will know, if within the wheel of modesty ye will call me with the
bell of courtesy, to give me a kindly hearing.

Now it is related that there lived a king of Fratta-ombrosa, Milluccio hight, who loved hunting so much, that he would leave the matters of the state and the most necessary things of his house undone to run after the trail of a hare or the flight of a wild fowl; and he followed this way so oft, that one day of the days fate and fortune led him in a forest, where was formed a thick squadron of the trees, which the sun's horses were unable to break. Here, upon a marble slab, he found a crow that had just been killed; and the king, beholding the blood so vividly with its bright red upon the white marble slab, fetching a deep sigh, cried, 'O heavens grant me that I might have a wife so white and red like unto that marble slab, and with hair and eyebrows as black as the feathers of this crow!' and he fell so deeply in this thought, and compared the two similes so much, that it seemed as if a marble statue was making love to another piece of marble. Having thrust this wretched caprice within his brains, and sought it with the longing of desire, in four pinches it grew from a toothpick to a bar, from a bow to an Indian vegetable marrow, from a barber's small fire-place to a glass-worker's furnace, and from a pigmy to a giant, so that he thought of naught else but the image of that thing which he had instilled in his mind and engraved in his heart, like stone to stone. Wherever his eyes turned, that form which he held within his breast stood before him, and forgetting every other matter, he thought and dreamt of naught but that piece of marble; so that his colour yellowed, and his figure lost its roundness, and he was fading slowly away; for this stone was a millstone which ground away his life; a gun which fired the match of his soul; a calamity which drew him to his end; a lodestone which firmly attracted him to itself; and lastly a stone which could never be set at rest.

His brother, Jennariello hight, seeing him fade slowly away, said to him, 'O my brother, what is the matter with thee, and what has taken thee that thou carriest grief in thine eyes, and the signs of despair in thy face? What has happened to thee? Speak, confide in thy brother; the stink of burning coals closed within a chamber killeth folk; powder mined under a mountain scattereth the pieces up in air; the itch closed within the veins putrifieth the blood; the wind kept within the body engenders colic; therefore open that mouth, and tell me what is the matter with thee; and at last thou mayest be certain, that where I may and can, I will lay a thousand lives down to serve thee.' And Milluccio in half broken words and sighs thanked him for his affection, saying that he doubted not of his love, but that his sickness was without remedy, because it was born from a stone, where he had sowed his desires without hope of plucking any fruit; from a stone, whence he never thought to gather even a mushroom of happiness; a stone of Sisyphus, which carried to the mountain all his designs, and when it had reached the top rolled down again. At last after many sayings, he related to him all which passed of his love. Jennariello, hearing this matter, consoled him the best way he could, and bade him be of good cheer, and not to give way to a melancholy love, for he would wander over the world till he found a woman who would be the original of that stone. Then commanding that a large vessel should be loaded with merchandise, and disguising himself in the attire of a merchant, the prince sailed towards Venice, the mirror of Italy, the receptacle of books of worth, the city greatest in marvels of art and nature; where getting himself a pass for the East, he sailed towards Cairo, and entering the city, he beheld a man carrying a falcon. And he bought it so as to carry it to his brother, who was so fond of hawking and hunting; and wandering on about the city, he met another man selling a handsome steed, and he purchased that also; but feeling tired, he entered a caravanserai, therein to rest from the troubles and travails of the sea.

Now the next morning, when the army of stars, by the order of the general of light, lifted up the tents from the palisado of heavens, and abandoned the place, Jennariello arose, and fared forth to gaze and wander about the city, looking around him like a lynx in quest of the damsel he sought, and he gazed first at one woman, and then at the other, seeking a damsel like unto the stone; and whilst he kept journeying from place to place, here and there, turning and glaring at all sides, like a thief pursued by bailiffs, and

fearing the detectives; at last he was met by a beggar, who was
covered with an hospital of plasters and a jew's rag-shop of rags;
and he said to him, 'O my lord, what is the matter with thee, that
I see thee so affrighted?' 'Must I tell thee my business?' answered
the prince. 'Yes indeed, so would I knead my bread; and tell my
reasons to the bailiffs.' 'Softly, O my handsome youth,' replied the
beggar, 'the flesh of man is not sold by weight; if Darius had not
related to his stable groom his disasters and vexations, he would
never have become the master of Persia; therefore it would not be
great matter, an thou wouldst relate to a poor beggar all thy trouble,
as there is ever found a small piece of wood which may be used
as a toothpick.' Jennariello, hearing the beggar speaking with so
much sense, told him the cause which had brought him to that
country, and the beggar, having heard him to the end, answered
him, 'Now thou shalt perceive, O my son, how we must consider
and keep in good account every one; that although I am but dirt,
yet will I be able to manure the orchard of thine hopes. Now, lend
me thine ears with great attention, and I, with the excuse of seeking alms, will rap at the door of a house where dwelleth a damsel,
daughter of a magician; open well thine eyes, look at her well, consider her, contemplate her countenance, measure her and take particular notice of her, and thou shalt find the image of the one so
much longed for by thy brother.' And thus saying, he went and
rapped at the door of a house not very far off; and hearing the rap,
the damsel, Liviella hight, looked out of the balcony, and threw a
piece of bread to the beggar; and when the prince beheld her, it
seemed to him that she was the very model of what King Milluccio
desired; and giving a largesse to the beggar, he thanked and farewelled him. Then he returned to his caravanserai, where he
donned a disguise, and taking two small boxes, he filled them with
all kinds of laces, pins, gems, and jewels, and returning under the
damsel's windows, he cried out his ware again and again, until at
last Liviella heard him, and called him, to have sight of the fine
nets, laces, ribbons, pocket-handkerchiefs, pins, rings and earrings,
and at last she bade him to show her something better, and he an-

swered, 'O my lady, in these cases I only carry some trifles and things of little worth, but an thou wouldst deign to come to my vessel, I would show thee somewhat of great worth in this world; as I have treasures of fine things, and worthy only to be worn by great lords and ladies.' Liviella, who was not wanting in curiosity (not to go against women's nature), said, 'By my faith, if my sire had not been out, I would have come to see them.' 'So much the better,' replied Jennariello, 'couldst thou come; because if he had been at home, perhaps he would not have let thee come and take thy pleasure; and I promise to let thee behold sumptuous stuffs, and jewels rare, and necklaces, and earrings, and bodices purflewed with gems and gold, and lace of great worth; in fact I desire that thou shouldst be struck with wonder.' Liviella, hearing of these wonders, called one of her gossips, and asked her to accompany her to the vessel, and they both went forth with Jennariello, and fared to the ship's sides, and mounted thereon, and the prince kept her marvelling and wondering over the sumptuous stuffs and wondrous gems, fit only for kings; and he dexterously signed to the captain to weigh the anchor and make sail, and before Liviella lifted her eyes from the goods, and perceived that they had sailed and distanced the land, they had gone a few miles; and when she discovered the deceit, she did the reverse of what did Olympia, because if the latter wept and lamented at being left upon the rocks, Liviella wept because she was carried from the rocks. But Jennariello related to her who he was, and where he was leading her, and the good fortune that was to be hers, and he drew in vivid lines the beauty of King Milluccio, and his valour, and his many virtues, and lastly the fond love with which he would receive her, and he did and said so much that she ceased her weeping and lamenting, and prayed the winds to send the vessel quickly to her goal, so that she might gaze upon the painting which the prince had painted with such lively colours.

And thus they sailed cheerfully on, until one day of the days they felt the waves under the vessel become troubled, and although the ship's master spake in whispers, for he was a man of great intelligence, every man cried out, 'Be on guard, because now we will have a storm, and may God watch over us.' At these words there bore witness a strong gust of wind; and behold, the sky was suddenly covered with clouds, and the sea-pigs came forth upon the sea. And the waves, curious to know the business of other folk, having not been invited to the bridal, would yet spring upon the vessel's deck. Some of the sailors were working at the pumps, and others were casting the water into the sea in tubsful; and whilst all hands were at work, one man at the wheel, another at the sails, because each worked in his own cause, Jennariello mounted the mizzen-top-sail with a very powerful spy-glass, so as to discover if any land was near where they could shelter.

Now whilst he was engaged measuring the distance of an hundred miles with a pipe two feet long, he beheld two pigeons, male and female, who rested upon the mizzen-mast, and the male said, 'Rucche, rucche;' and the female inquired, 'What is the matter, O mine husband, and why art thou lamenting?' and the male answered, 'This unhappy prince hath bought a falcon, which will no sooner be in his brother's hands than he will pluck out his eyes; and whoso will not bring the bird to him, or will warn him of the evil, will become a marble statue.' And after saying this say the bird rested a short time, and then again cried, 'Rucche, rucche;' and his mate said to him, 'And yet art thou lamenting! is there somewhat else new?' and the pigeon answered, 'There is something else, the prince hath bought also a steed, and the first time his brother shall ride him, he will break his neck, and whoso shall not lead him to him, or shall warn him of the danger, will become a marble statue.' And the bird rested again, and then cried, 'Rucche, rucche.' 'Alas! why so many times rucche, rucche?' rejoined the female pigeon. 'What other misfortune is in the way?' And the male answered, 'The prince is leading a fair bride to his brother, but the first night that they lie together, both the one and the other will be eaten by an hideous dragon; but whoso shall not lead her to him, or shall warn him of the danger, will become a marble statue;' and when the pigeon ended his say, he and his mate flew away, and the

tempest ceased to sway, and the sea calmed down, and the wind
fell from wrath. But a wilder storm arose in Jennariello's breast,
from the words he had heard from the bird, and more than four
times he was on the point of casting into the sea the cause of the
forthcoming ruin of his brother. But he was restrained by thoughts
of himself, and the first cause was that he feared in himself that
if he brought not to his brother these things, or if he warned him of
danger, he would become a marble statue; therefore he resolved to
look rather at his own than at his brother's weal, because the shirt
was tighter upon him than the gaberdine.

When they reached Fratta-ombrosa, he found his brother on the
shore, as he had been apprized of the arrival of the vessel, and the
king awaited for the coming ashore of Jennariello with great joy.
And when he met him, and beheld with him the one being whose
image was engraved within his heart, and confronted the one face
with the other, and perceived that not the difference of an hair was
to be seen between the twain, his happiness knew no bounds, and he
was nearly dying with the fulness of joyance; and embracing his
brother, said to him, 'What falcon is this which thou hendest in
hand?' and Jennariello replied, 'I bought it for thee.' And Milluccio said, 'It can well be seen that thou lovest me, because thou
soughtest to please me; and surely an thou hadst brought me a
treasure, thou couldst not have pleased me more than with the gift
of this falcon;' and he stretched forth his hand to seize it, when
Jennariello ready with a knife which he wore at his waistband, cut
off the bird's head. At this deed the king marvelled with great
marvel, and thought his brother had lost his senses, but desiring not
to trouble the joy of the meeting, spake not a word. After a time
he beheld the steed, and enquiring whose steed it was, he was told
it was his own; and when he heard this, a longing seized him to
mount it, and he bade his brother hold the stirrup, and Jennariello
did so, but when his brother was going to mount him, he drew his
knife and cut the steed's legs off; and the king was wroth with exceeding wrath, for it seemed to him that his brother did it in despite
of him, and his entrails burnt with anger. But he did not think it

time to show his resentment, desiring not to poison the first happy moments of his bride, whom he never tired of gazing upon and hending by the hand; and when they arrived at the royal palace he sent invitations to all the lords and notables of the land to a great festival, where in the saloon could be seen steeds of finest blood curvetting and prancing by the side of young colts in the shape of women. And when the ball was ended, a wondrous banquet followed, and thereafter they retired to rest, and the bride and bridegroom retired to their chamber. The young prince had no other thought in his mind but to save the life of the king, his brother, and of the bride, therefore he hid himself behind the newly wedded couple's bed, watching for the coming of the dragon; and behold, at the midnight hour, an hideous dragon entered that chamber: fire came forth of his eyes and smoke of his mouth and nostrils, and the sight of him would have caused the direst affright to the bravest heart, and a looseness that all the drugs of the druggists could not have cured. And Jennariello arose and drew his Damascene blade, and began to cut and slash right and left, and between others he drew a fendent with such power and strength, that at one blow he cut through one of the pillars of the bed; and at the noise the king awoke, and the dragon disappeared.

Milluccio, sighting his brother brand in hand, and the bed pillar cut through and through, cried with a very loud cry, 'Ho there, ye folk! help, against this traitor my brother, who hath come to slaughter me.' At his cries hastened to his aid some of his officers, who slept in the ante-room, and the king bade them seize his brother and bind him. And the king forthwith sent Jennariello to gaol, and as soon as the morning dawned, and the sun opened his bank to return the deposit of light to the creditors of the day, he summoned a great council, and related that which had happened; and since the deed in the night seemed to agree with the wrathful spirit shown in the killing of the falcon in his despite, and the cutting the legs of the steed, by unanimous voices Jennariello was condemned to die. And all the prayers of Liviella to soften the king's heart were powerless, and he said to her, 'Thou lovest me not, O my wife, since thou esteemest thy brother-in-law more than my life; thou hast seen him with thine own eyes, this dog of an assassin, hending brand in hand, which could have cut an hair's breadth through the air, come to make mince-meat of me; and if that pillar had not sheltered me (for me a pillar of life), at this very moment thou wouldst be widowed of me.' And thus saying, he ordered that justice should be executed.

Jennariello, hearing this sentence, and being reduced to such an evil strait for having done a good deed, knew not what to think of his painful position, because, an he spake not, it was wrong; and an he spake, it was worse; it is bad to have the itch, but it is worse to have the scab; for he would but fall from a tree into the clutch of the wolf; if he held his tongue, he would lose his head under the sword, and an he spake out, he would end his day within a marble prison. At last, after counselling in himself and thinking what was best, he decided to discover all to his brother, and whilst in any way he was doomed to die, he esteemed it better by far to make resolution to avow the truth to the king, and end his days innocent of the guilt laid upon his head, than to retain the true cause hidden within his breast, and thus be sent out of the world like a traitor. Therefore he sent word to the king that he desired to speak on a matter important to the state; and the king sent for him to his presence, where he began by speaking of his great love to the king, shown on several occasions; and after, of the deceit he had been guilty of with Liviella for his sake; and what he had heard from the pigeons about the falcon, and how he had brought the bird and so as not to become a marble statue had said naught of the secret, but had slain the bird rather than see his brother sightless. And when he had ended this part of the story, he felt his legs harden into stone, but he continued to relate about the steed, and when he had ended his say, he had become marble to his waist, hardening matters for which at other times his heart would have wept, and which he would have paid in ready money. At last ne came to speak of the dragon, and when he had ended he became a marble statue, and remained amid the saloon. When the king perceived this, he fell to weeping and lamenting, and buffeted his face, and rent his garments, blaming his error and the false judgment he had passed upon the best and most loving of brothers; and he mourned with excessive mourning for more than a year, and whenever he thought of him his eyes rained a flood of tears.

In the meanwhile Queen Liviella gave birth to twin men-children, beautiful as a full moon in her fourteenth night, and the like of them had never been seen in the world; and after a few months were past, the queen had gone forth one day of the days into the country for a few hours, leaving the babies in the saloon with their sire, who gazing at the statue amid it, his eyes rained tears, remembering the foolishness which had made him lose the flower of mankind; and behold, as he was thus lost in thought, a very old man appeared, with long hair covering his shoulders, and with a beard which covered his chest; and he bowed low before the king, and said to him, 'What wouldst thou give, O king, so that this handsome brother thine should return to life again?' and answered the king, 'I would give my kingdom.' 'This is not the thing required,' replied the old man, 'the price must not be wealth; but a life must with a life be paid.' The king, partly for love of Jennariello, partly because he knew himself guilty of injustice to his own loss answered, 'Believe me, O my lord, that I would give my life for his, and so that he would come forth from this stone, I would be content to be put within a stone.' The oldster, hearing these words, rejoined, 'There is no need to risk thy life in such a venture, because it is not easy work to grow up a man, but the blood of these thy children, anointing this marble, would bring him to life again.' The king replied, 'Children are easily brought into the world, witness the form of these my heart's core that we may have some more, but I would have back a brother like unto whom I can never hope to have another.' And thus saying, he made before a stone idol the miserable sacrifice of these two innocent lambs, and anointed with their blood the statue, and the prince returned to life and embraced the king with great joyance; and the king commanded that the two poor little creatures should be put in their coffins, and laid out in honour for their burial, as was fit and due to young princes.

In the meanwhile the queen returned from her outing, and the king bade his brother hide himself, and then said to his wife, 'What wouldst thou give, O my heart, that my brother should return to life?' 'I would give my kingdom,' answered Liviella, and the king replied, 'Wouldst thou give the blood of thy children?' 'That I would not,' answered the queen, 'I would not be so cruel as to pluck forth mine eyes with mine own hands.' 'Alas!' cried the king, 'to behold my brother in life again, I have murthered mine own children, and this is the price I paid for Jennariello's life.' And thus saying, he showed her the children within the coffin, and when she beheld the woeful spectacle she cried with bitter cries, and buffeted her face like one gone mad, and said, 'O my children, O props of my life, O core of my heart, O fountains of my blood! Who hath done this evil at the sun's windows? Who hath bled me from the principal vein of my life without a doctor's leave? Alas! my children, my hopes, my babes; O darkened light, O poisoned sweetness, O lost crutch of mine old age! Ye are pierced through and through by a sword, and I am pierced by my grief! Ye are drowned in your blood, and I am drowned in tears! Alas, to give life to an uncle, ye have slain your mother, because I can no more weave the web of my days without ye, O weights of the loom of this darkened life; needs must the organ fill its bellows with the wind of my cries, now that ye are taken from me! O my children, O my children, why do ye not answer to your darling mother, who gave you her own blood within your bodies? Now she will give it to you out of her eyes! But as my sad lot and fortune alloweth me to see the fountain of my joy and pastime dried up, I do not wish to live in sadness and fear in this world! Now step by step I will come to find you.' And when she ended her words she ran to a window to throw herself out therefrom, but when she was near it, her father entered within a cloud, and he cried, 'Stay, Liviella, for I, after having fared a journey, have done three services, revenged myself of Jennariello, who came into my house to rob me of my daughter, by changing him for a few months into a marble statue; and thee of the dishonour and evil thou broughtest upon me, in flying from me aboard a ship, by letting thee behold thy sons, two gems, cruelly murdered by their sire; and I have punished the king for this caprice of a woman with child which had come upon him, of constituting himself judge criminal of his brother, and headsman of his own children. But it was my will to shave and not to flay ye, and therefore it is my desire that the poison ye have drained should turn to sweet pastry. So do thou go and take thy children, and my grandchildren, more beauteous than ever; and thou, Milluccio, embrace me, I accept thee as my son-in-law and mine own son, and I forgive Jennariello his offence, because he did this in service of a worthy brother.' And when he ended his say, the children came, and the father was never weary to kiss them and embrace them, and to join the general enjoyance came also Jennariello, who, having passed the crucible of trial, now felt himself in macaroni broth, although with the pleasures reserved for him in his life he never forgot the dangers past, and thinking of the error of his brother, he perceived how careful mankind must be not to fall into the pit, as true is the say that

'Human judgment is ever false and wrong.'

PRIDE PUNISHED

Of the Fourth Day

THE KING OF BELLO-PÆSE, DESPISED BY CINTIELLA, DAUGHTER OF THE
KING OF SURCOLUNGO, WREAKETH VENGEANCE UPON HER, REDUCING
HER TO BAD PLIGHT, BUT AFTERWARDS TAKETH HER TO WIFE.

It was well that Ciommetella had quickly brought the magician
upon the scene, and thus thrown water upon the fire which burned
the spirits of all hearers, and left them breathless in pity for
Liviella. In the happiness of the poor child each felt happy, and
the mind of each awoke up to a lively expectation that Jacova
would enter the field of contest, and she, in the livery of her story,
setting lance in rest, entered the lists of their desire.

Whoso draweth the rope too tight will break it; whoso seeketh
misfortunes will reap disasters and trouble; whoso desireth to go
upon the mountain-top, if he falleth down, the damage is his own:
as ye will hear in what occurred to a damsel who, despising crowns
and sceptres, descended through necessity to the stables; but with
the head-breaking which cometh from Heaven come also the plasters; never came punishment without caresses, nor blows without
sweetmeats.

There lived in days of yore a king of Surco-lungo, who had a
daughter, Cintiella hight, beautiful as a moon: but who possessed
not a drachm of beauty that was not overweighted with a dose of
pride; and so great was her pride, that she thought no other person
in the world of any account; therefore it was impossible for the poor
father to find a suitable mate for her; no matter how good, or how
great, or how brave he was, none pleased her. Amid the many
princes who flocked to ask her in marriage was the King of Bello-
pæse, and he left naught undone to gain the affection of Cintiella;

but the more he tried to please her, the more she turned from him
in disdain; and the more cheaply he gave her his love, the more
niggardly she dealth with his desires; the more liberal he was with
his adoration, the more wanting was her heart; and not a day passed
in which the unhappy king did not say to her, 'When, O thou cruel
one, to whom so many melons of hopes have turned to so many
vegetable marrows, will I find in proof a red one? When, O thou
barbarous and cruel woman, will the storms of thy cruelty end,
and I be able, with a fair wind, to stand at the wheel of my designs to guide my vessel to thy beauteous port? When shall I plant
the standard of my love-longing and desire upon the walls of that
fortress, after spending such a time in beseeching and praying at
thy foot-stool?' But all these words were thrown to the winds;
she had eyes of such sheen to pierce a stone, but had no ears to
hearken unto the lamentations of whoso, wounded and stricken,
wept with sore weeping; rather she looked upon him with contempt
and wrath, as though he had done her some evil action, or gathered
up the grapes from her vineyard. At last the king, perceiving the
hard-heartedness and lack of sweetness of Cintiella, and feeling
that she cared not in the least for him, retired with his followers
and his goods to his own domains, saying, 'For ever will I retire
from love's play.' But he swore a strong oath to be revenged of
this damsel, who in hardness of heart was not a damsel but a Saracen
Moor, saying that he would cause her to repent with bitter sorrow
of having ill-treated and mocked him.

And the king departed from that country, and let his beard grow
long, and dyed his face and hands with a dark tint, and after a few
months donned the disguise of a peasant, and returned to Surco-
lungo, where by dint of largessing he got into the post of the king's
gardener. And he attended to his work and new duties as best he
could, until one day of the days he laid under the windows of
Cintiella a tray with an imperial robe within it all purflewed with
gold and diamonds; and the handmaidens of the princess sighted it,
and ran in haste to their mistress, telling her what they had seen;
and she sent word to the gardener, asking him if he would like to

sell it; and he replied, that he was not a merchant nor an old-clothes seller, but that he would most willingly give it as a gift if they would allow him to sleep one night in the saloon of the princess; and the handmaidens, hearing this, returned to Cintiella, and said to her, 'O our lady, thou shalt lose naught by it, thou mayest safely give this satisfaction to the gardener, and we shall have this sumptuous robe, fit for a queen to wear.' Cintiella was caught by that man who fisheth wiser folk than she, and took the robe, and allowed him have his desire.

The next morning, at the same place, he laid another robe of the same workmanship, which was no sooner seen by the princess, than she sent to ask him if he would sell it, for she would give him whatever he might ask. The gardener replied that he would not sell it, but would give it freely as a gift an they would allow him to sleep in the anteroom of the princess; and Cintiella, desirous to have the robe, let herself be drawn to give him this satisfaction. When the third morning dawned, before the sun came to strike the gun upon the tinder of the fields, the king laid on the same spot a sumptuous under-waistcoat of the same texture as the two former robes, and when Cintiella beheld it, she said as she said of the others, 'If I have not this under-vest, I shall not be content'; and sending for the gardener said to him, 'It is needful, O my good man, that thou shouldst sell me that under-vest which I beheld in the garden, and take thou my heart for it.' 'I do not sell it, O my lady, but an thou please, I will give it to thee as a free gift, and also a chain of diamonds, if thou wilt allow me to sleep one night in thy chamber.' 'Now thou art a most villainous fellow,' said Cintiella, 'it is not enough for thee to have slept in the saloon, and in the ante-room, but now thou must sleep in my chamber, and after a while thou wilt think of sleeping even in my bed!' The gardener rejoined, 'O my lady, I will keep my under-vest and thou thy chamber; if thou desirest otherwise, thou knowest the way. I am content to sleep on the ground, a thing that would be vouchsafed even to a Turk; and an thou beheld the chain which I would give to thee, perhaps thou wouldst give me a better weight.' The princess, partly for profit and partly by the rede of her handmaidens, who had helped the dog in his climbing, allowed him to persuade her to satisfy his want, and when evening came, and night darkened and starkened, the gardener, taking the chain and the under-vest, fared to the apartment of the princess, and presented the things to her. Then she bade him enter her chamber and sit in a corner, and said to him, 'Now stay there as if paralyzed, and move not, an thou carest for my favour,' and making a sign on the floor with a charcoal, added, 'An thou passest this mark, thou shalt leave thy hindparts behind thee.' Then bidding the handmaidens draw the curtains around the bed, she retired to rest.

The king-gardener awaited till she was asleep, and thinking it was high time to work in the territory of love, he arose from his seat, and laid himself down by her side, and before the mistress of the place was well awake, he gathered the fruits of his love; and when she awoke, and saw what had occurred, not desiring to make of one evil two, and in order to punish the gardener ruin the garden, made a vice of necessity, and contented herself of the disorder, and felt pleasure in the error; and where she had disdained crowned heads, was subdued by a hairy foot, for such seemed the king, and such believed him to be Cintiella. So the practice continued and the play, and she conceived, and saw herself grow rounder day by day, and she said to the gardener that she was ruined if her sire perceived how the case stood; and therefore they must think how best to remedy and eschew the danger. The king answered that he could not think of any other remedy to this evil than to leave the country, and he would lead her to an old mistress of his, who would give them a place where she could be brought to bed of her child. Cintiella, seeing in what plight she was reduced by the sin of her pride sans peer, which had carried her from rock to rock, allowed the words of the king to move her, and leaving her own home, she put herself in the hands of fate and fortune.

Now the king, faring with her for a long time, at length led her to his own home, and relating the whole story to his mother, besought her to dissimulate for a while, because it was his wish to repay himself for the slight which Cintiella with her pride had put upon him in time past. And therefore, setting a small stable in order within the palace, he made her live very miserably, letting her see bread at the length of a cross-bow.

One day of the days the king bade his handmaidens, when they kneaded the bread, call Cintiella in to help them; and meanwhile told her to see if she could get of it a cake for themselves to abate their hunger. The unhappy Cintiella, making ready the bread for the oven, before their very eyes was able to get from the whole a scone, and taking it when it was baked, put it in one of her pockets; but at the same time in came the king arrayed in his own raiments, and said to the handmaidens, 'Who bade ye allow this woman within the palace? Can ye not see that she favoureth rogues, and if my saying be true, and ye put your hands in her pocket, there will ye find the proof of her crime;' and they did his bidding, and found the scone, and at the sight they cried together to her shame, and the raillery and derision lasted all day. When night came, the king disguised himself once more, and went in to her, and finding her sad, and feeling scorned of the affront received, bade her not to mind what had happened, for necessity was the tyrant of mankind, as justly said that Tuscan poet that

> ' The an-hungered beggar
> Cometh to do an act, which done by others,
> In better state he would himself have blamed.'

Therefore, whilst hunger chaseth the wolf out of the forest, she could be excused if she did a thing which would not sit well in others. And she must arise and fare up to the lady of the house, who was cutting divers pieces of cloth for clothing, and offer her services to her, and try to take one piece, knowing that she was nearly on the point of child-birth, and she needed a thousand things. Cintiella, who could not disobey her husband, for as such she held him, fared up to the lady, and joining the handmaidens in cutting, she hid some napkins, and binders, and caps, and shirts, and put them under her clothes; but the king came once more, arrayed in his own raiments, and reproaching them again, as he had done for the bread, bade the handmaidens search her, and they finding the stolen things upon her person, she was again loaded with injurious epithets, and she returned weeping to the stable. Then the king donned his disguise, and ran after her, and found her in deep despair and told her not to allow melancholy and sadness to win upon her, that the matters of this world were of opinion only, and therefore she should try for a third time if she could gain some trifle for the babe she would bring to the light, and she would have a ready and good occasion so to do, because the lady had wedded her son to a foreign lady, and was going to send to the bride some robes of brocade, and cloth of gold, and other goods, and he added 'They say that the bride is just thy stature, and that it is her desire to have them cut upon her figure. Now the thing will be easy to thee, to try to get in hand some nice cuttings, so that we may sell them, and live in ease all our life.' Cintiella did as her husband bade her, and had even taken one foot of rich gold brocade, when the king again came, and making a great to-do with the handmaidens, ordered them to search Cintiella, and finding upon her the booty, they chased her out of the house in great shame. Donning at once his disguise as gardener, the king ran down to comfort and console her, because if he punished her in one way, in the other the love he bore her made him anoint her wounds, so as not to drive her to despair; but the wretched Cintiella, with the anguish of what occurred to her, thought that all was a punishment from Heaven for her arrogance and pride, and that for holding princes and kings of renown as her foot-cloths, she was now treated as a low-born chit, and because she had hardened her heart to her sire's rede, her face now reddened with shame at the servants' leers and sneers; and the wrath, and grief, and pain caused her to be brought to bed with child-birth pains, and the queen-mother was informed of the case, and she sent for her, and had her brought to her apartment, showing compassion of her sad state. And Cintiella was laid in a bed purflewed with gold and pearls, in a chamber covered with hangings of cloth of gold, and she wondered with excessive wonder and mar-

velled with greatest marvel, seeing the stable changed to a royal
chamber, and the straw whereupon she lay turned to such a precious
bed, and she knew not what had happened to her; and strengthening
cordials and sweetmeats were given to her so that she could be
brought to bed easier. But by the will of Heaven, without much
labour-pains she gave birth to two beauteous men-children, the like
of which had never been seen. As soon as she had been delivered,
the king entered, saying, 'And where is gone your sense and judgment to lay a cloth upon an ass? is this a bed for a low woman?
quick let her arise and be gone and give her a bastinado, and perfume with rosemary this chamber, that this pest may not be smelt.'

The queen, hearing this, said 'Enough, say no more, O my son;
enough and sufficient are the anguish and torments which thou hast
made this poor child endure, thou shouldst be filled to satiety, thou
hast reduced her to rags, and hast made her suffer so many trials,
which ought to satisfy thee for the contempt she showed to thee
when at her sire's court; but let the debt be paid by these two beauteous gems of great price which she presenteth to thee.' And sending
for the children, who were the most beautiful ever seen in the
world, she held them up to his embrace. The king, beholding such
beauteous babes, felt his heart soften, and kissed them, and embraced Cintiella. And she recognised him for whom he was in
reality, and he told her that whatso he had done was because of the
disdain with which she had treated him, a king of such puissance
and renown; but that from that moment he would hold her as the
crown of her head ever dear. Then the queen also embraced her
as her daughter, and her joy was the greatest of joyances, beholding
her two boys, and she drank deep draughts of happiness and content,
forgetting past anguish and regret; and ever after she remembered
to keep her sails down, thinking that

'The daughter of pride is ruin.'

The stories having ended for that day, the prince, desiring to rid
himself of the sadness of soul which Cintiella's story had brought,
called Cicco Antuono and Narduccio, and bade them do their part,

and they with flat caps on, and black tight-fitting breeches, and doublets well cut and trimmed with lace, came forth from a corner of the garden to recite the eclogue which followeth:

ECLOGUE

THE HOOK

Narduccio and Cicc' Antuono

Nar.   Lend me an half ducat, O Cicc' Antuono,
      And take this pledge.

Cic.   In faith, I would most gladly lend it to thee,
      If I had not this very morning made
      An excellent purchase.

Nar.   It is mine evil fate: but what didst purchase?

Cic.   I found a good occasion
      To buy an hook quite new:
      An he had asked of me a thousand crowns,
      As many would I willingly have spent on't.

Nar.   Thou art most prodigal in thy disbursements:
      An hook, the most that it may cost,
      Should be no more than two carlini.

Cic.   Indeed thou understandest not, Narduccio.
      These things are like 'my love returned to me':
      Know'st not that fishing-hooks are risen in price,
      Because they catch no longer fish, but crowns?

Nar.   How can they fish up crowns? I understand not.

Cic.   Thou art an ass, forgive me:
      Hast just come into the world?
      Knowest thou not that there is not a man
      Who holds not in his hand a fishing-hook?
      By its means he liveth in the midst of plenty;
      By it he dresseth richly, and groweth fat;
      It putteth a good paillasse underneath him;

By means of it he can shut up the pigs;
With it he shineth, becometh full at bottom;
With it, in fact, he ruleth all the world.

Nar. Thou strikest me with wonder and great marvel:
What shall we bet,
That thou hast fixed in thy head to make me believe
The moon is in a well?
And I must swallow, that it is a rare thing,
A bee philosophorum, this hook of thine?

Cic. Exactly, this is the bee,
Come forth from the efforts of genius.

Nar. O my brother, I have eaten
Bread from most bakehouses,
Nor have I ever heard it named;
Then either I am a fool, or thou'rt befooling me.

Cic. Open thine ears, and hearken,
For thou art a great simpleton.
Few people name it a fishing-hook,
Because from its first infancy
It bears a bad appearance.
Therefore great wits
Have changed its name;
Therefore in this age
All things wear masks.
The prince gives unto them
The title of presents or gifts:
The judge hath namèd them
A happy gage, a softening,
An honouring of the hand, or of the mouth.
The clerk is right; and Heaven knoweth
If it is more crooked than a dog's leg;
The merchant names it gain;
The craftsman, business;
The shopman, industry;
The rogue, craft, cunning device;

The watchman and bailiff, head-covering;
The bandit, preserved fruit;
The soldier, ransom;
The spy, a deed;
The whore, a present;
The pimp, gain or glove-covering;
The broker, *pour boire*, for a drink;
The commissary calls it provision;
And in fact every one gives to it his own colouring,
The corsair, of sponge,
The captain, of quiet life,
(And if he is not quiet, return to him,
For he carries matters beyond truth and ruin,
And I assure thee that he doth more war
With his hook than with the sword).
Dost thou want more? the poet,
Who despoileth of conception and of words
As many books as they put in his hands,
Of Horace, Ovid, Mafaro, and Nasone,
And giveth them the name of imitation.

Nar. I understand thee; by Jove, thou shouldst succeed
As a professor; thou art a clever servant
Of the four masters of the crucible;
Thou art an handsome boaster greedy of gain;
The pink of wile and guile, an thou wilt say
That all their knowledge in these days is hooked.

Cic. Hook and fishing-hook
Are one and the same thing;
'Tis enough that every man
Wears it at his waist-band,
Some of gold, some of silver, or copper,
Some of steel, and some of wood,
According to the person's rank and quality.
For instance, we will say of that great man
Who conquered the world:

To fish up all his kingdoms
He had it made of gold,
Set with diamonds and carbuncles.
And he who made Cicero
Salt so much of pork bacon,
He carried it of silver.
The others, in due order,
Following judgment or power,
Have it made as they can:
Enough that each may fish.
And therefore to this fishing
Various names are given:
Gathering, ravishing, wrapping up,
Lightening, lifting, scratching,
Shortening, setting things straight,
Blowing, cutting, switching up,
Picking, cleaning, catching up,
Hands-filling, helping oneself,
Playing at 'Wrap up Cuosimo,'
Or at emptying pockets,
Playing the part of prior, or playing the harp,
Shaking purses, or playing the spider's game.

Nar. Thou mayest say all this
With only a simple word:
Playing at triumphing in the way of murthering,
That depredations you may commit, and robbery.

Cic. Thy memory is bad, have I not told thee
That the world in these sad days of ours
Giveth to evil things the name of good?
And for naught else doth genius work and strive
But to set at work this fishing-hook,
Which catcheth, and is not seen,
Which pulleth, and is not felt,
Which grappleth, and is not touched,
And is always taking, picking, and hooking?

Nar. O my brother, I envy it not,
    All these things go afterwards down with the tide;
    And goods that are ill acquired
    Are never handed down to the third heir:
    Rich folk go to the bottom,
    And they behold their houses fall into ruin,
    The chimneys destroyed, themselves reduced to beggary:
    They wander through the world finding no mercy;
    And he spake well, a schoolmaster, who said
    That if all things go wrong, 'tis the fault of the millstone.

Cic. In these days the bigoted hypocrite
    Hangs by the neck with hunger;
    Whoso stealeth not hath no goods;
    Whoso taketh not hath no straw;
    Whoso gaineth not hath his soul in grief;
    And whoso never fisheth never feasteth.

Nar. And in restoring it
    Thou may'st give me three horses;
    Besides, very oft it happeneth
    That a gallows-tree is found,
    For some foolish simpleton who is fond of gain:
    A decree comes forth, that he be straightway led
    Astride an ass, as if he were a monkey;
    The court presents him with a paper mitre;
    At the market-place he seeth himself marked,
    And not to suffer hunger becometh infamous.
    He loseth his honour to enjoy an hour;
    For a few copper coins
    He gaineth a seat at the oars;
    The juice of the grape
    Becometh salt sea-water;
    To catch with his nails
    He gaineth three blocks of wood;
    The feathers become for him a pennon.
    What use to have so many coins

Of copper, silver, and red gold,
Ducats, and crowns and smaller pieces?
If, *par example*, after much search we find
That more monies we have, we are never content in mind.

Cic. If once thou triest this our hook,
Thou'lt never do without it; 'tis as the itch:
The more thou scratchest it, the more it itcheth.
Let us look round
At the arts and offices of this our world,
And thou'lt perceive that every man makes use of it.
Begin at the beginning, 'tis antinomy
Of whoso hath vassals on his fiefs:
Behold he sighteth a worthy farmer
Who hath a flock of growing pigs—
Today he cometh and asketh the loan
Of so many crowns, which he will soon return,
When it shall rain so much dried figs and raisins;
Tomorrow he sendeth for some barley
Which he will return at harvest-time;
Now he will borrow his ass, or oxen,
With plea that 'tis needful for the court.
This nuisance will last for such a time,
This bitter siege such a time will last,
That the poor farmer in despair
Useth hard language upon his lord,
Or dealeth him a cuff: O wretched man,
Better, far better had he broken his neck!
Behold, he is taken,
And cast quick into a pit;
Chains are put on his feet,
An iron band round his neck,
Handcuffs on his hands,
And a large bill upon the prison gates,
Saying, 'Ban and command, ho there, depart, ye folk!
For whoso speaketh to this man

Will pay six ducats penalty!'
In fact, thou mayest cry out whatever thou wilt,
Petitions send, beg friends to interpose,
He is never set free
Of so many draughts of vinegar,
Of anguish and of torments,
Expenses, and travail,
Unless he sendeth some agreement sweet.
At last when he hath realised the wants
Of a greedy wolf and him to surfeit filled,
Whilst this wolf murdereth him, 'tis said he hath graced him.

Nar. O accursed fishing-hook!
May evil reach the shameless forge
Where thou wert cast and riveted and tempered.

Cic. Hark to what doth the captain and master of arts:
Because from the full-grown ox
The calf doth learn how to plough.
He bringeth forth witnesses, embroileth papers,
Lengtheneth sentences,
Occupieth deeds and writings,
Sendeth to jail without cause;
And there the fishing-hook worketh for seven,
And where he should be dragged
And punished, he gains the name,
Of being skilled in his office,
Industrious, and of good sense.

Nar. This is more than true,
And if a man of weal returneth
With a clean purse, and clean of conscience
(A matter which hath happened
To me about twelve times),
Then every one doth say,
It is better he should withdraw,
Because 'tis not his art:
'Tis a pity to give him a patent,

   For he is an ass, and cannot get provaunt.

Cic. The doctor, if he be a rogue,
   Lengtheneth his patient's sickness,
   And with the apothecary holdeth share:
   If he is upright, he showeth too
   That amid all his prescriptions
   He also knoweth this secret,
   When he holdeth out his hand behind his back.

Nar. Thou canst not speak against this fishing-hook.
   For it is honoured and full of modesty;
   Thus 'tis and may be called a fatal price,
   For thou payest behind thee whoso helpeth thee filth.

Cic. The merchant never loseth
   His cap to the crowd;
   Giveth old goods to buyers;
   Linen full of starch
   To make it thick and weighty;
   He sweareth, affirmeth, and voweth
   That the rotten goods are new,
   That the crushed and undone are the best,
   And with fine words, and evil deeds,
   He beguileth thee, and showeth to thee
   The white for the black, and thou findest ever
   In the goods thou buyest something wrong,
   And when he measureth
   With gallant ostentation,
   He stretcheth the cloth, so that thou mayest find it scarce.

Nar. Therefore 'tis not a marvel
   When Heaven turneth its face against it,
   And for an error forgiveth the chase.

Cic. The butcher selleth to thee
   An old and sickly ram
   For mutton or young lamb;
   A bullock for a calf,

And ornaments it all
With flowers and golden paper,
To stir thine appetite.
He selleth bones for flesh, and against thy will
The weight is always greater than the joint:
In weighing the meat, may God and Heaven save thee,
He forceth down the balance with his fingers.

Nar. 'Tis matter enough to swell thy lungs with wrath;
'Tis this the reason that upon each feast-day
They dress with elegance as a baron might.

Cic. The oilman also cheateth at the measure:
To show thee that he filleth to the brim,
And that the oil doth reach the topmost mark,
He dents the bottom of the measure in,
Raising a hump in the bottom.
He mixeth bran with the oil
To give it body and colour:
Thou beholdest a golden froth,
And fillest thy finest pots,
And after thou shalt find the dregs,
Or rather a mixture of water and filth,
Which, put to burn, blackens thy lamp, is bitter,
And giveth a mournful light, and then
Shoots a shot and dies out.

Nar. There is not a foot of clean ground,
All good is past:
O thou corrupted world, how art thou changed!

Cic. The tavern-keeper hath decanters scarce;
All night he is in traffic,
And if he finds the cask
A little sour in taste, or not so thick,
He beateth up the whites of eggs in it:
But most of all he openeth
Good wine and bad wine,

Maketh of vinegar asprinio,*
Rather of water wine,
And with the fingers covereth the spout
So that it shooteth forth by slow degrees,
And the decanter's neck hendeth in hand
So that, deceived by the sight,
They never would perceive the lack of measure.

Nar. O wretched he, who falleth in their trap:
He needeth an iron stomach and a full purse.

Cic. The tailor keepeth for himself a banner,
From every cut, he seeth if there are some shreds:
He putteth the cotton on account as silk;
If thou with him go forth to buy some goods,
He will come with needles pinned on at his breast,
He'll bargain in thy favour,
And then return to the merchant for the pact;
But this is the least of salt:
In the list he tricketh thee,
And thou, in reading the account,
Wilt curse the point that bringeth such amount.

Nar. O blessed and most happy are the animals,
Who can stay naked
In the forests, vales, and plains, and appenines:
They are not ever subject to these ruins.

Cic. Listen, the old-clothes vendors in the Ghetto:
If thy caprice will push thee
To sell somewhat to them,
Thou shalt meet with a crowd
Agreeing in all matters,
Which taketh thee by the throat;
.If thou buyest a suit of clothes,
Thou'lt don it now, and tomorrow
It will be nothing worth, thou'lt find it torn,

* Vineyard cultivated near Naples in Terra di Lavoro from which are
gathered rather sour grapes from which wine is made called 'asprino,' *asprinio.*

'Twill last thee only from Christmas to Saint Stephen's,
And with damages and scorn
Thou goest pricked and painted.
But of what use to touch so many strings?
I should require a ream of writing-paper
In which to explain the gifts and all the arts,
Which do most honour to our fishing-hook,
Relating how many half-starved beggarly beings
By help of this waxed fat and rich became.

Nar. Accursed invention,
Honour's poison,
By which is ever seen
Dark the truth, and black all faith.

Cic. Thou mayest say whatever pleaseth thee;
But every one doth use it constantly,
And may I die enstrangled by a rope
If this same day I do not buy me one.

Nar. 'Twere better thou shouldst die of heart-disease,
For an thou use the fishing-hook in this world,
The fishing-hook will draw it out of the world.

I could not say if the head or the tail of the fine entertainment of the day pleased most, because if one was tasteful, the other sank deep into the bones' marrow, and the enjoyment of the prince was so great that, to demonstrate himself courteous and truly liberal, as a great lord should be, he sent for the lord of the wardrobe, and ordered that there should be given to the reciters a number of old hats, which had been his sire's, as a free gift from him to them; and now the sun had been called in haste to appear at the other pole, to help and lighten his estates, occupied by the shadows, wherefore the prince arose, and dismissed the company, and each one fared to his own hayloft, with injunctions to return the next morning at the time appointed and at the same place.

END OF THE FOURTH DAY

FIFTH DAY OF THE

DIVERSION OF THE LITTLE ONES

THE birds had already referred the rogueries and traps which had been laid and done that night to the ambassadress of the sun, when Prince Thaddeus and Princess Lucy repaired thus early in the morning to the usual place of meeting, where with the cool morning breeze had come nine of the ten women. And the prince, seeing this, asked wherefore Jacova had not come, and they replied that she had been taken ill with looseness whilst in full health, and Thaddeus commanded that another woman should be found in her place, to supply and act instead of the missing one. And thus, unwilling to fare far to seek one, they sent for Zoza, who lived vis-à-vis the royal palace, and she was received by Prince Thaddeus with many compliments, because he felt indebted to her, and for the inclination and affection he had laid upon her; and she with her companions gathered some flowers, one some blooming cat-mint, another some sweet lavender, another some five-leaved rue, and one one thing and another another; this one made a wreath, as if she would recite a farce; and another, a sweet posy; one would lay a full-blown rose upon her breast; and another hold a pink between her lips; and because it wanted about four hours for the midday hour, when the time would be ripe to begin their story-telling once more, the prince ordered that they should begin some games to entertain and amuse his wife. He bethought himself of Cola Jacopo the farrier, a man of great wit, so he sent for him, and when he stood in the presence, and the prince told him his want, Cola Jacopo, just as if he kept all kinds of inventions in his pocket, straightway found what Thaddeus required, and said, 'My lord and ladies, that enjoyment which hath not a bough of usefulness combined with delight in it is ever insipid, and therefore the entertainments and the wakes bring not a useless pleasure but rather a tasteful gain, because not only pass we the time pleasantly in this kind of games, but we excite and awaken our wits to the knowledge of giving ready and witty replies to whatso may be asked of us, as it happeneth in the game of games which I think of playing, and which is done in this manner. I will propose to one of these ladies one kind of game, and she, without taking thought about it, must answer that she does not like it, and the cause of her dislike to it, and whoso answer not readily, or answer out of purpose, shall pay a fine, and shall do the penalty commanded by the princess. To begin the game, I should like to play with the Lady Zoza a quarter of a ducat at small triumph;' and Zoza replied, 'I will not play this game, because I am not a rogue.' 'Bravo,' said Thaddeus, 'here the rogue and the assassin triumpheth.' 'If it be so,' rejoined Jacopo, 'then, as I have been expulsed, I shall play my quarter ducat with Lady Cecca at the failed bank.' 'I care not for it,' answered Cecca, 'I am not a merchant.' 'She is right,' said Thaddeus, 'this game is for them.' 'At least, Lady Meneca,' continued Cola Jacopo, 'let us spend a couple of hours at the game of discontented.' 'Forgive me, but that is a game only fit for courtiers,' answered Meneca. 'Thou hast hit the nail on the head,' said Thaddeus, 'as that race of folk are never in good humour.' 'I will,' rejoined Cola Jacopo, 'ask the Lady Tolla to play with me a forest of copper coins against four golden moutons.' 'Heaven forefend,' answered Tolla, 'this is a game of husbands who have a wicked wife.' 'Thou couldst not have spoken better,' replied Thaddeus, 'this game is just fit for them, for often and very often their game ends in rambutting.' 'At least, Lady Popa,' replied Cola Jacopo, 'let us play at twenty figures, and I will give you mine hand.' 'Say naught and let it be as if unspoken, for that is a flatterer's game.' 'She hath spoken as a Roland,' said Thaddeus, 'as this game hath twenty and thirty figures, transforming themselves ever so well, to put a poor prince within a sack;' and continued Cola Jacopo, 'Then, O Lady Antonella, let us not lose this time, by your life; but let us play for a large platter of fritters at the excise.' 'Thou hast found me in sooth,' answered Antonella, 'that is not bad, to treat me as a mercenary woman.' 'She speaketh sooth,' said Thaddeus, 'because this enigma called woman is very often wont to make thee pay tribute.' 'The devil, when shall we come to it?' continued Cola Jacopo. 'Am I dreaming? In this way the hour will pass, and we shall have no enjoyment, unless the lady Ciulla would play with me for a measure of lupine, the game of calling.' 'Am I a constable or a bailiff?' answered Ciulla; and Thaddeus answered at once, 'She hath spoken sooth; because it is an office worthy of a bailiff and a clown to call at court.' 'Then do come, O Lady Paola,' again said Cola Jacopo, 'and let us play at three of five and piquet.' 'Thou art mistaken,' answered Paola, 'I am not a court grumbler.' 'This one is a doctoress,' answered the prince, 'because there is no place where honour is more besmeared and backbiting goes on against the notables than in our own palace.' 'Without fail,' said Cola Jacopo once more, 'the lady Ciommetella will be pleased to play with me at Carretuso Merregnao,' and Ciommetella, 'Fine game hast thou chosen for me, only fit for a schoolmaster; in sooth thou hast found thy mate.' 'She must pay forfeit,' said Cola Jacopo, 'the proposal has naught to do with the answer.' 'Go,' answered the prince, 'bid thy teacher give thee back thy money for the answer from the strong-box of Seville, because the pedagogues play so well at Carretuso that, although they lose five, they still mark the game.' But Cola Jacopo turning to the last of the ladies said, 'I cannot believe that the lady Zoza would be so unkind as, like the others, to refuse my invitation, therefore she will do me a favour as she would play with me one ducat at outstripping.' 'Look at thy leg, for that is a game for little children.' 'Now 'tis she who must pay the forfeit,' concluded Thaddeus, 'because at this game even the old men can play, and therefore, Lady Lucy, it is your duty to condemn her to the penalty you think fit to adjudge to her.' And Zoza arose and knelt before the princess, and she ordered her as penalty the song 'The Neapolitan country-maid,' and the lady Zoza sent for a tambourine, whilst the coachman to the prince played a lyre, and she sang the following song:

THE NEAPOLITAN COUNTRY-MAID

An thou dreamst that the wound was deep,
   That I am grieved and heavy-hearted,
That thy unkindness haunts my sleep,
   Daughter, thou with thy wits hast parted.

Gone is the day when Bertha spun,
   Mingling my heartstrings with her threading;
The fight against folly and love I've won,
   My amorous tears no longer shedding.

Since the young cat hath oped its eyes,
   Now that the cricket hath tuned its singing,
Thy faulty beauty no more I prize,
   And my soul from thy glamour its flight is winging.

Now that the babe from the breast is weaned
   And the plate of his choice is with surfeit laden
Whatever thy fanciful pride hath deemed,
   He yearneth no longer for thee, O maiden.

The song was ended, and all were pleased it had suited their taste, when they found that the hour of the midday meal had arrived, and tables were spread, and they sat around them, and if they found tasteful viands, they also had better beverage; but when the wants of the belly were sealed up, and the table-cloth was removed, the command was given to Zoza to uncover the rim of the stories, and although the unlucky lady had her tongue rather thick, and her ears rather small, she did her duty beginning thus:

THE GOOSE

Of the Fifth Day

LILLA AND LOLLA BUY A GOOSE AT THE MARKET, AND THE BIRD DROP-
PETH GOLDEN COINS; A NEIGBOUR BEGGETH THEM TO LEND IT TO HER,
AND FINDING THE CONTRARY, ATTEMPTETH TO SLAY IT, AND CASTS IT
OUT OF THE WINDOW. THE BIRD, NOT BEING DEAD, TAKETH HOLD OF
THE HINDPARTS OF A PRINCE WHO IS DOING A THING OF NEED TO NA-
TURE. HE CRIETH ALOUD FOR AID, BUT NONE OF THE REALM CAN PULL
HER OFF FROM HIM BUT LOLLA, FOR WHICH REASON HE TAKETH
HER TO WIFE.

TRUE was the saying of that great man of weal, that 'The
craftsman to the locksmith, the musician to the musician, the neighbour to the neighbour, the beggar to the beggar'—there is not an
hole in the great building of the world whereupon that accursed
spider called envy doth not weave his net, which feedeth on naught
else but the ruin of his neighbour: as ye particularly shall hear from
the tale that I am going to relate.

Once upon a time there lived in very reduced circumstances two
sisters, and it was as much as they could do to gain a livelihood by
spinning flax from morn till night, which they sold; but they
dragged on their wretched life, and it was impossible but that some
day the ball of necessity would touch that of honour, and send it
out; for which matter Heaven, who is so great to recompense good
deeds, and so thin and slow in punishing the evil, put into the minds
of these two poor children that they should go to the market, and
sell some skeins of thread, so that with what they received from it
they should buy a goose. The women did so, and carried the goose
home, and they loved her so well that they fed her, and let her
sleep in their own bed, as if she had been their sister. But sweep
today and look tomorrow, the good day came, and the goose began

to drop golden crowns, in such manner that one by one they filled a
large chest, and the dropping was such that the sisters began to lift
their heads, and to look well fed and happy. Such was the show of
their prosperity that the gossips began to take notice of it, and one
day meeting together, they spake thus amongst themselves, 'Hast
thou seen, O gossip Vasta, Lilla with Lolla, who but a few days
ago might have dropped down dead with hunger, but who now
have become so well-fed and well-dressed that they live in luxury
like great ladies? Hast thou seen their windows always ornamented
with fowls and barons of beef, which stare thee in the face? What
can it be? Either they have laid hands on their honour, or they
have found an hoard.' 'I am astonished and am become a mummy
with exceeding marvel,' answered Vasta, 'O gossip Pearl mine, when
they were ready to sink, I see them in parvenus' splendours, which
seem to me a dream.' They said these things and others, stimulated
by their surging envy, and they bored a hole in the wall of the house
of one of the gossips that corresponded with one of the chambers
occupied by the two damsels, so that it might enable them to espy
their doings, and to gratify their curiosity; and they played the spy
for so long that one evening, when the sun whippeth with its rays
the banks of the Indian sea to give rest to the hours of the day,
they beheld Lilla and Lolla spreading sheets upon the ground; then
they made the goose walk thereon, and as soon as she was on the
sheets, the goose began dropping crowns until the very balls of her
eyes stood out.

When morning came, and Apollo with his golden wand exor-
ciseth the shadows to withdraw, came Vasta to visit the two damsels,
and after twisting and lengthening the conversation, she came to
the point, and begged they would kindly lend her the goose for two
hours, to make a few young ducklings she had bought take affection for the house; and she begged, prayed, and besought so much,
that the simpletons, partly because they knew not how to envy, and
partly not to cause suspicion on the part of the gossips, lent the bird
to her upon the understanding that she should return her at the
time appointed. Then Vasta went home where the other gossips

were waiting for her, and they laid clean sheets upon the floor, and made the goose walk thereon, but instead of showing a mint and a coining of crowns, out of her fundament there came forth a sewer of dirt, which covered the bed-linen with a dark yellowish matter, the stink of which filled the whole house like the flavour that cometh forth from the pot of stew on the holidays. When they beheld that sight, they thought to feed her well, so that she would make the substance for the *lapis-lazuli philosophorum*, to satisfy their desire. And thus they fed her so well and so much, that she was full up to her throat, and they then placed her upon a clean sheet; but if the goose had been rather loose before, she now discovered a new dysentery, indigestion playing a part. For which reason the gossips were wroth with exceeding wrath, and twisting the neck of the goose, threw her out of the window into a narrow street with no outlet, into which ordure and filth were cast. But as fate and fortune had decreed, that where least thou thinkest the bean will grow, passed that way a son of a king, hunting and birding, and on the road he was taken by a colic, and bidding his groom hold the reins of his steed and his sword, he entered that narrow street, and completing his service, he beheld the dead goose, whereupon he used it for a very obvious purpose.

Now the goose was not dead; so, turning her head, she caught hold with her bill of the fleshy part of the prince and would not let go, and he cried with loud cries, and his suite ran to his assistance, and tried to pull off the bird from him, but it was of no avail; she held firmly at her booty like a feathery weight or an hairy hermaphrodite. And the prince, unable to resist the suffering, and beholding the fruitless efforts made by his suite, bade them lift him up, and carry him in their arms to the royal palace, where he sent for all the doctors and sages of his realm to deliver him. They tried all kinds of ointment, and made use of pinchers, and used and sprinkled powders, but to no purpose. And perceiving that the goose was like a tick, and would not let go for quicksilver, a leech that would not drop for all the vinegar used, the prince ordered a ban to be proclaimed, that whoso would deliver him from this an-

noyance at his bottom, if it should be a man, he would gift him
with half of his realm; if a woman, he would take her to wife.
And folk, having put their noses to the reward, swarmed to the
palace-gate; but the more remedies they tried, the more the goose
tightened her hold, and pinched the wretched prince's back parts,
and it seemed as if all the prescriptions of Galen had been gathered
together, and all the aphorisms of Hippocrates, and the remedies
of Mesoe against the posterior of Aristotiles, to torment that unhappy prince. But by decree of the Decreer, amid so many who
came and went to try this trial, came also Lolla, the youngest of the
two sisters, and when she beheld the goose she knew her, and cried,
'O Niofatella mine, Niofatella;' and the goose, hearing the voice
of her beloved mistress, at once left her prey, and ran to meet her,
caressing her and kissing her, well pleased to change the back parts
of a prince for the caress of a country-maid. The prince, seeing
this marvel, desired to know how it had occurred, and Lolla related
the story from beginning to end, and when she came to the trick
played on the gossips, the prince laughed till he fell backwards;
and he bade them be taken, and whipped well with switches, and
sent into exile; and thereafter amid joyance and feasting he took
Lolla to wife, with the goose that could drop so many treasures for
her dowry. And he married Lilla to a rich husband, and they
lived happily together the most mirthful in the world, in spite of
the gossips who tried to shut the road of the two sisters to the riches
which Heaven had sent them, and they opened another way so that
one should become a queen, knowing in the end that

'An impediment is often an assistance.'

THE MONTHS

Of the Fifth Day

GIANNI AND LISI ARE BROTHERS, THE ONE RICH AND THE OTHER POOR.
LISI, NEVER BEING SUCCOURED BY HIS RICH BROTHER, DEPARTETH FROM
HIS COUNTRY, AND ON HIS WAY MEETETH REAL FORTUNE, AND BECOM-
ETH IMMENSELY RICH; HIS BROTHER BEING VERY ENVIOUS SEEKETH HIS
FORTUNE IN THE SAME WAY, BUT THINGS GO WRONG WITH HIM, AND
HE SAVETH HIMSELF FROM A GREAT MISFORTUNE ONLY BY HIS BROTH-
ER'S HELP.

THE fits of laughter enjoyed by the company at the misfortune
which happened to the prince were so long and frequent that it
was needful to make them come down from their high horse, else
they would have continued their laughter till the rose bloomed.
But Cecca signed with her finger that she was ready to relate her
story, and having sequestered all mouths, she began to say thus:

It is a true phrase 'to write in silent letters'; because to be silent
never brought evil or hurt to any one. The tongues of some back-
biters can never say a good word, and they cut, and sew, and use
the scissors, and prick thee; but do thou not care for them, because
they are always in question, and at the shaking of the bags it has
been seen, and is seen now, that where a kind word gaineth love and
usefulness, speaking evil begetteth enmity and ruin: and ye will now
hear in what manner, and will give me my just due in saying that I
speak sooth.

It is said that once upon a time there lived two brothers, Gianni
who was in easy circumstances, and lived sumptuously as a lord,
and Lisi, who had not even life; but as much as the one was poor
of fortune, the other was mean of soul, and would not have risen
from the night-vase to refresh the spirit of any one. His meanness was such that it caused Lisi to leave his country in despair, and

wander about the world; and he fared on and on until one night of the nights he reached a mean-looking tavern, after a day that had been an extremely bad day, cold and wet. When he entered that tavern, he beheld twelve youths sitting around the fire, and when they saw the unhappy Lisi black and blue, and stiff with the cold, first because of the advanced cold season, and second because of the threadbare garments which he wore, they had pity on him, and they invited him to come and sit near the fire. Lisi accepted the invitation, for he stood greatly in need of it, and warmed himself at the fire, and while employed thus, one of the youths, who had an angry and sulky face, enough to cause his interlocutor to smile, addressed him thus, 'O thou my countryman, what dost thou think of the weather?' 'What should I think of it?' said Lisi. 'It seems to me that all the months of the year do their duty; but we know not what we ask, we desire to lay down the law even to the heavens, and would wish to have things to our liking. We did not fish too deeply if it is well or bad, useful or loss; and of our very caprice and instability, in winter when it raineth, we should like to have the sun in Lion, and in the month of August, heavy rains and the discharging of the clouds; we do not think that if it should be so, the seasons would go from head to backside, the need would be lost, the harvest never be gathered, our bodies sicken, and nature itself have to carry its own legs. Therefore let us be satisfied, and let Heaven run its course; it is for this that it hath provided us with trees to remedy the severity of winter by giving us wood for fuel, and to shade us from the heat in summer with the leaves.' 'Thou speakest as a Solomon,' said the youth, 'but thou canst not deny that this month of March, in which we are now, is too impertinent with so much ice, and rain, and snow, and hail, and wind, and storms, and fogs, and tempests, and continual change, that it causeth one to be weary even of life.' 'Thou speakest evilly of this poor month,' answered Lisi, 'but thou speakest not of what is good and useful that its coming bringeth: because it is March that beginneth to set forth the spring, and the generation and procreation of things, and if naught else, it is the cause that the sun proveth the felicity of the present weather, by making it enter into the house of the Ram.' The youth was very pleased with Lisi's words, because he was the month of March himself, who had arrived in company of his eleven brothers at that tavern, and desiring for his goodness to recompense Lisi, who had not spoken a word against a month so unpleasant that not even the shepherds like to name him, presented him with a fine little casket, saying, 'Take this, look for all that is needful to thee, and try also, when thou openest this casket, to keep it always before thee.' Lisi thanked the youth in submissive and grateful words, and putting the casket under his head as a pillow, lay down to sleep.

As soon as the sun with the brushes of his rays came to retouch with light the shadows of the night, he farewelled the youths and journeyed on in his wayfare, but he had not gone fifty steps from the tavern, when he opened the casket and said, 'O thou my good, could I not have a litter lined with frisa,* with a little fire within, so that I could fare in warmth amid this snow?' He had hardly ended speaking these words, when a litter stood before him with two men attending beside it, who lifted him up and laid him within. And he bade them to fare towards his home; and when the hour for the midday meal came, he opened the casket, and said, 'Let somewhat of viands appear,' and at once the best things that could be desired seemed to drop from heaven, and the banquet was such that ten crowned kings could have dined of it.

One evening they arrived at the beginning of a forest, which allowed not even the sun to enter, because he came from suspicious places; and Lisi opened the casket, and said, 'In this beautiful site, where this river playeth counter-points against the stones and pebbles on the shore to accompany the song of the cool zephyrs, I should like to rest for the night;' and at once, behold, a tent was pitched of fine scarlet under a cover of tarpaulin, with feather beds, and a Spanish blanket, and web-like bed-linen; and asking for food, at once a table was laid under another tent, covered with silver

* ' Frisa'—a kind of woollen and thread texture, used by very poor folk until the eighteenth century.

fit for a prince, and viands appeared whose flavour could be detected from the distance of an hundred miles. And when Lisi had eaten his sufficiency, he took his rest, and when the cock, the sun's spy, informed his master that the shadows had fled, being tired, and that now it was time to follow them and crush them, he opened the casket, and asked for sumptuous raiments, and said, 'I should like to have a rich robe, because to-day my brother will see me, and I should like to make him feel covetous;' and the words were hardly spoken, when he beheld before him a robe of black velvet, with ermine trimmings and yellow linings, with a long end falling from one shoulder, and Lisi apparelled himself in it, and entering the litter, after a time arrived home.

Now when Gianni beheld him come so sumptuously arrayed and at his ease, he desired to know what fortune had betided him; and Lisi related to him what had passed with the youths he met at the tavern, and of the present he had received from them, but kept silence upon the conversation they had held together. Then Gianni sighed for the moment when he could take leave of his brother, and say that he was going to rest because he was tired. And when he left his brother, he straightway wended his way towards the tavern, and reaching there, he found the twelve youths, and he began to converse with them; and that same youth putting to him the question anent the month of March, he opened his mouth and throat, and began to say, 'Oh may God confound this accursed month of March, enemy of those infected with the French disease; hateful to shepherds; troubling the good humour; and ruin to the body; a month that an thou desirest to announce to some one his ruin, thou sayest, "Wend thy ways, March hath shaved thee;" a month that an thou desirest to give any one the highest title of presumptuous, thou sayest, "What cureth March?" In brief it is a month that would make the fortune of the earth, and the happiness of the world, and the prosperity of mankind, if the place were cleared of it by the squadron of its brothers.' The month of March, hearing this very complimentary address from Gianni, spent his time pompously in the house till morning, thinking the while how to serve him out for his fine speech, and Gianni being desirous to depart, he gave him a good leave-taking, saying to him, 'Always, when thou desirest somewhat, say, "Switch, give me an hundred;" and thou shalt see union pearls threaded in a rush.' Gianni thanked the youth, and began to touch of spur, faring onwards without stay or delay, nor would he make trial of the 'Switch' until he arrived at his own house.

As soon as he laid foot upon his threshold, he went to a secret chamber, so as to be able to hide the monies which he hoped to get from the switching, and he said, 'Switch, give me an hundred,' and the switch laid it down upon his shoulders, and bade him come back for the rest, doing the part of a composer of music on the legs and face in such a manner that, at his brother's cries, Lisi ran to see what had happened, and beholding that the switching would not cease, but went on like an untethered horse, he opened his casket, and by its aid caused it to stop. Then he asked Gianni what was the matter, and what had happened to him, and Gianni related to him the whole story, and when he ended, Lisi said to him that he had no one to blame but himself, since he had been the cause of his own hurt through his cross temper: he had done like the camel that, wishing to have horns, had lost his ears; and that he should learn another time to keep a bridle on his tongue, which had been the key that opened the warehouse of this misfortune, because an he had spoken well of the youth, perhaps he would have gathered the same fortune as himself, so much more that speaking well is a merchandise that costeth nothing, and bringeth gain usually more than one thinketh of. At last he consoled him by saying that he had better not seek more ease than that which Heaven had accorded to him, that his casket sufficed to fill up to crushing thirty misers' houses, and that he would be master of all his goods, because to a liberal man Heaven is treasurer, and that if it had been another brother he would have disliked him for the cruelties he had used towards him in times gone by, when he was in misery, but on the other hand be believed that his poverty had been the cause of his riches which had sent him fair wind, and carried him into good port, and therefore he would be merciful unto him, and he felt in his soul spirit to recognise the favour. Gianni, hearing his brother's words, begged him to forgive him for his past behaviour, and together in unison they enjoyed the good fortune sent them from heaven, and from that hour Gianni spake well of all things, no matter how bad they were, because

> ' A dog scalded by hot water,
> Is ever after afraid of cold water too.'

PINTO-SMAUTO

Third Diversion

Of the Fifth Day

BERTHA REFUSETH TO TAKE A HUSBAND; AT LAST SHE KNEADETH ONE
WITH HER OWN HANDS, AND HE IS STOLEN FROM HER BY A QUEEN;
AFTER TROUBLES AND TRAVAILS SHE FINDETH HIM, AND WITH GREAT
ART WINNING HIM BACK, FARETH WITH HIM TO HER OWN HOME.

THE tale related by Cecca pleased well all hearers, and Meneca,
who was ready on her horse to begin her own story, seeing that
everybody had open ears to listen, spake as follows:

It hath always been more difficult for man to save whatso he
hath acquired than to acquire again whatso he hath lost, because in
the latter event Fortune co-operates, and she ofttimes helpeth un-
justly, whilst in the former there is need of sound judgment. It is
often seen of a person who cannot discourse at ease, that not knowing how, he will rise and mount where all good is found, but for
lack of wit to keep the position, he unfailingly slideth down: as
ye will clearly see and will learn from the story that I am going
to relate, if ye are intelligent enough to understand.

There once lived a merchant who was blessed with an only
daughter, whom he greatly desired to see settled in life; but whenever he touched the strings of the lute on the subject, he found her
a thousand miles distant in thought from his intention, because the
empty-headed damsel, like an ape, hated the tail, and like territory
sold, or preserved game, she refused to have any intercourse with
men, and wished that it was always fair-day at her tribunal, always
holiday at her school, always court-feast for her bank, so that her
sire became sorrowful and filled with disappointment.

One day of the days he must needs go to a fair, so before departing he asked his daughter Bertha, thus was she hight, what she
desired that he should bring her upon his return, and she replied,

'O my father, an thou lovest me, bring me half an hundredweight of sugar from Palermo, and half of ambrosian almonds,* with four or six bottles of scented waters, and some musk and ambergris, and some amber; and bring me also about forty pearls, two sapphires, and a few garnets and rubies, with some gold thread, and above all a kneading-trough and a silver scraper.' The sire marvelled with exceeding marvel to hear these extravagant requisitions of his daughter, but unwilling to contradict her, he fared on his journey, and on his return he punctually brought the things whereof she had commissioned him, and when she saw them, she took them, and shut herself up in a chamber. Then she began to knead a quantity of almond paste, mixed with sugar, and rose-water, and perfume; and when it was ready she shaped an handsome youth, with hair of the threads of gold, and eyes of the two sapphires, and teeth of the pearls, and lips of the rubies. She shaped him so comely and graceful that he needed only the power of speech to be perfect.

Now Bertha, having heard it said that at the prayers and supplications of a certain king of Cyprus a statue became a living being, began to beseech, and pray, and supplicate the goddess of love that her statue should be imbued with life; and so much did she pray that at last the statue began to open its eyes. When she beheld this, she redoubled her prayers and supplications, and soon the statue began to breathe, and after the breath came the word, and at last the members of the body commenced to act in their usual way, and the youth to walk. Bertha, with greater joy than if she had gained a kingdom, embraced him and kissed him, and taking him by the hand, led him before her sire, and said to him, 'O my father and my lord, thou hast always said thou wast desirous to see me wed, and I, to please thee, have kneaded myself a husband according to my heart's desire.' The father, beholding this handsome youth, whom he had not seen go in, come forth of his daughter's chamber, wondered with exceeding wonder, and perceiving so much beauty,

* 'Mandorle ambrosine' = ambrosian almonds; the best kind of almonds in Naples.

grace, and comeliness (folk might have paid a copper coin each to sight his shapely form), was pleased that the marriage feast should take place forthwith. And folk came from all the parts of the world, and amongst them was a great queen in disguise, and when she beheld the perfect beauty of Pinto-Smauto (Bertha had named him thus), she took it into her head to have him for herself. Pinto-Smauto, having only opened his eyes to the malice and craft of the world about three hours before, knew not how to trouble water. His bride having bidden him do so, he accompanied to the head of the staircase all the foreigners who had come to honour the bridal feast with their presence; and he did likewise with the queen, who, hending him by the hand, led him slowly to her carriage, drawn by six horses, which was waiting in the courtyard, wherein she drew him, and bade the coachman depart for her own realm, where Pinto-Smauto, not knowing what had happened to him, became her husband. Such was his case.

Now Bertha awaited and awaited for Pinto-Smauto until perceiving that he came not, she went to the courtyard, to see if he was talking with any one, and to the terrace-roof to see if he had gone to breathe the fresh air: she looked in the closet of ease to see if he were gone to pay the first tribute to the need of life, but not finding him, she directly imagined that some one had stolen him for his great beauty. Then she bade a proclamation be published, but no one appeared to give any news of him; and at last she decided to fare on a journey around the world to seek him. Donning a disguise as a beggar, she wended her way, and after having fared a month's wayfaring, she came to the house of a good old woman, who received her with love and kindness, and hearing of her misfortune, and seeing moreover that Bertha was with child, felt so much compassion of her, that she taught her to say these three words: the first was, 'Tricche Varlacche,* in the house is raining,' the second, 'Anola Tranola,* fritters at the fountain,' the third, 'Backsides and drums, fritters and beans, and caraway-seed.' And

* 'Tricche Varlacche' and 'Anola Tranola,' childish words without any meaning, used in children's games.

she bade her say these words whensoever her greatest need came, for she would gain somewhat of benefit. Bertha marvelled to hear of this bran present, but said in her mind, 'Whoso spitteth down thy throat desireth not to see thee dead, and whoso taketh what is given never drieth up; every atom is useful; who knoweth what good fortune may be contained in these words?' and saying thus, she thanked the ancient dame, and farewelling her, continued on her wayfare.

After faring on for a length of time, she came to a beautiful city, Monte-retunno hight, and making her way to the royal palace, sought for the love of Heaven a resting-place even in the stable, for she was nigh to be brought to bed with child. When the young damsels of the court heard this, they bade the servants give her a small chamber on the staircase, where the unhappy Bertha rested, and whilst gazing out, she beheld Pinto-Smauto pass that way, whereupon she was ready to slide down the tree of life. Finding herself in such need, she thought it was time to make trial of the first word told her by the ancient dame, and so said 'Tricche Varlacche, in the house it raineth,' and lo and behold, a small gold cart encrusted with jewels stood before her, which went round the room alone, a thing most marvellous to behold; and the young ladies saw it, and related the wondrous sight to the queen, who without loss of time hastened to Bertha's chamber, and seeing the thing, enquired if she would sell it to her, as she would give her whatever she desired. The other answered that although she was but a beggar, she liked her joyance more than all the gold in the world; and therefore, an she longed to have the cart, she must allow her to sleep one night with her husband. The queen marvelled with exceeding marvel to hear this madness of the beggar-woman who was in rags, and for a caprice would give her so much wealth; but she decreed to win this good mouthful, and thought by giving some sleeping draught to Pinto-Smauto, she would make happy the beggar-woman, and well pay herself. And when night darkened, and the stars showed themselves upon the heavens and the glow-worms upon the earth, the queen having given the draught to

Pinto-Smauto, who always did whatever he was bid, she let him go and lay by Bertha's side. But no sooner had he laid himself down upon the bed, than he fell asleep, like a dormouse, whereupon the wretched Bertha, who thought that that night would suffice to pay her for all the past anguish, perceiving that no audience was vouchsafed to her, began to weep, and wail, and lament exceedingly, reproaching him with that which she had done for him; and she never closed the grieving mouth, whilst the sleeper never opened eyes till the sun came forth, dividing the waters, and separating the shadows from the light, when the queen came down, and taking Pinto-Smauto by the hand, said to Bertha, 'Thou art already satisfied,' and went her ways.

Bertha said in her mind, 'Such happiness mayest thou have all the days of thy life, for I have passed such a bad night that I will remember it for some days.' But unable to resist the longing and anguish, the unhappy damsel tried the second word, saying, 'Anola Tranola, fritters at the fountain,' and lo and behold, a golden cage appeared, with a beautiful bird within it, singing like a nightingale, and made of gold and precious stones; and when the young damsels observed the bird, they referred it to the queen, and she hastened to see him, and asked her the question she had done for the cart, and Bertha answered the same as before, and the queen, having lighted upon and smelt the wrath which burned within her, promised to let her sleep with her husband; and taking the cage with the bird, when night came, she gave the usual draught to Pinto-Smauto, and sent him to sleep with Bertha in the same chamber, where she had laid for them a sumptuous bed. And Pinto-Smauto slept heavily like one dead, and Bertha wailed, and wept, and lamented with the same lament as hitherto she had done, saying things which would have moved a stone to compassion, and weeping, and lamenting, and buffeting her face, she passed another night full of anguish. When the day arose, the queen came down to fetch away her husband, and left the wretched Bertha cold and frozen, whilst she bit her hands for the trick which had been played upon her.

In the morning Pinto-Smauto went down to the garden to gather

some figs, and out of the city-gates he met a cobbler, whose room
was next to Bertha's, and all the live-long night he had heard her
bemoan herself, and he had not lost a single word of what she
said, and so he referred to the king the weeping and lamenting of
the unhappy beggar-woman; and the king, who was beginning to
grow wise, when he heard this, imagined how this thing might be,
and thought in himself that, an it should be vouchsafed to him to
sleep once more with the poor woman, he would not drink the potion that the queen had prepared for him. Now Bertha longed to
essay the third experiment, and therefore said the third words:
'Backsides and drums, fritters and beans, and caraway-seed.' And
behold, some napkins of silk and swathing bands, all purflewed with
gold, appeared, and a cradle of gold stood before her; which things
being seen by the young damsels, they reported it to their mistress,
who bargained to have them as she had done with the others, and
receiving the same answer from Bertha, that an she wanted them,
she must allow her husband to sleep with her, the queen said to
herself, 'I lose naught in satisfying this country-woman, and taking
from her such beautiful things.' So she accepted the rich gifts from
Bertha, and when night appeared, and settled the instrument for
the debt contracted with sleep and rest, she gave the draught to
Pinto-Smauto, but he, instead of drinking it, kept it in his mouth,
and pretending to go and empty his bladder, he spat it out in the
next chamber, and after went and laid himself down by Bertha's
side; and she began the same song as the other nights, telling him
how she had kneaded him of sugar and almonds with her own
hands, how she had made his hair of threads of gold, and his eyes
and mouth of pearls and precious stones, and how he owed the life
given to him by the gods to her prayers and supplications, and lastly
how he had been stolen from her, and how, full with child, she
had wandered through the world in search of him with much labour
and travail (may kind Heaven guard from such trial any baptised
being), and how she had slept two nights with him, and given in
exchange two treasures, yet could not get a single word out of him,
and that this was the last night of her hopes and the end of her

life. Pinto-Smauto, who was awake, hearing these words, and remembering as in a dream what had befallen him, embraced her,
and because the night had come forth in her black mask to open the
stars' ball, he arose very softly, and entering within the chamber of
the queen, who was drowned in deep slumber, he seized the gifts
she had taken from Bertha, and the jewels and monies which he
found in her lesk, to repay himself for past travail, and returning
to his wife, they departed at the self-same hour. And they never
ceased faring till they issued from the confines of that realm; and
they rested in a comfortable lodging, where Bertha brought to the
light a beauteous man-child; and when she was able to leave her
bed, she arose, and they departed, and wended their ways to the
palace of her father, where they found him in good health. And
his joy and gladness upon beholding his daughter once more were
so great that he became boisterous and cheerful as a boy fifteen
years old, and they lived happily together.

The queen found neither her husband, nor the beggar-girl, nor
the jewels; and she rent her garments, and pulled her hair, and
buffeted her face; and folk were not wanting who said,

' Whoso deceiveth must not complain if he be himself deceived!'

THE GOLDEN ROOT

FOURTH DIVERSION

Of the Fifth Day

PARMETELLA, DAUGHTER OF A POOR COUNTRYMAN, MEETETH GOOD FOR-
TUNE; BUT IN PUNISHMENT OF HER TOO GREAT CURIOSITY, IT ESCAPETH
HER HANDS. HAVING PASSED MANY DANGERS, SHE AT LENGTH FINDETH
HER HUSBAND AT THE HOUSE OF HIS MOTHER, WHO IS A GHULA, AND
WITH HIS AID AT LENGTH BECOMETH FREE OF TRAVAIL AND TROUBLE.

MORE than one in that company would have given a finger to
have the ability and power to make for themselves a husband or a
wife at will, and especially was this so with the prince, who would
then have seen by his side a sugar paste instead of a rock of poison;
but the game having come round to Tolla's turn, she waited not
for the summons to pay her debt, but spake what follows:

To be excessively curious, and to desire to know too much, is like
carrying the match in hand in order to set fire to the ammunition
of our own fortunes; and whoso seeketh to know the business of
other folk, is often deceived in his own; and most times, whoso
diggeth in some strange place in search of an hoard findeth in its
stead a common sewer, wherein he falleth on his face: as happened
to the daughter of a gardener in the manner which followeth.

In long ages gone before, there lived a gardener, who was so
exceedingly poor that, however he sweated upon his labour, he could
hardly keep himself in bread. But he had three daughters, and he
gave them three pigs so that, when the young sucklings grew, he
could sell them, and thus save the amount as a small dowry. Pas-
quzza and Cicca, who were the two elder sisters, took their young
pigs to pasture, but would not allow Parmetella, who was the
youngest, to go with them, but sending her off, bade her take her
little pig to feed elsewhere. So Parmetella carried him into a
forest, where the shadows strengthened themselves against the as-

saults of the sun, and reaching a pasture-ground, amiddlemost of
which stood a fountain of fresh water, which like the hostess of a
tavern stood inviting with a silver tongue the wanderers to drink
half a measure, she found a tree with golden leaves. Plucking one
leaf she brought it to her sire, who with great joy took it, and sold
it for twenty ducats, which served to stop some of the holes in his
home; and he enquired of her where she had found it, and she answered him 'Take it, O my father, and seek to know no more, an
thou desirest not to waste thy fortune;' and returning the next day
she did the same; and she continued plucking the leaves until the
tree was left as bare as if it had been plundered by the autumn
winds. Then she perceived that the tree had a great golden root,
which could not be drawn forth by the hand; so she wended home,
returning shortly after with an axe, and straightway began to cut
at the root of the tree; and pulling it up the best way she could, she
beheld underneath it a beautiful staircase of porphyry. So great
was Parmetella's curiosity that she descended the stairs, and came
to a very large and dark cave, at the end of which she perceived a
light, and walking straight to it, she found an opening leading into
a fine plain, amidst of which stood a splendid palace, where one trod
upon gold and silver, and looked upon naught but pearls and jewels.
And Parmetella wondered with great wonder, and marvelled with
exceeding marvel at the sight of so much splendour, and perceiving
no living being within this magnificent abode, she entered a saloon,
where were hung many pictures, whereon were painted beautiful
subjects, and particularly the ignorance of a man believed to be
wise, the injustice of him who held the scales, and the wrongs
avenged by Heaven, matters truly to cause wonder, so living they
seemed; and amid the saloon she found a table laid with things to
eat and drink.

Parmetella, who felt her bowels ring, seeing no one near, took
her seat at the table like a handsome count at a masked party; but
whilst at the best of her enjoyment, behold, a beautiful slave entered, and he said to her, 'Stay, do not go away, as I want thee for
my wife, and I shall make thee the happiest woman in the world.'

Parmetella, although she felt small with fright, hearing this fair promise, heartened her heart, and contented herself in doing whatsoever the slave desired, and suddenly a diamond carriage was presented to her drawn by four golden horses, with wings of emeralds and rubies, which carried her high in air so that she might enjoy herself; and to attend upon her and do her service were appointed a number of apes clad in cloth-of-gold, and they forthwith changed her from head to foot and arrayed her as a spider in his web, so that she looked indeed as a queen.

When night darkened, when the sun, desirous to sleep on the banks of the Indian rivers without gnats infesting him, put out the light, the slave said, 'O my love, an thou art willing to sleep, lay thee down upon this bed; but when thou art well wrapped up in the bed-linen, put out the light, and be careful to do what I bid thee do, an thou desirest not to be deceived in thy spinning.' And Parmetella did as he bade her, and falling asleep, when no sooner had her eyes begun to feel heavy, than the black slave became a handsome youth, and he laid himself down by her side, and she awaking, and feeling that her wool was carded without being combed, nearly died with affright, but seeing that the matter was reduced to civil war, stood firm at the blows. But the next morning, ere the dawn came forth to seek some new-laid eggs to comfort her old lover, the slave jumped out of bed, and returned in his own dark form, leaving Parmetella curious to know which glutton had sucked up the first new-laid egg of so beauteous a chicken. And again the following night, when she lay down to rest and put out the light, behold, as in the night before, the youth came and lay with her, and when he was tired of playing at that game, he fell asleep. But no sooner had he shut his eyes, than she took up a gun which she had put near the bed, and applying the tinder, lighted a candle, and raising the coverlet, she beheld ebony changed to ivory, caviare into milk, and coals into cream and virgin lime. And whilst she stood open-mouthed, gazing at and contemplating this beautiful pencilstroke, the best ever given by nature upon this canvas of the marvellous, the youth awoke, and began to curse and swear, and he turned to her, and said, 'Alas, Parmetella, through thy curiosity I shall be obliged to stay another seven years in this accursed chastisement: thou wouldst put thy nose within my secrets, but now begone, break thy neck an thou wilt, and never mayest thou come before me, return to thy ragged shirts, as thou hast known thy fortune.' So speaking, he disappeared like quicksilver.

The unhappy damsel remained awhile stiff and frozen with affright; and bowing her head groundwards, went forth from the palace, and when she came outside the cave, she met a fairy, who said to her, 'O my daughter, my soul weepeth for thee, and for the misfortune which hath befallen thee; thou art faring to the slaughter-house, where thou wilt pass thy wretched person upon a hair-breadth bridge; therefore do thou remedy to this thy peril, and take these seven spindles, and these seven figs, this small juglet of honey, and these seven pairs of iron shoes, and wend thy way, and never cease thy wending until these shoes are worn out, and then thou shalt perceive seven women on a terrace-roof spinning with a spindle formed of a dagger and the bones of dead folk, and the thread is wound round the bones; and knowest thou what to do? Hide thyself most carefully, and when the thread cometh down, do thou draw off the bone, and put in its stead a fig, anointing the spindle with honey; because when they will draw it up, and taste the sweet, they will say, "Who hath sweetened my small mouth, may her small chance of fortune be sweetened;" and after these words, one after the other will say, "O thou who hast brought me these sweet things, let me see thee;" and thou shalt answer, "I will not, because thou wilt eat me;" and they will answer, "I will not eat thee, an God take care of my spoon;" and do thou stand firm on thy feet, and be stubborn; and they will continue, "I will not eat thee, an God watch over my spit;" and be thou firm and budge not; and they will reply, "I will not eat thee, an God watch over my broom;" and do thou believe them not at all; and if they say, "I will not eat thee, an the heavens watch upon my night-vase," do thou shut thy mouth, and let not issue forth from it a single sound, otherwise they will cause thee to leave thy life. At last they will

say, "An God guard me from thunder and lightning, I will not
eat thee:" then thou mayest go up, for they will not harm thee.'
Parmetella, hearing this, thanked and farewelled the fairy, and
fared on through wilds and wolds, mountains and plains, until
after seven years' journeying her iron shoes were worn out. And
she reached a big house with a terrace upon its roof, and there she
beheld the seven women spinning. So she did whatso the fairy had
advised her to do, and after a thousand games, and signs, and
raillery, they swore by thunder and lightning, whereupon she showed
herself, and then went up to them, where the seven said to her,
'O thou traitress, thou art the cause that our brother hath been imprisoned in that dark grotto for seven years in the shape of a blackamoor slave, but never mind, an thou hast known how to stop our
just revenge with the oath we have taken, with the first opportunity
thou wilt discount the new and the old fault. Now thou must do
as we bid thee: go and hide thyself behind that kneading-trough,
and when our mother, who would eat thee without fail an she saw
thee, cometh home, arise and come forth, and get hold firmly of
her breasts, which she carrieth like saddle-bags, thrown over her
shoulders, and pull as hard as thou canst, and let not go thy hold
until she sweareth the oath by thunder and lightning not to harm
thee.'

And Parmetella did their bidding, and the ghula swore by the fire-
shovel, by the small vine, by the pegasus, by the reel, by the rack,
and at last swore by the thunder and lightning, whereupon Parmetella let go the breasts, and showed herself to the ghula, who said,
'Alas, thou deservest a kick and straight gibbet, thou traitress: with
the first rain I will make thee carry the wash.' And the ghula
sought with a toothpick every chance to devour Parmetella, and one
day she took twelve sacks of pulse, as peas, beans, and other kinds,
and said to her, 'Traitress, take thou this pulse, and choose and pick
it, so that each sort be separate from the other: and if this evening
the picking be not finished, I shall swallow thee like three coppers'
worth of fritters.' The unhappy Parmetella seated herself near
the sacks, and said, weeping, 'O my beauteous mother, when the

golden stump shall fall upon me, that will be the time when the disputes shall cease, and my weeping; to behold a black face return to
white, this wretched heart hath become a thing of naught. Alas!
woe is me, I am lost, I am dispatched, I am going, there is no more
remedy for me; every moment I expect to fill the guts of the ghula;
there is no one to help me, there is no one to advise me, there is no
one to console me.'

Now whilst Parmetella was thus lamenting and weeping, behold
Thunder-and-Lightning appeared (thus was the ghula's son hight),
for the time of his exile had ended and the curse which had been
cast upon him had ceased. Although he was angry with Parmetella,
yet still his blood could not turn into water, and seeing her weeping
and wailing, he said to her, 'O thou traitress, what causeth thee to
weep?' Then she related to him all which had befallen her with
his mother, and how his mother meant to eat her; to which he answered, 'Arise, and hearten thine heart, as never shall what she saith
take place.' And scattering the pulse upon the ground, he made a
deluge of ants come forth, and they at once began to carry the pulse
away to separate heaps, so that Parmetella had no difficulty in gathering them up, and putting them in their separate sacks. When
the ghula came, and found the service done, she was in despair, and
said, "That dog of Thunder-and-Lightning hath played me this
trick; but thou shalt pay for it; take this fustian, it is for twelve
mattresses, and let them be filled with feathers by this evening,
otherwise I will do quick work of thee.' The unhappy damsel,
taking the stuff, and seating herself upon the ground, began to
weep, and wail, and buffet her face, making two fountains of her
eyes, when Thunder-and-Lightning appeared, and said, 'Weep not,
thou traitress, leave it to me, I will send thee safely in port: therefore scatter thine hair about thy face, and lay thou the mattresses
on the ground, and cry with loud cries, and weep, and lament, and
say, "The king of the birds is dead;" and thou shalt see what will
occur.' And Parmetella did as she was told, and behold, a cloud
of birds darkened the air, and beating their wings, they shook off

their feathers by basketfuls, so that by the end of an hour the mattresses were filled.

When the ghula came, and saw what had fortuned, she was wroth with exceeding wrath, and said in herself, 'Thunder-and-Lightning hath taken to do me mischief, but may I be dragged tied to the tail of a monkey, if I do not catch her at somewhat amiss, whence she will be unable to escape.' So, turning to Parmetella, she said, 'Haste thou, and run to the house of my sister, and bid her send me instruments of music, because I have given Thunder-and-Lightning in marriage, and we will hold a bridal festival fit for a king.' On the other side she sent word to her sister that the traitress was coming to fetch the instruments, and to bid her, when she came, to slay her, and cook her, and she would come and partake of the feast. Parmetella, hearing that lighter services were commanded of her, felt more cheerful, believing that time had sweetened her bitterness. O how crooked are human judgments! On the way she was met by Thunder-and-Lightning, who, seeing her go at a sharp pace, said to her, 'Where art thou going, O thou unhappy one? Dost thou not see that thou art going to the slaughter-house, and art building the gibbet for thyself, and art sharpening the knife? that thou art mixing the poisonous potion for thyself? that thou art sent by the ghula to be slain and eaten? But hearken to me, and doubt not; take thou this small loaf, and this bundle of hay, and this stone, and when thou shalt come to the house of my aunt, thou shalt find a dog, which will come barking to meet thee, and to bite thee, and do thou cast this small loaf at him, thus thou wilt shut his mouth; after passing the dog, thou shalt find a horse loose, which will come up to thee to kick thee, and to crush thee under foot, but do thou give him some fodder, so that it will stop his feet. At last thou shalt come to a door, which is banging continually, and do thou prop it with this stone, so that thou wilt ease its fury; then mount thou up above, and thou shalt find the ghula with a child in her arms. And she hath heated the oven ready to roast thee in it, and she will say to thee, "Hold this child; and await until I go up above to get the instruments of music;" but know thou that she goeth only to sharpen her tusks to pluck thee to pieces, and do thou cast the child, without any pity, within the oven, because it is ghula's flesh; take the instruments which are behind the door, and slide before the ghula cometh back: otherwise thou art lost. But beware, an thou wishest not to have any trouble, not to open the box containing the sounds.'

Parmetella did as her lover bade her, but as she was coming back with the music, she opened the box, and behold the things all flew out and about, here a flute and there a bagpipe, here a reed and there a spoon, and they made a thousand different noises in the air; whilst Parmetella ran after them, crying with loud cries, and buffeting her face.

Meanwhile the ghula came forth, and not finding Parmetella, looked out of the window, and called out to the door, 'Crush thou this traitress,' and the door answered, 'I will not harm that unfortunate who hath propped me up.' Then cried the ghula to the horse, 'Trample thou down this rogue;' and the horse replied, 'I will not trample upon her, because she gave me some fodder to munch.' Lastly the ghula called to the dog saying, 'Bite thou this coward,' and the dog answered, 'Let the poor thing go in peace, for she hath given me a little loaf.'

Now Parmetella, who meanwhile was crying aloud, and hastening after the instruments of music, was met in the way by Thunder-and-Lightning, who gave her a good scolding, saying, 'O thou traitress, wilt thou never learn, even at thine own expense? Knowest thou not that for this accursed curiosity of thine thou art in the strait in which thou findest thyself?' And having thus spoken, he called back the instruments of music, and they came, and he shut them up again, bidding Parmetella to carry the box to his mother. But when the ghula saw her, she cried aloud, saying, 'O thou cruel fate and fortune, even my own sister worketh against me, and refuseth to give me this satisfaction.'

In the meanwhile the young lady who had been destined as a bride for Thunder-and-Lightning arrived; and she was as hideous as a pestilence, a glandule in the flesh, an harpy, an evil spirit, a gibbet, an owl, a rotten cask, a consumption; and she was decked with a thousand flowers and sprays, which made her look like a newly opened tavern. Then the ghula prepared a sumptuous banquet; and because she smothered her ill-feeling under the mask of pleasantness, she bade them lay the table near a well, where she set her seven daughters, each hending a torch in hand, but she bade Parmetella hold two torches, and made her sit on the edge of the well, with the design that when she fell asleep she might tumble to the bottom.

Now whilst the viands came and went, and wine was drunk, and their blood began to feel heated, Thunder-and-Lightning, who was sitting between the bride (may evil befall her) and Parmetella, said to the latter, 'O traitress, lovest thou me?' and she replied, 'I love thee up to the terrace-roof;' and he rejoined 'An thou love me, give me a kiss;' and she, 'God forfend it, avaunt from me, keep thy sweet goods for whoso singeth after thee; may Heaven maintain her for thee for another hundred years, with health and men-children.' Then answered the new bride, 'An I even lived for an hundred years, I would always think of thee as a most wretched being, for refusing to kiss such an handsome youth; whilst I for two chestnuts allowed a shepherd to kiss me, pinching my cheeks.' At these words in proof of the prowess of the bride, the bridegroom swelled with rage like a toad, and the viands stuck in his throat; but with all he heartened his heart, and swallowed this pill, thinking in his mind that he would square up accounts afterwards, and settle the reckoning. But when the tables were cleared, he bade his mother and sisters go, and leave him with the bride and Parmetella, to wend to their rest; and he bade Parmetella pull off his boots, and whilst she was thus employed, he said to the bride, 'O my wife, hast thou seen how this lump of filthiness hath denied me a kiss?' and the bride answered, 'She was wrong, to draw back and not kiss thee, thou being an handsome youth; whilst I for two chestnuts allowed a shepherd to kiss me.'

Thunder-and-Lightning could not contain himself any longer, but with the lightning of disdain, and the thunder of deeds, and the mustard mounting to his nose, he caught up a knife, and cut the bride's throat, and digging a pit in the cellar, buried her there; and embracing Parmetella, he said to her, 'Thou art my joy, thou art the flower of womankind, the very ass of honour, and therefore turn thou those eyes to me, and give me thine hand, and uphold thy mouth, and let thine heart be near to mine, and I will be thine whilst the world is world;' and so saying, he led her to the bed, and both lay together, and played and joyed together till the sun led forth from the stables of water the horses of fire, and chased them forth to pasture in the fields sown by the dawn. When the ghula came in the morning with new-laid eggs to comfort the bride and bridegroom, so that she might say, blessed is he who gets tied with the marriage knot and goeth in bondage, she found Parmetella in the arms of her son, and hearing how the matter had ended, left them, and hastened to the house of her sister to concoct a plan, and devise a device, by which she could rid herself of this chip in her eyes, her son being unable to help her. But she found on her arrival there, that her sister, full of grief at the sight of her child baked in the oven, had cast herself herein and been baked; and the stink of the burnt flesh infected the neighbourhood, and the ghula, when she beheld this fearful scene, was distracted, and she wailed, and wept, and lamented, and so great was her despair that, ghula as she was, she became a ram, and ran around the house hitting her head against the walls until her brains were scattered about; and thus Thunder-and-Lightning lived with Parmetella, and made her and his sisters happy and contented, and they all lived peacefully together in joyance and delight, finding the truth of the saying that

'Whoso is firm of purpose ever winneth.'

SUN, MOON, AND TALIA

FIFTH DIVERSION

Of the Fifth Day

TALIA, THROUGH A CHIP OF FLAX, IS LEFT BY HER SIRE IN A PALACE,
WHERE A KING FINDETH HER, AND HAS BY HER TWO CHILDREN; HIS
WIFE, BEING JEALOUS OF HIM, GETTETH THEM IN HER POWER, AND
COMMANDETH THAT THE CHILDREN BE SLAIN, AND COOKED, AND GIVEN
AS FOOD TO THEIR SIRE, AND TALIA BE BURNT; THE COOK SAVETH THE
CHILDREN, AND TALIA IS RESCUED BY THE KING, WHO BIDDETH HIS
WIFE BE CAST IN THE SAME FIRE WHICH SHE HAD PREPARED FOR TALIA.

THE fate of the ghula, instead of causing an atom of compassion,
only excited pleasure, and every one rejoiced that affairs had fallen
out with Parmetella better than was expected. As it was now the
turn of Popa to reason and relate a story, she, who was ready with
her foot upon the stirrup, spake thus:

It is a matter known by experience that cruelty becometh the
hangman of him that exerciseth it; and whoso spitteth up to heaven,
upon his own face the spittle falleth. And the reverse of the medal
is that innocence is like a sprout of the fig-tree, easily broken; and
where the point of the sword of malignity remaineth in such a way
and manner that a poor man believeth himself dead and buried,
behold, he riseth again in his own flesh and bones: as ye will hear
in the story that I, from the cask of my memory, and with the
point of my tongue, will pierce and spin.

There once lived a great lord, who was blessed with the birth of
a daughter, whom he named Talia, and he sent for the sages and
astrologers in his estates, to foretell him what lot and fortune would
befall her; and they met, and counselled together, and cast the
horoscope over her, and at length they came to the conclusion that
she would incur great danger from a chip of flax. Her father
therefore forbade that any flax, or hemp, or any other matter of the

kind should be brought within his house, so that she should escape the predestined danger.

One day of the days, when Talia had grown into a young and beauteous damsel, she was looking out of a window, when she beheld passing that way an ancient dame, who was spinning, and Talia, never having seen a distaff or a spindle, was pleased to see the twistings of the spindle, and she felt so much curiosity as to what thing it was, that she bade the old dame come to her, and taking the distaff from her hand, she began to stretch the flax. Unfortunately one of the chips of the flax entered her nail, and Talia fell dead upon the ground. When the affrighted old woman beheld this, she hastened down the stairs, and is hastening still.

As soon as the wretched father heard of the disaster which had taken place, he bade them, after having paid for this tub full of sour wine with casks full of tears, lay her out in the palace (it was one of his country mansions), and put her seated on a velvet throne under a dais of brocade; and closing the doors, being desirous to forget all and to drive from his memory his great misfortune, he abandoned for ever the house wherein he had suffered so great a loss. Such was his case.

After a time, a king went forth to the chase, and by decree of the Decreer he passed that way, and one of his falcons, escaping from his hand, flew within that house by way of one of the windows, and not returning at the call, the king bade one of his suite knock at the door, believing the palace to be inhabited; but though he knocked for a length of time, nobody came to answer the summons, so the king bade them bring a vintager's ladder, for he himself would clamber up and search the house, to discover what was within it. Thereupon he mounted and entered, and sought in all the chambers, and nooks, and corners, and marvelled with exceeding marvel to find no living person within it. At last he came to the saloon, and when the king beheld Talia, who seemed as one ensorcelled, he believed that she slept, and he called her, but she remained insensible, and crying aloud, he felt his blood course hotly through his veins in contemplation of so many charms; and he lifted her in his arms, and carried her to a bed, whereon he gathered the first fruits of love, and leaving her upon the bed, returned to his own kingdom, where, in the pressing business of his realm, he for a time thought no more of this incident. Now Talia was delivered after nine months of a couple of beautiful creatures, one a boy and the other a girl; in them could be seen two rare jewels; and they were attended by two fairies, who came to that palace, and put them at their mother's breasts; and once they sought the nipple, and not finding it, they began to suck at the fingers, and they sucked so much that the chip of the flax came forth; and Talia awoke as if from a long sleep, and beholding beside her the two priceless gems, she held them to her breast, and gave them the nipple to suck, and the babes were dearer to her than her own life. Finding herself alone in that palace with two children by her side, she knew not what had happened to her; but she noticed that the table was laid, and refreshments and viands brought in to her, without seeing any attendants.

In the meanwhile the king remembered Talia, and saying that he would go a-birding and a-hunting, he fared to the palace, and found her awake, and with two cupids of beauty, and he was glad with exceeding gladness, and he related to Talia who he was, and how he had seen her, and what had taken place; and when she heard this, their friendship was knitted with tighter bonds, and he remained with her for a few days. After that time he bade her farewell, and promised to return soon, and take her with him to his kingdom. And he fared to his realm, but he could not find any rest, and at all hours he had in his mouth the names of Talia, and of Sun and Moon (thus were the two children hight), and when he took his rest, he called either one or other of them. Now the king's wife began to suspect that something was wrong from the delay of her husband in the chase, and hearing him name continually Talia, Sun, and Moon, she waxed hot with another kind of heat than the sun's and therefore sending for the secretary, she said to him, 'Hearken to me, O my son, thou art abiding between two rocks, between the post and the door, between the poker and the grate. An thou wilt tell me with whom the king thy master, and my husband, is in love, I will gift thee and largesse thee with treasures untold; and an thou hidest from me the truth, I will not let them find thee neither dead nor alive.' Our gossip was frightened with sore affright, and his greed of gain being strong above fear, blinding his eyes to all honour, and to all sense of justice, a pointless sword of faith, he related to her all things, like bread and bread, and wine and wine. And the queen, hearing how matters stood, despatched the secretary to Talia, in the name of the king, bidding her send the children, for he wished to see them; and Talia with great joy did as she was commanded. Then the queen (that heart of Medea) told the cook to slay them, and prepare several tasteful dishes for her wretched husband; but the cook, who was tender-hearted, seeing these two beautiful golden apples, felt pity and compassion of them, and he carried them home to his wife, and bade her hide them; and he made ready two lambs in their stead in a thousand different ways, and when the king came, the queen, with great pleasure, bade the viands be served up, and whilst the king ate with delight, saying, 'O how good is this priest of Lanfusa, O how tasteful is this other dish, by the soul of mine ancestors;' she ever replied, 'Eat, eat, that of thine own thou eatest.' The king heeded not for twice or three times this repetition; but at last seeing that the music continued, answered, 'I know perfectly well that I am eating of mine own, because thou hast brought nought into this house;' and waxing wroth with exceeding wrath, he arose and went forth to a villa at some distance of his palace, to solace his soul and alleviate his anger.

In the meanwhile the queen, not being satisfied of the evil already done, sent for the secretary and bade him fare to the palace and bring Talia thither, saying that the king longed for her presence and was expecting her. As soon as she heard these words, Talia forthwith departed, believing that she obeyed the commands of her lord, for she longed with excessive longing to behold her light and joy, knowing not what was preparing for her. And she arrived in the presence of the queen, whose face changed by the

fierce fire which burned within, and looked like the face of Nero;
and she addressed her thus, saying, 'Well come, and fair welcome,
O thou Madam Rattle, thou art a fine piece of goods, thou ill weed,
who art enjoying my husband; is it thou who art the lump of
filth, the cruel bitch, that hath caused me such a turning of head?
Wend thy ways, for sooth thou art welcome in purgatory, where
I will compensate thee for all the damage thou hast done to me.'
Talia, hearing these words, began to excuse herself, saying that it
was not her fault, because the king her husband had taken possession of her territory when she was drowned in sleep; but the queen
would not listen to her excuses, and bade a large fire to be lit in the
courtyard of the palace, and commanded that Talia should be cast
therein. The damsel, perceiving that matters had taken a bad turn,
knelt before the queen, and besought her to allow her at least to
doff the garments she wore. And the queen, not for pity of the
unhappy damsel, but to gain also those robes, which were purflewed
with gold and pearls, bade her undress, saying, 'Thou canst doff thy
raiment, I am satisfied;' and Talia began to take them off, and at
every piece of garment she drew off she uttered a loud scream, and
having doffed the robe, the skirt, the body, and the under-bodice,
she was on the point of withdrawing her last garment, when she
uttered a last scream louder than the rest; and they dragged her
towards the pile, to make cinders of her to warm Carontes' breeches;
but the king suddenly appeared, and finding this spectacle, wished
to know the matter, and asking for his children, heard that the wife
who reproached him for his treachery had caused them to be
slaughtered and served as meat for him. Now when the wretched
king heard this, he gave himself up to despair, and said 'Alas! then
I, myself, am the wolf of my own sweet lambs; alas! and why
did these my veins know not the fountains of their own blood; ah,
thou renegade bitch, what evil deed is this which thou hast done?
Begone, thou shalt get thy desert as the stumps and I will not send
that tyrant-faced one to the Coliseum to do her penance;' and thus
saying, he commanded that the queen should be cast into the fire
which she had prepared for Talia, and the secretary with her, be-

cause he had been the handle for this bitter play, and weaver of
this wicked plot, and he was going to do the same with the cook,
whom he believed to be the slaughterer of his children, when the
man cast himself at his feet, saying, 'In very sooth, O my lord, for
the service I have done to thee, there should be naught else than a
pile of living fire, and no other help than a pole from behind, and
no other entertainment than stretching and shrinking within the
blazing fire would be needful, and no other advantages should I
seek than to have my ashes, the ashes of a cook, mixed up with the
queen's. But this is not the reward that I expect for having saved
thy children, in spite of the gall of that bitch, who desired to slay
them, to return within thy body that part which was thine own
body.' The king hearing these words, his senses forsook him, and
his wits were bewildered, and he seemed to be dreaming, and he
could not believe what his own ears had heard; therefore turning
to the cook, he said, 'If it be true that thou hast saved my children,
be sure that I will take thee away from turning the spit, and I will
put thee in the kitchen of this breast, to turn and twist as thou
likest all my desires, giving thee such a reward as shall enable thee
to call thyself a happy man in this world.' Whilst the king spake
these words, the wife of the cook, seeing her husband's need,
brought forth the two children, Sun and Moon, before their sire.
And he never tired at playing the game of three with his wife and
children, making a mill-wheel of kisses, now with one and then
with other; and giving a rich gift and largesse to the cook, he made
him a gentleman of his chamber, and took Talia to wife; and she
enjoyed a long life with her husband and her children, thus knowing
full well that at all times

> ' He whom fortune favoureth
> Even in sleep good raineth for him.'

THE WISE WOMAN

Of the Fifth Day

SAPIA, DAUGHTER OF A BARONESS, TEACHETH CENZULLO, THE SON OF A
KING, WHO WILL NOT UNDERSTAND OR KEEP IN MIND THE ALPHABETICAL
LETTERS, TO BE PRUDENT; BUT RECEIVING A BUFFET FROM HER AND WILL-
ING TO BE REVENGED, HE TAKETH HER TO WIFE, AND AFTER A THOU-
SAND OUTRAGES, SHE HAVING PRESENTED HIM, WITHOUT HIS KNOWLEDGE,
WITH THREE CHILDREN, THEY BECOME RECONCILED AND UNITED.

THE prince and princess were pleased that Talia, despite her
travails, came to a good ending, for they hardly thought that amid
all this storm she would come safe into good port; but bidding
Antonella to do her duty, and uncover her story from its hidden
depths, she put forth her speech thus:

Three kinds of ignoramuses are to be found in this world, who
deserve, more than any others, to be put in an oven: the first, whoso
knoweth naught; the second, whoso is unwilling to know aught;
and the third, whoso pretendeth to know all. Of the second species
is he of whom I am going to speak to you: for, unwilling to allow
any knowledge to enter his head, he hateth whoso trieth to teach
him, and like a new Nero seeketh to withdraw the means of getting
bread.

There once lived a king of Castiello-chiuso, and he had an only
son, who was a blockhead, nor could he in any way be made to
learn the A.B.C., for if anybody spake of letters or of learning, he
became wild, and acted madly, and neither blows, nor words, nor
threatening had any effect upon him. Now the unhappy father
had swollen like a toad with rage, nor knew how to wake up the
wit of this son of his so as not to leave his kingdom in the hands of
a mameluke, fearing it to be an impossible thing that ignorance and
dominion could go together. At this time there was a daughter of

the Baroness Cenza who, for the knowledge which she had gained, at thirteen years of age had acquired for herself the name of Sapia, or the wise woman; and her good qualities having been reported to the king, he bethought himself to send his son to the baroness, so that she should bring him up with her daughter, believing that with the company and example of the damsel the prince might learn to do some good. Therefore he sent him to the palace of the baroness. Arriving there, Sapia began to teach him first the sign of the cross; but perceiving that he was casting behind him kind treatment and kind words, and that good rede entered one ear and came forth from the other, she one day lifted her hand and dealt him a buffet, whereupon Carluccio (thus was the prince hight) felt hurt and slighted, and what he had not done for kindness he did for shame and despite, so that in a few months he had learned to read; more-over, he soon passed the grammar, and knew all the rules, so that his sire was pleased indeed, and taking Carluccio away from the house of the baroness, sent him to study other things. In time he became one of the wisest men in his kingdom; but the blow he received from Sapia was so much impressed in his mind that it stood ever before him, and when asleep he dreamt of it, and he resolved to avenge himself or die.

In the meanwhile Sapia had reached a marriageable age, and the prince, who stood ready, match in hand, to set fire to the mine, took advantage of the occasion to be revenged, and said to his sire, 'O my lord, I confess that I have received my being from you, and therefore, I am under very deep obligation to you; but to Sapia, from whom I have received my well-being and my ability, I feel more than obliged; and therefore finding no way sufficient to repay her the debt, an it please you, I would take her to wife, assuring you that you would put a careful guardian over my person.' The king, hearing this decision, answered, 'O my son, although Sapia is not of a position equal to thine own, yet with her virtue set in the balance of our blood, it falleth down so much, that she can be well fit for this marriage; therefore, if thou art content, I am pleased and repaid.' Thereupon, sending for the baroness, the

marriage settlements were drawn out, and a marriage-feast spread
as befitted a great lord.   Then the prince asked the king to grant
him the boon that he might have a separate apartment, where he
might dwell alone with his wife.   The king, to please him, bade
a beautiful palace be prepared, separated from his own, wherein
the prince led Sapia.   And he shut her in a chamber, and gave her
little to eat, and worst to live upon, doing the while whatsoever he
could to annoy her, so much so that the unhappy lady became the
most desperate woman in the world, not knowing the cause of this
bad treatment which was meted out to her as soon as she entered
that house.   One day a longing seized her lord to behold Sapia, so
he entered her chamber, and enquired how she was.   'Pass thine
hand upon my stomach,' answered Sapia 'and thou shalt see how I
can stay so; what have I done to thee, and why dost thou treat me
worse than a dog?   Why didst thou ask me to be thy wife, if it
was thy desire to treat me like a slave?'   At these words the prince
answered, 'Dost thou not know that whoso doeth an offence writeth
it in sand, but whoso receiveth it writeth it on marble?   Remember
well what thou didst to me when thou wast wont to teach me reading, and know that I have taken thee to wife for no other reason
but that thy life may be ever a sauce of revenge for the injury thou
didst to me.'   'Then,' replied Sapia, 'I gather evil because I have
sown good.   If I gave thee a blow, it was because thou wast an ass,
and to make thee become wise.   Thou knowest that whoso loveth
thee maketh thee weep, and whoso hateth thee maketh thee laugh.'
If the prince was wroth before because of the blow received, he
was now still more angry because he was reproached with his own
ignorance; and so much the more, since he thought that Sapia
should give herself the blame for the error; instead he saw that
she, brave as a game-cock, replied to each of his peckings, and therefore turning his back upon her, he went his ways, leaving her in a
worse plight than before.   Returning a few days after, and finding
her in the same mood, he again went forth from her more ill-
pleased than at the last time, resolving in his mind to let her cook
in her own water like a many-feet.

In the meanwhile the king had renounced the goods of this life upon the column of a martyr's bed, and the prince was left lord and master of the realm, and he desired to go in person to take possession, and commanding a suite of knights, and noblemen, and soldiers to be got ready to accompany him, worthy of his person, he departed with them. Hereupon the baroness, who knowing the hard life led by her daughter, and wishful to remedy the evil, commanded a cave to be built beneath the palace of the prince, and passing through it, she was thus able to bring some refreshment to her daughter. And knowing of the king's intended journey, a few days before he departed she ordered some new carriages and sumptuous liveries, and arraying her daughter in rich garments, and sending with her a company of lords and ladies, bade her depart by a short cut, so that she should arrive one day before at the place where her husband was going; and she engaged the palace vis-à-vis the one where the prince would dwell. And Sapia, arrayed in fine array, stood at the window, and when the king arrived, and beheld this flower out of the pot of the graces, he fell in love with her at first sight, and did all things in his hand to obtain possession of her, and he enjoyed her, and left her with child, and gave her a necklace to wear in remembrance of his love. Then the king having departed to fare to other cities of his kingdom, she went back to her own home, and at the end of nine months brought forth into the world a son. And the king returned to the capital of his kingdom, and hoping to find Sapia dead, came to see her, but he found her more fresh and beautiful than before, and more obstinate than she had ever been, and she again told him that it was to make him wise, when he was an ass, that she had signed five fingers on his face. The king, in high disdain and wrath, departed, and intending to visit another part of his estates, bade his suite accompany him; and Sapia advised by her mother, did as she had done the first time, and once more she enjoyed her husband, who gifted her with a rare gem to wear on her head; and she conceived of him, and when the time of bearing was come, she gave birth to another son, and returned to her own home. And the same matter occurred a third time, and the king gifted her with a thick gold chain, set with precious jewels; and she conceived and bare him a daughter, who came into port in due time: and the king returned from his journey, and heard that (the baroness having administered a sleeping draught to her daughter, and having given out that she was dead) they were going to bury his wife; and after she was duly buried, her mother had her brought forth from the grave, and hid her in her own palace. Then the king after a short time held a festival, and treated for a new marriage with a great lady, and she came to the palace, and many feasts and entertainments took place, and at one of these banquets appeared Sapia in the saloon, with the three children, who were three jewels, and casting herself at the king's feet, she begged him to do her justice and not rob these children of their rightful position, as they were of his own flesh and blood; and the king was struck dumb with amazement, and was like a man in a dream. At last, seeing that Sapia's knowledge was great and reached unto the stars, and beholding before him three beauteous props for his old age, he softened his heart; and giving that great lady in marriage to his brother, and presenting them with a large estate, he took Sapia to his breast, letting the folk of the world know that

'A wise man ruleth the stars.'

THE FIVE SONS

Of the Fifth Day

PACIONE SENDETH FORTH FIVE OF HIS SONS INTO THE WORLD TO LEARN
A CRAFT, AND EACH RETURNETH WITH SOME EXPERIENCE; THEY GO TO
SAVE THE DAUGHTER OF A KING STOLEN BY A GHUL, AND RETURNING
WITH HER, DISPUTE AS TO WHO DID THE GREATEST DEED OF PROWESS
SO AS TO BE WORTHY OF HER AND MAKE HER HIS WIFE; BUT THE KING
GIVETH HER TO THE FATHER, AS THE PARENT STEM OF ALL THESE
BRANCHES.

As soon as the story of Antonella was ended, Ciulla, sitting erect
upon her chair, and glancing around to see that all listened with
attention, with graceful mien spake thus:

Whoso sitteth upon ashes possesseth a stupid and forgetful mind;
whoso walketh not seeth not, and whoso seeth not knoweth not;
whoso wandereth through the world becometh expert; and practice
maketh the skilful doctor; and the faring forth of his own hayloft
maketh man brisk: as I will explain to you in the tale which followeth.

There once lived a man of weal, Pacione hight, who had five
good-for-nothing sons, and the poor father, unable any longer to
expend with gain, resolved one day to get rid of them, saying, 'My
sons, God knoweth if I love ye; for at the best ye have come forth
from my loins; but if I am old, and work little, ye are young and
eat much, and I cannot maintain ye any longer as I have before;
every man for himself, and Heaven for all; therefore go ye to
gain yourselves masters, and learn some craft or service; but be
careful not to make any agreement for more than a year and when
the time is ended, I shall expect you at home knowing some craft
or virtue.' The sons, hearing this resolution, farewelled him, and
taking with them only a change of clothes, each went his way. At
the end of the year, they met at their father's house, where they

431

were received with caresses, and as they were tired and hungry, the table was laid, and they sat down. When they were at the best of their eating, they heard a bird singing, and the youngest of the five sons arose and went forth a-birding; and when he returned, cloth had been removed; and Pacione began to ask of his sons, 'Now do ye gladden my heart, and let me know what fine virtues ye have learnt in this time.' Luccio the eldest replied, 'I have learnt the craft of a rogue, where I became the chief of rogues, and the head-master of thieves, and the fourth in the art of marauding, and thou wilt not find a peer to this body, that can with more dexterity cut off knots, or steal cloaks, or wrap up and cut up washing, catch and lighten pockets, clean and put to rights shops, shake and empty purses, sweep and empty boxes; and wherever I can reach, I can show the miracles of hooking.' 'Bravo, in very sooth,' said the father, 'thou hast learnt the craft of a merchant, to make exchange and counterpoints of fingers, with receipts on shoulders, turning of keys, and casting of oar, and scaling of windows, and lengthening of rope; O unhappy me, if it had been better that I should have taught thee to work in the spinning-wheel, than feel my body go round like a spinning-wheel, thinking that every hour I may see thee dragged within a court of law, covered with a paper hat, discovered false, and consigned to work an oar, or an thou escapest this, see thee twist round one day at the end of a rope.' Then turning to Titillo, the second son, he said to him, 'And thou, what fine craft hast thou learnt?' 'To build boats,' answered the son. 'That is better,' replied his sire, 'that is a good and known craft, and thou mayest live all thy life with it. And thou, Renzone, what hast thou learnt after such length of time?' 'I can draw the cross-bow so straight that I can even blind a cock,' said the third son. 'It is also something, at least,' replied his father, 'thou canst live by hunting and birding'; and turning to the fourth son he asked him the same question, and Ghiacuccio replied, 'I know an herb that will cause a dead man to rise.' 'Bravo, O thou priest of Lanfusa,' answered Pacione, 'this should be the time when we should be saved from want, and cause folk to live longer than the

Verlascio of Capua.' And lastly asking of his younger son, who was named Menecuccio, what craft he knew, the son said, 'I understand the language of birds.' And the father replied, 'Whilst we were at table, thou didst arise to listen to the chirping of the sparrow; and as thou boastest of understanding what they say, do thou tell me what thou didst hear that bird that was upon the tree bough say.' 'It said,' said Menecuccio, 'that a ghul had stolen the daughter of the King of Autogolfo, and carried her on the top of a rock, where no news of her can be heard, and the father had published a ban that whoso findeth his daughter, and bringeth her to him, shall have her as wife.' 'If it be as thou sayest, we are rich,' cried Luccio, 'because I alone am enough to withdraw her from the arms of the ghul.' 'An thou trust to do the deed,' replied the old man, 'let us wend at once to the presence of the king, and if he give us his word that, an we save her, he will give us his daughter in marriage, let us offer him to find his daughter.'

So all being of one accord, Titillo in a short time built a beautiful boat, wherein they entered, and sailed, and arrived at Autogolfo, where they begged an audience of the king, and when they stood in his presence, they offered to win back his daughter, whereupon the king confirmed the promise. Being thus assured, they at once set out for the rock, where, as good luck would have it, they found the ghul, lying in the sun fast asleep, with his head resting on the breast of Cianna (thus was the damsel hight); and when she beheld the boat coming through the waters, she arose with the pleasure of the sight, but Pacione made a sign to her to be still and silent. Then landing and laying a heavy stone under the ghul's head, they bade Cianna arise, and fare with them to the boat, and as soon as they entered it, they took up the oars and rowed fast onward. But they had not gone far when the ghul awoke, and not finding Cianna by his side, he looked round the shore, and beheld the boat carrying her away, whereupon changing himself into the shape of a black cloud, he flew through the air to reach the boat. Cianna, who knew the ghul's art, recognised him at once in the cloud, and she feared with sore affright, so that she had barely

courage enough to warn Pacione and his sons, when she fell in a
dead faint. Then Renzone, who beheld the cloud coming nearer,
taking hold of his cross-bow, pulled the string and hit the ghul in
the eyes, thus blinding him, and the pain was such that he fell
straight down like hail into the sea. And they stood watching the
cloud, and when the ghul fell, they turned round to see to Cianna,
and she was stretched at their feet, white and cold, and to all ap-
pearances gone out of all life. Thereupon Pacione buffeted his
face, and plucked his beard, exclaiming, 'Behold, the sleep and the
oil are lost; behold our trouble and travail cast to the winds, and
our hopes into the sea; she hath already gone to feed in the heavenly
pastures, so that we may die from hunger; she hath said good night,
so that we might have an evil day; she hath broken the thread of
life, so that we may break the thread of all our hopes. It is well
seen that the design of a poor man never succeedeth; it is well
proven that whoso is born unfortunate dieth unhappy; behold, the
daughter of the king is freed, behold us returned to Autogolfo,
behold the wife won, behold the festivals of the folk, behold the
sceptre won, behold us fallen upon our backsides on the ground!'

Ghiacuccio hearkened to all this moaning, but at last perceiving
that the music lasted too long, and the song accompanied by the
lute of grief and pain counterpointing even to the rose, said,
'Slowly, O my sire, we will go to Autogolfo to live more happily
and consoled than thou thinkest.' 'May the sultan have such con-
sòlation,' answered Pacione; 'when we shall present this corpse to
the expecting father, he will make his suite count to us, but not
count to us monies; and where others with a light sail quickly and
happily have passed this gulf, we will instead be engulfed in it.'
'Be silent,' replied Ghiacuccio, 'where hast thou sent thy brains to
pasture? Dost thou not remember the craft that I have learnt?
Let us get ashore, and let me search for the herb that I hold firmly
in my brains, and thou shalt behold somewhat else than annoyance.'
The father, hearing these words, embraced him, and heartened his
heart, and as he was torn and dragged by his desire, so did he tear
and cast the oar, so that in a short space of time they reached the

shore of Autogolfo, where Ghiacuccio disembarked and sought for the herb, and running back to the boat when he had found it, and squeezing the juice in Cianna's mouth, she suddenly, like a frog who hath been within the grotto of the dog, and is afterwards cast into the lake of Aguano, returned to life. Then they fared to the presence of the king, who received them with great gladness; and he was never satisfied of kissing and embracing his daughter, and of thanking these folk that had recovered her for him. But being asked to maintain his promise, the king said, 'To which of you am I to give Cianna in marriage? This is not a millet-pudding, that I can give a piece to each. Therefore it is needful that only one take the bean from its shell; the others must be content with the toothpick.' Answered the eldest who was very cunning, 'O my lord, the reward must be according to the labour, therefore take thou notice of which is the one that hath done the most to gain this beauteous and tasteful mouthful, and after do thou justice, so that we may be pleased.' 'Thou speakest sooth like a very Roland,' answered the king, 'therefore relate ye what each hath done so that I shall not see wrongly, and be able to judge rightly.' And so they related each their exploits, and at last spake the king to Pacione, and said, 'And thou, what hast thou done in this service?' 'I think I have done a great deal in the matter,' replied Pacione, 'having made men of these my sons, and having by the strength of first teachings obliged them to learn the craft they know, otherwise they would be senseless fools, where now they have brought forth such pleasant fruits.' The king, having heard both sides, and ruminated and digested the rights of this and the other, adjudged Cianna to Pacione, as the source of the life and health of his daughter. And thus it was done, and the sons had a gift of monies, to use to their profit and gain, whilst the father for his great joy became sprightly and lively like a youth of sixteen, and thus came in his mind the true proverb that

'**Amid two disputants the third rejoiceth.**'

NENNILLO AND NENNELLA

Eighth Diversion

Of the Fifth Day

JANNUCCIO HATH TWO CHILDREN BY HIS FIRST WIFE; HE WEDDETH A
SECOND TIME, AND THE CHILDREN ARE SO HATED BY THEIR STEPMOTHER
THAT SHE LEADETH THEM ONE DAY INTO A FOREST, WHERE THEY LOSE
EACH OTHER. NENNILLO BY CHANCE BECOMETH A FAVOURED COURTIER
OF A PRINCE, AND NENNELLA CASTETH HERSELF INTO THE SEA, AND IS
SWALLOWED BY AN ENSORCELLED FISH, AND CAST UPON A ROCK. HER
BROTHER DISCOVERETH AND RECOGNISETH HER, AND AT LAST SHE IS MAR-
RIED BY A WEALTHY PRINCE.

CIULLA having come to an end of her career, Paola got ready to
run the race; clearing her voice with a good hem, and wiping her
mouth with a fine cambric pocket-handkerchief, she thus began:

Unhappy is he who, having children, hopeth to find them a good
teacher by giving them a stepmother; for he instead carrieth home
a machine for the undoing of their fortunes. There never yet has
been seen a stepmother who could gaze with love and affection upon
the offspring of another; and if unhappily one have been found,
we may safely call her a white crow. But amid so many that
ye may have heard named, I will mention one to you, to be added
in the list of wicked, conscienceless stepmothers, whom you will
think worthy of the punishment, which she purchased for herself
with ready money.

There once lived a man, Jannuccio hight, who had two children,
Nennillo and Nennella, whom he loved as the babes of his eyes.
But death having with the soft file of time broken the iron bars
of the imprisoned soul of his wife, he took to himself an hideous
witch, an accursed bitch, who no sooner set foot in his abode than
she began to be horse of one stable, and say, 'What! have I come
hither to clean the louse from other people's children? I wanted
just this to take upon myself the annoyance of others, and behold

ever near me these tiresome weeping children; it had been better an I had broken my neck than come in this hell to eat badly, and spend my days in bad plight, and sleep worse; and for the nuisance of these two crap-in-breeches, this life cannot be tolerated; I came here as a wife and not as a servant; I must think of some expedient, and find some place where these exacting creatures may go, or else I shall find a lodging for myself. It is better to blush once than to grow pale an hundred times, and I shall break the relationship for ever; I am resolved to see in very fact the construction of all, and break asunder all in all.' The wretched husband, who loved his wife, said to her, 'Be not angry, O my wife, for the sugar is very dear; to-morrow morning before the crowing of the cock I will rid thee of this incubus, and thou shalt be happy.' So the next morning, before the dawn shook the fleas from the Spanish red coverlet out of the easterly window, Jannuccio filled a large basket with viands, and carrying it on his arm, led the children to a forest, where an army of poplars and beech-trees besieged the shadows. And when they came to that place, Jannuccio said, 'O my children, stay here, and eat and drink merrily, there is naught wanting: do ye see this track of ashes, that I let fall as I go? This will be the thread that will bring ye out of this labyrinth, and lead ye to your own house.' Then giving to each a kiss, he returned weeping to his home.

Now like unto all animals summoned by the bailiffs of the night to pay the tax of necessary rest to nature, the children either wanting their natural rest, or fearing to stay in that steep desert place, where the waters of a river beat the impertinent stones which stood before its feet, in such manner that Rodomonte would have smiled, they fared slowly by the track of ashes, and it was midnight when they reached the house. When Pascozza, their stepmother, saw them, she acted not as a woman but as a fiend, lifting her cries to the heavens, beating her hands and feet, and snorting like a frightened steed, saying, 'A fine thing is this! Whence did these children shoot forth? Is it possible that there is no quicksilver, to destroy them out of the house? Is it possible, that thou wilt keep them here, to be the distress of my heart? Begone, take thyself off from before mine eyes, I will not tarry to listen to the music of cocks or the weeping of fowls; if not, thou mayest clean thy teeth if I sleep with thee, and to-morrow morning I shall fare to the house of my parents, for thou art not worthy of me, and truly I have brought thee too many fine things and house-furniture to see them soiled, and for the stink of others to be left to me; neither have I brought thee such a good dowry as to be the slave of children not mine own.' The wretched Jannuccio, who beheld the boat in a bad storm, and the matter becoming too warm, immediately took the little ones, and returned to the forest, where giving them another basketful of things to eat, he said to them, 'O my darlings, ye can see how that bitch of my wife holdeth you in hatred and distaste; she came to my house for your ruin and to be a nail in this heart of mine; therefore stay ye here within this forest, where the pitiful trees will shelter ye against the hot rays of the sun, where the river, more charitable, will give ye unpoisoned food, and the earth, more kind, will give ye a bellyful of grass without danger; and I will make you a track of bran, which ye may follow when the food faileth you, and thus ye will be able to come and seek help and provaunt.' So saying he turned his face aside, so as not to dishearten the poor little things by letting them see him weep.

When the children had eaten all the provaunt in the basket, they desired to return home; but an ass, son of evil fortune, had eaten up the bran that had been scattered on the ground; and they lost their way, and for two days wandered through the forest, eating the acorns and chestnuts which had fallen to the ground. But as Heaven ever holds the merciful hand over the innocent, a prince who was hunting passed within that forest, and Nennillo, hearing the barking of dogs, was affrighted with sore affright, so that he hid himself within the hollow of a tree. And Nennella set off running so swiftly that she came forth of the forest, and reached the sea-shore. Now some corsairs, who had chanced to land to get some wood, saw Nennella and took her; and their chief carried her to his own house, where his wife having died a short time before, he kept her as his own daughter. In the meanwhile Nennillo, who had hidden himself within the hollow of the tree, was surrounded by dogs, which barked so furiously that the prince bade some of his followers go and discover the cause; and when they found this beautiful boy, who knew not how to tell them who his father and mother were, being so very young, the prince bade a huntsman put him upon a load, and carry him to the royal palace. And the prince had him brought up with great diligence, and instructed in virtue, and amongst other things he had him taught to be the court-farrier, so that before three or four years had passed he became so clever in his art that none could equal him. Such was his case.

But let us see how it fared with Nennella. It had been discovered that the corsair with whom she dwelt was a sea-marauder, and the people came to make him prisoner; but he being on friendly terms with the court clerks, they advised him in time, so that he was able to escape with his family. Perhaps it was the justice of Heaven, that whoso had done evil upon the sea upon that sea should pay the penalty, and therefore embarking upon a slender vessel, they sailed, and when they reached amiddlemost the main, a storm of wind capsized the boat, and they were drowned, all save Nennella, who was not guilty of their thefts, and escaped this danger; because near the vessel stood a charmed fish, which, opening wide his big jaws, swallowed her. The child now believed that she had ended her days, when instead she found marvellous matter within the belly of that fish, beautiful valleys and plains, splendid gardens, and a fine palace with all its commodities, wherein she dwelt like a princess. And this fish carried her upon a rock, where a prince, it being then the greatest heat of summer, had come to breathe the sea air. Meanwhile a great banquet was being prepared; and Nennillo from one of the palace terraces was sharpening the knives upon this rock, delighting much in his office and desiring to gain therein some honour, when Nennella beheld him from the fish's throat, and cried in a choked voice, 'O my brother, O my brother, the knives are sharpened, the tables are spread, and to me my life

is tiresome without thee, within this fish.' Nennillo at first heeded
not the voice, but the prince, who was standing on another terrace,
turned, and hearing this music, beheld the fish. And when he again
heard the same words, he was wellnigh out of his senses with amazement, and sending some of his servants to the shore, bade them see
if they could find some means to cheat the fish and draw him ashore,
and continually hearing the words, "O my brother, O my brother,'
he asked of each of his followers if they had lost any sister. And
Nennillo replied that he remembered as a dream that when the
prince had found him in the forest, he had a sister, of whom he
had never since heard any news. Then the prince told him to draw
nearer to the fish, and see what was the matter, for perhaps this
fortune had been saved for him. And as soon as Nennillo neared
the fish, the fish laid his head upon the rock, and opened wide his
mouth, and out of it sprang Nennella, so beautiful that she seemed
a mermaid in the interlude of the coming forth of a nymph by the
exorcism of a magician from the jaws of an hideous animal. And
when the king enquired of the matter, she related to him part of
their trouble and travail, and their stepmother's hatred, but was
unable to remember the name of their father and their home; and
the king caused a ban to be published that whoso had lost two children answering to the names of Nennillo and Nennella within the
depths of a forest should come to the royal palace, where he would
hear some good news of them.

Jannuccio, who all this time had a sorrowful heart, and was disconsolate, believing that his children had been devoured by wolves,
ran with great joy to the presence of the prince, saying that he had
lost these children. And when he had related the story, how he
had been obliged to carry them to the forest, and so on to the end,
the prince reproached him severely, calling him a worthless man,
who had allowed a woman of naught to put her foot in his throat,
reducing himself to the wretched plight of sending two gems of
great price like his children to wander through the world. But
after breaking Jannuccio's head with these bitter words, he laid
upon it the plaster of consolation, sending for the children, whom

the father never ceased caressing, and embracing, and kissing. Then the prince made him doff his garment, and ordered that he should be arrayed as a gentleman; and sending for Jannuccio's wife, he let her see those two golden shrubs, saying to her, 'What would he deserve who should harm these two gems, and put them in danger of death?' And she answered, 'I would put them in a closed cask and roll them down a mountain.' 'Begone, and thou shalt have it,' said the prince; 'the ram hath used the horns against itself; now as thou hast pronounced the sentence against thyself, thou must pay it, for the hatred thou hast shown to these thy beauteous stepchildren.' And therefore he commanded that the sentence pronounced by herself should at once be executed. Then, choosing a very wealthy nobleman, he gave him Nennella to wife, and he gave the daughter of another nobleman as wealthy to Nennillo, presenting them with wealth sufficient to live upon; and their sire also; so that they needed the help of no one in the world for the future; and the stepmother, put within a cask, ended her life, crying out of the bung-hole whilst she had life,

'He who mischief seeks shall mischief find;
There comes the time when he shall be repaid.'

THE THREE CITRONS

Of the Fifth Day

CENZULLO OBJECTETH TO TAKE A WIFE, BUT CUTTING ONE OF HIS FIN-
GERS UPON SOME CURDLED MILK, HE DESIRETH TO HAVE ONE, RED AND
WHITE LIKE UNTO THAT WHICH HE HATH JUST MADE OF CURDLED MILK
AND BLOOD; AND FOR THIS REASON HE WANDERETH LIKE A PILGRIM
THROUGH THE WORLD. COMING UPON THE ISLAND OF THE THREE
GHULAS, HE RECEIVETH THREE CITRONS, AND IN CUTTING ONE OF THEM
HE GAINETH A BEAUTEOUS DAMSEL AS HE DESIRED. SHE IS SLAIN BY
A BLACK SLAVE, AND HE TAKETH IN CHANGE THE BLACK FOR THE
WHITE, BUT DISCOVERING THE TREACHERY, HE COMMANDETH THE SLAVE
TO BE SLAIN, AND THE FAIRY, RETURNING TO LIFE, BECOMETH QUEEN.

It is impossible to say how much the story of Paola pleased the
company; but it being now Ciommetella's turn to speak, the prince
having given her the signal, she spake thus:

Spake sooth that sage who said, 'Say not what thou knowest, and
do not what thou canst do; for both the one and the other carry
unknown danger and unexpected ruin'; as ye will hear of a certain
slave (speaking with respect of our lady the princess) who, attempting to do all the evil in her power to a damsel, caused so much
wrong in the question that she became the judge of her own error,
and sentenced herself to the punishment she well deserved.

The King of Torre-longa had a son who was his right eye, and
upon whom he had laid the foundations of his hopes; and he longed
for the time when he could choose his son a fair and wealthy bride,
and have the joy of being himself called grandsire.   But this
young prince was so wild and cold and exotic that, whenever they
spake of his taking unto himself a wife, he shook his head, and was
distant an hundred miles from that purpose, so much so that the
poor father, who beheld his son headstrong and obstinate, fearing
that his race might be lost, became wroth, and spiteful, and ill-
humoured like a whore who hath lost her account, or a merchant

whose partner hath failed, or a farmer whose donkey is dead.
Neither could the tears of his father move the prince, nor the
prayers of his lieges soften him, nor the rede of men of weal take
him off his feet; it was idle to put before his eyes the wishes of him
who had begotten him, the need of the people, his own interest
as he was the last and the full stop of his race; for with the per-
fidiousness, and obstinacy, and ostentation of an old mule that hath
a skin four fingers thick, he stuck down his feet, stopped his ears,
and hardened his heart so that no one could sound the alarm, try
as they might. But because as much is sure to happen in an hour
as in an hundred years, thou mayest not say, 'I shall not pass this
way.' It so fortuned that one day of the days, the table being spread,
and as all were sitting to their midday meal, the prince, wishing
to cut some curdled milk in the middle, and chattering the while,
and hearkening to the gossip that went round, accidentally cut his
finger; and two drops of blood fell upon the curdled milk, thus
causing such beauteous and such graceful blending of colours, that,
either it was a punishment of love, that waited for him at every step,
or the will of Heaven, to console that man of weal his sire, for,
though he had never been molested by the domestic colt, he was
molested and tormented by this wild colt of finding a damsel so
white and red like that curdled milk and his own blood; so one day
he said to his sire, 'O my lord, an I do not win my wish I am lost.
Never had I any longing for womankind, but now I long with
sore longing for a damsel like unto mine own blood. Therefore
do thou resolve to allow me to fare around the world, and lend
me thine aid, and provide me with the needful, that I may go and
seek this beauty like unto this curdled milk, an thou desirest to see
me in health and in life, otherwise I shall end the course of my
existence, and go to rack and ruin.' And the king, hearing this
beastly resolution, felt as if the palace had fallen upon him, and he
was stunned and amazed, and his colour yellowed, and when he
came to himself and could speak, he said, 'O my son, core of my
soul, eye-babe of my heart, crutch of my old age, what hath turned
thine head? Hast thou lost thy wits? Hast thou lost thy brains?

Either ace or six; thou wouldst not take unto thee a wife to give
me an heir, and now thou longest for her, to drive me out of this
world. Where, O where dost thou wish to wander in exile, consuming thy life, and leaving thine home: thine home, thy fireside,
thy resting-place? Dost thou not know to how many travails, and
troubles, and dangers thou exposest thyself in travelling? Chase
away from thee this whim; be thou corrected; do not wish to see
this life struck to the ground, this house fallen, this realm ruined.'
But these and other words which he said entered in at one ear and
came forth from the other, and they were all cast into the sea; and
the unhappy king, seeing that his son was a church-steeple owl, gave
him leave to depart, presenting him with a bagful of golden crowns,
and two or three servants to serve him, and feeling his soul departing
from his body, he looked out of one of the terraces of his palace,
and followed him with his eyes till he was lost to sight.

The prince, having left his sire wretched, and in despair, and embittered, wandered on through wilds and wolds, hills and valleys,
forests, and plains, and declivities, seeing various countries, treating
divers peoples, and always keeping his eyes open to see if he could
find the target of his desires. At the end of four months he came
to a port in France, where he left his servants at the hospital with a
pain in their feet, and embarking alone aboard a Genoese ship, and
passing the strait of Gibraltar, thence he took place in a larger vessel, and sailed towards the Indies, seeking from realm to realm, and
from province to province, and from land to land, and from street
to street, and from house to house, and from den to den, if he
could meet with the original of the beautiful image he cherished
in his heart. And he wandered, and twisted his legs, and moved
his feet so long that he arrived at the Island of the Ghulas, where
casting anchor, he went ashore. There he met an old dame, very
thin, and with an hideous face, to whom he related the cause that
had brought him in those countries. The old woman was struck
with amazement, when she heard the fine caprice and the capricious
chimera of this prince, and the travails and the risks he had passed
to gain his end, so she said to him, 'O my son, do thou swiftly dis-

appear, for an thou wert seen by my three daughters, who are the slaughter-house of all human flesh, thou wouldst not be worth three coppers; because half living and half roasted, a pot will be thy bier, and a belly will be thy grave; but let thy feet be an hare's, and thou wilt not have to fare far to find thy fortune.' When the prince heard this, he was affrighted with sore affright, and wondered with excessive wonder, and therefore he hastened in his way, without even saying by your leave, and he well rubbed his shoes till he came to another country, where he found a second old woman more hideous than the other, to whom he related the affair, and she said to him, 'Melt, depart from here, an thou wilt not serve as breakfast for my children, but hasten thee on, for night is near, and a little further on thy way thou shalt find thy fortune.' When the prince heard this, he wended on his way without tarrying a single moment, just as if he had a couple of bladders tied to his tail, and he fared so long that he met a third old dame, who was sitting by the side of a wheel, with a basket full of sweetmeats and comfits, and she was feeding some asses who, after eating, capered and jumped by the shore of a river, kicking at some swans that were there. The prince, coming to the old woman's presence and saluting her, re-lated to her the story once more, and the cause of his pilgrimage, and the ancient dame with fair words consoled him, and gave him a good breakfast, so that he licked his fingers, and arising from the table, she consigned to him three citrons, which seemed to have just been gathered from the tree, and gave him also a fine knife, saying, 'Thou mayest return at once to Italy for thy spindle is full, and thou hast found what thou seekest; wend thy ways therefore, and as thou art not far from thy realm, at the first fountain thou comest to cut one of the citrons, from out of which will come forth a fairy, saying, "Give me a drink"; and do thou quickly supply her with some water; otherwise she will melt like quicksilver; and be solicitous with the second, and quick with the third so that she escape thee not, giving her to drink at once, and thou shalt have a wife according to the desire of thy heart.' The prince, overpleased, kissed that hairy hand, which seemed like a porcupine's back, an

hundred times. Then, taking leave of her, he departed from that
country, and fared to the sea-shore, and there he took ship for the
Pillars of Hercules, and arrived at our sea; and after a thousand
storms and tempests he entered port one day's journey from his own
kingdom. And he arrived at a charming grove, where the shadows
formed a palace for those prairies which desired not to be seen by
the sun; and he dismounted at a fountain, which with its silvery
tongue called the folk to drink the cool, crystalline water, and sitting on the grassy carpet purflewed with flowers, and drawing forth
the knife, he began to cut the first citron, when behold, a beauteous
damsel sprang forth white like milk and cream, and red like a
strawberry, who said, 'Give me a drink.' And the prince was so
amazed that he gazed open-mouthed at the beauty of the fairy,
and was not dexterous enough to give her the water, so that she
appeared and disappeared at one and the same time. Whether this
was a staff laid upon the prince's head and back may be considered
by him who, longing for somewhat, hath it in his hands and loseth it.

Then the prince cutting the second citron, the same thing happened, and this was the second blow he received; so making two
rivulets of his eyes, the tears rained down his face and kept time
with the fountain, yielding in naught to its flowing, and thus weeping and lamenting, he said, 'Alas, how wretched am I, whenever
shall I gain some good? twice have I let her escape, just as if I had
the rope round mine hands; let the devil take me, for I move like
a rock, when I should run like a greyhound. In sooth I have done
it finely. Wake, thou wretched man, there is only one more left;
and at the third winneth the king; and this knife must give me the
fairy, or do a deed which slayeth.' And thus saying, he cut the
third citron, and the third fairy came forth, and said like the others,
'Give me a drink,' and the prince at once gave her some water, and
behold she remained in his hands, a fair, tender damsel, white like
curdled milk, mixed with red that seemed an ham from the Abruzzi,
or a sausage from Nola, a beauty without compare and without
peer, a whiteness and fairness beyond measure; and upon her hair
had rained the golden rain of Jupiter, from which love pointed his

arrows to wound the hearts. In that face love had painted all his wiles, so that some innocent soul should be hanged in the gibbet of desire; in those eyes the sun had lighted two luminous bodies, so that in the breast of whoso saw them fire should be set, and light-ning and fireworks of sighs should be drawn; Venus had passed near those lips, giving them the colour of the rose to pick with its thorns a thousand enamoured souls; in those breasts Juno had squeezed her own, to feed with their beauty all human desires. In very sooth she was so beauteous from head to foot that ye could not behold a more comely and graceful being. The prince's wits for-sook him, and he knew not what had happened to him, and he gazed in wondering ecstasy upon this charming child of a citron, this beautiful damsel, fair in form and of stature symmetrical, this tasteful fruit, and said to himself, 'Dost thou sleep, or art thou awake, O Cenzullo? Is thy sight charmed, or have thine eyes been turned, that thou gazest upon a white thing, that came forth of a yellow? What a sweetmeat is this out of the sour juice of a cit-ron?' At last finding that it was no dream, and that the game was true, he embraced the fairy, giving her hundreds and hundreds of kisses and pinches, and after a thousand loving words interchanged between them, that like a song were counterpointed by sweet kisses, the prince said, 'O my soul, I will not take thee to my father's country without that pomp and luxury worthy of thy beauty and worthy of a queen; therefore do thou climb this oak, where it seemeth that for our need nature hath formed it in the shape of a chamber, and await for my return. I will fare with all speed as if I had wings, and before this my spittle shall have dried, I will be back to carry thee, arrayed in sumptuous raiment, and accom-panied as it needs should, to my own kingdom;' and kissing her fondly, he took leave, and departed.

In the meanwhile a black slave-girl had been sent by her mistress to that fountain with a juglet, to fetch some water, and by chance beholding in the waters the reflection of the face and form of the fairy, and believing that it was herself, wondered with extreme wonder, and began saying, 'What is this, O wretched Lucy; thou

be made so beautifully, and thy mistress sendeth thee to fetch water,
and me must support this thing?' And thus saying, she brake the
juglet, and returned home, and the mistress asked of her why she
had done this bad service, and she answered, 'Me gone to little
fountain and knocked the juglet against a stone.' The mistress
believed this tale and swallowed this lie, and the next day gave her
a fine cask, to take to be filled with water; and she returning to
the fountain, and again beholding the same beautiful image in the
water, sighed deeply, and said, 'Me is not an hideous slave, me is not
a good for naught, me is nice and genteel, and yet must carry to
fountain barrel?' and saying thus, she brake open the cask, and made
a thousand pieces of it, and returned home to her mistress grumbling, and saying, 'An ass knocked against the barrel, and it fell
and brake to pieces.' When the mistress heard this, she lost her patience, and taking up a broomstick, laid it on the slave's back with
good will, so that she felt the effects for many days. The next day
the mistress took up a leathern pipe, and said to the slave, 'Haste
thee, run, thou beggarly slave, cricket-legged, broken-behind, haste
thee and tarry not, and do not pick and choose, and bring me this
full of water, if not I will weigh thee and slice thee like a many-
feet; and I will give thee such an hiding that thou shalt for ever
remember it.' And the slave ran in haste, carrying her legs like
lightning that is afraid of thunder, and filling the pipe, saw again
the beauteous image, and said, 'Me should be silly, if me carried
this water; 'tis better to marry than to be a slave; and this is not a
beauty to make me die a wrathful death, and to serve a coloured
mistress.' And when she ended speaking, she took a large pin, and
began to prick the leather pipe, which seemed a garden with a
fountain that opened so that the water poured out in an hundred
smaller fountains. And the fairy, seeing this, laughed loudly and
heartily, and the slave-girl, hearing this laugh, turned her gaze
upwards, and perceiving the ambush, and speaking to herself, said,
'Thou art the cause that me got a flogging, but never mind,' and
she said aloud to the fairy, 'What art thou doing there, O beauteous
child?' and the other, who was the mother of politeness, related all

that she had within, without leaving out one iota of what had fortuned her with the prince, whom she expected from day to day, and from hour to hour, and from moment to moment, with raiment and suite to company her on her journey to his sire's kingdom, where she would enjoy her life with him.   When the wicked slave-girl heard this, she bethought herself to gain this prize, and replied to the fairy, 'As thou expectest thy husband, let me come up and comb thine hair, and make thee fairer'; and the fairy answered 'Thou art welcome, like the first of May'; and the slave climbed up, and she held out the small white hand to her, which, caught between those black paws, seemed a crystal mirror within an ebony frame, and thus she rose up by her side, and beginning to unfold her hair, the blackamoor stuck a large pin in her head in the site of memory. The fairy, feeling the pin, cried, 'O pigeon, O pigeon;' and forthwith became a pigeon, and flew away, whereupon the slave undressed herself, and remained mother-naked, and making a little bundle of her apparel of rags which she had been wearing, cast it far from her; and there she remained upon that tree, and she seemed a statue of black stone within an house of emerald.

In a short time the prince returned with a large cavalcade, and finding a cask of caviare where he had left a tub full of milk, for a time his wits forsook him.   But when he came to his senses, he said, 'Who hath made this blot of ink upon our royal papers, whereon I believed I should write the happiest of my days?   Who hath covered with mournful hangings the newly painted white dwelling, wherein I believed I should have enjoyed my pleasure?   Who causeth me to find this black touchstone, when I had left a silver mine which would have made me rich and blessed?'   But the cunning slave, perceiving the wonder and exceeding surprise of the prince, said, 'Do not wonder, O my prince, that I am ensorcelled, and made white by bindings but of black behind.'   The unhappy prince, seeing that the evil had no remedy, like an ox growing horns, swallowed this pill, and bidding the blackamoor come down, dressed her from head to foot, beginning with her anew.   Then swelling and choking with rage, and with face distorted by wrath, he returned to his own country, and when six miles distant from the capital he was met by the king and queen, who had come forth to him, ye may suppose that they were received with that pleasure with which the prisoner receiveth the intimation of his sentence. And they were saddened to behold the fine proof of madness in their son, who had wandered the world over to seek a white dove, and had brought back instead a black crow; but as they could not do otherwise, they renounced the crown in favour of the bride and bridegroom, and put the golden circlet upon that hideous black coal face.

Now whilst bridal feast and banquets the most magnificent were preparing in all pomp and sumptuousness, and the cooks were plucking geese, slaying young suckling pigs, flaying lambs, making mincemeats, roasting capons, and preparing many other tasteful viands, a beautiful pigeon came to one of the kitchen windows, saying,

> 'O thou cook of the kitchen,
> What doth the king with that Saracen-woman?'

And the cook took no heed of it; but the pigeon returned a second time and a third time, repeating the same words, when the cook, marvelling with excessive marvel, hastened to his mistress to relate the matter as somewhat wonderful; and his lady, hearing this music, ordered that the pigeon should be caught, and slain, and made a stew of. And when the pigeon again returned, the cook did all in his power to catch it, and when he caught it, he obeyed the command of the blackamoor, and having scalded the bird to pluck it, quickly threw that water and the feathers into a flower-box on a terrace, where three days had not passed before a beautiful citron-tree sprang forth and grew in four pinches' time, and so it fortuned that the king looking out of his window from the terrace, and perceived this which he had not seen before, called the cook, and enquired whence it came, and who had nurtured it. And hearing from Master Ladle all the matter, suspicion entered his mind; and therefore he ordered that the penalty of death should be adjudged to whoso should damage that tree, so that no one should touch it, and that it should be tended carefully. And at the end of a few days three beautiful citrons began to grow, the same as those given to him by the ghula, and when they were ready to be gathered, he gathered them, and shutting himself within a chamber with a large cup of water, and with the same knife that he always carried hung at his waistband, he began to cut. And it happened to him with the first and second citron as it had occurred before; lastly he cut the third citron, when the third fairy came forth, and he gave her to drink, and as he had sought, the same damsel that he had left upon the tree remained with him, and he heard from her the tale of the evil and treachery of the slave.

Who can explain the joy felt by the king at this good turn of fortune? Who can describe the fond embrace, the kissing, the sweet epithets, the proud content, the exhilaration, the trembling of ecstatical bliss? Ye may think that he was swimming in sweetness, and could not stay in his skin, and his senses left him; and supporting her in his arms, he made her array herself sumptuously, and taking her by the hand, led her into the saloon, where the courtiers, and the grandees, and the nabobs of the land were gathered together to honour the bridal feast of their lord; and he called them to him one by one, and said, 'Tell me, O my lords, what chastisement would deserve whoso would do any hurt to this beauteous lady?' And the reply was, from one, that such a person would deserve a rope necklace; another, that he should be cast into the sea; another, that he should be hooted and stoned by a mob of ragamuffins; and one said one thing and one another. At last he sent for the black queen, and putting to her the same question, she answered, 'They deserve burning, and their ashes scattered from the top of the castle-walls.' The king, hearing this, rejoined, 'Thou hast spoken thine own sentence, and hast thrown the axe at thy feet, and thou hast built thine own gibbet, and sharpened the knife, and mixed the poison, because no one hath done her harm but thyself, thou ungrateful, wicked woman. Knowest thou that this lady is the damsel in whose head thou stuckest the large pin? Knowest thou that this is the beauteous pigeon that thou badest be slain and cooked in the baking-pan? What dost thou think of this? Shake thyself free and thou canst. Thou hast done a fine filthiness, and whoso doeth evil deeds evil expecteth, and whoso cooketh shrubs eateth smoke.' And thus saying, he bade his followers take her and cast her alive upon a pile of burning wood, and when she was burnt to ashes, they scattered them to the winds from the castle-walls, making the old saying true in the end, that

'Whosoever soweth thorns, let him not walk bare-footed,'

END OF THE TALE OF TALES

TENTH DIVERSION

Of the Fifth Day

ZOZA RELATETH THE HISTORY OF HER TROUBLES. THE SLAVE, FEELING
HERSELF TOUCHED AT ALL POINTS, DOETH SCISSORS, SCISSORS, SO THAT
SHE MAY NOT END HER STORY. BUT THE PRINCE, IN SPITE OF HER,
DESIRETH TO HEAR IT, AND DISCOVERING THE TREACHERY OF HIS WIFE,
CONDEMNETH HER TO DEATH, FULL WITH CHILD AS SHE IS, AND TAK-
ETH ZOZA TO WIFE.

ALL ears had been opened, listening to Ciommetella's tale, and
some praised the knowledge and taste with which it had been related, and some of the company blamed her for the lack of discretion and judgment she displayed in relating it in the presence of the
slave princess, and publishing the dishonour and infamy of one
like herself: and they said that she had run a risk to spoil the game.
But Lucy acted truly as Lucy should, shaking herself the while
the story was related, and by the trembling of the body could be seen
the strength of the storm which was within her heart, for she
saw portrayed within a story of another blackamoor slave the
facsimile of her own treachery and evil doing, insomuch that an
she could she would have caused the conversation to cease: but
partly because she could not do without the stories, like the spider
who cannot do without sounds, the doll having caused such fire to
enter in her soul, and partly not to give Thaddeus cause for suspicion, she swallowed this pill, thinking in her mind to show her
resentment, and to revenge herself in fitting time and place. But
Thaddeus, who was very pleased with this pastime, signed to Zoza to
relate her story, and she, bowing gracefully, said,

'O my lord, truth hath always been mother to hatred, and therefore I should not like, in obeying thy commands, to offend some
one of this company which surrounds me; because I am not used to

feign inventions, and to weave fables. I am constrained, therefore, by nature and by accident to speak the truth: and although the proverb doth say, "Piddle clear and show figs to the doctor," knowing that the truth is not at all times well received in the presence of princes, I tremble to say somewhat which may cause thee to be wroth.' 'Say what pleaseth thee,' answered Thaddeus, 'for from that charming mouth naught can come forth but honey and sugar.' These words were like so many knife-thrusts in the heart of the slave, and tokens of it could have been seen upon her face, an the black face like the white had been index of the soul: and she would have paid with a finger of her hand to have been fasting of these stories, for her heart had become blacker than her face, fearing that the former story might have been the prognostic of the coming disaster, as from the morning beginneth the evil day.

In the meanwhile Zoza began to charm her hearers with the sweetness of her words, relating her troubles and travails from the beginning to the end, first telling of her natural melancholy, the unhappy ill-omened presage of what destiny had decreed for her, carrying from the cradle the bitter root of all her misfortunes, that with the key of a forced smile constrained her to weep a rivulet of tears. She continued to the curse of the old woman her pilgrimage whereupon she suffered untold anguish, her arrival at the fountain, her ceaseless weeping, and the treacherous sleep which caused her ruin. The slave perceiving the vessel take to high seas, and that it was ready to founder, cried, 'Be silent, dry thy throat: if not, I will beat my belly and slay little George.' But Thaddeus, who had discovered a new country, had no more phlegm: so lifting up his mask and casting it to the ground, he said, 'Let her end her tale, and do not go into heroics about little George or big George: at last thou hast not found me alone; and an the mustard mounteth to my nose, it would be better that thou shouldst go under a cart-wheel.' And commanding Zoza to continue in spite of the wife, she, who desired for naught better than to obey the behest, continued to relate the finding of the broken pitcher, and the deceit practised by the slave to rob her of her good fortunes. And whilst speaking, she wept with sore weeping, and there was no one present who did not weep in sympathy.

And Thaddeus, who from Zoza's words and tears, and the silence of the slave, understood and fished the truth of the affair, gave Lucy a good talking-to, more than one would do to an ass, and obliging her to confess with her own mouth this treachery, ordered at once that she should be buried alive, with only the head out, so that her death should be delayed. And embracing Zoza, he bid all folk honour her as his wife and princess, and sent messengers to the King of Valle-pelosa, bidding him come to the wedding-feast. And with this new bridal-feast ended the greatness of the slave, and the entertainment of the stories. And let us congratulate them, and may they have health, whilst I have come on foot, treading softly, with a spoonful of honey in my mouth.

SONNET

To whomso hath read this book correctly

BY M.R.S.D.

An in these pages ye did find
Aught error, as ye whilom read,
Then to these faults be always blind,
For art must guile e'en Argus' head.

And if ye have found good in these,
And will their petty slips defend,
Then shut your eyes, and trust, like Mars,
That what was wrong will rightly end.

Ride not cock-proud on pack-ass' loin,
Go simply with the beggar's coin,
And ye shall with true wisdom join.

But peace to barking, currish pen!
When ye have read—then read again:
Read backwards, sideways. So godden!